DA

Liz Williams is the daughter of a stage magician and a gothic novelist, and currently lives near Brighton seafront. She received a PhD in the philosophy of science from Cambridge, and her subsequent career has ranged from reading tarot cards on the Palace Pier to teaching in central Asia. Her short stories have been published in *Asimov's, Interzone, The Third Alternative* and *Visionary Tongue,* and she is the co-editor of the recent anthology *Fabulous Brighton. Darkland* is her sixth novel.

LIZ WILLIAMS

DARKLAND

TOR

First published 2006 by Tor

First published in paperback 2007 by Tor
an imprint of Pan Macmillan Ltd
Pan Macmillan, 20 New Wharf Road, London N1 9RR
Basingstoke and Oxford
Associated companies throughout the world
www.panmacmillan.com

ISBN 978-0-330-42691-6

1 3 5 7 9 8 6 4 2

A CIP catalogue record for this book is available from
the British Library.

Typeset by Intype Libra Ltd
Printed and bound in Great Britain by
Mackays of Chatham plc, Chatham, Kent

Visit www.panmacmillan.com to read more about all our books
and to buy them. You will also find features, author interviews and
news of any author events, and you can sign up for e-newsletters
so that you're always first to hear about our new releases.

To my father and mother

ACKNOWLEDGEMENTS

To my agent, Shawna McCarthy, for all her help. To my editor at Bantam, Anne Groell, for everything. To Peter Lavery and Stefanie Bierwerth at Tor for making this a much better book!

To the Montpelier writing group for giving this a kicking when it needed it. To the usual suspects in Brighton and London for their invaluable input on the matter of drink. To James, for making a difference. To Pwyll Pen Annwn for making another one. And to Tanith, with thanks for all the books!

ONE

PLANET: NHEM

Aldur Eskind and I came in at Iznar spaceport, the only one in operation on this part of Nhem since the others had been so badly bombed in the war. Looking across the cityscape – the vitreous green buildings and darker jade domes against the rosy sky – it struck me that Nhem should have been a hot world, but it was winter for most of the year in these latitudes, with a thick frost lining the ground in the mornings and lingering in the shadows for the rest of the day. I did not mind that – it reminded me of Muspell – but the cold did not settle the dust and the air was so dry that my mouth and skin felt immediately desiccated. And there were other unsettling signs, too. When I dropped down onto the pitted ground of the space-port, I felt a disrupted current of energy rise up through my feet, making my spine tingle as though someone had drawn an unexpected finger down it. The sense that we Muspellians call the seith was immediately alert and jangling. It was more than the customary shift of a slightly different gravity. This was a blighted place, inimical to women. Aldur was staring at me impatiently.

'Vali? The flyer's waiting.'

'Sorry. I'm coming.'

'That wind blows in from the Salt Desert,' Aldur said as we hurried to catch the flyer, our hair whipping in the breeze. I pulled the cowl up to cover my head, not wanting to risk arrest. The flyer took us upwards, skirting the space-port and the old city and heading out over the sprawl of slums and suburbs. Aldur pointed out to a white waste of rock beyond the city perimeter. 'The Nhemish are constantly fighting to hold it back.'

'They wouldn't have to if they hadn't caused the Inner Seas to dry up in the first place.'

'They said it was the Hand of God.'

I snorted. 'Apparently they say everything's the Hand of God these days. That's what we were told in the debriefing, anyway.' I looked down across the city. The domes of the Most Holy floated above the old town like a collection of glass bubbles, green and unreal in the sunlight.

'That's where the Hierolath's chambers are located,' Aldur murmured into my ear. I glanced forward to check that the pilot could not overhear, but I kept my voice low all the same.

'Yes, I read the notes. I'll need a pass for the old city; it seems they've become obsessive about checking documents.'

'That shouldn't be too much of a problem,' Aldur said.

'Even for a woman. They'll give you a chip for the curfew period, as long as you're properly dressed.'

'As long as I keep my mouth shut, you mean.'

'Just remember that here, a speaking woman is like a talking dog.'

'Not what she says, but that she does it at all?' An old, old joke, as ancient as Earth itself. But here on Nhem, it was even less amusing.

Uneasily, I watched the domes shimmer into illusion behind dust and cold air. The pilot took the flyer into a small port at the city's edge. It wasn't as windy here, so we came down on the stabilizer fields rather than the under-carriage; the runway was pockmarked with potholes. A collection of tin sheds stood at the edge of the field. The pilot parked the flyer and Aldur and I made our way to immigration.

'*Where* are you from?' The clerk looked tired, or bored – or both – and I was grateful. The last thing I wanted was an encounter with a religious zealot. I'd have had quite enough of that by the time I was finished here. I smiled at him, but he did not smile back. His gaze slid over my face and away, as if he was embarrassed. It was strange not to have it linger. I had to remind myself that I looked different now. There was no reason for him to stare in fascinated horror at my face.

'I've come from Muspell,' Aldur said. He did not look at me, either. I had become a thing, not a person, and he would no more include me in his itinerary than he would mention his suitcase. He fanned a handful of papers in

3

front of the clerk. Most of them were forgeries. 'I'm with an aid agency. Green Globe. Here.'

'Yes, I have you on the list. You've been approved.' He sounded surprised. 'Where are you planning to stay?'

'A hotel called the *Argeria*. I don't know where that is.'

'I can arrange transport,' the clerk said. I got the feeling that he was eager to be rid of us. He had just stamped the last remaining document when a shadow fell across the desk.

'Let me see those.'

Aldur and I avoided one another's eyes. The clerk shuffled on the other side of the desk.

'Everything is in order; I've checked—'

'Check again.' I saw chilly blue eyes behind a visor. The green uniforms bore the wave symbol of the Unitaries. These were the Hierolath's own militia, harder cases by far than the poor little clerk. *Idhunn*, I prayed, *may you have done your preparation well.* Don't let me down. She never had before, but this was another world and Skald business rarely took any of us off Muspell.

The militiaman spent a lot of time looking from the laminated holographic image on my travel papers to my face. He would see no discrepancy, I was certain. Golden eyes, a long switch of red hair tucked under the cowl.

As different as possible from my real self – and from a woman of Nhem – as we could make it. I was careful not to look him in the face. There were penalties for that sort of thing, even for outworlders. Animals are not supposed to stare at humans.

4

Aldur himself had retained typical Muspell looks: a tall, thin-faced man, grey eyes, pale brown hair. I knew that he was originally from Nessheim, but he could have come from of the hundreds of islands in the Reach. I swallowed a lump of homesickness and concentrated on the matter in hand. It was not easy to look demure.

'*This* will have to adopt suitable attire before leaving the building,' the militiaman said, with a jerk of the head. It was addressed to Aldur, not to me. *Make sure you keep your pet under control.* 'And so will you.'

'I'm familiar with the dress restrictions,' Aldur said.

'You have gloves?'

'Yes, and facial masks.'

'Then put them on.'

They made me go in a separate room for that, offended no doubt by the sight of my bare hands. A woman inside, invisible behind her own mass of garments, helped me on with a slip-gown, a thing of flounces and folds. She moved with slow, dogged thoroughness, as though I was a difficult doll to dress.

'Thank you,' I said to the woman. 'I appreciate your help.'

She did not answer. She gave me a dull glance and I saw with a shock of realization that there was no awareness behind her eyes, no sentience. Of course I had known what they did to their women. Yet knowing and understanding are two different things.

The militiamen were waiting impatiently by the door, our documents firmly clasped in their fists. My clothing was only slightly less ornate than Aldur's. The male form was clearly almost as inflammatory as the female.

The Nhemish must have overactive imaginations, I thought.

'They're escorting us to the hotel,' Aldur said. It was the first mistake he had made.

'Do not speak to your property directly!' the militiaman barked. 'Do not look at your property when you address it.'

'How am I supposed to speak to her, then?' Aldur's voice betrayed an edge of exasperation and I hoped he was not about to say something unwise.

'You must speak to the air.'

And I was less than the air, here. But I had to let it pass. If we were successful, things would be changing here soon enough.

We followed the militiamen out of the building into the afternoon sun. From now on, the movements of Ettar Hestin and Tyu Ullasdottir, Green Globe aid workers, would be severely restricted. As a woman, Tyu – my own assumed self – would be expected to remain largely in the hotel, which suited me. Ettar – Aldur's persona – would be doing most of the liaison, or such was our cover story. And at least government paranoia was giving us a ride to the hotel.

The militiamen watched as we signed in, evidently fearing that something might be amiss with our registration, but all went smoothly. Aldur, carrying the bags with myself trailing behind, took a lift up to the rooms. They

6

were small, stuffy chambers, but high. From here, one could see all the way to the domes of the Hierolath's palace.

As we walked, I found myself frowning. There was something about Aldur, something about the way he walked, that reminded me of someone. I'd noted it when we first met, but then the details of the mission had preoccupied me and I'd pushed it to the back of my mind.

But I did not have to go far to look for the name; it was etched into my mind as sharply as my now-concealed scars.

Frey.

It was, I told myself, only a reminder of the last time that I had walked behind a man. Nothing more than that.

'We'll have to be careful,' Aldur said in an undertone, when we again met in the corridor. 'No fraternizing in the rooms. They have laws against that sort of thing, even in a diplomatic hotel.'

'If I have my way, we'll be out of here by morning.'

The rooms were certain to be bugged, but I did not think that any surveillance was likely to be very sophisticated, given the overstretched Nhemish resources. Any spare planetary funds had gone into the war effort, and what was left was now being channelled into the rebuilding of religious edifices. It seemed the Nhemish had made a great deal of the durability of their cities when they colonized the planet. The buildings were supposed to be eternal and unchanging, just like their deity-decreed social structure. I thought of the impermanent slums at the city's edge and wondered how they accounted for those. Perhaps the Nhemish simply pretended that they did not exist.

I told Aldur to stay in the room until curfew rang, and then go down to the lobby and make himself visible. I don't think he liked it, but he was under instructions from the Skald, and he did not argue. Then, locking the door behind me, I went into the small bathroom adjacent to my chamber and turned on the tap. At first, nothing happened, but eventually a thin stream of brown liquid trickled out, then stopped again. We had been warned that the water situation was critical here, and rationed. I cursed under my breath and took a packet of rinsing wipes from my bag. Drawn carefully over my skin, the wipe darkened it, but I had to be careful not to peel off the strip of synthetic skin that hid my scars. With equal care, I took my golden left eye out of its socket and put it in a travelling pouch. Replacing it with a darker eye, I changed the contact lens on the right eye, then sprayed the parting of my hair. Within minutes, the alteration spray seeped downwards to invade and colour the follicles.

Now, a dark-haired, dark-eyed woman stared back at me from the spotted mirror. I saw my own oval face and sharp chin, my pointed nose and arched brows, but although the colouring was now closer to my own, the unfamiliarly smooth skin made me blink, confronting me with a stranger. In the flounces of the slip-gown, I was no longer Vali Hallsdottir of Muspell, or the aid worker I had so briefly pretended to be. I was Nhemish, and nothing.

Impatiently, I waited for the call of curfew, sitting in the chair next to the window and watching the sky turn to a deeper rose behind the jade domes. Both of Nhem's moons were thin crescents, hanging delicately against the sky. It would have to be tonight. We had one chance, and a slim plan. Far beyond the city rose the mountains, indigo shadows, the summits touched with red where the last light of the sun was striking them. Perhaps those who had hired us were hiding there, praying for our success. I felt an immense distaste for what I had to do, growing to a bilious lump in my throat. It was almost as though I could feel the gathering force of the seith, hiding deep within as if chased there by these energies of an alien world.

The dusk grew, and suddenly the peace was shattered by an ear-splitting shriek. The siren for curfew had been activated. It was time to move.

I tucked the gown up around my waist, cursing the ruffles, and cautiously opened the window. There was no sign of any wires or trips, and no one below. I secured a cord to the sill, switched on the clamps, and slid out of the window, first dropping my pack. It was a long way to the ground. A flicker of movement caught my gaze and I looked quickly up. A pale face at the window swiftly withdrew, but it was only Aldur.

I picked up the pack and secured it around my waist. Apart from this, I wore the slip-gown, cowl, face-mask and gloves, and the light, all-encompassing sandals that were the only footwear permitted for women. I set off for the old town, keeping to the shadows. The map implant guided me. It was strange to be somewhere wholly unfamiliar, and yet to know exactly where I was going.

Aldur and I had studied the Hierolath's methodology extensively over the last month, and the despot followed a clear pattern. The streets of the old town would be almost deserted tonight. I planned to be in exactly the right place at the right time – or the wrong one, depending on how one looked at it. I glanced up at the moons. They were almost parallel now, moving into phase. It would not be long.

By now, I was almost at the gates of the old town. Iznar was typically Nhemish: an ancient city that had accreted in untidy rings around a central core. The old town itself was a mass of conical tenements, tumbling down beneath the Most Holy, built of fused green brick and glazed with a viridian sheen. The gate itself was guarded by two of the uniformed militia at its foot and a third man on the walkway that hung over the street. I veered away from the gate, heading into the maze of passages beyond. The map implant delivered instructions, in a small, cool voice. It gave me an illusory kind of comfort.

Along . . . then left . . . beneath the archway . . .

It did not look as though there was any way in, but as I ducked under the low arch I saw that there was a partially concealed entrance. I pushed through and found myself in one of the streets of the old quarter. The conical buildings on either side were shuttered, the doors fortified and placed several feet above the street. Iznar was, I remembered, prone to flash floods from meltwater in the spring.

Despite the shutters, I felt eyes on my back all the way. I searched until I found a pile of rubble, then secreted the pack behind it. This meant that I had to disengage the thin stringy film of the tabula; a Nhemish woman would have no need of such a device. There was a rudimentary translator in the map implant, but implanted tabulas never worked as well. I would just have to take the chance. It was not, however, likely that anyone would be engaging me in very complex conversations.

Once this was done, I sent out certain of the senses of the seith, its first and oldest messages: allure, connection, desire . . . It was hard to do on this alien world and I was taking a risk, but the only people on the streets tonight would be the militia, and they were the ones I needed to draw to me.

I had reached the end of the street when the shout came.

'There is one!'

I halted immediately and turned round, to stare trembling at the ground. A member of the militia was running towards me, weapon drawn. I gave a series of small frightened grunts. The militiaman struck me across the side of the head and I stumbled back against the wall. A companion panted up to join him.

'What is it?'

'A female.' He reached out and snatched the mask from my face. I did not look at him directly, not wanting him to see intelligence in my eyes, but I had the chance to take a quick glance at him all the same. Typically Nhemish male, pale face, blue eyes; could almost have been from Muspell. I wondered fleetingly how much they spent on their genetic programs, keeping the genders distinct. 'It'll do.'

'We'll take this one?'

'It'll save scouring the streets for another.'

I was aware of a sudden flood of mingled terror and relief. They would take me. It was happening. When he secured my hands, I sagged in his grasp. All I had to do now was submit.

TWO

PLANET: MONDHILE

Ruan and Eleshtra took one mur apiece to ride up into the Otrade, driving the rest of the little herd before them. The murai were glad to be out of the winter pens, after a season of storms and snow – too glad, Ruan thought. He was relieved when they were through the town gate and out onto the path that led up into the foothills. The town defences hissed down as they passed through the gate: he felt the energy travel through him like brief lightning, and sensed it rise once more when they were out.

It was good, too, to have his sister with him again. She had said nothing about what had happened in the south, and he did not like to pry. Her business was her own, after all. But he still worried about her, as though he were the elder and not a full three years behind. Eleshtra herself was no more than twenty-four, but whatever had taken place in the south had aged her, accentuated the bones beneath her skin. Ruan watched her with concern.

'I'm worried about the grey one,' his sister said as they rode. Ruan looked ahead and he saw what she meant. The mur was limping a little. A raw patch on one hind leg gleamed bloody in the afternoon sun.

'It must have happened on the way out of the pens,' he said. 'It'll be Gainen, I'm sure. She nips. I'll take a look at it when we get up into the hunting grounds.'

'I should have muzzled her in the pen,' Eleshtra said.

'She's very quick. Don't worry. It'll heal. It won't slow her down for long.'

Gainen glanced back, a cold, crimson stare as if she knew that Ruan was talking about her. Sometimes, he thought that they verged on understanding human speech; old stories of cross-breeding came uneasily to mind. His own mount tossed her long head and snarled through the muzzle, as Gainen slid through to the head of the herd.

'She wants to be herd leader,' Eleshtra said.

Ruan laughed. 'Better let her, then. It's not as though we have any say in the matter. They can fight it out amongst themselves. It's spring, after all. She probably just wants the rest to get a good look at her hind quarters.'

An hour later, they were high in the foothills. Ruan looked back to see the slopes marching into the distance, piling up against the mountain wall like layers of darkening cloud.

Ruan shivered. 'I don't like it up here. The land pulls at me.'

'I don't like it either. But it's a good hunting ground.'

'Perhaps that's why.' He looked further. The glaciers at the ridged summit of the Otrade were clearly visible

14

today, but Ruan thought that they were too clear. Rain was on its way.

'There's a storm coming,' he said to Eleshtra. 'We ought not to leave it too late to get back.'

His sister shrugged. 'What's wrong with storms?'

Ruan slapped his mount's arching neck. 'Nothing, if it was just me. But this one doesn't like the lightning.'

'Oh, very well,' Eleshtra said with a sigh. 'But it's not the same, watching it from the windows of the house. You can't feel it properly. You can't taste it.'

'I'll ride back, if you like. You take your time.'

'No, it's all right. I'll come with you. We're almost there, anyway.'

Ruan could feel the bounds of the murai hunting grounds, pulling at his senses: a prickling down his spine and inside his throat, telling him that this was not his territory.

Keep away. Keep away, or we will kill you.

The mur scented it as well, and this was as close as Ruan wanted to go. He looked up the slope, so innocuous to the eye, and drew hard on the reins of his mount so that the beast shrieked and danced.

'Turn her back!' Eleshtra cried and, with an effort, Ruan did so. He hauled her head round and sent her back down the hill. She resisted and pulled all the way, and it wasn't until they reached the lower slope that she stopped.

From the look of it, Eleshtra was having similar trouble with her own mount.

'Good,' Ruan said, looking back from among the trees.

The satinspine was starting to put out red buds, like flecks of raw meat against the glossy black bark. Through the branches, he could see that the rest of the herd was already high on the tawny slope of the hunting ground, like fleeing shadows. 'Another month, and the breeding season will be over. We can bring them back down, and hopefully some young as well.'

'I wonder if—' Eleshtra began to say, but her mount screamed and reared. From the corner of his eye, Ruan glimpsed a fawn streak among the trees, smelled sudden musk.

'Visen!'

Eleshtra dragged the mur back under control and kicked her sides. The mur sprang down the hill in a series of uneven bounds, but the visen was circling up. Ruan could see the narrow, eyeless head, the flange of its nose as it scented the air. It ran straight for Eleshtra.

He did not shout to warn her; she could already see it. He whipped the bow down from his shoulder, notched an arrow, and fired. It sang out, hissing over his sister's shoulder and burying itself in the visen's throat. The beast fell and lay twitching. Ruan, racing up, tore the muzzle away from his mount's jaw and she sank her teeth into the visen's flesh. He let her tear for a moment, until the visen was quite dead, then dismounted.

'Well, at least we have something for dinner,' he remarked.

Eleshtra was staring uneasily down at the corpse.

'Where did it come from? Why isn't it hunting with its pack? Why is it hunting at all in *daylight*?'

Ruan glanced around him. 'I don't know. We ought to go back.' With an effort, he picked up the visen's body, slung it over the mur's back saddle and secured it with a thong. The mur struggled as Ruan tried to put the muzzle back on. She lashed out, teeth narrowly missing his cheek, but he snapped the muzzle over her jaw and locked it tight. Then, he mounted quickly and he and Eleshtra set off through the trees.

There was no sign of the rest of the pack, but as they reached the trees something shrieked behind them, sharp and piercing and filled with rage. Eleshtra turned back in the saddle, eyes wide. 'That sounded *human*.'

'Maybe it was a child?'

'Maybe.'

They listened, but there was nothing more, only the rising wind in the trees and the thunder rolling in, high over the mountain wall.

THREE

PLANET: NHEM

The militiamen brought me in through the courtyard, my feet dragging across the inlaid mosaic. They had stunned me with a prod shortly before they took me from the cell, but lightly, so that I had not soiled myself. If I made any sound – they informed me through blows and nudges – they would use the prod again and I would be taken filthy and stinking before the Hierolath. After that, I knew, he would have my tongue taken.

I did not make a noise. Besides, the effects of the prod had made my tongue swell until it bulged fatly against my teeth. Breathing was difficult. I concentrated on getting air into my lungs and let the men take my weight. I did not attempt to maintain the effects of the seith. It had already done its work in drawing in the militiamen, and I would need it again in a little while.

The prod had made my vision dim and blurred, and I hung my head, but I took in what I could of the courtyard: the mosaic floor, the silent fountain, the grains of mountain sand that skittered across the floor like grass-coloured

18

fleas. It was a clear night, bitter cold, but I did not mind that. It was a reminder of where I had come from and where, I told myself firmly, I would be returning as soon as all this was finally over.

The militiamen knocked at the door of the Hierolath and waited for his reply over the intercom before hauling me inside.

'Just put it down there,' I heard him say. I recognized his voice from the newscasts and I knew that if I raised my head I would recognize his face, too. It was, after all, plastered across every wall in the fortress-citadel: a man in his sixties, ankle-length hair concealed within a skin bag, eyes like burning dots in the wells of his skull.

The militiamen dumped me on the floor.

'Stay,' he said in my ear, enunciating clearly, as one who speaks to a hound. 'Stay . . .' Then he left. I lay where I had fallen, curled and unmoving, for several minutes. I reached into myself and called upon the seith, sending information out into the empty air. It reminded me of fishing – the patient wait, the care – but I was not looking forward to what this would reel in.

A pair of sandals appeared before my face. I willed myself to stillness. A hand reached down and took hold of my hair. I was pulled upright, grateful for the swollen tongue that stifled my grunt of pain. He did not speak to me. I felt myself pushed and pulled through a door. The slip-robes were torn away. Beneath, I was naked. I looked dully at the floor, maintaining the seith, memorizing patterns. They did not believe in depicting words or symbols in this part of Nhem. The mosaic was tiled in random, muted shades, all in green once more – the colour of holiness. Then my hair was seized again and I was thrown face down on a pile of pillows. My legs were thrust apart. Now, I stared at the pattern on the pillow, a rough, loose weave. *It will not be long*, I thought, *it will not be long* – and felt a small, private wave of relief that the Hierolath seemed intent on rape only, and not an accompanying beating. He had said nothing, but when he entered me, he started shouting. I knew, from the fractured words, that it was because he had found me wet.

'Filth and slime! It is a disease, a poison, a toxin to men . . .'

The thing he thought I was would barely have understood him. I gritted my teeth a little harder, feeling the force of the seith increasing within. It was nothing like the impending release of sex; more like the warnings that play across the flesh before a storm. The Hierolath's rant became even less coherent than that as he pounded into me. There was a soft slap as something hit the floor. From the corner of my eye I saw the edge of a skin bag. Long, pallid, greasy hair whipped across my exposed flesh. I smelt lanolin and sour musk, like an old sheep. Swallowing hard, I kept my face closed and numb as he cried out the words for sickness that, in the language of his people, were the worst.

All I could think about was my brother. He had been gentler, and that had been worse.

The Hierolath began to punch me – flailing blows,

weak. He was not young, after all. I lay passive and still, but I could not stop myself from shaking. At last I felt him ejaculate and it was at that point that I released the pent-up power of the seith. I directed it at his solar plexus. He would not have mistaken it for an orgasm. But it left me shaking, all the same.

My hair was snatched up again and I was dragged from the couch and thrown to the floor. I lay, still trembling, on the cool mosaic. He was muttering and whispering.

'Where is it? Where has it gone?'

He was looking for the cleansing knife, I knew. The effects of the prod were wearing off. My tongue once more grew slippery and small. I pushed away the realization of wetness running down my leg and began to count, silently inside my head.

'Where is—'

Then there was a rustling thud, as if something old and papery had struck the floor. I lay and listened to the Hierolath breathing, to the sudden gasping sounds, then to the silence. I was still shaking, but this time I gave way to it for a moment. I curled up, hugging my knees, with the Hierolath's semen leaking onto the mosaic.

Eventually I put a stop to my incipient hysteria and sat up. The Hierolath lay where he had fallen, spreadeagled and half naked, with his robe hitched up around his knees. He was already starting to bloat and rot. Frowning, I flicked the robe aside and checked. Good. His toes were crumbling, becoming dust. I waited impatiently until the rest of the body was no more than a series of curls and whorls of ash, then I crossed to the window and opened it. The mountain wind blew in, redolent of snow from the heights.

I breathed cold air in and it helped me to feel a little cleaner. Soon the Hierolath's body was scattered to the four corners of the room. The head was the last to go. A sophisticated society would use DNA testing to check the room, but this was not a sophisticated society. I leant down to the crumbling skull and whispered, 'Old man? You did not ask "it" what "its" name was, but I am going to tell you. My name is Vali.'

Then, I gathered up the Hierolath's robe and wiped off the worst of the leaking semen. Peeling an acid patch from the outside of one molar, I set it to the hem and waited until it burned down to ash. It, too, was soon gone. Then I put my own torn slip-robe back over my head, gave a mocking bow to the mask, slid it securely over my face, and was gone through the open window, up onto the roof and then into the mountain dark to where the pick-up ship was waiting.

FOUR

PLANET: MONDHILE

The next day, Ruan once more found himself riding up into the Otrade. He and Eleshtra had told the satahrach about the visen, and what they had heard, and old Arrath had frowned.

'A voice, you say?' He sounded bemused and Ruan did not blame him.

'It sounded like a child,' Eleshtra said.

'But what would anyone be doing up there, apart from herding mur? Hunting, perhaps? But it would be foolish to hunt so close to the murai territory.'

'We thought it might be a mehed,' Ruan added. 'Sometimes the wanderers stray into strange places.'

'I am sure you are right,' the satahrach said. 'Without true consciousness, always in the bloodmind, they have no more wit than animals – and often a lot less. Animals, after all, know what to leave alone.'

'True, but that visen did not,' Eleshtra said. She stroked the fawn-cream, black-tipped pelt with one hand, stretching it across her knees as she sat in front of the fire.

'Hunting in daylight? I've never heard of such a thing. It's rare to see visen even in the night.'

'Rare and fortunate,' Arrath said softly. 'And the Otrade is not so very far away. If the visen have begun to change their hunting patterns, come closer to the settlements . . .'

'Someone should go and see,' Ruan said.

His sister laughed, and it struck him that it was the first time he had heard her do so since she returned from the south. 'Ah, Ruan. You haven't changed. Still wanting to take care of everyone and everything.'

'There is nothing wrong with that,' the satahrach chided. 'Especially in a world where we turn so much on one another, so often.'

'That is the natural way of things,' Eleshtra said.

'Even so,' Ruan remarked, 'someone should see.'

'So will you go?'

Both his sister and the satahrach were looking at him.

'I think I will,' Ruan said.

And so next day, early in the afternoon, Ruan set out, this time on foot. He took the bow with him, and a net, in case there was any bird-hunting to be had. He headed back up the path that led to the foothills, and at the place where he had killed the visen, he paused. Everything seemed the same: the black and crimson trees, the soft rich leafmould beneath his feet. Yet he could feel something, an apprehension in the air. He went cautiously up into the woods, bow at the ready. He could see where the visen had come from, now. There were tufts of creamy hair clinging to the thorns and he followed the trail it had made. It led him up onto a high ridge of rock, and there it disappeared.

There were marks in the shale, however, a little further down the ridge. Moving with care, Ruan edged his way down the bank. But cautious though he was, he missed his footing and slid. He did not notice the line of black energy until it was too late. He stepped right onto it, moving from the familiar, heavy pull of the rock beneath into something that shifted and changed and sucked his conscious awareness down into itself. His ears rang as if he had been trapped in a gong tower, and his sight was filled with sparks of dazzling, bloody light. It occurred to him fleetingly that this must be how an enemy would feel, snared in the energies of the town defences. A sense of disaster rose up inside him with tidal force.

Then it all went away. He was standing on the apron of scree, with a distant humming under the soles of his feet and a girl standing in front of him. She was perhaps twenty or so, close to his own age. She was smiling, displaying small, sharp teeth. Her moonlight hair was bound in four braids, which reached her knees and ended in clasps in the shape of silver stars. Her eyes were a pale frost blue. She wore hammered leather armour, interlaced with mesh. She said, 'Why are you standing there like a lump?' and then she laughed.

'I can't move,' Ruan heard someone say, and the voice was panicky.

25

'Oh,' the girl said, lowering her gaze and looking at him sideways. 'Then you'll just have to stay put, won't you?' She laughed again and turned to go.

'Help me,' the voice said, and Ruan wondered at it. It did not seem part of him. But the girl was already sauntering away down the path, her braids swinging behind her and the stars at their ends catching the sun. Dark energy rose up once more inside him, like a bottle filling with blood. Through the mist he felt the sun drop down towards the ridge of the mountains.

Much later, the girl came back again. He knew this because she clapped her hands once, behind him, and the haze gradually receded. Hands crept across his eyes. Ruan felt soft leather gloves and the prickle of talons against his forehead.

'Guess who it is!' he heard her say. He strained to strike her hands from his eyes but could not move a muscle.

'Let me go!'

'Why, of course,' she said. The clasping hands disappeared, and next moment she was standing in front of him. The dying light lent a crimson cast to her hair and the stars sparkled ruby as she threw back her braids. She held out a hand, smiled when he could not take it, then pushed him clear of the energy line.

Ruan fell to his knees in front of her, gasping on the stony ground. Nausea rose bitter in his throat. A hand came to rest gently upon his shoulder.

'You're not well,' the girl said. 'I'm sorry.' She sounded genuinely contrite. 'I didn't realize it would affect you so badly. You will forgive me, won't you?' She crouched beside him and he found himself staring into her pale eyes. 'Let me take you back to my clan house, just for the night. We'll look after you there.'

'I can't,' Ruan said. 'My family will be worried. I have to go back.' He reached for the comfort of the bow, but it had gone from his shoulder. It did not seem to matter, somehow.

'No, you don't,' she said, serene, and next moment Ruan realized that of course he didn't have to go back. It was as though a weight had been lifted from his shoulders. He felt light as air.

The girl helped him to rise and Ruan leaned on her as they climbed the scree. His head was pounding now, hammering with the aftershock of the energy and her presence. He was suddenly aware of the long lean line of her body against his, of her quick, sinuous step. But when he looked wonderingly into her face, he saw only concern.

'We're nearly there,' she said, reassuringly. 'It's not far now.'

Yet Ruan could still sense the energy, running in a parallel course through the rocks.

'It's over there,' he said. 'The energy line, I mean. Can't you feel it? I should go back.' The words sounded hollow, a whistle in the wind.

But she said only, 'Hush . . . Don't *worry*,' and she led him on, stumbling a little, up over the next ridge.

It was now close to dark. The sun was long gone behind the Otrade, and the first stirrings of the night breeze touched his skin. Marahan was flickering over the ragged lip of the mountains – the first star in the evening sky and a sure sign of spring. He could smell the resinous scent of ipher from the forest, sharp on the wind.

'Here we are,' the girl said, and smiled at him.

The tower rose up from the rocks below like a spine, white against the shadows. Then, as he took a step forward, it shifted into darkness, becoming barely visible. Startled, he stepped back and there it was again, bone-white in the dusk. It was perhaps a hundred feet high, massive at the base and ringed with high balustrades, tapering to a smooth summit.

'We get a lot of stray travellers here,' the girl said. 'But you're not like the other one. The vitki.' She spoke as though savouring the word.

'The what?' Ruan asked, puzzled.

Her grip on his arm tightened. Then, as if the skin of his senses had been torn away, Ruan once more felt the black line of energy. It ran straight to the tower, as channelled water runs to a deep, still pool; it must be part of the tower's defence system. Shock ran icy through him. The girl drifted by his side, hazy in the half-light. And without stopping to think, he snatched the hunting net from his belt and threw it over her head. She cried out, clawing at the net, but the tangle of metal burrs at its hem was already snagging itself in her hair. The metal stars flashed as she struggled, but he did not wait to watch. With her furious cries echoing behind him he ran, up into the rocks and away from the energy line and the tower. He did not look back, nor did he stop until he reached the ridge that led down to the town where his own clan house lay, and sanctuary.

That night, Ruan suddenly woke. He sat up on his elbows and looked around. Everything was as usual in the little chamber: the piled blankets on the narrow bed, the bows hanging on the wood-panelled wall, the carved chest that contained his clothes. The embers still glowed in the grate, casting a faint red light across the room. He could feel the energy of the town defences all around, encasing and protecting him. It was very quiet. But then something scratched at the wax paper of the window, a thin small sound. Ruan waited and listened. Moments later, it came again.

He slipped from the bed and padded across to the window, taking care not to walk where he might cast a shadow. The sound came once more, this time more insistent, like the claws of a bird against the thick paper pane. And now he thought he could glimpse it through the glow cast by the dying fire: a great wing, sweeping over the oblong of the window. He reached out to touch the latch.

'Let me in!' someone said. Ruan stumbled back from the window, banging his elbow on the wall. He swore.

'It's so cold . . .'

He knew that voice, he was sure of it, but he could not have put a name to it. He flicked open the latch. The window flew open in a whirl of snow and someone was there, surging across the sill in a cloud of dark-and-light. Stars flew in her unbound hair. It was the girl from the tower.

'It's you,' Ruan said, stupidly. The girl dusted icy crystals from her hands. She ducked her head, cocking it to one side, and smiled up at him.

'Of course. Who else?'

She was wearing different clothes, all in black and a kind of iridescent pearl. Her tunic was unlaced down the front, displaying the pale curve of her breasts.

'Why are you here?' Ruan asked.

'Why, I came to find you,' the girl said. 'You ran away. We can't have that.'

Her gaze held his. He tried to look away but could not. 'This is what I came for,' the girl said. She stepped forward. He felt her arms slide round his neck. Suddenly her arms were bare, her skin smooth and cold.

'Wait! How did you get inside the walls? Who are you? What's your name?'

'My name is *never mind*,' the girl murmured. He felt her tongue stroke his cheek, flickering delicately around the lobe of his ear. Somehow, he thought it should be rough, like an animal's, but it was feather-light against his skin.

He did not understand how she had removed her clothes, but now she stood naked in his arms, almost as tall. The stars glowed in her hair and he could not understand that, either. But it did not matter. *My name is never mind . . .*

Then she was moving against him. He touched her small breasts, the long waist and narrow hips, then slid his hand between her legs and found her wet. She gave a cold, fierce smile and caught his lower lip between her teeth.

There was sudden pain and the taste of blood, but he found that he did not care. Nor did it concern him when her claws raked his back and he was carrying her down onto the bed and taking her hard. She locked her legs around his waist and her eyes grew huge and blank, but the little smile never left her lips, except when she sank her teeth into his shoulder and he felt himself start to come.

Dizzy and faint, he was not certain whether she climaxed, but he heard her hiss and it sounded like victory.

And then she was no longer there, cool air where her warm flesh had been, and he was alone on the bed and bleeding.

FIVE

Planet: Nhem

The pick-up place was located in the hills to the west of the city. I slipped down through the old quarter, this time using the seith to minimize my passing presence, but it made little difference. The old quarter was quiet, like a hive stilled by cold. As soon as the Hierolath's absence was discovered, however, all hell would break loose and I did not want to risk still being in Iznar when that happened. The militia would be looking for a woman, and most probably an outworlder. The local women would be beyond suspicion. You would not suspect a dog or a cow, after all, of dispatching your leader – but then, those who had hired me were different. I needed to get out of the city and adopt a different disguise as quickly as possible.

Iznar was a gated city, tucked away behind massive walls. The western gates lay open during the day, but were closed as soon as curfew sounded. However, we had learned that they were opened once during the night, to let a militia team in from the desert and send another one out for the midnight shift. While this distraction was going on, I planned to go over the wall. But first, I found the pile of rubble where I had hidden the pack and retrieved it. I was relieved to find that it was still there, but somehow this also made me uneasy, as though things were going too smoothly. That was never a good sign.

I hung back behind one of the thick buttress walls, hiding in shadows, until I heard a siren sound midnight. There was an ear-grinding creak as the gates were winched open, then the tramp of feet as the militia team came through. When I peered round the corner, I saw that the guards at the summit of the gate were coming down the steps in preparation for the change-over. I crept along a back alley towards the wall. They were going into the guard-house at the base of the gate.

I took the hook from the pack and the length of fibreline, then spun it up and over. It struck the top of the wall, and held. It wasn't easy in the slip-robe, and I had to tuck the tattered thing up to free my legs. But I was up the line before the next shift emerged from the guard-house, thanking whatever deity might be listening that the Nhemish had imposed a ban upon cameras. Transmission of the human form was held to be soul-splitting and sacrilegious. Given their paranoia, it made something of a dilemma for the Nhemish security forces, but it was one that suited me.

Once at the top of the wall, feet grating against its surface and sending a little shower of sand down into the street, I pulled the fibreline up behind me, ran across the wall's narrow span, sank the hook into the rough stone of the opposite side and sent the line down, after a swift check to ensure that there was no one on the other side. The previous team had just gone through and it would not be long before the next militia team was sent out, but it gave me just enough leeway to spin down the wall and into the rocks on the other side, reeling the line in once I hit the ground.

I caught a brief glimpse of desert as I did so: a long expanse of rock, dunes sliding up like sea-waves, and then the spectral presence of the snow-capped peaks beneath a wash of starlight. Just as my feet hit the ground, the gate creaked again and the next shift came through. I dropped, face down behind a rock. But the militia went on, moving quickly towards the edges of the dunes. I waited until they were out of sight, then set the map implant to 'readout' and looked for the pick-up place.

It lay some five miles from the city walls: a flat plateau of rock nestling between crags, out of view of the city and invisible from anywhere but the plateau itself. I set off through the desert, muffled as much as possible against the cold. I was used to it, and there was no wind, but the chill still struck through to my bones and numbed me as I ran. Perhaps, I reflected, that was just as well. I could feel the Hierolath on me, a ghostly, tainted touch.

I kept an eye out for the patrol, but they were nowhere in sight. It wasn't just the militia that concerned me; I was not entirely sure what kind of wildlife might be native to this part of Nhem. The briefing had contained information about sink-larvae – as long as the body of a man – that burrowed beneath the ground and spun webs of mucus and sand in order to entrap their prey. And there was a kind of rodent known as a nightrunner, sporting a huge female form that leaped down from the crags onto her victims, while the tiny males followed a hundred-strong behind. I was not keen to make the acquaintance of either one and was careful where I put my feet. The infrared of the map implant delineated areas of softer, looser sand, and these I avoided, just in case. When I reached the sandstone canyon that led to the pick-up site, I was equally careful of what might spring from above.

If it had not been for the prospect of the roving militia and unwholesome local wildlife, I might almost have enjoyed the hike. It felt good to be out in clean, cold air again, even though this dry world was very different to my own. Away from the polluted pall that hung over the city, the stars were as lustrous and bright as any seen from the deck of an island-bound ship, the constellations in fiery, unrecognizable patterns. Somewhere up there was Muspell's sun, Grainne. I did not pause to seek it out. I would be seeing it soon enough, I told myself, just as soon as I rounded the pillar of rock that the map had directed me to and saw – nothing.

I stood staring in disbelief. This was definitely the place. The map coordinates all converged and were signalling red against my inner sight, but there was no sign of the ship. We had agreed not to use the comm channel except in emergency, in case the Nhemish picked up the frequency, but this was certainly an emergency. I put a call through to Aldur.

'Where are you? The ship's not here.'

But there was nothing from Aldur's channel, only a messy hum of static. The channel was patched directly into the map implant, which, like mine, had been set into the wall of Aldur's visual cortex. If the channel was down, that meant either that Aldur was dead, offworld, or that someone had removed it. Somehow, the last option seemed the worst of all. These things were meant to last for life.

Was it possible that my own implant was faulty, or that someone was interfering with the frequency and I had been directed to the wrong place? I scouted around the neighbouring rocks, but it seemed logical simply from the surroundings that this was the intended place for my retrieval. Everywhere else was too narrow, too rocky or too unstable for even a little rescue pod to set down, let alone the larger pick-up.

At that point, I heard voices. I ran behind an outcrop of rock and sprawled face down on the rough sand. Peering around an edge of stone, I saw the militiamen a little way below: four men in helmets, joined by a fifth, who was bare-headed. The plume of blond hair and his pale skin, combined with the camouflage suit, rendered him almost invisible against the rocks. He and the others conferred in staccato Nhemish, but they were too far away for my tabula to be able to pick up what they were saying.

After a few moment's conversation, two of the men wheeled away and ran up into the rocks, where they disappeared. I shrank back further against the rock wall, wary of being glimpsed from above. I did not want anyone creeping up on me from behind. The other three melted back into the shadows under the crags. I glanced up, to a sky empty of anything other than stars. Without the pick-up ship, it was pointless to move. I would have to wait until morning, then try to rig up a transmitter and send out on the panic channel to the nearest Muspellian ship. But if any of the militia came near, I thought, I would kill them. And what had befallen Aldur? He must have been captured or killed for that channel to be down. The notion that he might be offworld raised too many questions for me to want to contemplate it at the moment.

Leaning back against the rock, I reached out with the seith. The immediate vicinity was devoid of life, but I could feel the edges of the wind against the rocks, lifting the sand in tiny whorls and spirals and sending it skittering over the stone. The rock behind me still gave out a faint radiance from the day's sunlight – no real warmth, but the memory of heat.

But the area was disturbed, presences moving around me, and I knew that they were the militia. There were two of them, not very far away. And they were coming closer. They were stalking me, and from the nature of their movements I did not think they were after a terrified Nhemish woman, a stray animal from the city. They moved cautiously, as though the person they sought was dangerous.

So, I thought to myself, these men of Nhem were not completely stupid when it came to women. I crouched back against the rock, rising a little so that I was squatting, ready to spring if the need came.

And the next moment, it did. They rushed me in a pincer movement, one from each side of the rock. I heard a shout from below as their comrades realized what was happening. But I was already springing upward, leaping for a handhold of stone some three feet above my head. I grasped it and it held. I drew up my knees as the militiamen cannoned into one another below. It would have been comical if it hadn't happened so fast. They spun around, clasping at one another, but not falling. So I swung down, kicked one of them in the side of the neck, then threw myself up again, stepping onto the handhold and jumping up to the summit of the crag.

A shot hissed past my ear and sent a sparkling shower of burning sand to the canyon floor. I dropped flat. The other man had raced around the side of the crag and was climbing up the other side. A conveniently large rock took care of him. I leaped down to the body, checked that he was dead, and stripped him of his weapon. That, I felt, evened the odds considerably.

The remaining three were fanning out around the crag. I reached out with the seith, felt warmth and intent, a bitterness upon the air. I followed it, springing around the side of the crag and firing as I did so. A man fell in a spit of flame. I dropped, almost too late. A shot soared overhead, inches from my prone form. I smelled shattered rock, breathed in dust. Rolling over, I glimpsed him at the top of the crag and fired again. The head that had appeared over the edge of the rock jerked back, too sharply for a voluntary movement, and sank out of sight. I rolled again, down behind the rocks, and searched for the fifth man. That, I thought, was the commander.

He was better than the rest – probably the reason for his rank. He moved with more stealth; I could barely feel him against the edges of the seith. I wondered where he had fought and won his battles; in the incessant civil wars of southern Nhem, perhaps. It would not have been off-world. The Nhemish regarded any world other than their own as an abomination. To them, Nhem alone was the sanctuary cradle, chosen by deity. But wherever this man had fought, he knew what he was doing. I did not want to wait for him to come to me.

I inched around the edge of the crag, trying to get a better fix on him. I could not tell exactly where he was, only that he was close. I crouched in the shadows of the rocks, seeking, and the seith was suddenly baffled. It felt as though he was all around and yet nowhere, a presence spreading out to encompass the dark. I did not understand it until he was suddenly standing over me, right on the lip of the crag.

He and I fired at the same time. Rock exploded directly above my head, sending splinters of fractured stone in a needle storm against my face. My shot went wide but, as he raised his weapon again, something like a huge black arrow struck him from behind. He toppled over the crag, landing only a couple of feet from me and bringing the thing with him. I looked into a flat, snarling face.

From the corner of my eye I saw what looked like a waterfall pour over the edge of the crag and flow across the rock. There were burning pinpricks up the length of my leg. I sprang to my feet. Nightrunners: the males following the much larger female, an ironic counterpoint to the society of Nhem. The males were the size of dormice, nothing more than stomachs surrounded by a round ring of teeth. They swarmed up my leg and I brushed them off, but more followed. The female was the size of a lynx, but I did not have time to wonder how in the world they mated. Perhaps they stood on one another's shoulders. She raised her dripping face from the militia commander's throat and growled at me from the middle of a maw of needles.

I saw her long hind haunches bunch and ripple, like a cat about to leap, but then we were all blasted against the rock by an immense punch of air. Nightrunner males blew past me like squealing leaves. The female tumbled over and over, got to her feet and shook herself in wet-cat manner. The pick-up ship fell from the sky to hover on rocking blast-jets, a few feet from the crag. The hatch slid open.

I ran the short distance over stone and jumped from the lip of the crag to land sprawling, crushing several small furred bodies beneath me as I did so. The hatch hissed shut, the pick-up shot upwards, and staggering to the nearest screen I saw Nhem receding fast behind us: a red-gold sphere, with the crackling plaintive static of Nhemish air-space over the communications system, complaining of violation.

40

SIX

PLANET: MONDHILE

Ruan did not tell anyone what had happened at the tower, because it made him sound such a fool. It was like falling over your own feet. He felt as though everyone could see his ineptness, that he wore it like a patched and tattered cloak. And perhaps it really was visible, too.

Nor did he tell anyone about the dream. There were long scratches down his back and along his sides, and his lip hurt, but it seemed so improbable that the girl could have come to him in the middle of the night that he thought he must have done it to himself, in the throes of the dream – or nightmare, whichever it had been. Whenever he thought about it, which was often, it was half with pleasure and half with shame and he could not have said which was the stronger.

'Whatever is the matter with you?' Eleshtra asked the next day. 'You've been skulking in corners all morning. It's not like you.'

'I'm not feeling well.'

'You've probably caught a chill, out all day like that.' She looked at him. 'Did you find anything?'

'Of the visen? No. Not a trace.'

'Ruan?' She put a hand on his sleeve. 'Don't go up there again. When it's time, we'll fetch the mur together, and I'll ask some of the others to come with us. Visen are too dangerous to play games with.'

'Don't worry. I've no intention of going back,' Ruan said.

When she had gone, he went in search of the satahrach, going up the long stair of polished satinspine, past the door that led to the Memory Room and onto the landing that would take him up to the attics. At the window, he paused and looked out over the courtyard. The distant sound of someone tapping a piece of metal came from the forge along the street. The scent of blood drifted up from the courtyard as Eleshtra went by with a bucket of it for the mur. It was like looking down into a wet red eye. He heard the mur shriek in the stables as they smelled the approaching treat, heard Eleshtra mutter reassurances. A flock of sea-coloured ghows sailed over the roofs of the town, bickering over a fragment of fish that fell damply to the rooftop just below the window. Ruan watched them squabble and fight for a moment, and then they were off again, disturbing the morning peace. He turned from the window and headed for the attics.

He found the old man in the highest room of the clan house, fiddling with a piece of round glass, like the fragments found in the smoking mountains.

'What are you doing?' Ruan asked.

'They tell me you can see more clearly through this thing,' Arrath said. He held the glass and squinted through it. 'It comes from the south, like all useless objects.'

'And *can* you see more clearly?'

'I cannot. I cannot see anything at all, in fact.' The satahrach tossed the glass onto the table. 'Everything appears as though I am looking through smoke. Someone *should* invent something that permits one to see, when one becomes old. But I do not see what use a piece of this glassy substance is likely to be. The man who brought it said it was like an eyeball. But two bad eyes are not the same as one good one.' He picked up the glass again and handed it to Ruan. 'Here. You take it. Keep it as a lucky piece.'

Ruan shrugged and put the glass in his pocket. 'Thank you, Arrath.'

'And what do you want, by the way? To tell me about day-hunting visen?'

'No. I found nothing up there. The trail faded out. But I wanted to ask you about dark energy.'

'What about it? The land is full of it, in certain places. Currents of it run through the earth and the rock. It is like water, or a mineral. It is just something that is.'

'Can it be part of the defences of a place?'

'Of course. You know how the town defences work: energies of the land, corralled around this settlement,

43

recognizing only those who were born here. Dark energy works the same way: you can use it to protect a place.'

'And it can damage the people who live there? What about others?'

'If you live in such a place, you are part of it and it is part of you. Of course it can damage others, if they're idiot enough to seek it out and play around with it. Unless one is a certain type of person, it seeps into the bones like poison and infects the gall, which as you know is the seat of consciousness, causing it to swell. Why do you ask?'

'I could feel a line of dark energy in the foothills yesterday. It ran through the mountains. I wondered where it led.'

'As I've said, people do live on black lines. They feed off the dark energy until they are no longer part of the world. Their minds become warped by it, they have little concern for the pain of others. I heard tales of a clan who lived on a line like that, high in the mountains, years ago. It is unlikely that they are still there. Such people become weakened by inbreeding. They do not relate well to others, not even in times of festival or migration.' The satahrach paused. 'I would not go near people like that, if I encountered them. Dangerous and unstable folk.'

'I will keep well away from the line,' Ruan promised.

'Just watch where you are putting your great feet, that is all.' The satahrach said this with a sigh, as though he had little hope of being heeded.

Ruan went back down into the thin winter sunlight of the courtyard. The house defences were down. Eleshtra stepped blinking into the light, a bow in one hand. 'I'm going hunting, with Thia and the others. I don't know when I'll be back. We'll keep closer to town, though.'

He would have offered to go with her, but the women preferred to hunt together, without men. Ruan sometimes thought that it gave them the chance to gossip in peace, and so went back into the hall to sit down by the fire and warm his hands. The satahrach was quite right, anyone could see that. Yet he could not force the girl from the tower from his mind. He could see her as clearly in imagination as if she stood before him: the stars sparkling in her hair, her pale eyes full of challenge. He would not, he told himself, be returning to that dark line that ran through the mountains, or the dappled, shifting tower. He would never go there again. But staring into the firelight, he already knew that he lied.

SEVEN

PLANET: MUSPELL

The rescue craft was piloted by a woman named Inge, a calm blonde in her late forties whom I recognized from the Rock. She was one of the Skald's best pilots. I was grateful to them and glad to see her, and I said so. She greeted this with a small smile and a bow of the head, but she did not look up from the navigational display of the pick-up ship. I asked her if she knew what had happened to Aldur. She shook her head.

'I'm sorry, I've no idea. The Skald gave me specific orders: to collect you, and Aldur if he was there. But I was not to go in search of him, and there was no signature from his implant as I came in.'

'He must have been captured.'

'I couldn't wait.'

'I'm not blaming you,' I said. She could tell me no more. Wearily, trying not to think about Aldur or the rape, I found a pod-berth a little way along the cabin, stripped off what remained of my garments, and slipped into it. There was an immediate shower of dust from the ceiling of the pod, scouring me as clean as it could, then evaporating. It was not enough. I needed water – longed for Muspell's seas and rain – but this would have to do for now. I meant only to rest for half an hour or so, but when I woke I saw that I had been sleeping for sixteen hours, and Inge's serene voice was informing me that we were coming into Muspell space.

She lent me a jumpsuit, which looked too big, but I did not want to arrive on my home planet wearing the sad remains of my Nhemish ruffles. Reflected in the polished hatchway of the pod, I looked like a wet cake. I changed into the jumpsuit with relief.

Muspell loomed in the viewscreen: a marbled sphere, mostly sea, island-starred. The long skeins of the archipelagos of the Reach lay on the day side, stringing the planet like necklaces and half hidden by cloud. The other islands, of which the largest was Darkland, lay on the night side, the far face of the world. I could not see it, and was grateful. Muspell's stony little moon, Loki, was hanging over the planet's shoulder like a pestering neighbour, the mistletoe branch across its countenance clearly visible. They said that the early settlers – my ancestors – had taken this emblem, the legacy of meteor strikes, as a sign of the world's favour.

Inge brought the ship hard in under the moon to avoid the mainstream traffic coming up from Tiree: mainly cargo and executive craft, with a long passenger liner glimpsed briefly off the starboard bow.

'Heading up to Main,' Inge said, over her shoulder.

'That's the sky-ferry?'

'The first in the week.'

That reminded me that I had lost track of where we were on Muspell: late spring, now, with the equinoctial tides roaring up the Minch and the seabirds flocking over the islands. As we soared in over the sea, close enough for me to reach out and run my hand through the cold swell – or so it felt – I was overwhelmed with relief to be home. We passed the chain of islands that led into the big ports of Tiree and Coll, coming in over Tiree itself. The city lay below in a sprawl of warehouses and flats.

Tiree was not a pretty place, utilitarian and functional, and to my mind not really part of Muspell at all, despite its ancient name. Inge landed the ship to one side of the spaceport, in a bay marked with the signature runes of the Skald, and gave me a key to a rented room in the spaceport hotel. Designed for business travellers from off-world, this was bland and pleasant enough, professionally welcoming, but I had no intention of staying overnight.

At the desk I organized a wing out to the Rock, pausing only briefly in the room to wash the dye from my skin. It was good to be away from the stifling atmosphere of Nhem. I peered through the viewscreen of the wing, dim with sea-spray and rain, as I headed out of the harbour, and smiled with satisfaction at the cold surge below. I had already sent my report regarding the Hierolath's assassination on to the Skald. I had, also, received word that they were pleased.

The wing touched down with feather-lightness on the

ramp, sending up a shower of foam as it came in. The pilot stood aside to let me step down. The Rock towered above me, black and wet against the eggshell sky. The cavern doors were opening, the grind of stone against stone. I looked back at the quivering wing and walked through. The doors closed behind me with a last sea breath, and then I was enclosed within the fortress of the Skald.

Two women were waiting for me, dressed in water-armour and sealstock-fur cloaks.

'Idhunn is waiting for you,' one of the women said.

'Upstairs?'

'Yes, in the lamp room.' The woman smiled. 'You know the way, of course. But she sent us to escort you.'

'It's an honour,' I said.

'For us, yes.' After Nhem, it was good to be treated with respect, though the Skald behaved toward all visitors with equal courtesy, regardless of where they might have come from.

I followed the women up the long, worn flight of steps that led to the warning-lamp for shipping. I could have traced each one of the gald-stones that decorated the walls, although the fortress, so huge when I had first come here seven years ago, now seemed a little tighter, more cramped. I could not help wondering how often I had climbed these steps over the course of those years.

The women left me at the iron doors that led to the lamp room. I knocked, and the doors opened. I could see Idhunn's tall figure standing at the far side of the room, looking out to sea. Her hair fanned out around her shoulders – as pale as sea mist, though in Idhunn's case, it was due to age as much as the genes of Muspell. She turned and smiled.

'Vali.'

Looking at her now, she could be a girl in her twenties, her face unlined, the skin glowing, but the illusion did not last. She twitched her head, dispelling the effects of her seith, and was once more old.

'Come and join me,' Idhunn said. I did so. From this height, the curve of the horizon was clearly visible: all churning ocean until the gaze hit the islands of the Lesser Minch.

'I read your report,' Idhunn said. 'You must be glad to be home.'

'Nhem is not a pleasant place, it's true, but that was why I went. What I want to know is: why did I almost fail to make it out? Where's Aldur?'

'Vali . . . We don't know yet. Something's obviously badly wrong, but we don't think he's on Nhem any more.'

I stared at her. 'Then where is he?'

'Nothing happened to his implant, I'm sure of that – except that it was switched off. There was no record of any damage. There were traces of his communication channel going out through the Junction, then nothing.'

'The *Junction*? But that's halfway to Muspell. Are you sure?' He must have been talking to someone when he reached the Junction, if they had picked up those traces. But who?

'It was the night of your mission. In order to get there

as quickly as he apparently did, he must have left Nhem almost as soon as you arrived. The confusion delayed the pick-up.'

'But why? He knew what the parameters of the mission were.'

'We don't know. We're looking for him, Vali. That's the best I can promise you for now.'

'Find him,' I said. 'I want to know what happened.'

'So do we.' Idhunn paused, then went on, 'I've been talking to another operative – someone from Ghaith, not Muspell – deep in the Khas at Iznar. She's been there for a year now. She says that the place is a hornets' nest, filled with scurrying and twitching. Now that the Hierolath is gone, they're all jockeying for position.'

'Any winners?'

'It will be the boy.'

'And will it be for the better, I wonder?'

'That's why we were hired and you were sent. By the time the boy reaches an age to know his own mind – if he ever does – Nhem will have changed. Those who hired us will see to that.'

I smiled. 'The women's resistance. I wish I'd managed to meet them, but it was too risky. I should have liked to have met a woman who'd survived that breeding program.'

'There will be more, now that the Hierolath has gone and the factions are too busy fighting among themselves to seek out the secret laboratories. You have bought them time.'

'It won't be easy.'

'Remove the foundation stone, and the structure crumbles. These religious dictatorships are always brittle, built on personality cults as they are.'

The Hierolath was not a personality that I cared to remember. But he was gone, now. The Skald rarely meddled in outworld business – Darkland and the vitki were enough to keep us occupied – but on this occasion, we had been specifically asked to interfere and the Council had thought it a worthwhile cause. The resistance of Nhem had hired us because the Skald was run by women and they trusted us. Nhem had been a gender skirmish, and would continue to be so. Ironic, then, that I had been let down by a male accomplice. Ironic, but not, I thought bitterly, surprising. And I wondered, too, if any of it was quite as simple as that. I should like to know more about the Nhemish resistance, for all sorts of reasons.

I stared down at Idhunn's gnarled wrists, ringed with silver, at her hands gripping the old stone of the sill, and reminded myself to collect my own bracelets from my quarters. I did not feel fully dressed without them. Idhunn nodded in the direction of the Minch.

'Storm's coming up tonight.'

I laughed. 'I'll welcome it.'

'There's to be a dinner in your honour.'

'I'll be glad of that, too.' With surprise, I realized that I was hungry, though Inge had given me a ration pack on the pick-up ship. 'If no one minds, then I think I'll come up here after it, stand in the storm for a while.'

Idhunn gave me a sidelong glance.

'Get clean?'

'That's part of it. But I am made for this, Idhunn. You know that. It's what the Skald made me. It's what Frey made me.' There was a short silence after I spoke. I did not often say his name, and we both knew it. My brother's name I did not say at all.

'Do you still think it's worth the price? I will always ask, Vali. You know that. If you want to give up the game, go back to your family's hold, you know you can.'

I thought back to the rape, to the squalor of Nhem, then to the Hierolath's rotting corpse above that city of silenced women.

'Oh, it's worth it. If there comes a point when I change my mind, you'll hear about it. Scaraskae will always be there.' I was not sure whether I truly believed this. Nothing remains the same, and even though Scaraskae and its holdings had been in my family for over a hundred years, I did not like to take anything for granted. And what had Scaraskae given me? Not much, when all was said and done.

'Well,' Idhunn said with a sigh. 'The game's better for your presence, I'll tell you that much.'

After taking my leave of her, I went down to my own small chamber, set into the fortress wall. From here, there was an identical view to the one from the lamp room, only the angle was a little different. It was a comfort to look out over the same sea, and I threw the window open to dispel the stuffiness caused by my absence. Then, I took the

53

bracelets from the box. It had been my grandmother's and it was made from alder wood, a tree grown from the direct lineage of Earth, without genetic tampering.

Holding the hard wood in my hands reminded me of Scaraskae: the long slope of sea-meadow leading down to the foreshore and the alder groves, with the expanse of the fjord beyond. Closing my eye for a moment, I could almost feel its silence, away from the low stones of the house and the chattering of my family, my sisters and brother. It had been a long time since I had seen my sisters. As for my brother, if I never saw him again, it would still be too soon.

Even so, now that he was no longer there, I wished I could go back, but too much had changed and more would have to, before I could feel comfortable about returning to the hold. I would be little more than a ghost at Scaraskae these days – and besides, I belonged to the Skald now.

I slipped the bracelets onto my wrists: white sealstock bone for the Skald and silver for the Parliamentary Majority – to which every citizen of the Reach auto-matically belonged. Then I slid out of the borrowed jump-suit and rummaged in a drawer for trousers and tunic, and the fur-collared velvet jacket, which was the closest thing I had to formal wear. Under the clothes, I found the pen.

I sat back on my heels by the window and looked at it. I had not used it for over a year now, but it was a comfort knowing that it was still there. Some people, in response to trauma or despair, turn to the bottle or to drugs. Others starve themselves. I did none of these things. The scars on my face were not the only ones that my body bore. The tears that I wept were red. I cut.

It had started when I was young. My brother – I will not say his name, even now – and what he had done to me was the reason for it, and though the Skald had offered therapy, I had refused. I was private about my pain and I didn't trust counsellors: it seemed to me that too many of them had gone into the profession to serve their own needs and solve their own problems. Perhaps that was all part of the process, but I was determined that it should not be at my emotional expense.

Whatever the reason, from the age of thirteen onwards, whenever I was upset – which was a lot of the time – I had shut myself away in my room at Scaraskae, drawing thin red lines along my arms with a sharp little blade. My father had kicked my brother out by then, but I still took care to lock my door.

Sometimes I didn't even need to make the first cut; just touching the blade in my pocket was enough. No one ever noticed. The Reach is not a warm place and I wore long sleeves. Nor do we go in for communal bathing, though I had to pretend that I couldn't stand the heat of a sauna. Most of the time, the cutting did not leave a scar and I certainly wasn't trying to kill myself. It was hard to explain the satisfaction that I got from it; the absorbed state it produced that blanked everything else out, the peace that descended on me like a shroud. Hours could pass and I would sit, patiently etching lines on my skin. It did not hurt at the time; only later, and then the pain felt somehow necessary, as though I had earned it.

When I left home, I stopped cutting. I did not revert to the old habit until after my accident; during a particularly fraught and pain-filled day, I remembered it. It was like meeting an old friend. In that dingy room in Yetland, I found a blade, cleaned it in a flame, and began.

It was dark when I finally stopped. A movement at the door had broken the trance and when I looked up, I saw Idhunn standing in the shadows of the doorway and I felt ashamed, as though she had caught me masturbating. At that time I had not known her for long.

'How long have you been there?' I spoke from a dry throat and there was an accusatory note in my voice that I had not intended, the product of defence.

'Not long. I've only just got back, in fact.' She spoke neutrally, carefully normal, as if to let me know that she had placed no judgement on what I had been doing. She went on, 'How long have you been doing that?'

'It started ten years ago. I don't know why.'

'It's common enough,' she said, surprising me. I thought I had been the only one, some kind of neural freak to get peace from pain. 'A lot of girls in the seminary used to do it, when we were training – especially during the first year. Tuition in the seith can teach you other ways of dealing with things.'

'This is my way,' I said, still sounding far more defensive than I wished to.

'So I see,' Idhunn replied. 'Apparently it releases endorphins and that can give you a sense of euphoria.' Then she abruptly changed the subject to tell me about the evening meal. But she did not forget, because a while later, when we got back to the Rock, she gave me the pen.

It looked like an ordinary pen for writing, but when I tried it out on a piece of paper, nothing happened.

'It needs ink,' I said.

'It's not that kind of a pen,' Idhunn answered. She took it from my fingers and rolled up her sleeve, then ran the pen horizontally across her tanned arm. Immediately, a little wound appeared, a thin line of redness, a trickle of blood. She put the pen down on the table and held out her arm. After a moment, the wound and the blood vanished as though they had never existed.

'It's for you,' Idhunn said. 'I thought you might find it useful. Just in case.'

'Thank you,' I said, bemused. I ran the pen cautiously over the back of my hand, scribbling with it. I could see through to the muscle and bone, following the random path of the scribble. 'Wherever did you get this?'

'Oh, I just picked it up somewhere,' Idhunn said, evasively. 'Off-world; not here.'

'But what is it for? Is it a – healing tool, or something, for people like me? Or just a curiosity?'

'Not exactly,' Idhunn said.

'I can't think why someone would make such a thing apart from that.'

'People have . . . odd preferences, sometimes.'

I finally realized what she was talking about.

'Let's just say that, whatever you use it for, the holograph is better than the real thing,' Idhunn remarked. 'Whenever our tutor used to find the other girls at the seminary doing it, she would just give them a red pen. It seemed to work, quite a lot of the time. It gave me the idea.'

'I see,' I said. 'Well, thank you,' and we left it at that. I think, in many ways, it was the best gift that anyone has ever given me.

Now, seven years later and without stopping to think about it, I pushed up the sleeve of my shirt and began to draw. No one came to disturb me, and I felt again that strange, liminal trance-state. The afternoon settled down into an absolute quiet, with only the occasional rise of the wind, and the dim thunder of the sea against the shores of the Rock as the storm rose. I forgot about everything: my brother, Nhem, Aldur, the rape, the escape . . . even the seith.

But I did not forget about Frey. It was as though the past rose up before me on the screen of my mind, replaying our first meeting, over and over again.

He had come to the holding in Scaraskae. I was then in my early twenties and had gained some reputation in the district as a tracker. I took parties of hunters and botanists up into the ice-locked mountains at the back of the shoreline; bleak country, especially in winter, but it had been my family's home for generations and I'd had no other childhood, despite attending college in Coll. I was always glad to return, despite the savage weather, the empty landscape – or perhaps because of it. My brother was long gone.

On this particular day, I had only just come down off the mountain, and was taking the group I had been leading back to their wing on the shore. There were only three of them, all hunters, and they'd had a good trip. They were pleased and tipped well, and so I was pleased, too. I pocketed the money and then took our own small craft back to the holding. When I brought it up onto the shingle, there was another wing there: a sleek, pale vessel, the sort of thing owned by people with money. Flushed with recent success, I wondered whether it tokened another hunting party and I hurried up the shore to the holding.

He was alone in the kitchen when I went through the door. He turned to face me as I entered, and I caught my breath. It was like coming home to find a wild animal in the house: something quick and fierce, with one golden eye catching the firelight, the grey eye in shadow. He was in black, and the collar of his long coat was a thick pelt of fur that mingled with his pale hair. He grinned at me, showing teeth.

'You'll be the tracker, then.' His voice was soft, in spite of that feral grin. I remember failing to recognize the accent; it wasn't until later than I learned he was from Darkland. He came forward and I stood rooted to the spot.

I half expected him to touch me, with the proprietary air to which some men feel they have a right, but he did not. He stopped a few feet from me and I felt that he was studying me as an equal.

'That's right,' I said.

'Your name is Vali, I believe.' I saw something flare behind that golden eye, but the other remained as cold as the sea.

'You've heard of me?' I asked, trying to sound confident.

'Oh yes. I'm a tracker myself, you see. And I want an apprentice. So you,' he said, with utter certainty, 'are going to be mine.'

I opened my mouth to say something angry, about arrogance, but I did not speak, not then, not until a long time after that – and then only when Frey was no longer there to hear it. It was as though the air had stolen my words away and I felt myself submit, like a bitch in the pack.

It was a sudden and complete surrender and it left me chilled and shaken. Later, when he had explained the terms of his hire to me and gone away down the twilight shore, I told myself that it was nothing more than a powerful attraction, which I was even then starting to think of as love. I was very young, and knew nothing of the vitki. If neither of these things had been true, I would have resisted him. Or so I chose to tell myself.

*

At last, now, both the memories and the cutting stopped. I looked down at my arm, an apparent mess of red raw flesh, exposed bone, knotted sinew. As I watched, it all disappeared, the illusion melting into the sunlight until only my own bare forearm remained, undamaged except for the faint white tracery of old scars against the skin. I felt hollow and light, cleansed by memory and my own red blood. I put the pen in my pocket and went down the stairs.

EIGHT

PLANET: MONDHILE

Ruan reminded himself once again that he had no intention of returning to the tower in the mountains. It was simply that the weather was so fine in the early spring, with later light. And it was surely important to keep an eye out on the land around the town, check for signs of visen. The town's defences were geared against enemy humans, not wild beasts that were a part of the world – and they'd slipped through the gates before.

Although there was still frost on the ground in the mornings, the first white-green shoots of ittai and kith – the herbs that signalled the arrival of Rise-Month – were already starting to show. The snow birds would be flying north soon, in search of colder weather, but others would be returning south. The hunting was always good at this time of year. Saying nothing to Eleshtra, he packed the bow and the net and set out. Again, he went on foot.

To prove to himself that he planned to go nowhere near the tower, he began walking in the opposite direction, towards the shore, to where the migratory birds would be congregating along the estuaries. It was pure chance, he told himself, that a long v-shaped skein of serai dipped across the rim of the hills and headed up into the heights. Later, he would claim it was a sign. Later than that, he would believe that they had been a curse.

He veered north, following the skein. Others followed: oroth and the frail little gethi that always seemed to fly in their wake. Legend said that the gethi had been young men, cousins, who fell in love with a trio of huntresses and now were cursed by the land to follow them to the world's end. But that, Ruan thought as he watched them go, was nothing more than a story.

There were no tracks in these hills. Ruan made his way up the slope, feet crackling on the frost-brittle grass beneath the trees, following the path of an underground stream that seeped down the slope. He could feel it within the earth, still cold with snowmelt from the heights. If he closed his eyes, it seemed to him that he could see the stream itself, just above the ground, and he knew that this vision was the projected line of its energy. Minerals crossed it, interweaving, and beneath it all he could feel one of the lines of the world itself – not a big ley, like the Great North Road, but a lesser ley leading down from the pole, positive – rather than dark energy. The two could not coexist in close proximity, Ruan knew.

At the top of the slope he paused and looked back. There were more flocks flying up into the mountains, heading away from the wild coast to the calm lakes that lay among the snowfields. He was right, Ruan told himself, to head this way to hunt. He set off once more, in pursuit.

By the time he came to the reaches of the snowfields, it was late morning. The water-clear sky had darkened; there was a bank of cloud high over the peaks of the Otrade: an anvil mass promising thunder and probably more snow. There was a thin whip's edge to the wind; the last bite of Visen-Month, Ruan thought to himself, and that reminded him of the real visen that had threatened Eleshtra. It seemed unreal, a dream. But the oroth, with the gethi behind them, were flying in steady skeins across the mountains and he could smell them now, the mass of the flocks.

He hesitated for a moment, getting his bearings. The town lay behind him to the south-west. He could still feel the lingering pull of the clan house, but it was very faint. To the north, he could sense the huge bulk of the mountains, threaded with iron and silver, driving down into the earth and pulling the magnetic currents of the leys with them. There were other currents, too, but they did not concern him. He checked for water and found it: icemelt flowing from the lakes. If he continued to follow the little underground stream, it would lead up to the lake and the flocks.

Pleased with this simplicity, Ruan made his way up the slope. Sure enough, when he crested the next ridge, the lake lay below: a circle of dark water, crusted with ice at its edges. The flocks drifted across it, bickering for the cold-minnows that swarmed just beneath the ice at this time of year, ready to spawn and send their offspring on the long journey through the underground streams to the sea. More of the birds, latecomers, huddled in ruffled bundles of plumage at the lake's edge.

Not wanting to disturb the whole flock just yet, Ruan took out the bow and picked off a straggler along the ridge. It fell silently, a mass of dappled feathers, and he crept forward and picked it up.

There was obviously no point in killing more than could be carried or stored, and the need for dried flesh was diminishing with the end of winter. Ruan shot three birds – two oroth and a gethi – and decided that this was enough for the moment. He was just turning to head back up the ridge when there was a sudden flurry out on the ice. He stared, puzzled. There was something dark and flapping. The other birds were attacking it. Ruan saw a long neck with a razor beak strike out and recoil and then the bird was rising from the lake. It was a serai, but huge, and the feathers were jet black instead of the usual pearl. It took off for the ridge and landed clumsily some distance away.

It did not occur to Ruan to shoot it; he simply wanted a closer look. He had never heard of a black serai, and he wished to make sure that he was not mistaken – though he could not think what else it might be. He waited for a moment.

The bird was struggling to rise and Ruan wondered with dismay how badly it might be wounded and whether he would have to kill it after all. The serai was like a fragment of night against the snow-drawn contours of the ridge. The long neck was weaving around, snapping back and forth. Cautiously, Ruan walked along the top of the ridge, where only a thin layer of snow had settled on the spine of rock. The bird saw him and grew still. At first he thought it had hurt its head, then saw that the crimson droplet was an eye. It stared at him like a coal fallen from a fire.

Ruan drew closer yet, crouching down until he could have reached out and touched the bird. He looked at the fan of pinions spread out across the snow, the long, dangerous beak, the black claws banded with silvery striations. The bird watched him, unblinking.

'You're a beautiful creature, aren't you?' Ruan said. The satahrach would be interested to hear about this, he was sure. He would have to try to sketch it for Arrath when he got back to the clan house, but he had no skill in such things. He did not want to touch the bird – the chances of losing a finger from that fish-stabbing beak were all too high – and it was difficult to tell how badly injured it might be. He was reluctant to kill it on the off-chance, yet if it could not fly, it was doomed to a lingering death in the cold. Ruan stood, indecisively. The movement seemed to panic the bird. The great wings gathered up and it rocketed into the air with a blast that made Ruan stagger. He lost his balance, teetered wildly on the edge of the ridge, then fell.

Cursing, he rolled down the slope. The rocks were cushioned with snow and he knew that eventually he would hit a deeper patch and come to rest. But just as he reached the bottom of the slope the snow gave way beneath him and he was falling still, fast this time, through a sudden void. Blinded by snow, Ruan heard himself cry out, and then there was a sharp burn as his ankle twisted and the breath was knocked out of him.

He lay, gasping. The pain in his leg was so intense that he almost passed out, but then he began to breathe again and it receded, just enough. He wiped his eyes free of snow and sat up. He was lying at the bottom of a crevasse on a slide of ice. The walls of the crevasse rose sheer on either side, black and slick and frozen. A short distance ahead, the crevasse came to an end where the two sides met. Behind, there was a deep apron of snow. There was, all too clearly, no way out.

NINE

PLANET: MUSPELL

Next morning, the storm had blown out to sea, leaving the Minch glass-calm beneath a fragile green sky. I stood in the guest quarters where Idhunn had come to debrief me, absently gnawing at a strip of sealstock meat and looking out across the islands.

'Sit down,' Idhunn said. 'You're making me edgy.'

'Can't. Too restless.' I tore off a strip of the blubbery meat. The peace left by the use of the pen had ebbed away, drawn by the night's tide, and I was once more twitching.

'It's boiling out of you,' Idhunn said mildly. 'I can feel it. You're like a taut wire.'

I nodded. 'I need to get the seith together before I can concentrate on the next job. Whatever that is.'

She smiled. 'There's a wing waiting.'

Pulling on my leather coat, I ran down the steps to the dock, boot heels ringing on stone. The wing was cresting on a light swell. The cold air hit me like a body-blow. I spoke into the control panel, whispering activation runes. The panel answered.

'Destination?'

'Iscarray. South Shingle.'

I sat back as the wing eased away from the dock, spun in a spray of wave, then sped across the Minch.

It did not take long to reach the island. By the time the wing crunched up onto the shingle, it was still early morning. I could see a ring of brightness around the silhouette of the Rock, rising from the horizon's line. The sun was still coming up. I climbed the shingle bank and made my way through the coarse grass of the machair. A flock of moonfish rose as I approached, water falling in a glitter from the fans of their wings. I watched as they swirled out across the waves, avoiding the stabilizing jets that rose from the wing. There were no other signs of life. I walked up the long slope to the remains of the broch.

There was very little left: a squat ring of vitrified blocks, half-hidden by the heather. The main part of the fortification lay underground. Every time I came here, I thought of those early settlers, fleeing the irradiated north of Earth with their stock of stories and DNA. Shiploads led by the matriarchal parliaments of Iceland and Greenland, Orkney and Eire – places that had long since disappeared under the warmed and rising water – but possessing ideals which we still retained. No one else, it seemed, had wanted the sea-girdled, barren coldness of Muspell, except the northerners.

I did not know who had built the broch, nor which conflict had resulted in its vitrification, but I knew its reputation. It had always been strong in the seith.

Somehow, it seemed appropriate to step through the entrance of the broch rather than over the remains of the low wall. Once within, I knelt on drifting fine sand and wiry grass, my gaze seeking out islands: Arra, Sorostray, Afheim. Then I shut my eyes.

Immediately, I was back on Nhem in the middle of the rape: fear-filled and fouled. Everything that I had not allowed myself to experience during the course of the Hierolath's assault came rushing in on me. I dropped forward, distantly feeling coarse grass and sand under my palms. There was something sharp, but I ignored it. The reek of grease-encrusted hair and unwashed skin was overpowering. It was the smell that had been the worst, I realized now. And the older pain lay behind it, fresh and new behind the tarnish of time. Pain that I had sought out, again, in the Hierolath's palace, seeking – what? Transformation? To show that I could cope, that I was not afraid? These were thoughts I shied away from.

I took a breath for the air, a breath for the earth, a breath for the sea that surrounded me. But the recent past was too strong – I could feel him in me.

I took three more breaths, willing it away. I felt the seith rise up around me, powerful as a force-wall, my own personal temenos interacting with the temenos of the broch. During the rape, I had drawn it into myself until it lay hidden deep within, tiny as a seed. Now, I let it unfold and expand, slide past the boundary of my flesh and out, surrounding me like an invisible shell of energy. I felt it

70

encapsulated in turn within the ancient shields of the broch and the yet older seith of the island itself.

I drew this merging power into me, feeling the nausea and revulsion of the rape dissipate and be gone, down into the salt-cursed earth and the cold wind from the sea.

When I got back to the Rock, Idhunn was waiting on the water stair, her pale hair whipping in the breeze.

'Vali?'

'I'm all right. Better, anyway. I went to the broch.'

'Good,' she said, absently. 'That's good. Vali, we need to talk. But not here.'

Puzzled, I followed her up the stairs, wondering why she had come to meet me and expecting to be led into the lamp room. Instead, Idhunn took a turning away from the main stairs and led me up narrow winding steps to a metal door set in the wall. The passage we were in looked old; the door was arched, and etched with scenes from the Arrival. We were meeting in the council chamber of the Skald, I realized – a room over a thousand years old.

'Idhunn?'

'It's the only place I can be sure of not being overheard,' she said over her shoulder, by way of explanation.

'I don't understand.'

Idhunn ushered me into the room and closed the door securely behind us. I had only been in this chamber once before, the evening of my initiation into the Skald. It rose to a summit high above my head, delicately laced with vaulting carved out of the Rock and glittering with the dark-silver veins of the stone known as thorlight. The council chairs and desk ran in a ring around the chamber, with each name carved into the desk in gleaming lettering. Each time a new councillor was initiated, a section of the desk was removed and replaced – new wood for a new beginning. It was a sombre place, filled with shadows and the weight of age and difficult decisions. A single lantern hung from a filigree chain in the centre of the room. This lantern was, I knew, always lit, and legend said that it had been burning for a thousand years. I doubted that, but it was a pleasing thought.

Idhunn turned to face me and I saw that she was knitting her fingers together against the grey wool of her robe.

'We've found Aldur,' she said. 'Or, at least, we've found where he's gone.'

'And?'

'Vali, it is very difficult to tell you this. I wish I didn't have to.'

'*Tell me.*'

'The people who hired us, the women's resistance – you know they have holdings and laboratories in the mountains?'

'Yes, I knew that.'

'Someone tried to break into one of those laboratories, a day after you assassinated the Hierolath. He killed a woman who confronted him, and raided an information cache. He took material relating to the resistance's

72

attempts to reverse the breeding program on Nhem. He scrambled the monitors, but they managed to resurrect a partial image. It was Aldur.'

'Why would Aldur want material relating to the breeding program?' The notion chilled me.

'We don't know.'

'Where is he now? Do they know if he left Nhem?'

'We think he's back on Muspell. In Darkland.'

I stared at her. '*Darkland*? But why would he go there? He was from Nessheim. He wasn't a vitki.' Her face was still troubled and I could not understand why. Aldur had lied to the Skald and betrayed me for some sinister purpose of his own. Very well, so far so bad, but it wasn't the worst shock I'd ever received. Nessheimers and the other folk of the Reach had had their issues over the years, just like all the islands – though these days we were united, a strong society. If I'd thought about the matter, I would almost certainly have said that distant disagreements wouldn't matter to Aldur, but evidently I'd been wrong. Or perhaps someone had simply come up with a better price than the Skald could have given him. The mission to Nhem had almost cost me my life and I was angry, but I'd get over it. Did Idhunn consider me that fragile? *Was* I that fragile?

'All right,' I said. 'The bastard betrayed me and now he's fled to Darkland; who knows why? Why waste time worrying about Aldur? He's lost to the Skald.'

'Because his name wasn't Aldur,' Idhunn said.

'What?'

'When we'd got you out of there and were looking for him, I went back to the hospital where he'd had his map implant. They still had the blood samples that they'd taken when he was admitted.'

'That would have shown the hospital that he was who he claimed to be.'

'Exactly, except that the blood had changed.'

'Changed?' I was echoing her as stupidly as a seagull chick.

'It wasn't the blood belonging to Aldur Eskind any longer. And when I sent word out to Nessheim, to the census council, they told me that Aldur Eskind had recently been found drowned. A fishing accident, they thought. One month before he came to the attention of the Skald and we decided to send you both to Nhem.'

'So what are you saying? That Aldur wasn't an operative?'

'Aldur was an operative, but the person who went with you wasn't Aldur. It was – I think – the person who killed him and stole his identity.'

'But altering blood—' I looked at her, numbly. 'That's the kind of thing the vitki can do. So are you saying that the person who went with me was a vitki?'

Idhunn sighed, avoiding my gaze. 'Yes and no. We had the changed sample checked. Not "a" vitki. One particular vitki. Frey.'

I sank down onto one of the council seats. I remember staring at the name engraved in silver in front of me – gazing at it as though it held the answers to the maze my life had suddenly become – but I cannot now remember whose name it was.

'Vali?' With a start, I realized that Idhunn was standing behind me and that her hand was on my shoulder.

'If you had asked me a month ago,' I said – and my voice sounded nothing like my own – 'I would have told you that I would know Frey anywhere. That if his shadow so much as crossed the corner of my eye, I'd know immediately who he was. Apparently that isn't the case.' But even as I spoke, I remembered that moment in the hotel on Nhem, when I had walked behind Aldur and something about him had caused that fleeting moment of familiarity.

I felt Idhunn's hand shake a little on my shoulder as she took a deep breath. 'Apparently not. It isn't any failing on your part, Vali.'

'How can you say that? The man who did to me what he did to me? And I didn't even recognize him, for all these much-vaunted powers of the seith? I thought he was Aldur,' I said, and my voice sounded lost and small. 'I didn't *know*, Idhunn.'

'None of us did. How could we? He was perfectly disguised, right down to the fake DNA.'

'I didn't know that was possible.'

'It's possible, but it's rare.'

'But why?'

'Because he wanted to set you up, apparently. I don't know why he went to all that trouble, Vali.'

'He could have just killed me when we got to Nhem. Why didn't he? And what did he want with that lab?'

'I don't know,' Idhunn repeated. She hesitated. 'How much do you know about the vitki?'

I opened my mouth to answer but as I did so, I realized that what I actually knew was very little. 'It's so hard to separate fact from rumour,' I said. 'There are so many myths surrounding them. All I really know is that they're supposed to have come from a renegade bunch of psych-geneticists who left the Reach over a thousand years ago and settled in Darkland – which at the time was supposed to be much too dangerous to sustain a viable colony, though no one seems to know why. I always assumed it was because of the animal life.' Unconsciously, I had put my hand to my face as I spoke.

'That's about the sum of it,' Idhunn said. 'But Darkland isn't just dangerous because of the beasts that live there. It's very hostile terrain and people are said to disappear, though no one knows why. As for the vitki themselves – yes, you're right. They didn't just leave the Reach, they got kicked out because they disagreed with the demo-cratic principles of equality we'd brought from Earth. They believed in the superiority of the male.'

'They still do.' I was thinking of Frey, and Nhem.

'And the lines of experimentation that they were taking were considered not only unethical but insane. They were experimenting on humans – prisoners captured in war raids, but not just that. Some of the experiments were on children, snatched off the streets. It was as though they knew no limits.'

'But what was the experimentation for?'

'Oh, the usual. They wanted to breed a super-race. Enhance the psychic capabilities of humanity, do things that back in humanity's cradle would probably have been considered magic.'

'So do we, Idhunn. That's what we do.'

'But the Skald's taken the long way round. Meditation, discipline, devotion – I don't say we're perfect, or that there haven't been short cuts. The use of psychoactives testifies to that, and sometimes it's got out of hand. The witch-hunts of Muspell's past testify to that. Five hundred years ago – well, that's an old, sorry story. But we have what we have – the seith – by use of means other than an enforced breeding program and the elevation of one section of the community over the other. There's nothing arcane about the seith. It just uses abilities that our ancestors didn't understand properly and didn't know how to harness. But having those abilities doesn't make you special.'

'Because everyone's got them. They just use them to different degrees.'

'Yes, exactly. But the ancestors of the vitki wanted to claim that enhanced abilities made you a superior being and that because they had those capacities, they should therefore lord it over everyone else.'

'But we've never had a government that tolerated those sorts of ideas.'

'No, of course not, which was why the vitki got thrown out and went to Darkland, which no one else wanted. There were too many of them to imprison – resources were strained at that time – and killing them was seen as too extreme. So the councils made a deal and they went into exile. Unfortunately, once they'd gone to Darkland, no one could keep track of them and I'm not sure that anyone really wanted to; I think there was an attitude of "out of sight, out of mind". But of course it left the vitki free to practise whatever they wished. And as far as we know, they chose to regard their exile as an opportunity – setting up laboratories in the deep forest and the mountains, and starting all over again – eventually coming up with a breed of people with some very weird abilities that the rest of us don't quite understand.'

'If that's the case,' I said, 'if they're so powerful, why haven't they tried to finish what they started? Spread out to the rest of Muspell?'

'There are two reasons. One is that the vitki are known to be extremely divisive. Not every Darklander is a vitki; they took slaves with them. But the vitki remain the elite. They have a clan system, as the rest of the north does, and like the rest of the north they seem to spend a lot of time in incessant bickering and breaking up into smaller and smaller factions. Their beliefs could be a unifying ideal, but everyone wants to run the society that results from it.' She paused. 'That's why when Frey originally came to the Reach, claiming to be a vitki fugitive, everyone could understand why he was running from Darkland. Clan rifts, differing ideals. I don't think anyone believed that he was some starry-eyed prodigal returning to the path of righteousness, but it was thought that he'd be useful to have around because we might learn something about the vitki.'

'And the other reason?'

'That they've simply taken their time getting ready.'

'Are you suggesting that this is something they now plan to do?'

'There's been an increase of wing-building along the Darkland coasts. Satellites have shown us that, and a lot of activity in their wing-yards and air-yards. Darkland is into a lot of things, including high tech. But we don't know whether they're actually planning an invasion.'

'So how are we to find out?'

'Well,' Idhunn said, 'that's where you come in.' She must have seen the look on my face because she added quickly, 'You don't have to make the decision now. Think about it. But you're one of the best.'

'Because Frey trained me.'

'No, more than that. Because he trained you and you surpassed him.'

'You'd never get him to agree with that.'

'I don't have to,' Idhunn said, serenely. 'He's not here, is he? But I said it often enough when he was.'

'He wouldn't have paid any attention.'

'No, I know. Even though he sought our protection, he didn't approve of the Skald; said we were all meddling old women who didn't have any respect for men. I don't think I've ever been so flattered. And Tyri said that it finally proved to her satisfaction that the man knew his arse from his elbow after all. You need to shake off that lack of confidence, girl. Doesn't make much of an appearance, but when it does, it always seems to follow a sentence with his name in it.'

'He stripped me down,' I said, 'until I didn't know who I was any more.'

'That's right. And then you built yourself back up again. Oh, I know what these vitki do. It's all mind games, all party tricks, until you don't know which way is up.' She sounded uncharacteristically bitter. I wondered, for a moment, if there was a Frey in Idhunn's past, as well.

I looked out to where the sun glittered on the water, beautiful and illusory. *And then you built yourself back up again.* But from what, to what? As a sea-reader and tracker from a tumbledown holding in Scaraskae, to the assassin of the Skald, who used sex only as a weapon, and who had taken a vow of celibacy unless she intended to kill. I blinked. Suddenly, it seemed a long, strange road from that girl to myself, but it had only been seven years. It seemed a lifetime ago to me now, perhaps more. And now I had a chance to go after the man who had made me what I now was.

'Think about it,' Idhunn said again, gently.

So I thought.

TEN

PLANET: MONDHILE

The day wore on, dimming into a green strip of twilight above the crevasse. Ruan lay a little distance from where he had fallen. He had tried to crawl to the snowbank, with faint hopes of being able to clamber up it, but the powdery snow gave him no purchase and eventually the exertion sent pain lancing through his ankle, which in turn sent him down into unconsciousness.

It was very strange, out here in this icy prison. It felt almost warm. Ruan could sense the sun spilling over his face and he opened his eyes. The light was very bright, summer-golden, and the air was filled with a distant fragrance. Ruan sat up. The sun above him was bringing out the flowers; petals and stamens uncurling from the sides of the crevasse, great silvery buds opening into tongues of furry snow. Ruan had never heard of such a thing as ice-flowers and he watched in wonder. It did not occur to him that this was unreal, that he might be dying. He simply lay and watched the flowers unfurl around him, releasing their strange faint scent into the air of the crevasse.

Then it was dark. The sides of the crevasse were glistening with cold. Someone was flying above him, face lit with green fire. Ruan cried out. The figure swooped and landed. Stars sparked in the lantern light, flickering over the floor of the crevasse as someone knelt.

'Can you hear me?'

'It's you,' Ruan said. It seemed entirely reasonable that the girl from the tower should be bending over him, the girl whose name was *never mind*.

'Yes, it's me. Are you badly hurt? You're half frozen.'

'I think my ankle's broken,' Ruan said. Pain arrowed up his leg as she touched him.

'It's certainly badly swollen.' He glimpsed her smile. 'Does it hurt very much?'

'It's agony!'

'We'd better get you up,' the girl said. She stood, unwrapping an intricate leather harness from herself. She knelt again and hooked it around Ruan's chest and beneath his arms, lifting him up by the shoulders. 'This will hurt you more, I warn you.' She did not sound particularly regretful.

'How will you get back up?'

'Gith will lift you, then he'll send the harness down again for me. We have the sledge, you see, and the pack.'

'Gith?' Ruan asked.

'My brother.'

Ruan thought there was a question he ought to be asking, and after a moment's thought, he located it. '*Never mind*? How did you find me? And who are you?'

'My name is Gemaley,' the girl said. 'It doesn't matter how we found you.' She gave his cheek a soft pat with a black-gloved hand. 'We can talk about all that later.' She turned and signalled with the lamp. It was, Ruan saw, attached to her belt. 'Gith? You can bring him up now.' It sounded more like a command than an instruction. 'Maybe it would be best if you took the light.' She detached it from her belt and clipped it onto Ruan's harness.

'It's such an odd colour,' he said. 'How does it work? I've never seen anything like it before.'

'I told you,' Gemaley said. 'Later.'

There was a pull on the harness. Slowly, unsteadily, Ruan began to rise. His ankle blazed, and for a moment, everything went dark. Then he swung around, dangling on the end of the rope, and the light shone down on Gemaley's upturned face. She was still smiling. The green light made her look like a corpse, glittering over her sharp teeth and the pale hair. She gave him a little wave as he rose and then the light was shivering off the upper wall of the crevasse and Gemaley was gone in the darkness below.

Ruan was dragged over the lip of the crevasse by someone with rough, uncertain hands.

'Are you Gith?'

'Don't speak,' a voice said urgently into his ear. 'She won't like it.'

'But I spoke to her down there,' Ruan protested. He

rolled over onto his back, feeling packed snow hard against his spine.

'If she hears us talking between ourselves, she'll think we are plotting. Be silent.' A narrow face floated over his own, a look of Gemaley about the nose and jaw, but the eyes were wide and dark.

'Why would she think that?' Ruan asked, but Gith was already unfastening the harness and stumbling over to the edge of the crevasse. 'Gemaley!' Ruan heard him cry. 'I'm going to throw this down to you.'

Ruan lay where he had been dragged, staring up into a clear starry sky. He kept thinking of the stars that secured the ends of Gemaley's hair, as though their sharp points had lodged in his mind and could not be freed. Dimly he was aware of sound and voices, but they were fading. Soon, there was nothing but the night.

When he next woke, the stars were moving fast overhead, streaming past him as though caught in a celestial river. He saw a great icy ridge pour after them, ringed with icicles, and realized that it was he who was moving. He tried to sit up, but could not. There was a band across his chest and wrists, holding him down. His ankle throbbed and pulsed.

'Gemaley!' he called.

'Don't worry,' he heard her say. 'It won't be long now. It won't be long,' and then she laughed, though he could not for the life of him think why.

It was growing colder. He felt as though he was floating above himself, detached from his numb, hurting body. He blinked up at the stars as the sledge sped on, wondering vaguely what Gemaley had meant by 'the pack'. Pack of what? A mur's feet would not be able to cope with these conditions. And thus wondering, he faded again.

ELEVEN

PLANET: MUSPELL

There are times when the selk speak. For most of the inhabitants of the north – in cities like Stronsay and Tiree, or the landward towns – this is little more than legend, although the people there are aware of the origins of the selk. But to the islanders of the Reach, what the selk have to say is not merely a local curiosity, a remnant of long-ago attempts at genetic modification. It is of crucial importance. The islanders' livelihoods depend on the sea – on fishing kelp, and the hydrobarriers that supply so much of the north with its power – and who best to report on the sea than those who live in it? The northern seabeds are unstable, and the whole region suffers from terrible shifts in tide, the result of Loki's sharp lunar pull.

Unfortunately, the selk are not capable of speech all the time. They suffer alterations in their level of sentience, and for much of the year they resemble nothing more than the creatures of old Earth that are their ancestors, or, nowadays, the ordinary sealstock of Muspell's waters. But during the spring, their mating season, the light changes

behind their sad dark eyes and you can see someone looking back at you. They remember their names, and the
story of their lives. You need a tabula to decode what they
have to say, but it is articulate, detailed and shows an
intimate understanding of their environment, if nothing
else. They show little interest in humankind, or what
might be happening elsewhere on Muspell. Perhaps with
so short a time available for consciousness, they need to
concentrate their energies, or perhaps they simply do not
care.

And so, seven years ago in the middle of spring, I set
out from Scapa across the ice, with Frey Gundersson, vitki
of Darkland, to hear what the selk had to say.

It was a bleak morning when we set out, and there had
been a heavy snowfall overnight. The snow-clearers
had already been out and the streets were passable, but by
the time we reached the harbour the clouds were building
up again over Direfell. The hired vehicle, a Mauler, trun-
dled slowly down to the edge of the harbour, heavy tyres
grinding on packed snow. Frey turned to me and gave that
fierce grin.

'Could be a better day. But I've seen worse.'

I nodded in anxious agreement. I agreed with him a lot
in those days. He got out of the vehicle and walked down
to the harbour wall, tall in the close-fitting ice suit. It
looked almost like armour under the long leather coat; the
lights along the harbour wall caught it in a black gleam.
I should have been watching the weather, but instead, I
watched Frey. I did that a lot, too, in those days – covertly,

because he said it irritated him when I stared. He was then in his mid-thirties, but he looked older from the back because of the grey hair. It wasn't until you saw his face that you realized his real age: a countenance typical of the islands, all narrow planes and blades of bone, but with something lying under it, as though waiting to burst from the skin. There was a reason for this. At that point I suspected, but did not know. There had been rumours, of course, and I had chased them as persistently as a snow hare, especially the rumours regarding other women.

Now, Frey stood at the harbour's edge, gazing out to sea. I stared at him from the relative warmth of the Mauler. Eventually, over his shoulder, I glimpsed an arrow of hull and white wake. A wing was coming to take us across the Minch to the scarp of the icefield. I climbed out of the Mauler into a blast of cold air. My own clothes were less imposing than Frey's – not a vitki's ice suit, but slick-wear under a woollen fisherman's sweater, then oilskins. When I put the hood up, Frey said I looked like something peering out of a burrow; things that live in burrows on Muspell are not pretty. I kept the hood down in all but the worst weather.

'She's late,' Frey said, scowling.

'How do you know it's a woman?' I squinted through the mist of spray. It was a heavy sea this morning: a churning swell out on the Minch that made the wing slap up and down as it came. I could barely see that there was anyone at the helm, let alone their gender. I tried to keep my voice light, but Frey's scowl darkened.

'Because I spoke to her over the link last night. She owns the wing.' He turned to face me. I always had difficulty looking at Frey directly, because his gaze was so strange – that one grey eye, the colour of storms, the other golden as sunlight. And yet, the golden eye was the colder. It was this eye that had caused the rumours; this, and the fact that he came from Morvern in Darkland. There were parts of the north where you could claim that Darklanders had three heads, and have been believed. Sometimes, I wondered about it myself.

'Where's she from?'

'Inguish, from the accent. But the wing's registered in Coll. Did you get the gear out of the vehicle?'

'Not yet.'

The grey-and-gold gaze sharpened. He did not have to speak.

'I'll do it now.'

'The instruments are in the small case. Be very careful. I don't want it knocked about.' He was once more staring hungrily out to sea.

'I'll be careful,' I said, but he had stopped listening. I trudged back up the slope to the Mauler.

By the time I'd fetched the instrument cases and the packs from the back of the vehicle, the wing was docking. The pilot brought her in with a showy twist, sending a plume of spray up over the harbour wall. I heard her shout something in greeting and Frey's reply. I forced myself not to look round. This was stupid, I knew, and I hated myself for it. Every time he spoke to another woman, the fear rose up in me like something winding and alive, changing my voice and my face, turning me into someone clinging and petulant – the kind of woman I despised. The kind of woman I had never been, until Frey gave me reason to start behaving like that.

I picked up the lightest instrument case and carried it carefully down to the dock. I didn't know what it contained. It was vitki gear, and the price for poking one's nose into vitki business was high, or so I'd been warned – even when the vitki in question was an outcast.

The pilot, invisible underneath oilskins, was tying the wing to the ringpost as I approached. As I came down the ramp to set the case by Frey's feet, she turned. I saw very blue eyes and a mass of hair that was such a dark red it was almost black. The hood framed her face (she looked unlike anything that might peer from a burrow). Frey gave his feral smile. My heart sank. I was aware that my nose was starting to run and my only handkerchief was in the pocket of my pack, in the Mauler.

'You'll be Gundersson and Hallsdottir?' the woman called up. Frey had been right; she had an Inguish lilt, and a deep voice.

'That's right. And you'd be McGuirey?'

'Last time I checked.' She was smiling back. My heart slipped another notch.

'Where's the rest of the gear?' Frey said to me, without looking.

'I took it out of the back. It's waiting.'

'Good. Could you go and find the harbour-mistress?

She'll be in the office. You'll need to give her the paper-work for the Mauler so that the hire office can collect it.' All this was said without a turn of the head and McGuirey was staring back. Shit, I thought: But I'd look like an idiot if I protested, so I did as he asked me.

The harbour-mistress, when I finally found her, was the sort of woman I'd hoped the wing's pilot would have been: in her fifties, layered in woollens, with red-veined cheeks. How could you bring a wing all the way from Inguish in a filthy sea and still remain pale and serene? I began to hate McGuirey in earnest. I handed over the paperwork and the harbour-mistress spent an age poring over it. I swear she was moving her lips. The little office was stuffy after the cold morning air, warmed by the kind of oil heater that smells of burning fur. I couldn't even see out because the windows had steamed up. I stood, fidgeting, while she laboriously copied the details into a tabula.

'I'll need the ignition keys,' she said at last.

'We'll drop them off when we've unloaded.'

'Nasty day to go anywhere. Where are you headed?'

'Urusay. The ice.'

'Be breaking up soon, I'd have thought. What're you going out there for?'

'Selk.'

The harbour-mistress grunted and her face grew sour. A lot of islanders thought it was unlucky to talk about the selk, especially at this time of year, but she did not seem suspicious – that would be the province of the long autumn, when the selk pupped. Hunting sentient life was forbidden, but there were always a few outworlders who trickled through in autumn, after skins, and not a few city people, too. Selk fur was beautiful and the farmed pelts, grown on gene-racks, were worn a lot on the streets of Stronsay and Tiree. It was difficult to tell the difference, but the wearers of the poached skins knew, and I suppose it added an extra frisson to a winter wardrobe. I was sure that the reason so many city people refused to believe that the selk could speak was not due to a disdain for superstition, but denial and guilt.

The harbour-mistress eventually finished with the papers and I hastened back to the dock. Frey and McGuirey were roaring with laughter, but they stopped as I came down the slope.

'Get the stuff loaded up. McGuirey's getting restless,' Frey said, and gave that feral grin again.

'Can you give me a hand? I don't want to drop the big case.' I did not like the edge in my voice.

'I'll get her started,' McGuirey said, with a sharp glance in my direction. Frey and I walked back up the slope. He was ambling along as usual, that loose stride, but I could feel the annoyance in him like a steel wire tightening.

'Vali? What's the matter?' His voice was soft but cold.

'Nothing.'

'Good.'

He picked up the big case and I took the packs. We loaded them onto the boat in silence, then Frey went back to the Mauler. McGuirey was staring out to sea.

'Weather's coming up from landward.'

'Is that going to be a problem?' I was not very familiar with the Urusay end of the Minch in those days.

'Shouldn't be. Don't know yet, though. Depends if the wind keeps easterly.' She untied the rope with a practised hand. 'Your man there. Where's he from?'

I hesitated, then decided to tell the truth. 'Morvern.'

'Thought so.' She gave a little nod, as though something had been confirmed, and I wasn't sure that it was merely the question of Frey's origins. 'Unusual, to find an undisguised Darklander in the Reach.'

She was watching me closely and I grew flustered, not knowing what to say. Eventually I muttered, 'He's working for the Skald.'

'Yes, I know. Even more unusual. Do you know why he left Darkland?'

'Political reasons.' Pettily, I tried to sound mysterious, but it wasn't difficult. I had no real idea why Frey had fled his home country.

You're one of the few people I can talk to, Vali,' he had said one night, as we lay entwined in bed. 'You understand me.' His voice was uncharacteristically warm and I had been too flattered to reply that no, I did not think this was true. He had said once that he told me a great many things, but when I added it all up, it amounted to very little.

'How long will it take to get out to the ice?' I asked McGuirey, partly to change the subject and partly out of a genuine desire to know.

'Three hours or so direct, but if the weather starts coming this way I might take her up past Erren rather than risk too much open sea.' She smiled. 'It's a long time in a little craft.'

I thought that I could have liked McGuirey, if it hadn't been for Frey. I thought that I could have liked a lot of women, and I still tried, but there was always his shadow in the way.

When the shadow came back we climbed into the wing. McGuirey touched the tiller, which was a sophisticated thing for a craft this size; one of the Wayfinder models. I'd been reading up about the Wayfinders recently and they were not cheap. Whatever McGuirey's main business was, it was unlikely to be just ferrying people here and there across the Minch if she had spent money on this kind of equipment.

Neither Frey nor McGuirey spoke as we set off, and I was not inclined to make conversation. It would have been difficult in any case, over the roar and smack of the waves. Once we were out of the harbour, the sea rose to a heavy, rolling swell, dousing us with spray. I turned my head and watched Scapa, falling behind into a line of grey stone and white fields. Soon, even the great dark bulk of Direfell was gone, vanishing into cloud. I looked at Frey. He was staring ahead, towards the ice.

TWELVE

PLANET: MONDHILE

The stars had fallen. Above Ruan, there was only darkness. The smooth glide of the sledge had stopped, but it was still freezing. He was being jolted along.

'Careful!' he heard Gemaley snap.

'I'm being careful!'

'Not careful enough.'

Light flared up and Ruan saw that what he had taken for night was in fact the wall of the tower, looming above him. His head was lolling to one side. There were hands beneath his shoulders and legs; he was being carried up a flight of steps.

'Wait!' Gemaley's voice was a whiplash.

Ruan felt a shudder of lightning cold – the tower's defences, presumably, going down to let them in.

'Open the door!' There was the sound of scraping; metal against stone, setting Ruan's teeth on edge. As they came in through the door the wall of the tower changed again, shifting from glossy blackness to that shimmering white. It frightened Ruan beyond measure, though he could not have said why.

'Where are you taking me?' he asked.

'Upstairs. To my own chamber.' This was Gemaley's voice.

'I need to see your satahrach.' His ankle had passed to a point beyond pain. He thought with longing of home and of old Arrath, who never made a fuss, was always matter-of-fact about sickness, who healed so many.

Gemaley laughed. 'We don't have one.'

'But every clan has someone!'

'Oh, but we don't need one. Not here.'

He was still trying to make sense of this as they carried him up the stairs. The tower seemed to swing and turn around him. One moment it was as though he was looking up into the tower itself, but the next he was peering straight down the spiral stairwell, with the hall a very long way away. His head felt inflated to gigantic proportions. And underneath all these impressions lay something else, something dark and twisting and alive, that muttered with satisfaction at his presence.

THIRTEEN

PLANET: MUSPELL

McGuirey took us up through the chain of uninhabited islands known as the Rhos. I stared out at the sheer granite walls, rising out of the heaving ocean, white-capped with generations of seabird droppings, as though there had been a recent snowfall. It was certainly cold enough, though Frey had thrown back the heavy coat and was standing in the prow, facing the wind. Occasionally McGuirey glanced at him. I had grown sourly accustomed to women staring at Frey – a gamut ranging from open desire to admiration – but McGuirey's expression was unreadable. It bothered me. It was a deviation from the norm, yet another unsettling factor in my relationship with Frey.

McGuirey leaned forward and tapped me on the knee.

'See that? That's the Old Woman. We're coming round the reaches of Selsay, and in another half an hour or so you'll be able to see the edges of the ice.'

I nodded, looking at the pillar of rock – the marker to the true polar north. At the prow, Frey's face was fierce, turned to the magnet of the pole. McGuirey said, 'I wish your man there would sit down. He'll fall in if we hit a big wave.'

'He's used to the sea,' I said loyally, though I felt a small, swift flare of something under that; a pleasure that she had criticized him.

McGuirey snorted. 'No one's that used to it.'

'You should tell him,' I said.

'A vitki? From Darkland? He'll listen, you think?' She laughed . . . 'Look – what's that over there? A flying cat . . . I don't think so!'

I hid a grin. A little while after that I squinted through the spray and saw something huge and white ghosting up over the horizon.

'Iceberg,' Frey said over his shoulder.

'We'll be coming into Yetland in a few minutes,' McGuirey called back. She steered the wing through a suddenly choppy stretch of sea, veering between ice-walls. The wing bucked and plunged and even Frey sat down with a bump. I've never been seasick apart from once, when the Tiree ferry got stuck outside the harbour overnight in a storm. But everyone threw up then, including the crew.

This run was nearly as bad, but much shorter. When we reached the long low sea-wall that signalled the approach into Yetland, I felt green. But McGuirey and Frey looked as pale and composed as ever.

McGuirey took the wing into the dock and helped me ashore. My legs felt wobbly and I stumbled, a very bad sign – and for a Reach islander, a humiliating one. Frey paid no attention. He strode up the shingle, leaving McGuirey to secure the wing and myself to bring the packs ashore.

'When is he planning to head out?' McGuirey said, in an undertone. 'It'll be dark in a few hours. He'd best wait till morning now.'

'I think he wants to get going straight away,' I said.

She looked at me. 'And there'll be no argument from you?'

'Look!' I said. I forced a smile. 'Another flying cat!' I was his apprentice, I told myself. I did not have the right to question, but it still felt wrong.

But McGuirey was correct. Frey registered our papers at the harbour-master's office and immediately disappeared to collect the ice-rider.

'I'm surprised he hasn't hired a dog team,' McGuirey said, coming up to join me outside the office. 'They're supposed to be a traditional lot, the vitki.'

'He was making noises about it, but it's off the agenda now, for some reason.'

'Did he say why?'

'No, he didn't.'

She looked at me curiously. 'He doesn't tell you a lot, does he?'

'Look, I—' It seemed oddly difficult to explain. 'I'm just the apprentice. My mother was a tracker. Tracking is what I was born into, and it's what I do best.'

McGuirey nodded. 'So they signed you up with him?'

'He's one of the best.'

'But you'd never be a vitki.'

'I know that. You have to be born into the clans, a Darklander – and there aren't many women who are vitki, anyway. If any.'

'If that sort of thing interests you, I'd have thought you could have joined the Skald.'

'I don't know much about the Skald,' I said. 'Isn't it just a meditational order?'

'Oh no,' McGuirey said. 'They're much more than that.' She hesitated. 'A Darklander in the Reach. That isn't exactly a common occurrence. How did it come about?'

I couldn't help wondering that myself; it was a question I had asked a lot over the last few months and never received a satisfactory answer. I mumbled something and McGuirey shot me a sharp look. I was going to ask her more about the Skald, but Frey was coming back again.

'We have an ice-rider. They're preparing it now.' It was clear from his manner that I was expected to go with him then and there. I said good-bye to McGuirey with an odd pang of regret and headed off down Yetland's single street, lined on either side by shacks. This wasn't just the gateway to the pole; it was the poorest outer edge of the island chains. Half the houses seemed to be boarded up, the inhabitants long gone – probably to Tiree or Stronsay to earn some kind of living in the mines or the foundries. I thought they'd have done better to stick to the fishing, myself, but I didn't know the circumstances. Up here, away from the comparative calm and affluence of the rest of the Reach, the clans went to war over the fishing grounds – secret battles conducted far out in the reaches, under cover of darkness. No one asks too many questions if a fisherman doesn't come home. In the inner islands, everything was licensed and controlled as rigorously as possible, but that was not the case up here.

A gap between two of the rundown houses afforded me a glimpse of sea. I saw a gleam and a white wake behind it – McGuirey, heading back to Inguish. Despite that moment of regret, I could not pretend that I was not relieved to see her go. Now, it was just Frey and myself.

The ice-rider was at the back of a house that seemed more prosperous than the rest. We went through a weed-filled yard that led down onto the shingle. A man bent over the rider, checking the blades.

'This is Gunner Low,' Frey said. 'Owns the yard. Low, this is my assistant, Vali Hallsdottir.'

Low nodded. He was a tall man, dressed in waterproofs and a sweater, with blond hair and a great sweeping moustache. He smiled at me and I saw a flicker of interest in faded blue eyes.

'Get her off the shingle,' Frey said, a little sharply. 'I want to make a start.'

'Give me a hand and I will,' Low said. It took me a moment to understand what he'd said; the accent was very thick in these parts. He seemed not to notice that Frey was a Darklander, nor to care. Perhaps we sounded the same to him. Together, we pushed the rider down into the water, blades retracted, and loaded up.

'You want me to run through the sail controls?' Low asked.

'I know how to handle an ice-rider,' Frey said. Low's blond eyebrows made the faintest movement upwards. Avoiding my gaze, he reached out a hand and helped me into the rider. It was much narrower than McGuirey's wing, and cramped. Frey took the pull cord and started the rider up; it roared into life with a rattle. Low frowned. 'Sure you don't want a final check? Sounds a bit choked to me.'

'It'll be fine,' Frey said tightly. A moment later, we were out onto the slender gulf of water that separated Yetland from the start of the icefield. A few minutes after that, the blades hissing out of the rider and the sail unreeling out, we were up onto the ice itself and veering north, with the great white plain reaching before us all the way to the pole.

I had no idea where we were heading, and little knowledge of the landscape. We followed the coast for a while; the ice was wetter here and made for easier going, but it was also less stable, and soon we veered off into the main field.

Frey, I had heard, had done his initiatory years out here – the ingsgaldir period that everyone born into a vitki clan must undergo. The harsher tests, which had apparently been commonplace up to a hundred years ago, had been outlawed earlier in the century by the local parliaments, but everyone suspected that these things still went on. No one believed that Darkland told much of the truth to the parliaments of the Reach. I could not help wondering what Frey might have done, or undergone, and I was forced to admit to myself that this mystery was a large part of the attraction.

He seemed to be in no doubt as to where we were heading, though I did not understand how. The selk were migratory, and difficult to track. Perhaps this was more evidence of what were said to be the vitki's enhanced senses. I thought of Frey's fierce yellow eye and wondered.

As the rider glided on, I fell into a kind of trance. Ice and sky merged into one and I watched the clouds pile up on the horizon with a kind of contentment. Out here, there was nothing – just Frey and myself and the ice. And this was, I felt, how things should be. If I could just be with him, never set eyes on anyone else, everything would be all right. Then, I could let him get on with the work of transformation, re-making me into a suitable companion . . .

The sail snapped above me and I blinked. I had been thinking something, but I could not remember what it was. Frey turned to me and smiled, and the thought, whatever it had been, faded. It could not, I told myself, have been anything important.

The nights in the north are long and light in summer, but at this time of the year twilight still fell relatively early. It was very clear now, and as the rider sped on I watched Muspell's fiery sun crawl down towards the horizon. But next minute Grainne was finally gone. The sky deepened to an aqueous green and the evening star – Muspell's companion world of Idhunn – hung low over the icefield. They said in the islands that if you could see her reflected in the ice, you would gain your heart's desire before the year was out. But then, I already knew what my heart's desire was, or thought I did.

It grew dark quickly after that. Frey took the rider along the base of a ridge, and steered it to a halt.

'We'll camp here for the night,' he said, stepping down onto the blades.

'Are we far from where we're heading?' I asked.

'No, not so long. If we set off tomorrow, early, then we should reach it by dawn. Dawn's a good time. The selk like to catch the early fish when they rise.'

'And what about . . . anything else?'

Frey laughed. 'What kind of . . . anything else?'

'I've heard talk of fenris.'

'They might come out this far; it depends on the time of year. But they're solitary creatures, not pack animals. We've got the rifle.' He smiled, not pleasantly. 'And there are other ways of dealing with them.'

I wanted to ask, but it struck me that he was probably referring to vitki business, and I'd learned that it was best to keep quiet about that.

We ate some of the supplies: wind-blasted strips of salt fish and a lump of blubber, followed by a handful of dried fruit. In the lights of the rider, I caught a glimpse of my own reflection in the polished edge of the sail and wished

I hadn't. My hair, usually thick and silky, was a tangled black mass and my face was encrusted with salt. I looked small and hunched and unkempt. I thought of McGuirey. How did some women manage to remain sleek in the worst of conditions, whereas the rest of us suffered from running noses and puffy eyes? It must be some kind of gene, I decided.

'What are you thinking about?' Frey asked. He always asked when I was least expecting it, but at other times when I volunteered my thoughts, he seemed barely to be listening.

'The selk,' I lied. 'I've never heard them speak before.'

'Haven't you? I have. Once.'

'What happened?' I ventured.

'It was on the shores of Urusay, which is one of the volcanic mountains in the north of Darkland. I was alone. It was during my ingsgaldir.' His gaze slid towards me, then away. He would not be able to talk about that, I knew. 'A misty day, with the fog swirling over the shore and an oily sea. She was singing. I thought it was a woman. I climbed over the rocks and there she was. Selk. She did not see me. I listened to her sing.'

'Isn't that supposed to be dangerous?'

'It's a myth that they lure people onto the rocks. Why would they? The song involves sonar, to check the location of prey. Their understanding of sonic technology is supposed to be sophisticated. Someone wrote a paper on it at the language institute in Tiree.'

'Was it beautiful? The song, I mean.'

'Beautiful enough.'

'I wonder what they'll say this time. If we find them.'

'Oh, we'll find them,' Frey said. I could see the glint of the golden eye as he turned his face to the light. 'Don't worry about that.'

FOURTEEN

PLANET: MONDHILE

Ruan woke to find himself blinded by light. At first, he thought that it was morning and that the night had been nothing more than another dream, but then he moved and the stab of pain through his ankle made him realize that it was real. He was in the tower. The ceiling arched above him; black stone, glistening with a kind of inner brightness. The light was coming from two lanterns, set on tall poles. He raised his head. Gemaley sat cross-legged at the end of the bed, eyes bright. She was naked under a curtain of hair. She was flicking one of the star clasps between the fingers of one hand, to and fro, to and fro. Fascinated, Ruan watched as it caught the light. He could look at nothing else, not even Gemaley.

'Are you feeling better?' Her voice seemed to come from a long way away.

'I don't know.'

'Then I'll have to make you feel better, won't I?' she said, and slid forward until she was lying beside him, face down. She was still holding the star clasp and it looked sharp. With a careful flourish, she drew one of its points down his arm. It left a thin, stinging red line in its wake. Ruan snatched his hand away.

'What are you doing?'

'You'll have to get used to that, you know,' Gemaley said.

'What are you talking about?' His arm burned, momentarily eclipsing the pain of his ankle. Her words were an echo of something, but he could not remember what it might be.

'If you're to stay with me, you'll have to get used to it,' Gemaley said, patiently.

Ruan had no intention of staying with her, and becoming accustomed to pain was the last thing on his mind. Getting out of the tower as quickly as possible had become his principal goal, and in the morning he would have her send word to the clan and ask them to bring him home.

He thought he had said all this, but Gemaley was still gazing at him and suddenly he was not sure that he'd even opened his mouth.

'*Does* it hurt?' she asked, idly, tracing the scratch made by the star.

Of course it does, Ruan tried to say. Instead, he nodded. Gemaley leaned across and licked the scratch, her tongue slowly travelling up his arm. He tried to move, but he felt anchored to the bed. Gemaley's pointed tongue flickered down his chest, then his stomach, and began paying delicate court to the tip of his cock. Everything became focused on that one touch, her claws sliding up the inside of his thigh, her fingers closing around his erection and gliding up and down, up and down . . . Then, abruptly, she stopped and sat up.

'It's just a game, this,' she said. Lost in a haze of arousal, he barely heard what she said. He squinted up to see that she was above him, her hand slipping over the bare skin of her stomach and leaving a thin bloody trace in its wake. 'That's what I want.'

'I've never—' He disliked the sight of these fragile wounds, drawn in her own blood, but at the same time the wet redness was enticing and Gemaley seemed to sense this. She dipped the tip of one finger in the smear of blood and, retracting a claw, held it out to him.

'Here,' she said, very gently, like someone feeding a bird, and he sucked the blood from her hand before he could stop himself. The bloodmind roared in his head, a distant sea, and he forced it back.

'There, that's better,' she whispered, sounding like a woman with a very young infant, murmuring to it, before sending the child out into the cold world.

'Gemaley?'

'More,' the girl said. She took his own clawed hand and with it drew a bloody line down her belly until the pale hair at her crotch was sticky. Ruan watched his own actions with a remote, fascinated disgust, but he did nothing to stop her, and when her claws were once more fastened in his own flesh he did nothing to stop that, either, because he was already coming into her blood and her juices as she rode him, hard, and smiling still.

It was morning. He could feel it, sense the sun coming up over the edge of the Otrade, but no light penetrated the room in the tower. The windows were heavily shuttered. The lamp still burned, but it was guttering. Gemaley was gone. He felt sore and over-used, but his ankle had ebbed down to a dull, numb pain, with an occasional flicker of agony if he moved without due care. That suggested that it had not been such a bad break, if indeed it was broken at all. Perhaps the ligaments had been torn and the bone was intact.

He sat up nonetheless, and crawled to the edge of the bed. He had to get out of the tower. He swung his legs over the side of the bed and hopped naked to the door, leaning heavily on the lamp table as he did so. It was undignified, but dignity, Ruan felt, had long since disappeared. He was not surprised to find that the door was locked. Squinting through the keyhole, he saw only darkness. It was impossible to tell whether the key remained in the lock, but Ruan was inclined to think that it was not. Besides, the door fitted closely to the floorboards; one might have slid a hair between them, but not a key.

His ankle was beginning to hurt again, in slow ripples of pain that brought nausea in its wake. He was glad not to have eaten for so long, but then again, he was also ravenous. He crossed to the window and found that the paper panes and then the shutters could be unlatched. He threw the shutters open, leaning awkwardly on the windowsill as he did so. A blast of cold air met his face and he shivered.

He was very high up. The wall of the tower fell away beneath him, and even now, within it, the stone still shimmered and changed, altering with the light. Looking out, he could see the glaciers of the Otrade. The snowline had crawled a little higher up the slopes, but only a little, and the air was bitter cold. Breathing too deeply made his lungs hurt, and there was a band of pain across his chest for which he was inclined to blame Gemaley. Below the tower, there was only the forest – a great carpet of satin-spine and ipher. A thin, angry cry rose up from among the trees. It did not sound like anything human. Visen, perhaps, or altru. It made him shiver more than the cold. He took a last look at the pale sky and drew the shutters closed.

Sitting back down on the bed, Ruan considered his options. At present, they seemed few. Escape was out of the question until his ankle had healed. He supposed that he could try asking Gemaley to reach his clan by appealing to her better nature, but he was by no means sure that she had one. If not Gemaley, then someone else. Gith? But Gith seemed terrified of his sister and Ruan doubted that any appeal to him was possible. But if he was afraid of her, might he not also resent her? Ruan knew too little about the young man to say.

Gemaley and Gith. It was likely that they were of the

same litter. But there had to be other people in the household. There had to be elders, even if there was no satahrach – which would in itself be peculiar. Gemaley was far too young to be running a place of this size on her own, and she could not long have returned from the wild. Ruan had estimated Gemaley to be around twenty or so, like himself, which meant only a few years of civilized behaviour. If one could call Gemaley's behaviour civilized . . . There had to be other people, and surely they would ask questions. You did not simply bring someone in out of the storm and incarcerate them, not in any usual household. But this household, all too clearly, was not usual.

And there was another issue, too: the treacherous self which whispered that it would not be so bad to stay here with Gemaley. It was difficult to think about her without the images of the previous night intruding. He could hardly believe that someone so beautiful would take such an interest in him. It was flattering, terrifying, and ultimately it bewildered him. Even now, with his ankle hurting and thoughts of flight jostling for principal place in his mind, he could not stop thinking about her.

And he was certain, too, that this was just the way she wanted it.

FIFTEEN

PLANET: MUSPELL

I woke before dawn to find Frey standing on the ice, looking out to the thin grey line of the horizon. My breath steamed as I crawled out of the fleece bag, and the inside of my nose crackled with cold. When I touched my hair, it felt brittle.

'You're awake? Good.' He handed me a strip of fish. 'I want to get going.'

It was a better wind today, rising up with the sun. The sail of the rider sprang up to catch the breeze and we were off. Huddled in the cradle of the hull, I watched as Frey's face angled in and out of the light, looking as pale as a ghost's. I thought of the fenris, the great beasts that roamed the ice, and the morning wind seemed colder. The landscape of the icefield was changing, too, from a flat plateau to a series of carved canyons where icicles hung as delicately as lace. I did not know what had made those canyons, unless it was the wind. In a little while, the whole field would crack and foam into the waters of the northern

Minch. For now, I took note of the snow patterns, assessing the direction of the wind.

The rider skimmed through the canyons without slowing. It had a navigation system, I knew, and I wondered whether this had been pre-programmed. Did anyone map the ice, or was the terrain simply too changeable? The journey was making me realize how limited my understanding was, how limited I had been back in Scaraskae, in spite of my nights alone in the forest house of my grandfather. I did not think that Frey could see much in me. He had taken me on as a favour to my family, slept with me out of kindness . . . My thoughts spiralled downwards until they were as bleak and dark as the water that lay beneath the ice. But I was lucky that he took some interest, at least. Very far within, a small voice reminded me that I had not always thought like this, but the wind reached that voice and froze it into silence.

As we reached the end of one of the long canyons, the sun touched the edge of the horizon. In the pale new light I saw that there were islands in the ice; pinnacles of ivory rock, streaked red with something that could have been iron deposits. They reminded me of great bones, beasts stranded in the icefield to die. But Muspell had never had large forms of life, until humans arrived, and had started the experimental programs that had led to the fenris and the selk.

The nearest island was swarming with movement. It startled me, until I realized that the rock was alive with seabirds, the little arrow-tailed terns that are known as sea-ghosts. Alarmed, they sailed up as the rider glided beneath the rock, a cloud of white against the shadowy sky. Frey cursed under his breath.

'I don't want to startle the selk,' he said. 'If they think there's fenris or something about . . .'

'You said they would know when we were coming,' I reminded him.

'And they will. But not just yet. I have to find them first.'

This was news to me – he had handled the rider as if he knew exactly where we were going. 'How will you find them?' I asked, but Frey did not reply.

A little time later, he took the rider in under the lee of an island and stopped.

'Wait here,' he said. 'I'll be back in a while.'

'Where are you going?' I asked.

'To do some scouting. Stay here. I don't want you in the way.'

I knew better than to ask if I could go, but that small frozen voice within me was once again beginning to thaw. I might not ask, but I would go, I decided.

'All right,' I said, meekly.

I watched Frey stride off across the ice, footprints in the snow melting behind him. That, I thought, eyebrows rising, was a trick worth learning. I had no idea how it was done. He moved fast. Soon, he was nothing more than a shadow between the peaks of the islands. It was then that I slid down the side of the rider and followed. Frey might have vitki tricks, but I was still versed in tracking. I did not

115

take a direct route, but came up round the back of the rocky outcrops, head low, concealed under the white lining of my anorak.

As I neared the rock the sea-ghosts, which had settled back into a noisy flock, grew quiet. I was afraid they would start up again. Be calm, I thought. Nothing is wrong. Be still. It was just a hope, nothing more, but to my surprise the birds did indeed settle. I put it down to coincidence, and my own relative unobtrusiveness.

When I caught up with him, Frey had climbed one of the outcrops and was standing on a lip of rock, his coat whipping around him in the early morning wind. The sun was now up, sending a cascade of wan golden light out across the ice, and the sky was a clear azure. Even if Frey looked back, I was not sure that I was visible against the glare, but I did not want to take the chance. I took refuge beneath an overhang of icicles and watched.

Frey's standpoint seemed to me to be a good place to look for the selk. It was not far from the water, which I could see in a thin blue line across the icefield, and Frey was facing it. He raised his hands and cried out, a long wailing fall of sound. It made my skin crawl, as though pricked with a thousand icy pins. I had no idea what he was doing; calling the selk in their own tongue of Shelta, perhaps. But there was an animal, predatory quality to it that made me doubtful that the selk would respond. I wondered again about Frey's origins.

And then I saw them. At first I thought that they were lumps of ice, broken away in the early melt and bobbing about in the water. But then the ice changed direction and began moving purposefully towards the shore, and I realized that the lumps were the selk themselves. One by one, they heaved themselves onto the shore and waited.

Frey walked towards them, moving swiftly and surely over the ice. I felt a brief, bitter pang of regret that he had not bothered to take me with him, had not wanted me to come after all. But if the selk spoke, I wanted to hear it. I crept from beneath the icicles and moved closer, still under the overhang of the snow that covered the outcrop, until I was only a few yards from Frey and the selk.

Close to, I could see that they were really not at all that similar to the sealstock. Instead of tapering to a tail, they had long hind legs, bunched and folded beneath them like the legs of a frog, with immense webbed feet. Shorter forelegs – displaying the powerful muscles of a swimming creature – were curled against their breasts. I glimpsed slender fingers, ending in hooked claws. Their faces were not the round, dog-like countenances of the sealstock, but narrower, with splayed, intricate noses and wide mouths that, if opened, looked as though they would split their heads in half. At the nape of the neck, the skull was massively thick – a great bulge of bone and fat beneath the white-cream pelt. I wondered if this was a protection against water-borne predators grasping them by the back of the neck. Some of them were clearly female, as I could see rows of mammary teats along their undersides. Nor were their hides as grey and wrinkled as those of the sealstock, but dappled and opalescent, a creamy white upon pale grey.

I was close enough to see when the foremost selk opened its wide mouth and spoke. I did not recognize the language at first, but then Frey's tabula hummed and the words floated out onto the air.

'You are one of the old enemies. We recognize you. Why have you come?'

Frey laughed. 'Don't you know? To hear you sing.'

'We do not sing to order, vitki. We are not your choir.' There was a murmur of agreement from the others.

'Oh, but I think you are, you see,' Frey said. 'Sing for me.' It was a command, not a request, and the selk hissed at him.

'Sing,' Frey said, and then he cried out something, a chain of syllables. It meant nothing to me and the tabula was silent, which meant that it was unable to translate. Underneath the thick hood of my anorak, the hair crept up at the nape of my neck. The cry sounded atavistic, inhuman, more like the invocation of a rune than a word. And a change passed over the broad faces of the selk. One by one they opened their mouths and began to sing. Fragile sound drifted over the ice like cloud, and as it did so, I saw the light go out behind their dark eyes.

Frey pointed to the sea. 'Go, now. Go on.'

A moment later, the selk obediently turned and hauled themselves towards the waves, but just as the last one, the leader, reached the edge of the ice, it gave itself a sudden shake, like a wet dog. Its neck was too thick to allow it to

look over its shoulder, but it twisted around and I saw that
it was once more aware.

'You cannot hold us for long, vitki,' it said, softly, with
menace. 'Remember this.' Then it was gone into the sea
and Frey gave a snarl of disappointment and frustration
that made me grow even colder than I was already.

He melted back against the rock. I thought he was
about to climb down, and it struck me that it would be best
if he found me back at the rider as instructed rather than
out here on the ice, spying on him. I hastened back,
following my own footprints and the marker signs that I
had noted along the way. I had taken a circuitous route.
Hopefully Frey would return the way he had come, and
not see my footprints in the snow.

Somehow, I was relieved to find the rider still there. I
slid into its meagre protection and waited. When Frey
returned, I pretended to be checking the readouts. I held
my breath, but he gave no sign that he knew I had
followed him.

'What's the weather prediction for the next few hours?'
he said, without preamble.

'Clear. There's a gale blowing up near the pole but it
shouldn't affect us.'

'Good. I want to take you out on the ice, later.'

'Why?' I looked up, interested.

'I want to show you something.'

Perhaps he had merely wanted to try out whatever
experiment he had made upon the selk, I thought, make
sure that they would sing. But the memory of what I had

seen formed ice-deep within me, travelling through the marrow of my bones. He had done something to the selk, something forbidden. I did not know this for certain, but I could feel it.

I realized that Frey was watching me closely. 'Vali?' He spoke very quietly. 'What's wrong?'

'Nothing. Just concentrating on these readouts.'

'Good,' he said, and vanished round the other side of the craft.

We trekked for most of the morning, heading north-west through the ice canyons. It was unnerving terrain for me; I'd been up in the glaciers of Ushant before, but they had been narrow bands of ice sandwiched between the mountains, not this white wasteland. My face was protected by a mask, but even under this the skin felt brittle and cold and the goggles lent everything a yellow hue as the light grew stronger. Frey walked as though he knew exactly where he was going. Towards midday, he halted.

'Stop.'

I looked up from my own trudging steps to find that we were standing close to the edge of a cliff of ice. I could see it curving around, and estimated that it must be nearly a hundred feet high. At its base stretched a colossal bay, iced over but fractured and hammered into patchwork pieces by the spring thaw. I could see shapes moving on the ice, small and pale – but this was an optical illusion. Close to, they would not be small at all.

'What *are* they?'

Frey handed me the binoculars. 'Have a look.'

I peered through and was immediately confronted by a snarling face. I stumbled back and heard Frey laugh as he caught me by the arm.

'Careful . . . They're half a mile away, you know.'

I looked again and saw golden eyes set deep in gaunt wells of bone. The beast was enormous; perhaps fifteen feet from nose to the tip of the feathery grey and white tail, and dappled, like shadows amongst snow. The muzzle was very long, with no fur, and fringed with teeth. It was snapping and tearing at something bloody, and when I steadied the binoculars I saw to my horror what it was eating. I lowered the binoculars from my eyes.

'It's a selk.'

'Yes, of course. They're the fenris' main prey up here.'

'But the selk are sentient now.'

'So?'

'It's—'

'Oh, don't be sentimental, Vali. Listen to me. That's why we came.'

'What?'

'To hear the selk speak. But more than that. To call them in.' He gripped my arm. 'You know what you are, don't you?'

'No.' I wanted to pull free; he was hurting me. But I did not dare.

'You are like me, Vali. If you had been born in Darkland, you would have become a vitki. It's all about control, you see. You and I – we're not like other people. We're different. We're *better*.'

121

'I don't understand.'

'This is your ingsgaldir, Vali. You'll know what to do when the time comes.' He turned to the bay below and gave that long, strange cry. And then he disappeared.

I blinked. One minute he had been standing in front of me, and the next moment, he was gone.

'Frey? Frey, where are you?' I called and called, but there was no reply. I looked out over the icefield. I couldn't see any of the pale forms of the fenris, either, but there was a column of storm brewing up far out in the channel and the wind told me that it would be heading this way.

I had no idea what I was supposed to do, or what an ingsgaldir initiation involved. My best chance, I thought, lay in getting back to the ice-rider. I turned and started back. I was a tracker, I told myself. I had noted the signs, the marks of wind erosion on the columns of rock, the patterns of snow and ice and the fall of the light. I could find my way back easily enough and this must be some kind of test, surely. Perhaps this was all that an initiation was; the proving of oneself against a harsh environment. But when I went round an overhang of ice, a fenris was standing there in front of me.

It was very still. The snowy coat merged with the ice behind it, so that the golden eyes burned like stars. Its long jaw fell open to reveal the shards of its teeth. It made a sound, deep in its throat, and paused. I stood, rooted to the spot. I could not move or speak. I felt the world blur, shifting strangely. Suddenly, I was seeing it differently: assessing the land as a predator might; looking for the nooks and crannies in which prey might be hiding, scanning the ice for selk. But I couldn't hold it. I blinked and I was human again.

That was all it took.

The beast was on me so quickly that I did not even have time to cry out. It slammed me down against the ice, knocking the breath out of me. I felt a wave of fetid heat. I don't remember much, only an eye like fire and the pain as it tore at my face. I felt its tongue, rasping behind the teeth, obscenely huge. I thought it was panting, but somewhere, deep within me, I knew that the sound was coming from my own throat.

Then there was a blue-white blast, the terrible eye disappeared behind a red wall, and the ice shuddered beneath me. I turned my head and stared into a glazing eye, a mound of dappled fur that seemed as big as a mountain. Someone was pulling at me, rolling me over. The side of my face felt intensely cold and I could only see out of one eye. In the other, there was only brightness.

'Hallsdottir! Vali, can you hear me?'

But I could not understand why Frey was speaking in a woman's voice.

'Can you hear me?' the voice repeated. I moved my jaw and there was a nauseating rush of pain. My vision went dark. More coolness about my face, a feeling of restriction, then a sharp sting in my hand.

'I'm going to get you to the rider,' the voice said. I was being dragged across the ice. I could feel my heels gouging through the snow. I was lifted, up and over, but the agony was ebbing away now, and I was drifting off. I do not remember the rider's sail going up, nor the vehicle being steered round nor the long glide as we headed into the morning wind.

When I came round, I found that I was wrapped in something fleecy and soft. I explored it with my fingers, finding curls and twists of greasy wool. I opened my eyes. A gust of wind was rattling a pane and stirring the wool beneath my fingers. I was in a small, shabby room, but the perspective seemed strange. It took me a moment to realize that one eye was bandaged. I put up my hand to feel a thick pad of something taped over it, and across the left half of my face. I was lying on a narrow board-bed, piled with sheepskins and woollen blankets. An old-fashioned chest painted with stylized boats stood by the bed, with a water jug and a glass on it. My mouth was very dry and tasted foul. My tongue felt furry and thick. I tried to reach for the glass but my hands were shaking and weak. I sank back onto the bed.

'Ah, you're awake! Don't try to move. Do you want some water?' It was a woman's voice, unfamiliar, and I remembered then that someone had been speaking to me out on the ice. I had not recognized it at the time but now, strangely, I did. 'You're not McGuirey,' I said.

'No, but Ellen is here.' The voice was low and soothing,

a Reach accent, but I couldn't place the island. 'She's downstairs, having a chat to Gunnar.'

'Who are you?'

'My name is Idhunn Regnesdottir. I've come from the Skald.' She came to stand by the side of the bed and I looked up to see a woman in her sixties with a long grey plait, wearing heavy trousers and a felt sweater.

'What happened to me?' I said. A terrible thought struck me. 'Where's Frey?'

'You were attacked, by a fenris, out on the icefield, the day before yesterday. Ellen shot it, and brought you back.'

'*Where's Frey?*'

Idhunn's blue gaze was very steady as she looked down at me. 'We don't know.'

'Is he dead?'

'We don't know.'

'I have to find him! He might be hurt. I have to go back!' I struggled out of the imprisoning fleece and sat up. The movement almost made my head burst.

'You're staying right there,' Idhunn said. 'It's snowing outside, working up to a blizzard. Listen to the wind.' She pushed me back with a firm hand and I didn't have the strength to rise again. But I kept pleading with her, begging her to take me back to the ice, until she said, very insistently, 'Right. You're drinking this.' She held something to my lips and I swallowed a thick, bitter liquid. Moments later, the room was swimming and I was falling fast into a deep sleep.

When I next woke, it was dark outside. A lamp

illuminated Idhunn, seated in the chair, knitting. She was saying, '. . . in any case you have no proof, and you can't just start flinging allegations around, not with Darkland looking over your shoulder.'

'What are you talking about?' I asked. The attack and Frey's absence flooded back over me in a great hot rush of dismay. Idhunn looked up, startled.

'Vali? How are you feeling?' Ellen McGuirey came across to the bed and touched my hand.

'I don't know. Have you found Frey?'

'No. But we're certain he's alive, Vali. The rider you took has gone.'

'What do you mean, gone? I remember being in it.'

'That was mine, Vali. I followed you in my own vehicle, and we came back in it.'

I did not understand. 'Why did you follow us?' And the answer came back, obligingly: *because she wants Frey. She set the beast to attack you, and now she will go to him.*

'No!' I cried. I sat up in bed.

'Vali, calm down,' McGuirey said.

'Bitch!'

'Ellen, I think you'd better wait outside,' Idhunn said. McGuirey gave me an unhappy glance, but she did as the other woman suggested. Idhunn sat on the edge of the bed and took my hand in hers. I felt all the rage and betrayal gradually seep out of me, as though it was bleeding out.

'Vali, you need to listen to me. Gunnar Low asked a rescue crew to fly over the area where you were attacked. They went this afternoon. There's no sign of the rider that you and Frey hired. The body of the fenris is also missing. We're assuming that Frey took the body of the animal and has gone off in the rider.'

I stared at her, uncomprehendingly. 'But why? To look for me?'

'Vali, if he had gone in search of you, he would be back here by now. The tracks left by Ellen's vehicle would have been clear enough.'

'But why didn't McGuirey – Ellen – try to find him? How did she know that the fenris hadn't killed Frey and attacked me?'

'Because she knows what Frey is, Vali.'

'Frey is a vitki.'

'Frey is also something called a beast-caller.' She paused. 'That must have seemed like an almost magical talent, once. But it's just a neurological configuration that imparts a particular tonal note to the voice on a suitable frequency. When our ancestors discovered that, they started breeding it into the population. It's more common in the south than here, because that's where they breed so much stock, and the horse families guard it pretty carefully. But the Darklanders do it as well. Just not with horses. And Ellen's been making enquiries. She's pretty sure that Frey has fenric blood, is some kind of human–animal cross-breed. It was attempted, once.'

'There were rumours,' I said.

'Well, there would be, wouldn't there? Given his appearance, his abilities and his origins, it would be pretty obtuse of people not to notice.'

'It's illegal,' I said.

'It's illegal here.'

'It's illegal *everywhere*. Even in Darkland.'

'You think that matters? They still did it. Frey would seem to be the living proof of that.'

'But that doesn't mean—' I broke off.

'What, that he didn't call the creature to attack you? No, it isn't proof. But Ellen's an adept in the seith. She didn't like what she felt from your man. That's why she followed you.'

'The seith?'

'It's a set of disciplinary meditative practices that the Skald use. And a term for the sense that they generate.'

'I don't believe Frey would hurt me,' I said. 'I can't understand why he would bother.'

Idhunn's face was anxious. 'Sometimes the vitki make – bargains.'

'With whom?'

'With *what*, more like. With things that aren't human.'

'But the fenris aren't intelligent. They're not like the selk.'

'We don't know that. We don't know as much as we'd like to think about the legacies of the genetic engineering programs. There are all sorts of things out there – especially in the north, in the forests. Things that aren't just folktales, but real; things that people made for their own purposes in the distant past. Especially where Frey comes from.' She put her hand on mine. 'Vali, someone who you obviously care about a great deal has let you down very badly. Let the Skald help. Let me take you back to the Rock, sort out your wounds – which aren't as bad as they might have been, but they're bad enough. And let me sort out what I think that vitki has done to your mind.'

'What?'

'Ellen spoke to someone at your college in Stronsay. You'll probably think we've been prying into your affairs – and to some extent I suppose that's true – but under the circumstances it seemed justified. The people at the college remembered a somewhat withdrawn and unhappy, but essentially balanced young woman who took a quiet pride in her skills, which are apparently considerable – not a jealous neurotic who doesn't want to let her lover out of sight for a minute. Ellen McGuirey saw a lot on that ride to the icefield, you know. Now, the goddess knows we can all be thrown off course by a bad love affair, but I don't think you're quite the type, somehow.'

'I never used to be,' I said, surprising myself.

'One isn't,' Idhunn said, very dryly, 'until one runs into the wrong sort of man. If "man" is the right word.'

SIXTEEN

PLANET: MONDHILE

It was noon before the door once more squeaked open. Gemaley stood in the entrance, holding a bowl. She was not wearing her combat leathers today, but a blue tunic and a darker skirt, which looked too big for her, and which was wrapped round her hips. It made her appear to undulate as she walked. Ruan's gaze was snared like a bird.

'Ruan?' she purred. 'How's the ankle?'

'Still painful. But I'll be all right. Gemaley—'

'I've brought you something. I caught it myself.' She gave him an uncharacteristically shy smile. 'I hope you're hungry.'

'I'm starving.'

'That's always a good thing,' Gemaley said.

'Why?'

'Because then you'll appreciate your food all the more. Here.' She uncovered the contents of the bowl – lumps of meat on a bed of green leaves, glossed with oil. The meat was slightly seared, the inside raw and oozing.

'It looks fine,' Ruan said. Gemaley handed him the

bowl, then sat down on the bed and watched him as he tore into the meat.

'Is it all right? It's altru. A young one.'

'You catch the young?' Ruan had been trained only to hunt mature beasts, to preserve the breeding stock.

'Why not? There are plenty of them. Sometimes we don't bother to bring them back; we leave them for the visen to finish off.'

'That's a waste,' Ruan said.

'Not for the visen.'

'Why do you bother? You surely can't want to encourage them.'

'Oh, you know,' Gemaley said, vaguely. She looked away, flicking her hair so that her face was hidden behind its veil. It was clear she wasn't going to answer him. Ruan sighed and decided to change the subject.

'Gemaley, when I fell, it was because I saw a bird. A serai, but a black one. I've never seen such a thing before.'

'Haven't you? I've seen them up in the heights. They're like ordinary serai, but bigger. I think they're beautiful.'

'So do I, but trying to get a closer look at the bird led me into the crevasse.'

Gemaley put her head on one side. 'Is that such a bad thing, Ruan? If you had not fallen, you would not be here.' She brushed back her hair, then put her hand on his. Her fingers felt cool and fragile. 'That's not so terrible, is it? A few days here, while your ankle heals . . . And we can get to know each other better.'

'And then I'll have to leave,' Ruan said, conscious of mingled relief and regret.

'Of course,' Gemaley said. Her eyes widened a little, as though he had expressed a doubt, and he wanted to believe her, but he could not quite manage it.

'You said you didn't have a satahrach. But what about your elders? Can I talk to them?'

'There are no elders here,' Gemaley said.

Ruan stared. 'What happened to them?'

Sickness. It must be. It was the only reason he could think of, and if Gemaley had lost her family – it would explain a great deal.

'They died,' she said, indifferently. 'But they were very old. Now, there's only Gith, and me, and our sister Tian, who you have not met. She wants to meet you, though. Maybe I'll even let her.'

'Your clan's elders. Gemaley—' he suddenly felt very sorry for her, thinking of his own crowded household '—when did you start to lose them?'

'Seven years or so ago. There were four of them. They died over the course of a year.'

'Oh, Gemaley. You couldn't have been long back from the wild, surely?'

'I have never been in the wild. I grew up here.'

Ruan stared at her in disbelief. 'But no one spends their childhood in a house.' The idea seemed unnatural. He felt briefly and compellingly claustrophobic.

'I did. And Gith and Tian, too.'

'Do you remember it?' Ruan asked, hesitantly.

'Some of it.' Again, that disturbing smile, like lightning across her face. 'And you, Ruan? Do you remember your childhood?'

'No, of course not, not really. It was normal. I was put out into the wilderness when I was six months old, I survived, I came back when I was fourteen and became self-aware. I learned language gradually, like everyone else. It was a usual sort of childhood.'

'And mine was not,' Gemaley said. He could not tell whether she was simply stating a fact or whether she felt that he was criticizing her. He knew, with sudden realization, that he would not like to anger her, and some of Gith's nervousness was explained.

'But this is a special kind of place,' he said hastily, trying to make amends, and was rewarded by a brilliant smile.

'Yes. Yes, it is. And I'm looking forward to showing it to you, Ruan. When you're well enough.' She curled up beside him on the bed, hair fanning out around her, and drew him down.

That night there was a storm. Ruan was awoken by a splintering crash of thunder, right over the tower. The shutters rattled. Gemaley was once again gone and he was surprised to find how long he had been sleeping. He threw aside the covers and hobbled to the window. The wind tore the shutters from his grip when he opened them.

There was a long race of cloud over the northern peaks, suddenly lit by a blaze of lightning, forked and blue. Clouds ran before it, revealing bands of clear sky. Ruan glimpsed a thin crescent moon, Embar, with Elowen a half quarter just above the mountains, a smear of brightness. He knew that it was late, and the evening star was nowhere to be seen. Instead, the midnight star Rhe hung high above the tower like a lantern, a fiery blue. It reminded him of Gemaley's eyes, of the stars in her hair. He thought back to the afternoon, of Gemaley naked beside him, back arched, eyes wide open. She never seemed to close her eyes, not even at the moment of climax. The memory was at once disturbing and arousing, and with an effort he forced himself to stare at the star and put thoughts of Gemaley from his mind. The cold air helped.

The room was filled with a gust of wind and the shutters banged. Cursing, Ruan reached perilously out and pulled them back. The forest below roared under the sudden lash of the gale, trees tossing, and snapping together. As he leaned out, there was another crack of lightning and he saw something in the shadows, far below. It stood under the trees, but he could not sense anything there, only a blankness, as if a piece of the world had been detached and taken elsewhere. Then the lightning flashed again and he saw it – a tall figure, standing in the snow under a satinspine.

In the next flash, he saw a face turn upwards to look at him and it filled him with horror. He dragged the shutters closed and leaned trembling against them. He told himself that it was just the cold, but he sought sanctuary beneath the covers nonetheless, turning his back to the window and the storm.

SEVENTEEN

PLANET: MUSPELL

Once Idhunn and I had left the council chamber, I spent most of the rest of the day in the lamp room, curled in the window seat above the racing waters of the Minch and thinking back to what had happened seven years ago out on the icefield.

After I had recovered a little from the fenris' attack, Idhunn kept her promise and had me brought from Yetland to the Rock, where most of my real healing had taken place. They had not been able to save the sight in my left eye, despite consultations with a vision specialist in Tiree. I underwent a degree of reconstructive surgery on my face, but it was prolonged and painful and I asked them to halt procedures before the final round of operations. I regretted that, a little, but I had reached a point where I couldn't stand surgery any longer. Being messed about with, being touched, being cared for – it had all grown too much for me.

Now, I crossed to the reflective surface of the lamp and gazed into it. Usually, I avoided mirrors, but not today. In the silver curve, my scars were clearly visible – three long grooves down my cheek, as though an angry woman had scored my face with her nails. When I myself grew angry, as now, the scars darkened to a livid crimson beneath the pucker of flesh with its false eye. People often stared at me. I often challenged them.

Despite the element of regret, there was a part of me that was glad I had kept the scars. They were a reminder of how badly I had been hurt, and not just outside. The Skald had brought in a healer to deal with the emotional wounds, and at first I resisted it.

My family had never been ones to seek counselling, seeing it not so much as a sign of weakness, just as a non-necessity. No one really wanted to face what my brother had done; it was easier to just let it freeze over. And everyone knew that the cure for a broken heart was just to give it time, get over it, move on, let *that* wound close up as well. But, eventually, the curse of spring will come.

Still, Idhunn had insisted this was different. 'If Frey had simply been some idiot boy, I'd have said yes, go about the business of forgetting him. Get drunk, complain to your friends, throw stones at the waves. But Frey is a vitki, and was responsible for you nearly getting killed. That leaves tracks in your psyche, Vali, that are as visible to me as an animal's footprints in the snow would be to you. And we have to get rid of them.'

Even now, trained as I was in the seith, I did not really understand what the healer had done. She was a middle-aged woman, on the heavy side, with unruly hair. She looked, as she often said, as though she had been dragged through a hedge, and she had a fondness for large, shapeless pieces of jewellry that, in my view, did not suit her. Her work consisted mainly of placing me in a light trance, which I always fiercely resisted, but to which I invariably succumbed. Then, she would stand next to me and place her hands over my head.

This was all she did, or appeared to do. I was more than somewhat scornful, though I said nothing to Idhunn or the other women of the Skald, all of whom I was gradually getting to know. But over time, perhaps three months or so, someone like the old Vali began to creep back; venturing opinions that were not Frey's opinions, no longer aching quite so much for his touch and his body, starting at long last to resent what I now recognized as continual put-downs, and constant undermining.

When the women of the Skald sat around the communal rooms with a bottle of peat-flavoured whisky, complaining about their men, I began to join in. And over time, I found myself swinging from one extreme to another. I would have no further use for men, I decided, and it was unlikely that any of them would have any use for me, looking as I did. With the scars and the single eye, I looked like a crone in a fairy tale, and sometimes I felt like one, too. *That's that*, I thought. *I'll be a crone, then.* And I asked the Skald to make me what I became. A killer. The valkyrie legends of the north of Earth had not been forgotten, and I embraced them.

Now, I gave my reflection in the curve of the lamp a

hard, appraising look. I had not set eyes on Frey from that day to this, or so I'd thought. The Skald had made enquiries, but there wasn't enough proof to send a legal enforcer after him, and the vitki were a law unto themselves in any case. There was a long and sorry history of enforcers who had been dispatched to Darkland, and never heard of again.

I spent many hours rehearsing what I would say – and do – to Frey if I ever ran across him again, and it had occurred to me more than once to try and track him down myself. Idhunn had managed to talk me out of that, so far, but now it seemed that sending me after him was what she wanted. It suited me.

I was due to leave that evening. I would be travelling light to Darkland – a pack containing my weather gear, a few instruments, and a range of weapons: a bolt-firing bow that could be assembled from a palm-sized series of fibre strips, a pulse-firing sidearm, and a number of knives. Of them all, I preferred the knives; they seemed to fit well with the sense of the seith, for some reason. Idhunn and I skirted around the issue of what the weapons were actually for. The question of wild animals was raised. But it did not matter. We both knew that my target was information.

That, and Frey.

Early that afternoon, I stood waiting on the steps of the Rock. The wing came round the side of the Rock in a flurry of spray, a showy halt that was somehow familiar. When I climbed into the passenger seat, I realized why. The pilot was Ellen McGuirey.

I hadn't seen Ellen since those bleak days in Yetland. She spent most of her time out in the Reach, on Skald business, but we had exchanged regular notes by tabula. My embarrassment at my own jealousy was still present, to some degree, and it made me uneasy about encountering her again. I had to remind myself that I was a different person, now.

McGuirey had changed remarkably little and I felt a stab of envy at the waving dark hair, the blue eyes and smooth skin. She smiled when she saw me, in apparently genuine pleasure.

'Vali! How are you?'

'Well enough. You're looking good.'

'And so are you.' Her expression was serious, and I knew that she was referring to more than my appearance. 'You've just come back to Muspell?'

'Just returned. Skald business.'

'Like myself. Only in my case, it's the sea, not space. It's been too long, Vali. When you get home, we must get together.'

'I'd like that,' I said.

We talked a little on the way to Tiree, carefully avoiding the subject of Frey. I did not know how much Idhunn had told her, and instinct led me away from the issue. The trip took several hours, even by wing, and when we reached the ragged coast outside Tiree I was surprised to find how late it was. McGuirey moored the wing at the edge of the harbour. We had time for a snatched meal at one of the harbourside places, a pasty and a beer, and then went in search of accommodation.

We found some in the same vicinity – a dingy place, with paint peeling from the walls, eroded by the constant salt wash of the sea air. The man on duty at the guest house tried to overcharge us but after some brief bargaining, Ellen and I beat him down.

Tiree was a sprawl, I thought, looking out of the back window of the guest house; low-rise tenements and light industrial factories. Not a pretty place. After the clear air of the Reach, the air stank of chemicals and pollutants, and the sea had an oily sheen. Wherever humans went, they seemed ultimately to foul a place, I thought, whatever the original intentions might have been. You'd think we would have learned from Earth. But then at the other extreme were folk like the Gaians, who tailored and manicured their environment to such a pristine degree it was almost unreal.

I shut my eyes and thought of the islands, imagining myself back on the Rock. I could have stayed. I could have gone home to Scaraskae and the holding. My parents would have been glad to see me, I knew. I'd been avoiding them, too. Seeing my mother's expression as she looked at my ruined face had been difficult to bear. When I returned from my mission, I told myself, then I might go back to Scaraskae and cash in some of the land credits that were the Skald's payment to me for my services. I would buy a holding of my own, near the rest of the family, and undertake tracking for the locals, or for licensed hunters from Tiree.

And then it would be over. I would have buried the past and come to terms with it. I did not tell myself, in so many words, that I would do so by burying Frey.

EIGHTEEN

Planet: Mondhile

Next morning, Ruan's ankle was considerably better – not yet well enough to entrust it with his full weight, but healed sufficiently to allow him to limp along. He dressed, wishing that Gemaley had brought him some water in which to wash. He smelled of her, the cool, resinous scent of her hair, an animal musk. It made him feel curiously insubstantial, as though she was taking him over, piece by piece – slowly starting to consume him.

He limped across to the door and rattled the handle, expecting it to be locked as usual. But to his surprise, the door opened. He found himself looking out into a long hallway. He stepped through.

The hallway was panelled, with a wood that was probably satinspine, but it was difficult to tell under the layer of dust and moth-webs. The hall did not look as if it had been cleaned for years. Ruan could not see Gemaley doing much housekeeping – but that was usually the men's task, anyway. Perhaps Gith was too cowed . . .

Halfway up, however, the panelling stopped and the

143

walls reverted to the natural stone of the tower, that odd gleam. Ruan made his way as quickly as he could along the hallway. It was not so much that he was considering escape – if he dwelt on it, that seemed unlikely – as exploration, the preliminaries to flight. If he could at least figure out a route down to the main part of the tower, he could start planning his way home. The tower's defences were another matter. He needed to think about that.

At the end of the hallway lay a flight of stairs, leading down to a door. Ruan hobbled down them. This door, too, was unlocked. When he stepped through – taking care to leave the door ajar behind him – he was in yet another hallway, curving round what was presumably the outer wall of the tower.

And someone was singing.

It was a thin, small voice, and for an unnerving moment Ruan wondered if it might be a child. Gemaley's words about growing up in the tower returned to haunt him. What if there were other children here? He thought of the voice he and Eleshtra had heard shrieking with rage, on the day of the visen's attack.

Apart from his own childhood – as barely remembered as a dream – Ruan had only seen a few children, and those from a distance, hiding in the mountain scrub or fleeing down the slopes. Feral and dangerous, they were not folk he, or anyone, would willingly seek out. Gemaley's alleged childhood seemed like something out of the distant past, out of legend.

He paused for a moment, listening. The song was con-

tinuing, wordless, a stream of sound. It occurred to him
that it might not even be human at all. He thought again
of the black serai he had seen, the bird that had led to him
being here, but they had never been known to sing. This,
however, was the tower, and things seemed very different
here.

Cautiously, he made his unsteady way down the
corridor. He was afraid of being overheard, but the song
did not falter. It was coming from a room at the end of the
hallway. The door, Ruan observed, was half open. He edged
along the wall and peered in.

The singer was sitting on the bed. At first, with a jump
of the heart, he thought it was Gemaley, as the long pale
hair was the same. But then the girl turned her face to the
door. She had the same slanting eyes as Gemaley, but they
were a darker, yet somehow less intense, blue. And where
Gemaley's pointed features lent a delicacy to her face, this
girl's looked merely pinched.

She said, in a little, breathy voice, 'You can come in, if
you like.'

Not knowing what else to do, Ruan stepped through
the door. The room was a mess; the ceiling trailing with
moth-webs in which the bodies of wall-beetles and dis-
carded wing cases hung like dull jewels. A splintered chest
stood at one end of the room, looking as though someone
had attacked it with an axe. Clothes spilled out of it and
were strewn across the floor, amidst mounds of what
looked like earth. Ruan could not imagine why anyone
would bring soil all the way up here; there was no sign

of any plants. Back at the clan house, the satahrach's chamber usually looked as though a strong wind had recently swept through it, but one had the sense that somewhere, there was an underlying order. Old Arrath always seemed to know where to find things, at least. This was just squalour. And a peculiar smell permeated the whole room; a pungent, vegetable odour, only slightly diminished by the cold. The window stood wide open.

The girl on the bed was gazing at Ruan with a fixed, blank stare. The pinpoint pupils were like holes in the expanse of blue. He could hear her breath, wheezing in and out of her lungs. She sounded like someone with water fever, and for a moment, Ruan was afraid. But if she had water fever, she would be red in the face and unable to sit upright.

'What's your name?' Ruan said. He remembered Gemaley saying something about another sister, whom he had not yet met. This must be her.

'Tian. And you are Ruan, my sister's new find.'

Ruan did not like the sound of that. The girl smiled as she said it, but it was wistful, not like Gemaley's lightning smile. She patted the bed. 'Sit with me.'

Ruan hesitated for a moment, then perched on the side of the bed. He did not want to get too close to Tian. She looked too child-like for him to trust her, and she was, in any case, Gemaley's blood relative. That seemed to render questions of trust immaterial.

'Are you like the other one?' Tian asked. She frowned,

146

peering at him, and it was then that he realized that her sight was poor. 'No, you aren't. You are like us.'

'What "other one"?' Ruan asked. He had an ominous feeling that he was about to be given some ghastly revelation – a tale of another young man whom Gemaley had found, seduced, and . . . then what? Something Gemaley had said was nagging at the back of his mind. He searched for it, but it was gone.

'The one who is staying here.' Tian spoke as though it was quite a normal thing, and Ruan relaxed, but only a little. 'The vitki. I thought perhaps he had come to see you.'

'No, I've seen no one except your sister. Who is he? And what's a vitki?' But he'd heard that word before, and again it had been something Gemaley had said . . .

'I don't know. Gemaley found him.'

Gemaley seemed to do nothing except wander about the landscape gathering up stray men, Ruan thought resentfully. And with a slight cold shock he realized that he was jealous.

Tian's attention seemed to have wandered. She was gazing through the open window. The paper pane rattled in the breeze, a sound that set Ruan's nerves on edge.

'Didn't Gemaley tell you where he'd come from, this man?'

Tian smiled. 'Gemaley doesn't tell me anything. She says I wouldn't understand. Perhaps she's right.'

'She told me that your clan are all dead. Is that true?'

'Yes, it's true.'

147

'You must miss them very much,' Ruan said.

She stared at him blankly. 'I don't think about it. They're gone. We're here. It's enough, Gemaley and Gith and I, and the ones who pass through.'

'Tian – what happens to these visitors?' Once again, that ominous sensation began to crawl up Ruan's spine.

'They come, and then they go away again. That's it. I don't talk to most of them. I don't like talking to people. I won't talk to the other one. He frightens me.'

'You're talking to me,' Ruan said.

'That's different.' She was still gazing out of the window. Ruan wondered what she was looking at. Perhaps nothing, if her sight was so weak.

'I'd like to meet this other visitor,' he said.

'I don't think Gemaley would like that.'

'We're not talking about what Gemaley would like,' Ruan pointed out.

'It doesn't matter. If Gemaley doesn't want you to, then you won't.'

That was enough to make Ruan resolve to seek out this man, whoever he might be. He rose painfully from the bed.

'Are you going to tell Gemaley that I came to talk to you?' he said.

She looked vague. 'Maybe. Maybe not.'

Ruan did not want to tell her to keep quiet, as he had a feeling that it might have the opposite effect.

'I like secrets,' Tian murmured. He decided to take that as reassurance, however obscure.

'So do I,' Ruan said. He waited for her to say something

else, to seal their apparent complicity, but she did not. She continued to stare through the window, looking at nothing. She did not turn round when Ruan left the room.

His ankle was hurting again, and he briefly debated returning to his chamber. He did not, after all, want to anger Gemaley – and then he stopped himself. She had no right to lock him in; he was a guest, and should have some freedom within the household. She might be his lover, but she was not his owner.

Along the hallway lay the top of a spiral staircase, and now Ruan remembered being carried up here when he was first brought into the tower. He hobbled down it, clinging tightly to the metal rail. It must have been polished, once, but now the iron was rusty and sharp to the touch. Moreover, the stairs were damp. Squinting upwards, Ruan suspected that there were probably holes in the roof. Peering over the rail, he could see into the depths of the tower; a round patch of hall, far below.

Above him, the singing began again. It was eerily repetitive, despite the lack of words, and it made him shiver. He was beginning to feel feverish – first hot, then a clammy flush spreading across his skin. He told himself that he would go only a little further, but his ankle was burning again now, a throbbing, rhythmic pain. He did not want to fall down these steep stairs and risk a broken neck or, at the least, further confinement in the tower.

With a curse Ruan bowed to the inevitable and returned to his room. The singing followed him, all the way.

NINETEEN

Planet: Muspell

Next morning dawned calm, with a slight swell lapping against the sides of the harbour wall and a pearly haze across the outer reaches of the channel. I dressed in what Idhunn assured me was typical Darkland gear, which I would conceal under my greatcoat, and checked that the Darkland currency with which they had issued me was still safe. Back on the Rock, the medical team had once more covered my scars with a skin patch and I wore a false eye.

I had breakfast in my room with Ellen, who would be returning to the Reach that morning, while I took a wing alone to Darkland. Neither of us said a great deal, except towards the end of the meal, when she swallowed a final mouthful of ham and said, 'Vali, yesterday, when I said you were looking well, I hope you didn't think I was being insensitive. I actually meant it.'

I nodded. 'I know.'

She went on, haltingly, 'You must know, then, that I wasn't just referring to your appearance, though it's probably easier than you think for people to see past your scars. It's more a question of your spirit. When I first met you, with that vitki, you seemed utterly cowed, as though any mind of your own that you'd possessed had just been squashed under his personality. You were like a little shadow, trotting along behind. But now, you are your own person.

'In the days after you were hurt, when I sat watching you, I saw your self come back again, bit by bit, like a scared wild thing. And now you are entirely your own woman again. I wanted you to know that.'

She paused and looked down at her plate. 'I was in a – difficult – relationship once. I recognized that expression you wore because I'd seen it often enough in the mirror. It was always very subtle. He'd give me a look and I'd wonder if I'd said the wrong thing. I'd say something else and a week later it would be repeated back to me, but changed, just slightly, so I'd wonder what I'd really said. Bit by bit, piece by piece, he stole my soul away.'

'And what made you leave?' I found it hard to imagine the self-contained, quietly confident McGuirey as someone else's pawn.

'I didn't. He left me, for someone younger, and when he described her to me, I realized – a long time later – that she had all the qualities he'd worked to diminish in me. Her age had nothing to do with it. He'd succeeded in breaking me down and once he'd done that, he moved onto someone else. It took me a long time to understand what he'd done to me, and also what I had been complicit in. The

Skald and its practices helped me, just as they seem to have helped you.'

'It sounds as though you're well rid of him,' I told her. 'I wonder what happened to the poor girl he left you for?'

'Oh, her,' Ellen said with a grin. 'She ditched him after a few months. She was a playwright. He turned up as a character in one of her plays. *Lampooned.*'

'Oh, good for her.'

'I went to see it four times.' She turned away from the table and stretched, arching her arms above her head. 'It was a long time ago. But I haven't forgotten that I promised myself never to return to that situation, and I never have. And neither should you.'

'No. No, I never will.' The words seemed to echo around us, a shadow across the edges of the seith. 'Thank you, Ellen. I'll have to make a move soon.'

'So will I. You take care, where you're going.'

She had not asked, and I was not sure whether the Skald had told her – probably not, given the relative secrecy and nature of this mission. But I had the feeling that she knew anyway. 'Good-bye, Ellen,' I said on the steps of the boarding house. 'You take care, too.'

I watched as she walked across to her wing, her pack slung over one shoulder, and I waited until she had steered the craft out into the outer harbour, navigating past the moored lines of boats and wings. The last I saw of her that day was the wing picking up speed, heading toward the Reach in a sparkle of sunlit spray. Then I went over to the harbour-mistress' office, and asked for a wing of my own.

The Skald had already arranged a craft for me – one of their own tech boats. It had stealth capability; even approaching the apparently empty coasts of eastern Darkland, I did not want to risk being seen – and none of us really knew what kind of detection devices Darkland possessed. Infraction of their shipping regulations was known to carry a heavy penalty; no one who had violated their territorial waters had ever returned. It was hardly reassuring.

The Skald had promised to try to get me out if I got captured, but neither Idhunn nor I had any real confidence in this promise – the will was there, but the ability would be lacking. It seemed strange that it had proved easier to rescue me from Nhem – another world – than would be likely from a nation on my own home planet.

The wing was waiting on the other side of the harbour and I attracted not a few envious glances from people working on their boats as I made my way down the dock towards it. It was a slick, sleek thing, arrow-shaped, with long flaring vanes on either side; these were retractable and could be adjusted, depending on speed and the need for manoeuvrability. It was a sombre indigo in colour, but I knew that it had a camouflage function if I decided not to use the stealth capabilities, which could sometimes interfere with the navigation array. The moment I set sight on it I wanted to get it out there and moving. The heavy air of Tiree suddenly seemed even more oppressive.

I let the harbour-mistress know that I was leaving, deactivated the locking mechanism, and stepped in. The wing handled beautifully, sliding out through the narrow channels between the other craft, and out of the harbour mouth into the open sea. I touched the controls and the wing accelerated to maximum speed as though shot out of a bow.

Out here, the sea had risen to a surge but the wing's movement felt like a smooth glide. Signals from other shipping fed neatly into the navigational array in moving bands of crimson and sapphire, and all I had to do then was sit and watch as cargo ships, tankers, freight barges and the occasional opulent clipper slipped past with the transience of dreams.

I passed islands again – Muish, Eith, Eilish – but there was little time to study the scattering of villages strung along their heathery slopes. Soon, the islands grew barer and balder, but covered with flocks of seabirds. As the wing glided past the long slabs of granite that marked their shores, I saw grey bodies basking in the sun, but this close to the inhabited shores, they were only sealstock, not selk.

Soon even these crags fell away and there was nothing between myself and Darkland except the stormy reaches of the western ocean. Once we had been travelling for a couple of hours and were safely away from the shipping lanes, I took the wing up to maximum speed again and activated the stealth mechanism. I did not know how far out the Darklanders set their surveillance, but I was

certain that it was a long way outside their official navigational boundaries.

Clicking onto the array itself, I asked for an ETA and
after a moment the pale blue of the comm screen array
flickered into life, with the information that it would take
about fifteen hours to reach Darkland waters. It would still
be light, in this northern spring, but in any case their time
zone was some hours behind that of the Reach. I should
make Darkland by late evening, if all went smoothly.

But it did not. Some six hours out of Tiree, the rolling
swell changed to a choppier, higher sea and storm clouds
began to gather on the western horizon. I could not help
seeing it as a bad omen, as though the vitki somehow
sensed my presence and were summoning the weather
against me. I told myself that I was being superstitious,
that this sudden fear that gripped me in its cold claw was
nothing more than a legacy of my ordeal at Frey's hands,
but I could not shake it off, no matter how much reason-
ing I applied.

Eventually I sat back in the pilot's chair and tried to
send the fear into the seith, to disperse it. This was only
partially successful, for the storm clouds were growing,
massing up in the distance like a great heap of coals. As I
watched, I saw a flicker of lightning along the line of the
horizon, a strange and livid rose red. We were heading
straight for it and the swell was rising.

I slowed the wing a little, to improve its handling, and
turned the controls back to manual. If I was going to hit a
storm, I wanted to have maximum control over the craft

rather than relying on the array. It may have been that the array would do a better job, but I did not like the idea of putting my trust in the machine. The words of the old fisherpeople of the Reach – my grandmother among them – floated into my mind: *always pilot your own ship*. It was a saying they applied to every situation – including, as I recall, those to which it was barely appropriate. But it was an adage born out of two thousand years of experience, from an age that had always seen technology, and I thought it would be wise to heed it.

Under manual control, the wing handled well. I took it along the walls of the swell, turning its stabilizing jets to the highest setting and flying down sea-water canyons. The wing sailed up just as the clouds broke, taking me into the storm. Those clouds, which had been on the horizon only half an hour before, were now directly overhead and the viewscreen of the wing was illuminated by flashes of lightning through the streaming spray.

And then it happened. I misjudged the angle of a wave, caught the tip of one of the vanes and the wing somersaulted.

It took place so quickly that I barely registered it. Strapped securely into the pilot's chair, I tumbled over and over with the movement of the craft. The wing came to rest upside down. I looked into a heaving ocean. Claustrophobia and fear rose into my throat like bile. Praying that the vanes had not become hopelessly buckled, I activated the stabilizing jets on the upper side of the wing – which now faced the water. After a heart-

rending few moments, it shuddered and rose, raising me –
still upside down – several feet above the water. Increasing
the thrust on one set of jets turned me the right way up
again, but when I moved the wing forward, it was listing.
One of the side vanes had been damaged. The stealth
mechanism was still working, as far as I could tell, but I
was not entirely confident that the navigational array and
feedback mechanism remained undamaged. It could be
feeding me erroneous information and the wing might
be in plain sight of Darkland surveillance, for all I knew.

But there was no way of making absolutely sure, so I
flew on into the storm. By now, the sky had become so
lowering, it was immaterial that it was still the middle of
the afternoon. Darkland indeed! I could see nothing
physically through the mist of spray that covered the
viewscreen in long runnels of water, and was forced to rely
on the array for piloting the damaged wing. At the
furthest left-hand side of the screen a small tracery of
green indicated land – an estimated hundred and fifty
miles distant. If this storm kept up, it was going to be a
long battle ahead to keep the wing upright and flying,
though a great deal easier than sailing a boat would have
been.

The day settled down into a monotonous cycle of flying
from wave to wave. Now, I longed for nothing more than
to be able to see the coast of Darkland, steadily growing at
the edge of the screen into a chewed mass of fjords.

At last, the storm started to abate and the clouds lifted
a little, to reveal a sullen evening sky and a great wall of

cliffs and inlets ahead. I immediately saw how Darkland had gained its name, no matter what the practices of its inhabitants might have been. The cliffs comprised masses of vitreous black stone, shining wet in the dying storm-light and gleaming with iridescence.

I studied the navigational array and saw that Hetla was some twelve miles along the coast, but there were satellite indications of settlements strung in a ragged band down the shoreline. I could not see any, but doubtless they were concealed within the fjords. I chose a seemingly uninhabited inlet and, hoping I was doing the right thing, steered the wing towards it. The cliffs grew closer, looming over the boiling sea, and I had to fight to take the wing into the fjord's mouth without foundering on the rocks. This would be a nightmare coast for traditional shipping: rocks that rose in slabs, and needle teeth far out beyond the shore, half hidden by the tide and the racing currents yet low enough beneath the waterline to snag and sink an unwary vessel.

Once inside the fjord, however, the sea grew suddenly calm; an icy jade green, clear enough for me to see the rocks far below through the viewscreen. Above, the side of the fjord rose some two hundred feet, straight up and glassy smooth, into the uneasy air. If the whole inlet was like this then climbing would not be easy. However, I'd had experience on equally treacherous terrain – cliffs on Mohla and Farasay – and I was reasonably confident of my ability to scale it. Not, though, if someone noticed me from above. It was a pity that no one had developed a stealth mechanism for people as well as craft – but that was what the seith could do, to a limited degree. Unless, of course, one was being observed by people already versed in it, such as the vitki.

The wing glided up the channel, which in some places was so narrow that I had to bring in the vanes to avoid them brushing against the rock walls. At the end of the fjord lay a small stony apron of shingle and I brought the wing to rest on it and drew the vanes in completely. There was a shudder as the damaged vane slid into its sheath and I held my breath, hoping that it was not too badly buckled to retract, but it went in all the way. Then, keeping the stealth mechanism active, I set the camouflage mechanism as well, just in case.

Through the viewscreen, the nose of the wing shimmered and became shingle-coloured, almost invisible even to me. The wing was now as secure as possible, though it could be no help in getting me up the cliff. The hover jets could not lift it all that way.

Once the wing was shut down and camouflaged, I collected my gear from the hatch and stepped outside. Darkland's coast smelled no different to the rest of the north; an odour composed of sea-water, rain, ancient weed and shellfish, with an underlying dank musk that after a moment I identified as bull sealstock. I looked at the wing and to my satisfaction saw nothing, only a bare patch of shingle. Then I looked up the sheer wall of the cliff. Even in the dying light it emitted a faint sheen, plummeting straight down into the shingle. There were no visible handholds. I walked round the perimeter of the beach to see if there was any sign of a path leading up, but there was nothing. It was very quiet, with only the hush and lap of the sea against the edge of the shingle. I found it ominous.

There was no option but to use the laser piton against the wall, carving out foot- and handholds as I went. I did not like leaving such obvious traces, even in such a remote location, but it was either that or risk the wing's presence in a place more accessible to the possibly populated shore, and I did not want to take that kind of chance.

If I started now, I could be at the summit before darkness descended, and this spurred me on. I took out the piton and held it a couple of feet up the wall, cupping my hand over the top of the device to conceal any betraying glow. After a moment, there was a curiously sulphurous odour and the rock melted away under the beam of the laser. A few inches were enough. I made another depression, higher up, then began to climb.

It took perhaps two hours to scale the cliff. There was some satisfaction in knowing that it would be a lot quicker on the way down, with handholds already in position. I just hoped I wouldn't have to do it in the dark.

Above me, the clouds had sailed out to sea to form towering columns of cumulus on the far horizon, visible only in a narrow strip at the fjord's end. The sky above me was a darkening blue, with the faint sparkle of early starlight scattered across it. I fought back another wave of foreboding. This was still Muspell, I told myself, still home . . . but it did little good. It looked like the north, like the Reach, but it didn't feel like it. Despite the familiar landscape, this place felt alien and strange.

At last I reached the top of the cliff and hauled myself cautiously over the lip of the summit. I don't know what I expected to find – a circle of angry vitki, perhaps – but there were just trees: conifers rustling in the slight breeze, thickly compacted together to form a forest wall a short distance from the cliff. Looking down the coast, I saw a scatter of lights, which I decided it would be prudent to avoid. My destination was the ship- and air-yards of Hetla. If I came across Frey . . . but I had, deliberately, given no thought as to how I was to find him. As I had told Idhunn, a month ago I would have sworn that I would have been able to sense him, even in three hundred Darkland miles, but after Nhem, it was evident that I couldn't pick him out from a crowd when he was standing two feet away from me.

The old, familiar feeling of helplessness and failure washed over me. I wondered if he still looked like Aldur, or whether he had reverted to his original appearance. And I wondered – again – what the reason for this deception had been. It was a roundabout way of trying to kill me, but then Frey seemed to prefer roundabout ways.

Skirting the edge of the trees, I glanced inwardly at the map implant. Hetla lay on a wide fjord down the coast, not far away. I did not like the thought of a vitki-run city at night. It seemed best to make my way along the coast just after dark, hopefully before whatever lived in the deep forest began to stir, and then camp for the rest of the night until dawn. Once the sky started to lighten, I would make my way to the wing-yards and try to get some idea of what was happening.

The prospect of finding Frey seemed increasingly remote. I could hardly start asking around. I did not know how visible I might be – in any sense of the word – and as a non-Darklander I would have to rely, even more than I cared to, on the seith. Whether that would serve to hide me or to betray me, I was not certain.

I did not want to venture deep into the forest. Even as the thought occurred to me, there was a long, low cry from among the trees. I was familiar with all the wildlife of the rest of the north, but I could not tell whether this was bird or animal. A hunting owl, I hoped. I set off along the strip of short grass and earth that formed the cliff's edge, although there were still places where I was forced to make my way through the trees, and amongst thickets of thorn and bramble. The trees themselves had been blasted back by the wind, trained and twisted into unnatural, north-streaming shapes, but the low iron-coloured briars grew densely. It was slow going, but by midnight I estimated that I was almost in sight of the city outskirts.

Fighting my way through a grove of thorn, I suddenly stepped out onto a long slope, leading down to the cliffs of another fjord. Hetla lay beyond, illuminated in a long skein around the sharp curve of the fjord's mouth, but strangely dimmed as though seen through rain. If the lights were anything to go by, then the city was low-rise apart from a few tall structures at the outskirts – too narrow for apartment blocks – and burning red at the tips. I thought they might be watchtowers. Further up the fjord, towards the mouth, I could see the occasional flare from what looked like a refinery. It reminded me of the industrial coast outside Tiree, which still relied on natural gas for much of its energy.

I retreated back to the edge of the trees and unpacked the pad-bag, which inflated from a thin strip of film to a body-length thermal unit. I slipped inside it and lay listening to the cries of the creatures in the forest, while the baleful red eye of one of the watchtowers winked through the trees. The seith would wake me if anything approached, or so I hoped. It would be another few hours until dawn.

I woke just as the sky was changing to grey above Hetla. I crawled out of the pad-bag, deflated it to its carry size and stood looking out across the fjord. In daylight, Hetla extended further along the shore than I had thought. Parts of it must remain unlit at night and I wondered why.

I found myself looking down on rows of long grey sheds, extending out over the sea. The entire perimeter was guarded by lines of razor wire and a tower with weapons placements. Some kind of prison, perhaps? But for such an installation, one would have thought that it lay too close to the fjord's mouth, and the vulnerability to threat of attack. Whatever it was, I could smell a strong, sour, fishy odour rising up from the sheds and tainting the breeze. Some kind of processing plant? But surely you didn't need a gun tower to guard fishmeal or a canning factory . . .

Behind me stretched the forest, and in daylight I found it even more forbidding. These conifers were not like the eld-spruce and pines of the Reach but, like the brambles, they had deep grey trunks, and in the light wind from the sea, the dense needles seemed curiously insubstantial, like drifting smoke or captured cloud. I turned my back on them.

Further along the fjord I could see the city proper – ranks of oddly glistening buildings, some domed. I raised the binoculars to my eye. At the end of the fjord, rising up directly from the grey-green waves, was what looked like a cluster of official buildings – tall oblongs of pillared stone – but with no signs of activity yet. It was a style of architecture that I did not know.

The wing-yards themselves, a jumble of cranes and docks, lay across the fjord. The yards were huge, and no wonder when one saw what was being produced. Four war-wings lay berthed at the far end; huge whales with sleek black hulls. When their vanes were extended, they would be even larger.

Two more were under construction in dry dock and even this early in the day, there was work being done on them. I could hear the faint grinding sound of machinery drifting accross the water. I used the binoculars to take a couple of shots of all the vessels, then transmitted it back to the Rock. But whatever was there would surely have been picked up already from the satellite overview.

If I was to get down to the yards themselves, there were two choices: sailing across the fjord or travelling through the city. Sailing meant that I would either have to go back for the wing, or steal a boat, and I was reluctant to risk either. Besides, although I disliked the look of the place, I was curious to see what Hetla itself was like. I wondered if the city had border posts; whether one needed passes or documentation or implants to enter. Perhaps the vitki could simply smell intruders. In any event, I would soon find out.

I followed the cliff for some distance before coming to a road. This led down between buildings, but they were shuttered and it was impossible to tell whether they were shops or dwellings. There was a curious delicacy to them. Some had tall stalagmite spires that gleamed and glistened, reminding me of the canyons out on the icefield.

Despite my Darkland clothes, I felt highly conspicuous as I followed the slope of the roadway. What if the Skald had got it wrong and my attire was no longer in fashion, subtly betraying? But there were no guard posts or entry-ways, and as I walked on, the city began to come alive around me, men and women throwing open fragile wooden shutters and preparing for the morning. A narrow vehicle passed me at speed, sending a scatter of frost in its wake. Apart from the shine of the unfamiliar buildings, it could have been anywhere on Muspell and I began to feel a little easier.

What had not been obvious from the cliff summit was that the city was filled with trees that merged in with the dark background of the buildings. All were conifers – tall, pointed cones like the cypress that grew in the far south of the Reach, the colour of cloud, and giving off a heavy scent that was more highly perfumed than ordinary resin, and making the air seem narcotic.

I began to feel tired, despite having slept reasonably well up on the cliff, and I wondered if the trees had been planted deliberately, perhaps to have some effect on the population. Certainly the faces I saw around me seemed dulled and incurious. No one looked my way for long – perhaps the Skald had got my dress code correct after all. I took some pains to appear as thick-witted as they did, but it was not difficult. My head was beginning to pound. Surreptitiously, I reached into the pack and took an analgesic, but left the amphetamines for the moment. I did not like doping myself up, but it might become necessary.

By mid-morning I had reached the cluster of buildings I had seen from the cliff. They were even more imposing up close than they had been from afar. Tall basalt pillars rose out of the water. There was no way of telling whether they had been deliberately built this way or if this part of Hetla had been flooded. The sea level had risen through-out the north from natural climatic change and shifts in the polar ice, and if Hetla dated from early times then it might explain the position of the buildings. Each one was carved, with spirals and runes like sculptures of ice, and all had the same cold gleam. Hetla was more like some natural configuration, wind-hewn from a glacier, than a man-made city.

I saw wings coming and going, a constant flow of activity on the water stairs; mainly men, dressed in the leather-and-black that seemed to be standard Darkland gear. But there were women as well and my presence did not seem to attract a great deal of attention, apart from the occasional disdainful look. Darkland women tended to be tall and white-blonde and their dress was immaculate: high-collared tunics over long straight skirts or narrow-legged trousers – the sort of thing you couldn't get away with if you were short – worn under opulent furs. I saw several women in coats that might have been selk and wondered again about the fur trade here. There was also a preponderance of the crimson amber fur that was so rare in the Reach, catching the icy light like droplets of blood.

It occurred to me that the breeding programs might have run to more than the seith and its associated abilities. All the faces had a likeness, with pinched noses and pointed chins. There was not a great deal about them to remind me of Frey – a good thing.

By now, the sun was high, casting a cold silver glitter over the waves. I walked along the esplanade that bordered the strip of sea between the shore and the buildings. In spite of its strange appearance, the place had a businesslike, almost military air. I had somehow come to regard Darkland as less efficient, more chaotic than the rest of the north, but this eerie city had the unified atmosphere of a culture that knew where it was going – the direction of which the rest of Muspell would almost certainly disapprove.

The cranes of the wing-yards loomed ahead, sunlight glinting from their spines. The yards seemed to be in full swing now, the roar and hum of machinery filling the air, but I could hardly stroll up to a gate and press my nose to the wire, so I headed up the hill behind them, to a residential district that overlooked the slope of the fjord. It seemed seedier than the other side of the bay: small, run-down blocks of houses with shutters blasted by winter wind and salt spray, backed by the narcotic conifers. It did not look promising in any sense of the word, but then I had a stroke of luck. I found a bar.

I had no idea whether it was customary for the women of Darkland to enter a bar on their own, even in the middle of the day, but Frey had shown no sign of surprise whenever I'd suggested a drink, so I decided to take a chance. This particular establishment was as tattered as the rest of the district, with only a red neon sign outside (illustrating, with great originality, a beer mug) to indicate its trade. I pushed open the door and tried to keep the relief from my face when I noticed a number of other female customers. They could have been whores, but I did not think so. There was a general lack of coquettishness or, indeed, any great attention to appearance; they spoke together in low voices.

Everyone glanced up when I came in, then looked away again. Either they were genuinely uninterested or doing a good job of feigning it. The interior was as dingy as the outside, with the kind of floor to which one's feet stuck. Half of one wall was filled with leaflets, mainly dog-eared political exhortations to support the state. I tried not to shudder. A few of them were tidal schedules and I took note of both high and low tides for the time of year, just in case anything affected my chances of getting the wing out of the inlet.

I walked to the bar and in the local Gaelacht, ordered a beer in my best Darkland accent, adopted from Frey. It came more naturally than I thought it would, and although under the circumstances this was a good thing, I still wasn't relaxed.

Two of the women sitting near the bar looked up when I spoke.

'You're from Morvern?' one of them said. Seemingly, my new accent was good enough to be recognized. I had no option other than to ignore her or nod. I nodded.

'From Fetlar, or Westray?'

I chose Westray, hoping that this wouldn't turn out to be a place against which she held some deep-seated grudge. She was a stocky woman in her early fifties, with close-cropped grey hair and blue eyes. I wondered whether she had ever resembled the tall, disdainful looking girls I had seen in the government quarter. Somehow, I doubted it.

'I'm from Uister,' she replied, a name that meant nothing to me.

'Ah yes,' I said.

'You working here?' She indicated a chair.

'Down near the docks.' I did not say what I was doing.

'Working on the wings?' Her companion was younger, a thin girl with a weatherbeaten face. She looked as though she'd spent a long time at sea. Neither of them seemed like vitki, but after the last experience with Frey, I wasn't inclined to trust my own judgement.

'Maybe.'

The older woman shot her companion a warning glance. 'Don't ask stupid questions, Eilish. You know they can't say.'

'And what are you doing here?' I asked the older woman, conversationally, just as though we were neighbours far from home.

'Construction. You know what it's like up in Morvern these days.'

I nodded and tried to speak with feeling. 'I know.'

'No work, ever since the edict. Everything's being channelled into the war effort.' She spoke neutrally, but I could see from her face what she thought of that. 'You've seen Sule forest?'

'Not recently.'

'Blighted, all of it. The war effort, again.' She drained her beer and set the empty mug down on the table. 'We'd best get back.'

The younger woman, Eilish, nodded sullenly and they stood.

'Good meeting you. Good-bye.'

'Good-bye,' I said. I watched them go through the door and sipped my own drink in the sudden silence. No one

170

else was paying any attention to me, but the encounter with Eilish and her friend had sent the adrenaline flooding through my body, with the threat of impending discovery. Anyone versed in the seith would be able to sense it, as though I had acquired a red shell around me.

I took another sip of the beer and damped my emotions down. I had no idea what the woman had meant by the forest being blighted for the war effort. Darkland was a modern state. It did not need wood for either fuel or ships, so the apparent ruin of a forest made no sense. I kept my ears open, but the rest of the bar was filled with idle chatter about fishing and the local hunting. Such talk reminded me of my own hunger. I went back to the bar and bought a portion of salt herring, which I chewed while debating what to do next.

The two women had been sitting in a shadowy corner, close to the bar itself. I was grateful not to be in full view of everyone, and even more grateful of it when the door swung open and two men came in. They wore garments that were close to uniforms, and yet not quite formal enough: long grey coats, high-necked sweaters beneath, dark trousers tucked into knee-length boots. As they walked across the room, the long coats changed subtly to take on the colouring of the surrounding shadows, and it seemed for a moment that I glimpsed the beat of wings about their heads.

One was in his mid- to late forties, grey-haired and somewhat plump with a round face and cold eyes. The other was an older man, slightly stooped, not tall. They were wearing collar insignia shaped like moths, but even without these, I knew them. It was as though two wild beasts had walked in and stood, snarling. They were vitki.

They stood by the door, looking around them. I did not throw the seith around me, or do anything sudden. Instead, I let the invisible shields of the seith slide up and harden, until I felt protected by a wall of solid air. The vitki showed no sign of having noticed anything, but I could feel their presence. In their unassuming garments they were twice as threatening as the Nhemish militia.

This is it, I thought. *This is where they stride over and demand the documentation that I have not got.* I fought hard to keep down the rising panic; sat sipping my drink and ignoring them, just like everyone else in the bar. No one in that kind of place ever has a reason to be pleased by the sudden appearance of the authorities.

But the vitki did none of the things I had feared. Instead, they simply turned on their heels and walked out, without saying a word. Neither did the patrons of the bar exchange meaningful glances or sighs of relief. Everything carried on as before and I found this almost more unnerving than an interrogation would have been.

After a reasonable interval, I, too, got up and left. I didn't feel sure enough of myself to start asking questions and it was time to get as close as I could to the wing-yard. When I went through the door into the chilly afternoon light, the vitki were nowhere to be seen.

*

I loitered around the upper part of the town for the remainder of the afternoon, watching the wing-yard. There were trucks going in and out, gliding on hover jets and sending up waves of dust from the roadway. It took a while for them to pass through the gate and a queue formed.

I stood in the shadows, debating my choices, but a flapping tarpaulin on the back of one of the trucks decided me. I ran forward and dived beneath it, finding myself in a loading hold full of spare machine parts. The truck was starting to move forward so I wasted no time, but sat down on a coil of steel cable in the shadows and grew as still as I could. I folded the seith around me in its invisible mantle, imagining images of machine parts, wire, cable – until, I hoped, I merged into the background as success- fully as the wing had, in becoming part of the shingle. Once this was done, I simply sat and waited.

There was a burst of light as the tarpaulin was drawn back and from the corner of my eye I saw a face peering into the back of the truck. The man gave no sign that he had seen me. I felt his gaze slide over the seith and away; he noticed only what he expected to see. I did nothing, merely stared ahead. I heard him murmuring to someone out of sight, presumably noting component parts and quantity. The truck was open to view and the machine parts were low down; there was nowhere for a person to hide. I was aware of them scanning the base of the truck, probably for stowaways or explosives, but then the tarpaulin was fastened down again, this time securely, and the vehicle moved on. I did not let my guard drop, but maintained the concealing field of the seith until the truck came to a halt. Then I rose and, moving cautiously to the edge of the tarpaulin, peered out.

We were in a warehouse, a large, hangar-like building with low artificial lights. A small group of men were huddled together in the middle of the hangar, looking at a checklist. I did not want to be in the truck while they unloaded the parts; the seith would conceal me only so far, especially if vitki became involved. They had not noted me on the bar – or, worse, had done so and taken no action. Why?

I slid out from under the tarpaulin to the floor and dived behind a stack of cables. From here, I wormed my way along the oily floor to a set of racks, containing more equipment. It did not look like the kind of area that would be used very often; the racks were full up, and I noticed that most of the unloaded parts were being stored in empty areas on the other side of the warehouse. Looking up, I saw no sign of security cameras directly overhead, although there were clusters closer to the doors. I crouched down with my arms round my knees and settled once more into the seith, keeping an eye on the walkway beyond the racks.

Outside, I could sense night starting to fall. Gradually, the activity in the warehouse slowed, then stopped altogether. I heard the huge double doors at the front of the building rattle shut as the last of the workers left. When I was certain that the hangar was empty, I slipped out from my hiding place and edged along the wall to what appeared to be an office. The door was unlocked. I made a quick scan of the office, but the papers on the table showed nothing but lists of inventories, more or less what one would expect in a warehouse.

There was a camera by the door, gliding slowly round. I was afraid of an alarm sounding if I triggered it, so I judged the angle and its speed and dodged it instead, stepping quickly to another door. This one was locked, but it was a standard lock and easy to pick. I was out into the wing-yard by the time the camera swung back again.

With the warehouse now behind me, I was looking directly up into one of the dry docks and I caught my breath. The war-wing was enormous. I could see the vane bays along its sides, and the folded struts of what would eventually be the vanes themselves. But the thing was immense, the size of a battleship, and bigger than any I had ever seen before. It was a similar mottled indigo to my own wing and I was sure that this enormous craft had stealth capabilities; weapons too. There were gun place-ments all along its sides and pulse cannons mounted at the prow. I was too far away to see the stern, but I was sure that it, too, had cannon positions. I thought of this titan suddenly appearing off the shore of Tiree, firing hard, and swallowed a lump of foreboding. The Reach had nothing like this.

I did not waste too much time in staring at it, but set the implant to taking pictures and transmitting them back to the Rock. Knowing that Idhunn would soon be poring over them made me feel oddly and falsely reassured. Keeping to the shadows, I went round the corner of the warehouse to another vast bay. A war-wing lay in this one, also. There was a fragile tracery of tech around its base that I did not recognize; wires and cables looped in peculiar configurations. I spent some time trying to make sense of it, but eventually I sent this image, too, to the Rock.

At the end of the bay stood a large low building, made half of black basalt and half of the vitreous icy material I'd seen on the stalagmite-spire buildings. There were no lights on. I tried the door and was surprised to find that it opened easily. The room was empty. I felt no presence of life. Inside were rows of computer equipment – adjacent screens running the length of the room and displaying shifting displays that, after a moment, I recognized. They showed the sea between Darkland and the Reach, all the shoals and currents, all the reefs and island chains. A red tracery of lines wove between them, and I guessed that the computer was planning routes for the war-wings.

Closing the door gently behind me, I went across to the screen and started transmitting. I was so absorbed in what I was doing that when I heard the slight sound, it startled me. I spun round, but there was no one there . . . It would have been good to have a printout or a download of the screen information, since the surrounding tech might have baffles to interfere with the camera in the map implant, but I did not want to risk touching anything.

At the end of the room, a separate screen showed a map

of Darkland itself, covered in a rash of red and gold blotches. I did not know what they represented. Settlements perhaps, or areas of military production. I transmitted it anyway, and it was as I was doing this that I noticed the figure. He was standing by the wall, arms folded against the long coat, watching me. I leapt up and around to face nothing. As I stood in front of the screen, heart racing, he stepped out of the air. The coat got paler, catching the light, then faded to grey.

'I was wondering when you'd notice,' the vitki said, gently reproving. 'Not as good as you think, are you?'

I did not say anything. The implant was still loading, transmitting his image to the Rock. He was the younger and shorter of the two vitki who had been in the bar that afternoon, the one with the plump face.

'I think we'll turn our audience off, don't you?' he said. He stepped forward and touched me lightly on the side of my head. There was an instant of searing brightness and I felt the map implant sizzle and die. 'That's better,' the vitki said. His hand was a blur as he brought up the stick. It touched my arm, there was a second lightning pulse, and then I was folding down to the floor. The last thing I noticed was that he had polished his boots that morning.

TWENTY

Planet: Mondhile

Gemaley did not come to him that night. Ruan told himself over and over again that this was doubtless a good thing, but secretly he was disappointed. The ache in him was not merely physical; it was as though a piece of her spirit had locked with his, a puzzle half-completed. He lay staring into the dark, waiting and hoping for the creak at the door that betrayed her presence. It did not come. He tried to lose himself in fantasies of her, as though this might somehow summon her up, but it did no good. At last, too restless to sleep, he rose from the bed and went to the window.

It was early morning. Elowen hung low over the peaks, starting its downward path towards the sea. Ruan closed the window against the cold and stepped back. His ankle stung a little, but it was continuing to heal. He could put some of his weight on it now, and though he was still lame, walking should not be too difficult. Another day. Another day will heal me and then I can go. But in his mind, Gemaley came to stand before him, smiling a little, letting the tunic slip from her shoulders to reveal her small, pale breasts. Her shimmering form seemed to dance before him in the darkness. He did not let himself think. He went to the door and opened it, then stepped out into the shadows of the hallway and down through the house.

This time, no one was singing. The door to Tian's room was firmly shut and the hall was silent. He took the stairs carefully, but it was much easier than the previous day. He came out onto a narrow landing, overlooking the main hall below. Nightsight made shapes from the shadows – a flickering at the edges of the eye – but he ignored it. He thought of the figure he had glimpsed down among the trees and felt a fleeting shiver of unease. But if anything moved, he would see it.

He had no idea where Gemaley was to be found, but how big could the tower be? He would work his way down. There was no reason to be unsettled. He was a guest, not a prisoner. Gemaley was his lover, he was entitled to go looking for her. So why, then, did he feel so furtive? Nerves, Ruan told himself firmly, and resolved to ignore them.

Soon, he found himself down in the main hall. It was vaguely familiar from the night on which he had been brought here. Looking up, he could see the spiral tier of galleries disappearing into the dark. He looked towards the main door. What if it should be open? After a moment of indecision, he went over and pulled at the huge iron handle. The door did not move. That was that, then, Ruan thought with a brief, guilty pang of relief.

A door immediately to his left led into a long, curving room, clearly the main hall of the tower. The floor was covered with pelts, soft and dusty. The embers of a fire still burned in the grate, and this made Ruan feel more at home. But there was little in the way of furniture – nothing resembling the carved, polished settles and tables of the clan house, or the chests in which the utensils were so carefully stored. The clan hall ran like clockwork, with everything in its place.

Here, Ruan stepped closer to the fire and saw that the thing that was hissing in it was the knob of a chair back. They had been burning the furniture. A cold draught was coming through the torn edges of the window, making the paper flutter and hum like an instrument. Ruan frowned. This was unlike any clan house he had ever visited. Everything was going to ruin and neither Gemaley nor her siblings seemed to care what happened to it. Compared with the strong connection to place, to home – possessed by Ruan and everyone else he knew – this attitude was inexplicable. It must be shock, he realized. The loss of their family had sent both Gemaley and Tian to the edge of desperation, and the brother was clearly little better. They needed help. His help, perhaps.

Lost in a dream of saving Gemaley, Ruan walked back to the hallway. There were other doors, but they were locked, or perhaps simply stuck. He went up the stairs to the first landing and it was then that he heard the sound.

It was a raw rhythmic gasping, instantly familiar. Gemaley, when she made love. She must be having a dream, Ruan thought. He did not want to consider any other possibilities, not yet. It was coming from a room on the far side of the landing and the door was ajar. He would wake her, he thought. Perhaps she had intended to come to him, but had fallen asleep. He would surprise her. An inner voice counselled that surprising Gemaley at such a point might not be the wisest plan, but he decided to ignore it.

He pushed the door open. Gemaley was indeed within, but she was neither dreaming nor alone. She straddled a man, a stranger, just as she had ridden Ruan himself on those previous nights. The man's face was turned away from the door, hands reaching up to grasp the rungs of the bed. Gemaley's eyes were open wide, as usual. She was holding his wrists and Ruan could see the glint of her talons in the moonlight that came through the open window. Her lips were drawn back in that familiar snarl as she rose and fell – less, it seemed to him now, with desire than in triumph. Neither of them had seen him. Shocked, he was unprepared for the hand that grasped his shoulder and hauled him back.

'What are you doing?' someone hissed into his ear.

Ruan spun away from the restraining hand and turned to see Gith. Gemaley's brother was standing facing him, but in the shadows, ghost-pale.

'What do you think you're *doing*?' Gith snapped, again.

'I wasn't spying on her, if that's what you think. I just wanted to find her.'

'How dared you?'

'She's *my* lover, you know. I—' but then, belatedly,

Ruan realized that neither the words nor the tone had been of accusation, but of astonishment. 'What?'

'You have to come with me,' Gith said, still sounding amazed. 'It isn't safe.'

He seized Ruan by the wrist and pulled him toward the stairs. Bewildered, Ruan went with him.

'That man. Who is he?'

'He is the man from the forest.'

'You mean someone who lives in the forest? An outcast – mehed?'

'Not mehed. He calls himself a "vitki", but I don't know what that means. He isn't human,' Gith said. He turned to glance at Ruan and his face was fearful.

'What do you mean, "not human"? He looked human enough to me.' The sight was burned upon his eyes – Gemaley's face. Ruan tried to think about something else and failed.

Gith plucked urgently at his arm. 'He isn't like us.'

'A ghost?'

'No, he's real. He has earth senses. But he is . . . different.' Gith paused. They were now high in the tower, standing at Tian's door. Gith rapped sharply on the mottled wood. There was the sound of movement from within, and then the rattle of a bolt being drawn back.

'Gemaley?' Tian peered fearfully through the door. 'Oh. It's you.' But she gave a faint smile when she saw Ruan. 'And you, too.'

Gith slipped through the door, gesturing for Ruan to

join him. As before, the windows were wide open, letting in the night air.

'Gemaley's downstairs,' Gith told her. 'With the stranger.'

'Does he have a name?' Ruan asked.

'I told you. He is the man from the forest.'

'But he must have a name,' Ruan said.

Tian sat down on the bed again against the musty pillows, arms folded tightly around her knees. 'He has speech. He is aware; you can see it in his face.'

Gith stared at her. 'When have you spoken with him?' he asked, and the jealousy was clear in his voice. It did not seem to trouble his sister. She reached down and took a crease of the bed cover, twisting it between her fingers. Something about the action reminded Ruan of Gemaley.

'I've watched him,' she whispered. 'Even though he makes me afraid. When he is with my sister, when he is alone. He lives in the trees, not far away. I've followed him.'

'You?' Gith said, almost scornfully. 'You never leave the tower.'

'I follow him in my dreams,' Tian said. She still wore that faint, unnerving smile, an echo of her sister's.

'Dreams aren't real, Tian.'

'Mine are.'

'You said you'd seen this man with Gemaley,' Ruan said. 'What did they talk about?'

Gith laughed. 'They don't *talk*. They just fuck. That's what my sister does.'

'Do you care?' Tian asked Ruan, softly. 'Is that why you're asking?'

'I just want to know who this man is,' Ruan said, frustrated. 'Your brother says he isn't human.'

'I don't know what he is. Perhaps the trees made him. The forest conjures things up, sometimes. They never last very long.' She stole a look at Gith. 'But it wasn't true, what I said. They do talk sometimes. They talk about the energy under the tower. He seems very interested in the dark well. And they talk about the mountains and the creatures that live there. My sister *loves* birds.' Her face was innocent, but the words were not. Ruan thought back to the black serai with the garnet eyes and shivered. Tian saw this and her small smile grew. 'You've met her creatures. Or some of them, anyway. But not all.'

'What do you mean?' Ruan said. Tian's smile was smug, as though she knew something that he did not, and she was savouring his ignorance.

Gith reached over and gave his shoulder a little shake. 'You don't know us. You have to be careful. Gemaley – she has moods. She's not a kind person. She never has been. It's different for Tian and me – we're her family, we belong to her. But you are just a game.'

'She's been kind to me,' Ruan said defensively, but even as he spoke the words, he knew they were not true.

'When your ankle heals, you should leave. As fast as you can. And not come back.'

'I intend to,' Ruan said, but with a sinking heart he knew that wasn't true, either.

TWENTY-ONE

Planet: Muspell

I was, not to my surprise, in a cell when I came round. Just three walls and an empty space. I could not see any barriers, but I had no doubt that they were there; the seith was warning me away from the space with a pressing urgency and I knew, if I had doubted it before, that this was a vitki stronghold and vitki tech. Beyond me the room was empty; I could see a desk, a screen, a chair and that was all. There were no windows. I sat down on the bench, an integral part of the cell wall, and waited.

It was, again, some time before I realized the vitki was there. He was standing right at the edge of my vision, a shadowy figure with arms folded. Slowly, I turned my head to look at him. I thought he might be expecting some murmur of alarm or irritation, but I said nothing, only stared. My gaze met his – pale blue and ice-cold. He said, 'Very good. A lot of people are much slower.'

I did not respond.

'So. Let's see.' He stepped forward. 'You are Vali Hallsdottir, of a place called Scaraskae, on Ushant. A woman of the Reach, first a tracker, now an assassin and agent of the Skald. You were born in ColdYear 10, attended college and put your tracking skills to good use in taking hunters into the forests of Ushant. In the summer of VeilYear 10 you were introduced to a Darklander named Frey Gundersson and he trained you a little in the ways of the vitki, which was almost certainly a mistake, but never mind that now.' He spoke pleasantly, by rote, neither conversational nor interrogative. 'After an accident—' it was possible that there was the slightest pause after that word '—you recovered under the protection of the Skald, who trained you further in the use of the seith, and you now work for them as an assassin.'

Again, I said nothing. This was entirely correct, but all of it was more or less common knowledge. He took a step closer, until he was only a foot or so from the invisible barrier that separated us. Again, I saw a shadowy flicker of wings – around his shoulders this time. I blinked, and it was gone.

'You like sea-mint tea first thing in the morning, two cups. You used to eat a lot of meat, but since your accident you prefer fish or blubber, and vegetables, as meat tends to upset your digestive system. You used to cut yourself to relieve tension, but now have a less "invasive" method – a device designed for the sado-masochistic market. Your scars have a tendency to ache or itch if there is rain on the way, and you often wonder if you're imagining it. I,' he added, as if confiding in me, 'have sometimes experienced the same phenomenon with an old wound on my arm. It's a good predictor of the weather, but I wish it would find a less painful way of doing it . . . You would like a pet – probably something that doesn't need feeding every day – but you recently told your sister, who kindly offered to supply you with a cat, that you did not think it would be fair as you travel so much.'

I remained silent, but this time it was from bewilderment and not a little fear. I had no idea how he knew these things. I did not know whether he had exceptionally good surveillance techniques, or whether he was plucking the knowledge out of my mind. Either possibility was deeply alarming. When I looked at him, there was no suggestion that he expected me to respond, or that he was fishing for information. He was simply telling me, as though I might not know.

He went on, 'You're here as a spy, of course.' He did not seem to expect me to answer, either. 'In case you're wondering how I came to find you, we knew someone was here, and I saw you in the bar earlier on. You were doing a good job of concealing yourself, but not quite good enough. If you had been born here, and had come to the vitki early, we would have made something of you, no doubt about it.'

I was genuinely interested to know the answer to this.

'Some think the vitki are all male.'

'The members of the Skald are not all female, are they?'

'No. But most are, and the upper echelons are all women. That's common knowledge.'

He conceded this point with a slight nod. 'It's certainly

the case that there are far more male vitki. Years ago, when our ancestors reverted to more primitive social models, they believed that women were not capable of such things, but clearly this is nonsense. Nowadays, we are more progressive, and whatever you may have heard, many of us espouse full equality between the sexes. Some of our most prized vitki operatives are women.'

'And if I came to you now?'

His eyebrows raised, just a fraction. 'Are you offering?'

'No.'

'I thought not. But it's an interesting question. If you came to us now, we would have to undo most of the training techniques with which the Skald has imbued you. They follow a particular path which we consider long and unwieldy – unnecessarily so. You would have to undergo a degree of genetic enhancement to improve your intuitive abilities and often that does not work well in adults, for reasons that we don't really understand. I am not, by the way, telling you anything that the Skald do not already know.' A slight smile informed me, not that he was not so naive as to spill secrets, but that he was simply being polite enough to keep me informed. 'Also, there are other issues with genetic tinkering. It has a tendency to cause infertility in female subjects and we would want you as part of the breeding stock. That is, in fact, what you would be destined for under ordinary circumstances.'

I was not sure that I had understood him correctly.

'What do you mean, "ordinary circumstances"?'

'Capture.'

'You're putting me into a breeding program?'

'No,' he said patiently. 'I said that this is *ordinarily* what would happen. However, we have other plans in mind for you. Now, then.' He went on, so that there was again no expectation that I might ask 'what other plans'. He seemed to have no desire to see me play games. Whatever business he had in mind, we were already down to it. 'It would be a good idea for you to rest. It's late and we can discuss all this in the morning.' Without giving me a chance to reply, he was out through the door.

I sat back down on the bench and thought about what he had said. The prospect of a breeding program was disquieting enough, but I found it even more ominous that the vitki seemed to have an entirely different agenda for me. Even from the little he had told me, this nameless man knew me better than any other person except Idhunn. If he had been watching me, then how had he done it? If he had stolen my memories and preferences from my head, then how had he done that? There was no way that a relatively simple piece of technology like the map implant could retain emotions and tendencies.

But what I could not shake off was the impression that he wanted *me* – not just any Skald agent or inhabitant of the Reach, but me myself, just as Frey had wanted me. With Frey, I had mistaken it for love – it must be, I had thought at the time, blinded by my own desires and needs; later in the relationship, I had thought that any young and vulnerable woman would have sufficed for Frey's purposes. But now, listening to this calm-voiced vitki, I was no longer sure.

Yet if it really was me that the vitki wanted, why? Idhunn and I had been right when we said that everyone had seith abilities. They were not entirely evenly distributed among the population, but theoretically, given enough time and training and patience, even the slowest person could achieve as high a level as I had. It was not really analogous to intelligence; the variation was not nearly so great.

But perhaps the facts of the case did not matter as much as what the vitki themselves believed. If Idhunn had been right – and I had no reason to doubt that she had – when she said that the vitki believed in a super-race, perhaps their own arrogance was causing them to see in me something that wasn't really there, some ability, some potential. Perhaps this was what Frey had been looking for.

I did not expect to sleep, but it overtook me nevertheless. When I woke, I was still in the cell. The vitki who had spoken to me was no longer there. Instead, his place had been taken by a woman behind the desk, she was also wearing the moth insignia, but did not have the presence of the vitki. Her pale hair was confined in an elaborate metal fillet and her face was as chiselled and hard as marble. When she glanced up, however, I saw that her eyes were silver. At first I thought it was a trick of the light, but as she continued to stare impassively at me I realized that it was their natural – or unnatural – colour.

I did not bother smiling at her; there was no point in

trying to win friends. And from the expression on her face as she stared at me, she was as underwhelmed as I was.

'Don't try anything,' she warned me, but her tone sounded reluctant. I got the impression she'd have preferred it if I'd tried to storm the barrier and got zapped back. It would, I suppose, have provided entertainment. She had a pallid air, as though she didn't get out enough.

'I have no intention of trying anything,' I said. That, of course, wasn't true. My hopes had risen the moment I saw her, because whatever else she might be – in spite of the storm-warning of danger and dark around her – she wasn't vitki. And I'd had an idea.

I sat cross-legged on the bench and closed my eye, thinking about how the seith takes information from the environment and turns it into metaphor, one that is most readily understood by the viewer. Without direct visual sight, but with the steady drip of information provided by the map implant, I was nonetheless still able to see, though the information that the seith was providing was very different. Now, as I looked into the scene in front of me, I realized that the seith was translating differently this time. I felt that what I was seeing was the reality, and the cell I was imprisoned in was merely a physical overlay, a distraction to what lay beneath. I was in a room looking out onto an expanse of shoreline, and the room was full of birds.

They were black. I could not be sure at first whether they were crows or ravens, but soon realized from the curve of the beaks and the wedge-shaped tails that they were the latter. One brushed past my face and I recoiled, but I had been close enough to see its feathers shimmer into a sudden pattern of data. What I was seeing was not some kind of esoteric illusion, but the information structure that underlay this part of Darkland's system. However, the data contained in the birds' feathers passed too quickly and was too fragmented, for me to make use of it now that the map implant had been fried. I tried to shut out the brushing wings and go deeper.

Eventually, the birds and the room began to fade away, until I sat within a circle of cold grey nothing. It was as though a bank of mist had swept in from the sea to cover me, blanking everything else out. From very far away I heard a faint crackling hiss and knew that the cell containment field had been deactivated. At the back of my mind a voice told me that from the point of view of the guard, I had simply disappeared. I could dimly sense her, standing just beyond the fog bank, and without thinking about it and thereby collapsing the fragile shield of the seith, I rose and walked from the cell into the room.

Once there, I had to let myself see, because I did not know the layout of the building and could not feel it through the mist. I let the seith drop. The guard whirled round and came for me. She sent me crashing to the floor. I clapped my hands to the side of her head, but she merely shook herself like an animal and I felt her teeth snapping at my throat. The silver eyes were wide and blank; I wondered whether she was transmitting information. I also wondered, in the moments before she got her hands round my throat, what the hell she was. I reached up and broke her grip, and her thumbs with it. My knees locked round her waist and flicked her over, and the instant I was on top I plunged both thumbs into her silver eyes and blinded her. She made no sound at all, only a kind of empty gasping. Then I hacked her across the throat and she lay still.

Moments later, I was up and running. I snatched her weapon from the desk, looked through the window; perhaps fifteen feet to the ground – an acceptable drop. Outside, it was night. The window was sealed shut and certainly wired with an alarm. I did not want to waste time fiddling with it. I shot it out and dived through.

I hit the ground in a roll, coming up onto my feet. The alarm was going off now; a deafening siren shrieking out across the wing-yard. I could see the black bulk of one of the war-wings above me and I raced towards it, intending to conceal myself in its shadow. The wing-yard would be wired with motion sensors, but hiding might buy some extra visual time. There were shouts from behind me, but I was hoping that no one would start shooting for fear of hitting the wing. I bolted under the towering craft and ran along the edge of the dry dock. I heard a cry – 'Head her off!' – but whoever spoke was already too late. I had reached the limits of the wing-yard. I did not pause, but leapt from the side of the dock – a twenty-foot drop into the water.

It was very cold, but not lethally so. The milder currents that curled up from the south warmed the

Darkland waters, and this led to an immediate change of plan. Instead of diving under and coming up further along the shore, I struck out for the opposite bank, swimming like sealstock, up and under, holding my breath for as long as I could. For those of us who are used to northern waters, that's a long time. I was aware of the trails of wings streaking overhead and dived a little deeper, praying that I wouldn't encounter orca or their ilk. Our ancestors had proved somewhat over-enthusiastic about saving the whale. Even sealstock could be nasty, if they thought you were a threat. A bite would be bad enough, but teeth covered with toxic bacteria would make it far worse.

At last lack of air forced me to surface for a breather and I found myself in the middle of the channel. The wings were running along the shore, following the line of the wing-yard. They must have thought that I was hiding there. That suited me. I took several deep breaths and struck out again, heading straight ahead.

Dawn was coming up as I reached the opposite shore, reminding me that I had now been in Darkland for over a whole day. It felt like several months. As I swam, and the light grew, I realized that the way ahead would be hazardous; fencing had been put in the water, protruding several feet above the surface and 'armed' with shockwire. It ran out from the shore, then extended along the coast on either side, so that I would have to swim some distance to avoid it and what it contained – which turned out to be the series of stinking sheds that I had glimpsed from the cliff. By now, I was growing tired. I still had the weapon, slung over my shoulder. I hoped to sneak through the sheds unobserved, using the seith, but if it came to a fire-fight I would shoot my way out and make a dash for the forest and my own wing. Reaching the edge of a stone walkway, I pulled myself onto it.

The walkway led along the water's edge and between two of the long sheds. I could hear the whirring of machinery – perhaps a generator – and sounds coming across the water from the wing-yards. If I was observed by a camera, then there was probably a central system that would relay my image through to the vitki . . . I would just have to take good care not to be spotted.

Initially, my intention had been to make my way as quickly as possible through the sheds and up onto the cliffs; I did not want to linger. It was the sound that stopped me in my tracks. Something was singing.

It did not sound remotely human, nor like a bird. It was very high and sweet, but with a base note that travelled up my spine and into my gut, as though I were listening to something immensely loud; the kind of sound that you feel rather than hear. And I could feel it in the seith, too. Whatever was producing it was doing so on two levels at once. Then, slowly, more voices joined in until the sheds were reverberating with the noise. I looked wildly around me, but the sheds were silent. No one had come running. I knew what it was and I could not resist. The doors of the nearest shed were covered in wire mesh and when I looked through, I saw them, row upon row.

There had been no need for Frey to take me out onto

the ice to meet the selk, though perhaps this installation had not been here seven years ago. The selk were confined in narrow tanks, with transparent sides made foul by dirty water. Tubes led away from the tanks, presumably carrying waste and nutrients, but in each tank was a long pallid form. Against the shadows of a snowfield, I thought, they would be almost invisible. In the tanks, they looked like a collection of mutant ghosts.

The selk closest to me was singing. The wide mouth was open, displaying rows of sharp teeth, and its eyes were tightly shut in a nest of wrinkles. I shifted a little against the door frame, however, and its eyes snapped open. They were not like the welling black pools I had seen before, but palest blue, surrounded by a ring of white. They were human eyes in that animal face, the eyes of a Darklander. The selk's mouth pursed, closed, opened again.

'Help me . . .' I heard it say. The words were oddly formed and accented, but still comprehensible.

'I don't—' but the others had seen me now. The singing had stopped and they were crying out.

'Help me, help us, help . . .'

There was a blare of static from one of the loud-speakers high on the roof of the shed and I did not wait to hear more. I bolted for cover. Behind me, a great wailing cry went up from the imprisoned selk and I felt a wave of someone else's pain touch the edges of the seith and travel through it. It nearly brought me to my knees. But the alarm was already going off and I could not free them all, even if I had been able to get into the shed. I did not know how to open the tanks and detach them from the equipment, nor whether they would be able to make it out to the open sea in the limited time available before their captors sent out boats and trawl-nets and guns.

Thus I reasoned as I ran from the selk, and their pain continued to blast out at me, like the shockwaves from an explosion.

I ducked behind one of the sheds at the sound of running feet. Two guards sprinted past me, Darklanders clad in some kind of uniform, but not vitki. Their weapons were at the ready and I tensed in anticipation of gunfire, but that would make no sense – they would surely want to subdue the selk, not kill them. More guards ran past and I kept quiet and still. But somehow, although I did not know how the selk had known me for friend and not enemy, I did not think that they would betray me, and the sudden disturbance in the sheds provided me with a much-needed distraction. Swallowing guilt, I fled for the outer perimeter and the cliff.

The wire fence, which ran just under the sheer cliff, was a lethal hazard for anyone aiming to enter the compound from above, but useful for someone who was trying to get out. I climbed swiftly up the wire, balanced on one foot just beneath the razored edge at the top, then sprang for the cliff. It wasn't easy: it dismayed me to find how much I'd come to rely on the map implant to compensate for my missing eye. I found a handhold in the dense foliage – a leafy covering of some kind of creeper – that covered this part of the rock, and began to climb. I looked back once, fearing that I had been sighted in my dash for the wire, either on camera or by one of the guards, but everyone below seemed occupied by the commotion in the selk shed. I could hear the selk, crying out in high thin voices, but I did not know what they were saying. If it was indeed words, then it wasn't any language that I recognized; it must be in their own tongue of Shelta.

I was halfway up the cliff when the edges of the seith rippled and I felt a sonic blast shudder through me – the selk compound fell into a sudden and ominous silence – a low setting, but enough to stun. Had whoever was in charge simply clubbed the selk with some kind of sonic device? It felt as though they had, but I could not afford to stop and wonder. I climbed on and upwards, heading for the top of the cliff.

The creeper made it a fast climb and I was at the summit within twenty minutes. As I ran for the cover of the trees, a little black air-wing shot overhead, very low, and I threw myself flat among the bushes. I had no doubt that they were looking for me and this made it impossible to take the quicker but more exposed cliff path back to the fjord and my own machine. I would have to make my way back through the forest.

I set off through the thick undergrowth, taking a last look out to sea. It was still early in the morning, with a pearly mist hanging over the water and hiding the line of the horizon. A fresh, grey day, typical of the north in spring, with Grainne like a silver wheel, rising up through the clouds to burn off the morning fog. Among the trees, however, it was shadowy and still. I could hear the wing passing overhead, but they had little chance of spotting me through the trees. The seith would go some way towards baffling the infrared detectors, but only so far. With the map implant fried, I had to rely on the markers I had noted – or at least thought I had – on the previous day. It did not take me long to become hopelessly lost.

As the morning wore on, it became clear to me that I had strayed well past the point where the edges of the fjord should have become visible. This was not only potentially disastrous given my circumstances, but also professionally embarrassing. The trees grew a little less thickly here, and the ground beneath them was covered, not with the leaf-litter or needles that one might have encountered in a wood in the Reach, but with a thick ashy substance. The trees were different, too: the smoky conifers being interspersed with other varieties – principally a tree that bore waxy cones among its needles, like the candle trees of the south. As I stared up, wondering what they were called, I noticed movement.

At first, I thought it was no more than a bird in the branches, although I had seen none and the absence of birdsong was conspicuous in this forest. But then it moved again – a quick, urgent rustling high in the branches – and the seith shrieked alarm. I moved round the tree to get a better look and that was when I saw it.

It had been nailed to the upper branches of the tree and its wrists were tied. I saw a thick, sticky blood, like red sap, oozing out of the wounds in its flesh. Its limbs and torso were like those of a human, but the flesh was stretched too tightly over odd-shaped bones and was a pale, translucent grey. I could see no sign of any genitalia, though the thing was naked. Stringy hair fell down its back and its narrow head drooped forward, but as I stared, aghast, the head went up, swivelling like an owl's on the bony, ridged neck as it looked down at me. Its eyes were white around a vertical black slit. It opened its mouth, displaying a ring of teeth, and hissed.

As if the thing had spoken some magical word, the nearest candle-cone flared up in a glare of white burn. One spark caught another, and then the whole tree – and the thing nailed to it – was blazing. I heard it shriek, but I turned my face away; the light was too bright to bear. A shower of something that looked like red hot feathers fell to the forest floor, but I was already running, away from the burning tree and the dying thing in it.

I headed south, guided by the dappled sunlight, and came out gasping, onto the edge of a cliff. Here, it looked as though storms had sheared away the cliff. A pile of rocks lay far below with a white ring of surf surging round them and the edge near me was a tangle of exposed tree roots. It would not be possible to follow the coast at this point and I did not recognize any of it. A tracker's intuition told me that I had come too far and had overshot the fjord, and that my wing now lay back to the west. I made my way back into the deeper forest where progress was easier.

It was still hard enough going, however. The thorny

scrub that covered the forest floor snatched and tore at my clothing, and my feet were beginning to blister. Somewhere, too, a thorn had worked its way into the sole of my foot and even though I managed to tease it out, it still made me limp.

Just after midday, the sky started to darken and I looked up between the trees to see a bulk of livid stormcloud begin to build up over the forest. I was not too worried about that; the canopy was thick enough to keep out the worst of the wet, but the idea of stumbling about in the rain while I tried to find the fjord was not appealing. I had not heard the air-wing for some time.

I sat down against the trunk of a tree in order to try and get a feel for where I was. Closing my eye, I could sense that the sea still lay to the south, but did not know whether the forest retreated from the coast at this point. I decided to make for the cliff's edge again, and see if the going might be any easier. One thing was a relief: I had landed at a point where I had at least been able to move along the bare clifftop. If I had brought the wing in any further east, I would have been battling through the forest all the way.

Here, the conifers were densely packed, their rough bark weeping red tears like the amber drops worn by the women of Hetla. The scent of resin filled the air, making me drowsy and confused. I felt as though I was being watched, and I grew alternately hot and cold. As I stood hesitantly among the trees, the clouds parted and in a sudden shaft of sunlight I saw the underside of a huge bracket fungus split open and release a sparkling shower of spores. My throat and lungs were immediately raw, as if scoured, and I fled back through the undergrowth. The forest seemed full of a horrible satisfaction, as though the whole place was aware of me.

I headed in the direction of the coast, but after only a little distance I came out into a clearing; a perfectly circular area amongst the trees. Immediately, I ducked back behind the bole of a red fir, because there was a cabin at the edge of the clearing right next to me. It was a standard northern building; made of logs and tarred over, with a low wooden roof. A water barrel stood to one side, but there was no sign of any garden, such as a house in the Reach might have had, set with summer herbs and rows of beans. I was close enough to extend a hand and touch the boards. I could sense someone moving about inside. The place reeked of the seith. Whoever was inside was a practitioner, and here, that meant vitki. Very cautiously, I edged out from behind the red fir and peered through the window.

I could see someone inside: a small, hunched shape bent over a grate and dressed in skirts. A woman, and from the way she moved, not young. I relaxed a little. But then she straightened and stretched, and I caught a glimpse of her profile behind a skein of wan hair. Not young, but not old either and still beautiful. She sat down in a chair and reached down to take something out of a basket.

I glanced round the room. It was a typical cabin interior; set with a wood-burning stove and a low table and benches. Through a door, I caught sight of a modern range, similar to the one used by my own mother, who liked the latest in kitchen equipment. But the rafters of the room were hung with bones: the long expanses of femurs; hands ranging from the tiny claws of mice to human knuckle bones; a row of spines, twisting in the heat from the stove. I looked back at the woman in the chair. She had a skull in her lap, which she was polishing with a cloth – and she was staring straight at me.

I did not stop to see any more. I ran, springing across thorn bushes and scrub, tearing my way through dense thickets and letting the branches whip across my face. Running through my mind was the thought that I still had the weapon I had stolen from the guard; there was no reason for me to be afraid of some forest wife – but something deeper told me that if she had wished it, the weapon would have been rendered useless.

I did not stop until I found myself staggering by the edge of the cliff. The sea roared below, driven by the storm and thundering up onto a bank of shingle. I was at the place where I had hidden the wing. I did not pause to check if anyone was following me. I ran along the edge of the cliff then climbed down, grasping my own handholds of the day before. The glassy rock was slippery with rain and spray, and the salt burned into the scratches on my hands, but I did not care. What with selk imprisoned in sheds, war-wings looming over the shore and people like the witches in old folktales living in the forest, I just wanted to get out of Darkland. I was almost sobbing with relief when I dropped down onto the shingle and ran for the wing.

And that was when the round-faced vitki stepped out of nowhere into my path.

TWENTY-TWO

PLANET: MONDHILE

Next morning, back in his own room, Ruan awoke to find Gemaley coiled at the foot of the bed. The events of the previous night flooded back with a rush of dismay. She was not looking at him. Her pale eyes were downcast and he wondered whether she was ashamed. But then she said, 'You've been prowling around.' She smiled. 'Are you a nightbird, my Ruan?'

'I wanted to find you,' Ruan said. He felt at a loss; he did not know what else to say to her.

'And so you did find me. Why didn't you come in and talk to me?'

Ruan stared at her. 'You were with someone. A man.'

'So?'

'Your brother says he is known as the man from the forest.'

Gemaley laughed. 'Gith says a lot of things.'

'Who is he? Gith told me that he wasn't human, wasn't even an outcast.' He was trying not to sound too accusing, but he could tell that he was failing, from the sudden closed tightness in her face.

'You're questioning me, are you?'

'I just wondered—'

'You think you know what you saw?' Her tone was low, edged with danger, and with an accompanying contempt at his own cowardice, Ruan felt a twinge of fear. He had a sudden, swift image of sighting the visen along the arrow – *that* young man had not been so afraid. And Gemaley was only a girl, not a wild beast.

'Gemaley—'

She rose from the end of the bed and walked to the window, stretching. Today, she wore the leather leggings and a tunic made of some flimsy material that looked as though it had been assembled from a patchwork of other garments. He could see the big, uneven stitches.

'It's a fine day,' she said, throwing back the shutters, as though the previous conversation had never taken place. Sunlight streamed in, turning the tunic to a transparency of blue and green, as though she was clothed in water. Her hair streamed down her back to the floor like a streak of foam.

'Gemaley, I didn't mean—' He meant to sound firm and reasonable, but the words were apologetic.

'Can you walk now, do you think?' She turned to glance at him over her shoulder, gave a half-smile. 'You seemed to manage the stairs well enough last night.'

'Are you angry with me?' He did not care if she was, he

thought. She had no right to be, and yet he very much hoped that the answer would be 'no'.

Gemaley frowned. 'Of course not. Why would I be?', but she flicked him a look as if to say that he knew very well she was. 'You didn't answer my question.'

'You didn't answer mine.'

'That's true,' Gemaley said musingly, as though this had only just occurred to her. She came back to the bed and touched his hand, stroking it with long, cool fingers. 'But I want to show you something.'

'What is it?' He should tell her that he planned to leave, Ruan thought. But perhaps the ankle was not quite strong enough to carry him back to the clan house. It would be stupid to risk another fall, and perhaps this time there would be no Gemaley to help him. Unless he asked her to go with him – but something in him cowered at the thought of taking her home. He did not understand why this should be, yet the idea was so uncomfortable that he immediately forced it away. No, he could afford to stay another day, or perhaps even two. It would be the sensible thing to do.

Something screamed a warning in the back of his head, but he shut it out.

'I want to show you something in the hills,' Gemaley said. 'It's not very far. I don't want to tire you.' She undulated against him. Ruan took a breath. He half expected her to smell of the stranger, but she did not. She smelled only of herself and immediately he wanted her.

He reached out, but Gemaley was already gone and standing by the door, poised on one bare foot.

'Oh, I brought you something to eat,' she said. She pointed to the table, where a bowl of meat was sitting. 'I'll come back in a little while.'

'Gemaley, wait—' but she was gone.

Ruan got up, went to the table and forced down the meat. It tasted strange, as though it was old; perhaps it was. He wondered where the three got their food from. Gemaley hunted, that much was obvious, but he couldn't envisage her growing anything. Tian seemed ensnared in a permanent dream and he did not think that Gith was the crop-tending type, either. Maybe they were still using stores from the days when the rest of the clan were still alive.

Suddenly, he felt very sorry for them. They seemed so lost. Then he thought of Gemaley, astride the stranger, and his heart grew small and cold. It was so hard to believe that she felt anything for him, and yet . . . He had to leave, and not look back.

Ruan dressed and went down to the main hall. His ankle was much better, almost normal now, with only the occasional stab of pain. Ruan decided to ignore it. To his surprise, the hall looked almost welcoming. A patch had been put over the tear in the window and the grate had been swept. There was even a fire burning in it. Gemaley and Tian sat on pelts in front of it, Tian braiding her sister's hair with neat, deft fingers. The scene was so startlingly normal and domestic that Ruan stood open-mouthed in the doorway for a moment before stepping inside.

'There you are,' Gemaley said, without looking up. She was staring into the flames as if hypnotized.

'It won't take long,' Tian said. She sounded less ethereal this morning, too. Gemaley's hair spilled over the pelts as though part of the same animal; something silver and black, with a fawn dapple. Tian peered at the last plait, then secured it with a star clasp. Gemaley rose fluidly from the pelts piled by the fire.

'Are you ready, Ruan?'

'Yes.'

'Then let's go.' She did not thank her sister for the braiding, Ruan noticed, but treated it as though it were no more than her right. Tian stared after them and it was impossible to interpret the expression on her face. Resentment? Admiration?

It was wonderful to get outside. The tower's defences were down and the sensation of the dark energy that still surrounded the tower had subsided to a kind of background throbbing, like a distant storm. It occurred to Ruan then that during his time in the tower, he had ceased to notice the energy, and yet when he had first encountered it, its power had rooted him to the spot. When had it changed to become no more than this remote interference? Ruan could not seem to find the answer.

'The energy,' he said to Gemaley, who was striding a little way ahead of him down the slope. 'The black line. I hardly notice it any more.'

She turned, to stand looking at him with her head on one side, as if amused. 'Don't you? That's good.'

'But I don't understand why.'

Gemaley shrugged. 'I'm sure it's just one of those things.'

'Why would it just – disappear?' Ruan said.

'Perhaps you're changing,' Gemaley said. 'Perhaps it's getting used to you. You think too much, Ruan. Don't worry about it. Come on.'

He followed her along a high ridge that led from the tower through the forest, a rocky edge that allowed him to look down on the tops of satinspine, the tips of each twig starting to crimson with the coming spring. The sap was rising in the trunks, weeping out, and the air was pungent with resin. Looking back, the tower rose out of the forest like a squat ghost, a ruin's spirit. Gemaley walked sure-footed, the clasps of her braids catching the morning sunlight. Surely, he thought, she was no more than a fragile, clanless girl. How was it that he had become so afraid of her anger, when she had not displayed any towards him? His desire for her, however, was more easily explained.

It had occurred to him that she was taking him to her lover of the night before, the man from the forest – the vitki, whatever that was. The stranger might be a danger to him, though Ruan could not see why – unless Gemaley had told him that they, too, were lovers. And the odd thing that Gith had said, that the man was not human. Ruan admitted to himself that he was eager to find out. If it came to a fight, he was not afraid of that. And now, in the sunlight, the events of the previous night seemed barely real, something out of a dream. Like Gemaley herself.

It was not easy, making his way along the sharp rocks of the ridge, and it was impossible to keep up with Gemaley. Ruan took careful note of their route. If Gemaley suddenly wandered off, then he wanted to be able to find his way back again. But if that happened, then surely it would be the ideal opportunity to leave the tower behind and head for the clan house? This thought, too, Ruan put aside for the moment.

'We're nearly there,' Gemaley said over her shoulder.

'Where are we going? To your lover?' the words were out of Ruan's mouth before he could stop himself, but she only frowned, as if bewildered rather than annoyed.

'Who? No, I told you – there's something I want you to see.' She sprang down between the rocks and he saw a narrow trail leading through the trees. His people rarely bothered with tracks. This one looked as though heavy bodies had crashed through the undergrowth.

'This is a beast-path,' he said, wondering.

'That's right.'

'What made it?' Something large, clearly – wild mur or altru, or perhaps visen. He did not like the thought of heading off into the shadows of the trees with such creatures waiting.

'Oh, something or other . . .'

He was beginning to become alarmed by this vagueness of hers. She seemed entirely too unconcerned. A member of his own clan would have avoided the place, or checked carefully before using it. Gemaley headed down the beast-path as though she did not have a single care. Ruan hesitated for a moment, then followed her. He did not want her to think he was a coward, even though his intuition was shrieking a warning.

He kept his eyes and ears open as they made their way through the trees. There was a strong, pungent odour along the beast-track, and the marks of narrow, clawed feet in the scoured earth – visen, then. Ruan thought of a fanged shape springing out of the darkness and shivered. He was glad when the trees thinned up ahead, and Gemaley brought him out onto the shore of a small lake.

The lake reminded him of the one on which he had seen the serai; the same kind of round hollow, in between steep, snow-covered slopes, its surface partly glistening with ice. Oroth were paddling about on it. And indeed, as he watched, there was a flurry of white wings above the trees and a flock of serai glided down onto the band of clear water in the middle of the lake. Not just white wings, either. The black serai was there, too, a coal among snowflakes.

'It's that bird,' Ruan said, startled.

Gemaley smiled at him. 'Yes, you've seen it before, of course, haven't you? Stay there. Watch.'

She walked swiftly to the edge of the ice, then out across it.

'Gemaley!' Ruan called. He ran after her, with a sudden terrible vision of the ice cracking beneath her boots; Gemaley going down into freezing water without a sound.

The image was so real – Gemaley's face, peaceful and dead beneath a grey-green gloss of ice – that he blinked. She held out a warning hand.

'Stay where you are, Ruan.'

When she was some distance out on the ice, she raised a hand and cried out, a long fluting call. The fluttering serai grew still. Ruan saw the black bird raise its long neck. Gemaley cried again. The black serai surged up out of the lake, water falling from its wings in a shower, and settled on her crossed wrists. He saw her arms dip from the weight.

The bird's serpentine neck slid toward her face and Ruan held his breath, thinking of that razor-beak so close to her eyes. But Gemaley only laughed, touched her lips to the tip of the black beak in a brief, mocking kiss, then tossed the bird up, into the air once more. It flew off towards the mountains and he watched it until it disappeared, becoming a fleck of night against the glacier wall. One by one, the rest of the flock took off and flew after it – as if drawn upwards by its presence – a necklace of birds. Gemaley walked swiftly back across the ice with dancing steps and came up to join him, wearing her small, triumphant smile.

'How did you do that?' Ruan asked, amazed. 'They are wild creatures. I've never seen anyone lure one of them before.'

'I don't know.' She was being vague again. 'I've always been able to call them. But only the black ones.'

There were a dozen questions he longed to ask her. Did

you summon the bird that lured me to my fall? Did it somehow tell you what it had done? Did it bring you to me? But he asked none of these things. He followed her back, down the beast-path and along the ridge to the tower, drawn in her wake as meekly as the white serai, following their dark companion.

TWENTY-THREE

PLANET: MUSPELL

If it had not been for a break in the storm clouds, I would barely have seen him. It took me a moment before I realized that he had been using the shielding of the wing as a cover. I brought the stolen weapon up, but it was too late.

'Vali Hallsdottir.' I recalled, too, that he had never told me his name. 'Drop the gun.' I had a dizzy moment of failure and despair. He was armed, cradling the gun loosely across one forearm, and he could have had a clear shot if he'd wanted it.

I threw the gun down on the shingle. 'You've come to imprison me again.'

'Is that what you think? I would have expected you to be long gone by now. I've been waiting here half the morning.' He sounded reproving again, and a little annoyed, as though I'd stood him up. 'What happened, did you get lost?'

'How did you find the wing?'

'We tracked it in.' The vitki smiled a small cat smile.

'You knew I was here?'

'Of course. We picked you up on one of the scanners on your run up to the coast.'

'Why didn't you stop me then?' I felt like a mouse, casually swatted to and fro by a clever, subtle paw.

'I wanted to see what you'd do. I didn't know who you were, at that point, but I knew you were a good pilot from the way you took your wing through the storm, and that suggested Skald to me.'

'Then if you knew I was Skald—'

'As I said, I wanted to see what you'd do. Who you might have come to see.' He was still smiling, but he was watching me carefully through those pale-lashed eyes and I sensed that he was looking for answers, other than the ones I might have already given him. Somewhere over my shoulder, I seemed to hear the rattle of bones.

'You think we have contacts over here?'

'You headed straight for the wing-yards. But when I saw you in the bar and realized to my delight who you were, I also realized something that I have only slowly come to understand.' The rain was easing off now. The vitki sat down on a nearby rock, but he was still watchful and still cradled the gun.

'About what?'

'Our ancestors – yours and mine – were extremely superstitious at times. They believed in gods, which on the whole we do not. They spun coincidences into magic, and there I find myself rather more in sympathy with them. Just as I was in the middle of debating a particular issue with myself, you see, the universe throws someone at me out of the storm. A person who is ideally placed to help me.'

'What are you talking about?'

'I'm talking about Frey Gundersson.'

I found that I was gripping my shoulders, wrapping my arms around myself as if to ward off a blow, or the cold.

'Frey?'

'I thought you'd come here to find him. Have you?'

I was about to lie, but then I thought, why bother? 'He was a secondary goal,' I said.

'Ah. I see. You were sent to spy on the wing-yard, but since you were going to Darkland anyway you thought that you might as well try and find a trace of your treacherous lover, perhaps even get a chance to kill him. Is that it?'

'What's Frey to you?'

'Oh, Frey and I go back a long way.' He spoke lightly enough, but there was a tension underlying the words. 'But if you'd come simply to kill him, you'd have had a wasted journey. He isn't in Darkland. He isn't even on Muspell.'

'Then where the hell is he?'

'He's gone offworld, and I don't know why. But believe this, Vali. I want him found. I want him brought back, or dead, just as much as the Skald does. Just as much as you do.'

'Why?'

'Reasons.'

'Why not send one of your own operatives?'

217

'You think I trust one of my own operatives?'

I gaped at him. 'You'd trust an enemy spy over one of your own?'

'Frankly, I trust your hate more than I would a compatriot.'

'So you think I'd . . . what? Work for you? Believe you?'

'I don't think you'd object too much at the end of the day to being my clockwork soldier, Vali. Your pride may baulk at the idea, but you're too pragmatic to take offence for long. I plan to wind you up and let you go; pursue him until your batteries run out or Frey lies dead. So I'm not going to make you any offers, cut any deals, or tell you any stories. I'm simply going to give you the details of where Frey is then cut you loose.'

I did not like the sound of any of this. 'And how do I know that he's really where you say he is?'

'Think about it. I don't need to set a trap. You're here on the shore, I've got your weapon – you might be able to use the seith, but not against someone like me. There's a small war-wing blocking the mouth of the fjord and your own vehicle relies on wave-interfacing. It can't take you directly upwards, where you would in any case be shot down immediately. So why would I go to all the trouble of setting some elaborate trap when I already have you exactly where I want you? *If* I wanted you, which as I've said, I don't. Not just yet.' He cocked his head on one side and studied me. 'You'd have made a good addition to the breeding program. Perhaps you still may.'

There was no point in throwing a tantrum and telling him that I was not his plaything to be used or manipulated. I did not think he was interested in that kind of game. And there was little point in pressing him on the question of why he wanted Frey found, since he clearly had no intention of telling me. 'Very well, then. Am I to understand that once I've got the information about Frey's whereabouts, you'll let me go?'

'You'll be as free as a shearwater to fly back to your nest on the Rock.' He lowered the gun, though I noticed he did not take his eyes off me. 'In fact, you're free to go now. All the necessary data has been downloaded into the comm system of your wing.'

'In that case, I'd like to leave.'

'Then so you may.' He rose from his rock and glanced out to sea. 'One last question. What did you make of the selk?'

'It's illegal to incarcerate sentient creatures and anyway, it is immoral to treat anything as they're being treated.'

'I'd have expected nothing less.'

'Then why ask?'

'Oh,' the vitki said. 'Curiosity. Have a good trip back. And by the way, if you're wondering who I am, my name is Thorn Eld.'

I climbed into the wing and lowered the hatch, checking to see if the message system was flashing. The screen displayed an unknown, scrambled code and a set of data points, including a map of a world I did not know. I left

Thorn Eld standing on the shingle and backed the wing onto the water. Then I sped down the fjord. A black war-wing was riding the water in a froth of spray, just beyond the headland. As I passed it, I saw a scull hit the waves and shoot off in my wake, heading in the opposite direction to collect the vitki.

That was the last I saw of Darkland. I set the wing's acceleration to maximum and flew over the waters to the Reach, and never once looked behind me.

I did not return to Tiree, but took the wing west to the Rock itself. Seventy miles out of Darkland, the weather calmed and I was able to get through to Idhunn, whom I found as frantic as I had ever heard her.

'We had your last transmission, then nothing. I didn't know what had happened.'

'I'll tell you,' I said, and I did so as the wing sped across the miles of ocean. I told her as much as I could about the wing-yards, the war-wings, Hetla and its layout, the forest . . . everything, down to the last detail.

When I had finished my account, Idhunn was silent. Eventually she said, 'This vitki who interrogated you, this Thorn Eld. He doesn't show up on your broadcast, Vali.'

'What?'

'Tell me what he looked like.'

I did so. This time, Idhunn's silence became so pro-tracted that I was not sure whether the link still held. 'Idhunn? Are you receiving me?'

'Yes. Sorry, Vali. I was looking something up.'

'And?'

'There's no sign of anyone resembling him on our data-bases, but that doesn't mean a great deal. Although if he were a principal operative, as he seems to be, one would expect some record somewhere. But the vitki are hard to pin down.'

'He certainly knew enough about me.'

'How much of that could he have got from Frey?'

'A lot. From the past, and also from our time on Nhem.' Gradually, I realized, I was becoming used to the notion that Frey had been with me all that time, watching me from behind another man's face. I did not like it, to put it mildly, but if my time in Darkland had accomplished any-thing, it had at least lessened the state of raw shock into which the news of Aldur's possible true identity had plunged me.

'A lot? But not all?'

'No, not all.' I paused. 'Idhunn, he told me things about me that I barely even realized myself. It's as though they have a spy in my head. I've been wondering about the map implant, whether Frey could have done something to it, to tap into my mind and relay information back.'

'That's – quite paranoid, Vali. I've never heard anything to suggest that Darkland has that kind of technology. I'm not sure whether anyone does, to be honest. But if it will reassure you, I'll ask the medics to take a look at it when you get back and see if there's anything unusual about the implant.'

'They'll need to in any case,' I said. 'The vitki fried it. I might even need a new one – in fact, could you ask the medical staff to undertake an implant? That would give me a bit more confidence in what I'm carrying around in my head.'

'Of course.' She sounded relieved. 'I'll set it up now. They'll be waiting for you when you get back.'

And that, I thought with satisfaction as the wing spun past the first of the outlying rocks of the Reach, would not now be long.

Idhunn stood hovering by the bedside as I was preparing to go under for the implant replacement. The Skald's medical wing was a series of sunlit rooms on the eastern part of the Rock, catching the morning light and lapsing into a calm, sea-coloured dimness as the day wore on. It was a peaceful place. You could almost enjoy being ill here, and I was glad of the momentary respite, even though part of me wanted to get on my way, after Frey. *My clockwork soldier*. It was a bitter thought, but if I wanted to find Frey, did I really care?

'It's unlikely that anyone tampered with your implant,' Idhunn said again, frowning. 'That would take more science than Muspell has got. Unless they got it from somewhere else.'

She seemed anxious to reassure me, but I was not convinced. The technologies used by the vitki were too close to the supernatural for comfort. The sacrifice of ethics for knowledge was a bargain that the Skald had long ago stopped short of making, and I agreed with that. But if there was a way of accessing vitki knowledge and using it for our own purposes . . .? But it would still have come from the same dark source. I wanted to believe her, but I was glad when the medic appeared and touched a tranquillizer to my arm.

The next thing I knew, I was waking up with a sore tightness behind my eyes and Idhunn telling me gently that the operation was over, and had been a success.

They left me alone after that. I sat cross-legged on the bed, gazing out to sea and cautiously playing with the new implant. It was a more sophisticated version than the last, and despite a headache I enjoyed testing it out. Within it, too, I discovered a partial plan of a world that I did not know, yet was recognizable. I had glimpsed it on the navigational array of the wing, heading out from Darkland.

It was called Mondhile.

Later, I stood with Idhunn in the lamp room, looking down at the plans scrolling across the Rock's array. Idhunn twitched the pale skein of hair over one shoulder and bent forward for a closer look. 'So this is the place that the vitki wants you to go to.'

'Never heard of it.'

'Strangely enough, I have. And I've been doing some research while you were recuperating.'

'Tell me.'

She grimaced. 'It's one of the lost colonies. A little back-water place, the sort of planet that no one much bothers with unless it suddenly turns out to have something that someone wants. The Mondhaith haven't had contact with the outworlds for sixty years.'

'So what is it about this place that so intrigues Frey, I wonder?'

'That, Vali, I could not tell you. It's possible it's a free-lance contract that he hasn't mentioned to the vitki. Mining, something like that. A lot of the corporations seize on the old colony worlds, the primitive places. Go in, strip it bare, get out. Without bureaucracy to deal with, it can be a lucrative enough way of working if you've got the transport.'

'Perhaps. But I can't help feeling that if Frey's there now, it would be for reasons concerning their war effort.'

Idhunn frowned. 'Maybe. But he took a lot of trouble to go to Nhem with you, didn't he? And that wasn't to do with Darkland's war plans.'

I shifted uneasily. The tightness was growing behind my eyes and I did not think it had much to do with the new implant. '. . . that we know of. But I can't help feeling it's connected.' We stared at one another for a moment. 'Is Mondhile a warm world?'

'Where you're apparently going? No. Mountains. Cold. Lots of snow.'

I smiled. 'My kind of planet.'

'And there's something else I found in the records, too. They understand the seith.'

'The Mondhaith?' Frowning, I ran a hand down the slick, gleaming surface of the lamp. 'How human are they? Do you know?'

'More than some of the lost colonies, less than others. There have been changes, apparently, the result of genetic manipulation of some kind, long ago. The eyes are odd, appear blank, the nails have become claws. They're not so physically changed, but they have a connection to their world, perhaps even stronger than our own seith. They can detect minerals deep in the earth, feel the flow of water. Their sense of direction is very marked. They seem tied to their world's magnetic pole. They migrate, all together, every few years. They would make wonderful dowsers and trackers.'

I frowned. 'So that might also be an attraction for the vitki? The people as well as the world?'

'Perhaps. But they might find them uncooperative. The Mondhaith regard people who can't sense the land as nothing more than ghosts – crippled. That's why someone from Muspell has an innate advantage, through the training of the seith. The Mondhaith shouldn't see you as a ghost, but as like themselves.'

'And Frey.'

'Yes. And Frey, too. Oh, and their child-rearing practices are pretty bizarre. I imagine anyone who felt strongly about children's welfare wouldn't take to that society.'

I wondered what she meant. 'I can't say I'm the maternal type.'

'That's probably just as well. But everything we know is in the dossier.'

The lamp intensified as the dusk drew on. A line of brightness showed above the horizon, all that remained of sunset beneath the cloud shadow.

'And we could learn from them, perhaps,' I said.

'Perhaps we could,' Idhunn echoed, lost momentarily in the turning glow of the lamp.

I perched on the windowsill and studied the dossier as the details once more unveiled themselves across my inner sight. A strange place, Mondhile. A world where people sent their children out into the wilderness when they were only a few months old, children who lived like animals until they reached puberty and made their way home. I thought of a man with one golden eye and one grey eye, who had sent me to the beasts on the ice; and of the selk, speaking in their brief time of consciousness. Connections, but the puzzle would not quite add up.

An hour later, I turned the dossier off. Apart from the illumination coming from the lamp itself, it was completely dark. Idhunn was still staring out to sea.

'Where does this come from?'

'A Gaian anthropologist, who chose to stay on Mondhile after some kind of failed religious mission. She attached her report to a record pod and sent it into orbit. The pod was damaged slightly, so the report isn't as complete as it might have been originally.'

'A religious mission. Typical of the Gaians.' *Holier-than-thou* was not my favourite attitude.

226

Idhunn smiled. 'Most of them died, apparently.'

'Killed?' I always found it hard to feel sorry for missionaries, though I suppose this was a failing on my part.

'I'm not sure. If they were, it was probably accidental, given that the locals tend to see ordinary humans as "not quite there". But there are things in the anthropologist's report that are not clear and that I don't understand.'

I thought back. 'There's mention of something she calls the "bloodmind" – I got the impression from the notes that it might be some kind of ritual. It talks of people entering a particular state, but the text just isn't clear. I wondered if it could also be a reference to something like the seith.'

Idhunn shook her head. 'I don't know. A kind of intuition, perhaps?'

'And "house defences". What are those, do you think? I thought this was a primitive culture.'

'It sounds like a kind of moat. It's hard to tell.'

'But they let this anthropologist stay, yes? Is there any indication of what happened to her?'

'She wasn't a young woman when she went out. She'll be long dead by now. The Mondhaith are a bit longer lived than many human types, but not by much. And her record pod wasn't found until much later. It was all slower than light travel in those days – cold-sleep and colony ships and the like.'

'She was brave to stay,' I remarked.

'I doubt she had a choice.'

I went to bed early that night, but I did not sleep well. Darkland haunted my dreams. I found myself in that cottage in the forest, with the rattle of bones at my back. The vitki was smiling as he leaned forward, but I could not move. I woke, sweating, to find that it was just after dawn. I threw open the window, but not even the cold sea-wind could blow the shreds of the dream away.

'You'll be taking a wing to the port at Tiree,' Idhunn said, later that morning. It was not a good day for travelling. Another gale was roaring up the Minch, making the morning as dark as twilight, and sending a thunderous sea surging around the edges of the Rock. I did not regard it as auspicious.

'And then?'

'And then leaving on the six o'clock sky-ferry to Main.'

'And from there?'

She sighed. 'It's going to be a question of a series of ships, out to the edge of the system and Hatha-Khar, then a chartered craft which clips past Mondhile on the Alsturan run. They'll send you down in a hired drop-boat.'

'That must be costing the Skald.'

'Try to make it a quick trip, is all I'm saying. After the information you sent back on the war-wings, we'll be needing you here.'

I gave her a thin smile. 'I'm not planning on seeing the sights. Whatever they might be.'

TWENTY-FOUR

PLANET: MONDHILE

Ruan and Gemaley got back to the tower in the early afternoon, and despite his lingering fear of the place Ruan was glad to be out of the forest and the weather and under a roof once more. When they came into the hallway, Gemaley turned and put a solicitous hand on his arm.

'You ought to rest. You're more tired than you think you are.' Her face was once again filled with concern and he could not help a moment of doubt. Was it real, or just a convenient mask that she wore? Her eyes revealed nothing.

At first he thought, or hoped, that it was an invitation to an afternoon in bed, but he quickly realized that Gemaley had no intention of following him up the spiral stairs.

'What are you going to do?' he asked her, and hated how wistful it sounded.

'I have things to attend to,' Gemaley said calmly and before he could say anything more she disappeared into the main hall. Ruan hesitated for a moment, then went up the stairs. She was right; he was tired. His ankle was aching, though not badly, and he knew that it was almost healed. He collapsed onto the bed with the afternoon light filtering in through the paper pane, and fell asleep.

At first, there was nothing. Then the dream crept over him, detail by detail. He was in a low, dark room, surrounded by wet slabs of stone. Light, from a source he could not see, glinted from the walls. And he could feel the dark energy beneath the tower, a churning abyss coiling up from the heart of the world itself, ready to pull him down. In the dream, he knew he would be lost if that happened – not merely dead and fleeing into the spirit world of Eresthahan, but unsouled and disembodied – and in terror he flattened himself back against the wet chill of the wall. But the wall itself was moving, pushing him away, and then the light was fragmenting, breaking, becoming wings that whirled around him and brought stabs of agony in their wake as they seized him and carried him upwards. He cried out, and woke.

He knew immediately that it was close to sunset. The light was falling obliquely across the floor, filling the room with a red glow. Ruan realized that he was hungry; he had not eaten since the morning. He was not inclined to wait until Gemaley decided to bring him something; he disliked this growing dependency. He resolved to go in search of food.

He listened carefully as he passed Tian's door, but there was no sound from within. Perhaps she was downstairs in the hall, by the fire. That was a welcome memory in this bleak place. He hoped it was lit tonight, that someone had been out hunting – but that someone would surely be Gemaley. If not, then perhaps he would go hunting tomorrow. The thought struck him that this was foolish; if he was well enough to hunt then he was well enough to leave, and he snatched at the thought, but it was gone.

In the fading light, the tower had a strangely deserted feel, as though it had been abandoned many years ago and the people whom he knew were no more than spirits. He smiled at the notion. Gemaley, with her pale hair and eyes, could indeed be a ghost; summoned up from the world of the dead to torment the living. But then he thought of her flesh against him, her body next to his, warmth and scent and wetness and the touch of her hands, and knew that without question she was real.

Such an odd family . . . He wondered whether they had ever been on a migration. Surely they must have done, given their ages, at least once, but it was impossible to think of them as being anywhere but the tower, especially Gemaley. It was as though she was the spirit of the place itself, its presiding force made body and bone – and an impenetrable darkness within.

When he went into the hall he saw that the fire was indeed lit, though burnt down low. The room smelled unpleasantly of stale smoke, unlike the fragrant wood that the clan house burned in the evening. Ruan picked up a poker and stirred the embers; the only wood to hand was the leg of a table. He hesitated, then pushed it into the fire and it blazed up.

Ruan straightened and looked around him. There was no one to be seen. He walked out into the hall and behind an unlocked door found a chamber that had evidently been the stove room. The stove was still there, though filled with ash. Its top was covered with old food, burned and blackened. Ruan eyed it with distaste, but there was charcoal in the pit and meat on the table: a haunch of something that looked like wild mur, from the blue veins that ran along it. Ruan tore some chunks off, then pushed them with difficulty onto the blunt spit and lit the charcoal.

He watched as the meat cooked. There were no herbs hanging in the kitchen, no sign of a vegetable store or any pantry. Like the rest of the tower, the stove room seemed to be sliding into decay. But the meat was decent enough; fatty and succulent. Ruan ate it with his fingers, then went in search of water.

He found a tall barrel outside, just by the door that led out. Rainwater was evidently carried down from the roof, and purified by a series of filters, as with all these northern houses. But the pipe was cracked, probably from being frozen, and an icy scum had formed on the surface of the water that was left in the barrel. Ruan picked up a handful of snow from the step instead, first checking to see that it was clean, and ate it.

It was a clear night. A lack of prickle against his skin told him that the tower's defences were down. He could see the little crescent of Embar hanging above the tower, and the stars were beginning to blossom, out in the east. Through the trees the western sky still held the last of the sunset; a gilded redness. Ruan suddenly felt ice-cold. Tomorrow, he would leave, but now he wanted warmth and at least the illusion – and possibility – of companionship. He was about to go back into the stove room when he heard someone cough.

It was a faint sound, from deep within the trees. At first he thought it was an animal, but then he heard it again, unmistakably human. Footsteps sounded around the tower, just out of sight. Ruan peered round the curve of the wall to see Gemaley, her long leather coat hunched up around her, heading into the trees. Without stopping to think, Ruan followed.

She walked quickly, weaving between the arms of the thorn-stripe bushes. Ruan pursued her at a safe distance, then stood and watched as someone came out of the deeper forest to meet her.

'You're late, girl.' It was a man's voice, carrying clearly in the cold air. Ruan's heart pounded in his chest. He saw Gemaley shrug.

'I said I'd meet you at sunset.'

'You've no sense of time. Sunset's over.' The voice was deep and accented, with a rasp as though the owner of it was unwell. Presumably this was the person that Ruan had heard coughing. He seemed to stumble over some of the words, as though Khalti were not his first language, and there was a curious hum to his voice, like a very faint echo. This must be the stranger whom he had seen with her, the man from the forest. He sounded human enough, apart from that echo.

'You are obsessed with the day, the hour. What does it matter?' Gemaley said.

'To you? Nothing. You're a peasant. You live your life like an animal. Some of us have things to do.'

'What things?' Gemaley's voice held a trace of contempt, but she sounded more uneasy than Ruan had ever heard her.

'I told you before,' the stranger said, very quietly, as if reining back impatience.

'You can see it, when the time is right. You see? I understand time well enough.' Gemaley was defensive now, and that too was new.

'I don't know what you're talking about. Why can't I see it now?'

'Because it is ebbing. There is nothing to see. This is when we are idle, my brother and my sister and I. When the tide rises, then I will show you.'

'And when is that?'

'You expect me to know the exact day?' Gemaley sounded amused again, but the stranger clearly did not share it. Ruan saw the man reach out and grasp her shoulders, giving her a shake.

'Yes, why not?'

'Perhaps three days, then. I can't tell you exactly.' Gemaley now sounded sullen and, Ruan thought, a little afraid. 'It isn't like a woman – connected with the moons. It isn't a sea.'

Even with the echo, the man sounded exasperated, Ruan thought.

'Have you never kept track?'

'Why would I?' Gemaley was growing angry, and it made his spine shiver. 'Tell me that. What need would I have of such a record? Why are you so timid, that you need to pin the world down?'

To Ruan's surprise, the man let go of Gemaley's shoulders and laughed until he went into another fit of coughing. '"Timid", is it? You have no idea who I am, do you? What I am, where I come from.'

It was Gemaley's turn to laugh and Ruan thought that he had never heard anything so cold. 'And where is that? Eresthahan?'

'What does that mean?'

'The land of the dead.'

'Oh, you have no idea,' the man from the forest said softly. 'But you'll see, one day.' He leaned forward and gave Gemaley a lingering kiss.

'I'll see, will I?' she said, when he stepped back. The light note was back in her voice but there was still something brittle in it, as though her words would break if one could touch them; snap like icicles.

'If you want to.' Now he was teasing, too.

'Why not? I'm getting bored here.'

'That's no surprise. You're meant for more, girl. Stay here and you'll grow old and withered, dry as a moth in a web. But out there – that'll be different.' He hesitated and a note of genuine enquiry entered his voice. 'Why *have* you stayed here, Gemaley? Why haven't you gone somewhere else? Your world has towns. I've— heard tell of them. Maybe not very large ones, but they would give you greater scope than you have here.'

'What would I do in a town? I know no one. I have no clan there. Such places are always tightly knit.'

'There are festivals, or so I've read.' He laughed again. 'Festivals or orgies, depending on how you see these things. Have you seen anything like that? It's connected to what you're going to show me, isn't it?'

'You think I'd tell you everything?'

'I don't think you've been anywhere. I think you sit here like an insect queen, ready to pounce and catch your prey. Like that boy you've got up there in the tower.'

'Ruan? But Ruan's sweet.'

Hearing her say this, Ruan felt himself flush with pleasure, but somewhere at the back of his mind, a voice told him that this might not be the compliment it seemed. He thrust the voice away.

'He's "sweet", is he? You've got him snared like a fly in one of those flower-mouths I've seen among the moss.'

'Oh, he's free to go,' Gemaley said. 'If he wants to.'

'Is he? How many are there, down in that cellar of yours?'

'How many what?'

'Travellers.'

Gemaley gave a single short laugh. 'What, you think I lure them here and then kill them? Why would I do that?'

'Because you're . . . a little mad, maybe?'

'Do you think I'm mad?' Gemaley asked.

She did not sound as though she cared one way or the

other about his answer, but he said, musing, 'I don't know. I don't know whether you're mad, or whether you just look at the world in a different way.'

'Aren't they the same thing?'

'Perhaps.'

The calf of Ruan's injured leg was growing cramped and he shifted position – only slightly, but it was enough to bring the stranger's head up like a hunting mur. 'What was that? There's someone watching.'

'It's probably Gith. He likes to look, when he thinks it's safe. Especially if he thinks I'm fucking someone.' She laughed. 'Not that I mind. I like an audience, sometimes.'

'Well, I *don't*. What about the boy?'

'What about him? What does it matter?'

'Perhaps it doesn't,' the man said, but there was an edge to his tone that made Ruan feel that it would be prudent to back away. He moved as silently as he could through the trees and in through the stove-room door. It was by now quite dark and he sought his chamber as one who seeks sanctuary.

TWENTY-FIVE

PLANET: MUSPELL

I had to wait at Tiree spaceport because the transit was delayed – a nuisance that I could have done without. To pass the time I went in search of a bar, but the only one I could find was an ostentatious place in the front of the Arrivals building that looked as if it had prices to match. Before finding a seat, I went into the toilet – decorated, wall-to-floor, with something slick and shiny that reflected anything that moved, in an unnerving infinity of images – and checked that the camouflage was still holding.

I looked neither like myself, nor the Nhemish woman I had so recently been, nor the Darklander. My hair was a nondescript brown, curling over my shoulders, and my two eyes were hazel, and unremarkable. A pleasant enough face, slightly round, typical of Tiree. My scars were once more covered. It would do, I thought, until I got into the hire shuttle that would take me to Mondhile. Once I was there, it wouldn't matter what I looked like. Judging from the details of the debriefing, I could not pass for a local, and the only human who was likely to recognize me – the only outworld human there, as far as I or the Skald knew – was Frey, and he could see through any disguise I might assume. The shadowy dream of the vitki came back to haunt me. I turned from the mirror and went back into the bar.

As I'd guessed, it wasn't cheap, but the beer was drinkable; some kind of light wheaty brew from the south. It came with a bowlful of salted seaweed, reminding me that I had not eaten since breakfast, although they usually fed you on inter-system flights. I sipped slowly, studying the dossier on Mondhile through the implant. It sounded an odd kind of society; tightly knit clans, but no importance placed on parental connections. That alone suggested something that had strayed very far from the human norm; an upbringing closer to that of animals. And they were said not to have any real awareness until they returned to the clan houses at puberty, like those migrating shearwaters that return to the burrows where they hatched, even though they have flown a world away. I trusted that the Mondhaith were not as stupid as shearwaters, but you never knew . . .

There was other information in the report, but I'd studied it already back at the Rock. From what I'd read, it seemed there was a reasonable chance that the Mondhaith might leave me alone. But I could not count on it, and I hoped that I'd find the place where Frey's shuttle had landed, as fast as possible. He would have hidden it, concealed the traces, if he had any sense – and as vitki, he had more senses than most.

I sat in the bar, surrounded by glossy wood and glossier travellers, staring at the landscape of an unknown world as it unfolded before my inner eye. I gazed at sketchy coasts and vague mountains, wondering where Frey had been heading, or whether he'd had any firm idea of a destination. Knowing Frey, the answer was probably yes, but I did not have enough information with which to out-think him. I would just have to track him as best I could, and take it from there. I tried to pretend that I was doing it for the Skald, and for myself, but the vitki's words still echoed in my mind: my clockwork soldier.

The bar was filling up. I'm not comfortable with crowds, but it felt pleasantly strange to be walking around without everyone covertly staring at me – that's what two good eyes and an unscarred complexion can do. I suddenly longed to be myself again; for the silence of the Rock; for the sea and storms. I finished what was left of my beer and went back out onto the concourse. The intersystem transit was finally up on the flight display. I made my way to the gate and registered: my documents; an eye-scan; a pin-scratch blood test. Muspell's requirements were not as strict as those of Nhem. After that, I went through a barrage of security checks, and an assessment of my weapons licensing – which was watertight; Idhunn and I had made sure of that even before I left the Rock. Licensing varied from province to province; I did not want to run into stumbling blocks in Tiree that did not exist elsewhere in the Reach. The official spent a lot of time looking at the serrated knife I carried, but just as I began to grow uneasy, he said, mildly enough, 'Nice knife.'

'Thanks. It was custom made.'

'Yes, I thought so from the grip. You'll have to hand all this in.' He was even a little apologetic, though he shouldn't have been. Hijacks happened.

'Of course.' I handed everything over and tried not to feel naked. Then he moved on to the next passenger and I was being shunted forwards to the gate. I could see the dim bulk of the transit a little way ahead, lights blurred in the rain. The gale that had been such a storm up in the Reach had lessened by the time it hit Tiree. Now though, it was merely raining heavily and drearily. It felt more like winter than spring. A squall hit the windows, but no heads turned. The passengers all looked like locals. I blended in without difficulty. No heads turned to look at me and the seith remained placidly intact. After a short wait, we were ushered onto the transit. I found a seat by a porthole. I don't like sitting in the aisle, it makes me feel claustrophobic. Here, at least, I could see out to the dismal weather and then the stars. Two businessmen in cloakjackets took seats adjacent to me and began conversing in low voices about something to do with construction. I detected eastern highland accents – long vowels, a grumbling delivery – and amused myself by speculating on where exactly they might be from. If I grew too curious, I told myself, I would ask. People were inquisitive on Muspell, for no good reason.

There was a brief rumble, then a shift and glide,

causing the rain to streak across the recess of the porthole. And then we were out to the centre of the spaceport. I heard a small, calm voice echoing through the cabin: *Clearance to rise.* The transit went up, compensators whirring. I felt a brief pressure pushing me back and down into my seat, and then nothing.

I squashed my face against the porthole and looked down. Tiree was a spiral of lights below, rimmed by the black swell of ocean. I could not see the islands. We were heading east across the northern wastes and then Loki was hanging there, seemingly just outside the window.

Muspell fell away once more. I leaned back in my seat and closed my eyes. A crew member came to stand beside the seats.

'Would you like a sleeper?'

'No, I'm all right.' The seith would work as well as a drug, and leave me fresher. I set an internal clock for seven hours time, closed my eyes again, and drifted away.

When I woke, the businessmen beside me were still sleeping, one of them uttering small snorts. I touched the map-plan set into the seat in front of me and studied it. Muspell was far to the back of the display; the outer planets were closer. The gas giant Fellheim was shown as a great red ball. We had reached the edges of the system. The waystation of Main lay ahead.

It seemed to take a long time to dock. I waited impatiently in the queue of passengers. Finally, the doors opened and we were herded through into the main port and an endless procession of scans and documentation.

The port had that antiseptic atmosphere common to all these places. I felt mildly contaminated, as though the port disapproved of me. I retrieved my weapons and went into the toilet to put them in their proper places. I did not want to have to be fiddling about with them in the probably confined space of the shuttle. Then I headed in the direction of the shuttle-bay.

At first, soft carpet muffled my footsteps and the walls were painted a delicate lilac, but as I followed the directions for the shuttle-bay, Main began to betray its more antiquated origins: the old mining station that it had been before the galaxy opened up once more, making the need for waystations imperative. The gloss paint gave way to bare walls festooned with wiring; the floor became a grille encrusted at the edges with rust. I began to wonder how safe it might be. I paused briefly to study the instructions that I had been given. The shuttle was due to depart in an hour and was located in Bay 6. I looked at the directions on the wall panel and realized that I'd come the wrong way. Cursing, I turned back, and it was then I became aware that I was not alone.

At first, I thought it was merely another straying passenger like myself, but the movement was too hasty. I reached out with the seith. Someone was standing behind a stanchion, just round the corner. They were breathing hard, causing the edges of the seith to ruffle as though someone had brushed against my clothing. I did not make the mistake of calling out. The seith told me only of their presence, not their nature or intentions, but I decided that they were almost certainly hostile. I had the choice of contacting the station's security, or dealing with the situation myself. It was not a difficult decision. I drew the serrated knife and edged to the corner.

I could hear them now. The breathing was ragged, as if indecisive. They were coming forwards, a purposeful quick, stealthy tread. I wondered, fleetingly, whether this was a planned attack or simply an opportunistic crime. All sorts of people populated the remote parts of the way-stations. In this day and age, station managers did not have the resources to pay for additional security nor, indeed, the money to bribe planets into taking back dissidents of whom the planets were only too happy to be rid. But then the person came close enough for me to smell him, and I knew that this was no random attack.

It was only a faint odour, the subtlest underlay of spice and dust, but it was enough to bring back the memories of the back streets of Iznar and the Hierolath's palace. This person came from Nhem. And that made me think of Frey.

This raised all manner of questions with which I was unprepared to deal right now. My heart hammering, I gripped the knife more tightly and stepped round the corner. It only took a moment. A foot behind the ankle, a couple of strikes to the elbow and shoulder and he was gasping on the ground with a broken arm and my knife at his throat. He was not, I thought, a professional, or insufficiently trained if he was. Not Frey. Not Frey. Besides, he was too short. I looked down at the top of a dark head, blond at the roots. Nhemish, then. His skin had been stained to disguise its natural pallor, but it was turning grey with pain.

'And you are?'

'Plague of filth! Let me go.' He twisted round, trying to glare up at me, but it only put more strain on the dislocated shoulder.

'Not before you talk. Who sent you, why? I don't have time to waste.' I increased the pressure of the knife at his throat, drawing thin beads of blood. He struggled, but he wasn't in any position to break free and he knew it. I considered killing him, but then there was the problem of what to do with the body.

'I don't talk to animals.'

Of course, given the views of the Nhemish, he just had, but this was no time for pernickety semantics. 'All right,' I said. 'I'm calling security.' Since I'd broken his arm and was holding a knife to his throat, it was doubtful whether I could pass myself off as the fragile victim of an attempted rape, but I was worried about missing the shuttle. If I did, then it would be another few days before I could get to Mondhile and Frey. Perhaps I could tell them that he'd tripped over his own feet.

There was a console on one wall. I spoke the emergency code common to all waystations and the console clicked on.

'There's been an accident,' I told it. 'In the corridor leading to Bay 6. Someone fell and struck his head. He's unconscious – I think he has a fractured skull.' Moments later, this was more or less true. I let the body slump to the floor and raced for the shuttle-bay.

An assassin from Nhem raised some serious questions. How had they connected my Nhemish persona with myself? How had they linked that with the death of the Hierolath? And how had they known enough about my movements to track me down here? Frey and his fellow vitki were one of the more obvious choices. All of these issues were a matter of concern, but I just did not have time to deal with them.

I reached the bay just as the gate was closing and found myself to be the last passenger on the shuttle; they had reserved a seat at the back of the craft. The other occupants glanced at me with a mixture of curiosity and mild annoyance as I made my way down the aisle. I glared back; it wasn't as though I'd delayed departure. We sat on the docking ring for another fifteen minutes while the pilot gained clearance. I used the time to send a report to Idhunn. Let the Skald deal with the Nhemish assassin for now. It would cause all manner of bureaucratic headaches if they requested that he be released into Skald custody, and I suspected that Idhunn would simply ask that he be sent back to Nhem. The thought made me smile; I did not think that Nhem was a culture that rewarded failure.

If they were this determined to track me down, there would probably be another attempt, but so be it. I'd cross that bridge when I came to it. For now though, it was the reach into empty space, and then Mondhile.

*

I dozed all the way from Main to the Junction, trying to ignore the faint hum of conversation and instruments around me, but it was a bumpy ride. The seith helped, holding me in a cradle of its own, but I was glad when the lights once more came on to full beam and I saw from the seat display that we were coasting down into Junction space. I checked the tabula and saw that a message was already in from Idhunn.

'Your assailant's dead. Killed himself in station captivity after cursing everyone around him, apparently. Some kind of poison capsule. No loss to the neighbourhood, if you ask me.'

So that was a problem postponed, at least. Unless they'd sent others after me, which was likely. Idhunn had no answers to the questions that really bothered me.

'Security told me that he was from Nhem, but no name or any identifying marks. Fingerprints had been removed, retinas modified. They're doing a DNA test now. It's all basic alteration, nothing fancy.'

And that led to yet another question: if they wanted me that badly, why hadn't they sent someone with more experience? The assassin had smelled of fear, and that tended to be in short supply in the security forces, even Nhemish ones. As far as I was concerned, too, the issue of whether he had actually been sent to kill me was still outstanding. What if he'd been dispatched to hire me, instead? But that was unlikely, given the nature of the Nhemish, unless I'd somehow been awarded the dubious status of honorary male. Such things had happened before on other

LIZ WILLIAMS

worlds, in various peculiar circumstances, but lurking round corners was a stupid way to go about contacting an assassin.

I could not worry about this now. Mondhile and Frey lay ahead.

After the scramble to reach the Junction, I then had a day to wait before the shuttle came that would take me to Mondhile. I hired a sleeping-pod and spent most of the next few hours in it, then woke to go over the anthropologist's report once more and speak to Idhunn over the tabula. Reception was not good and we got only a handful of words in one another's conversations; fragments scrolling across the screen. Eventually the transmission broke up and that meant that I was separated from the Skald and would be working entirely alone. The thought helped me to concentrate, to run a mental itinerary of everything I knew about Frey that might help me to find him.

Hate should go a long way towards that, I thought. It was strange to look back on the girl I had been, too unsure of herself to see that what had masqueraded as love had been manipulation and mind-games. It had taken a long time in the Rock for that realization to penetrate, and when it finally had, I'd felt stupid. I still did, given what had happened on Nhem.

Idhunn said that this is what the seith really is: learning to trust the sequence of cues and clues that the world gives you, the knowledge at the edge of things. Intuition is not a supernatural sense, but simply the very swift processing of information from one's environment. I should not feel stupid, she said. I had only been young, and Frey was a vitki, raised on deception as if it had been milk. It took me even longer to believe her and sometimes I was not sure that I did, even now.

Remembering Frey made me restless. I slid out of the sleeping-pod into the corridor, first checking to make sure that there weren't any more Nhemish assassins lurking in the vicinity. Carrying my equipment with me, I set out for the docking bay.

The Junction was built like a spindle, and always made me feel that some huge presence was dangling it from a thread, turning it ceaselessly and spinning out our lives. But perhaps I had spent too much time listening to the legends of the Skald . . . The lift that carried me travelled through the vast hollow interior of the Junction, so that as I hurtled downwards I could see the small ships coming in, drifting amid the enormous spirals of the docking mechanisms which reminded me of the DNA double-helix. Most of these vessels were no more than pods and shuttles. I would be taking one of those dandelion-seed craft, with its thin parachute web, down to the surface of Mondhile. I had travelled in these things before and they always made me nervous, surely too fragile and frail to withstand the forces of planetary entry? And accidents could happen to anyone, seith or no seith. But that, too, was not worth worrying about just yet.

I found the pilot of the shuttle in one of the rudimentary, standing-only bars that surrounded the docking hub. Named Narmai Cane, she was a short, thickset woman with no neck, but surprisingly long and delicate hands. Her accent was heavy, but I could not tell where she came from; one of the outlying worlds, perhaps, or a cross-breed. Hatha-Khar, the nearest inhabited world to the Junction, was also one of the oldest colonies. Cane exuded a reassuring air of quiet competence and she was drinking flavoured water rather than alcohol, always a good sign in a person who is about to transport you through no-space.

'I can't tell you much about the place,' she said, when I asked her. 'Small world, lots of sea, lots of forest and mountains from the look of it. I've never touched down – why would I? There's nothing there.'

I smiled. 'Nothing for you, perhaps.'

'Well, I'm not a geologist or a miner. And I don't care much for other cultures, as long as they leave me alone.'

I wasn't sure whether it was meant as a rebuff, but then she added, 'I've seen too much of them. It's why I'm here,' and at last I placed the accent. She was not from Hatha-Khar after all, but another close-world named Gallowen, which had suffered wave after wave of invasion from other systems – a rarity in this part of the galaxy. The invaders weren't human, of course; interstellar invasion costs too much to be worth our while. The human colonists had braved it out for a few generations, with little choice, but as soon as space opened up, the bulk of them moved elsewhere and left the planet to the religious wars of the neighbours. I was glad that Muspell was too far away from any alien systems to be on the invasion routes.

'Have you dropped anyone else off there recently?'

She gave me a shrewd glance. 'There's only been one, and I'm sure you know that. Gave his name as Thoren Eim. Tall, quiet. Odd eyes. Said he was a geologist.'

'That's right.' I did not want to give her too much information and it was unlikely that she would have recognized him as vitki, being an outworlder.

'Work for rival corporations, do you?'

'Something like that.'

'Well, it's none of my business. I'll drop you off, and make the pick-up. But I can't wait. You'll have to be there.'

'I'm not sure when it will be. How many windows can you give me?'

'Two, for the next month. After that, I don't know. My route's due to change. You'd be wise to take the last opportunity, at least. I don't think it's the kind of planet you'd want to get stuck on.'

'When did the other passenger ask to be collected?'

'In eleven days' time.'

'And that's the next window?'

'Yes.'

'Then you'd best do the same for me,' I said. I did not want to tell her that in all likelihood, only one of us would be coming back. As she said, it was none of her business.

The ship was old, but it was in good repair. As we walked through the docking hub I could see a host of places where the hull had been patched, but I doubt that it would have been so visible to an unpractised eye. I wondered whether it had been a Gallowenese ship, and whether it had seen war. The pods were strapped to its sides, their webbing folded. From this distance, they looked barely big enough to carry a doll. I thought of plummeting through atmosphere in one of these things and winced.

'How long will it take?' I asked Cane.

'A few hours. You're prepared?'

'As much as I'll ever be.'

The old ship roared and rattled on take-off like a leaf in a strong wind. Cane handled it calmly, her broad face betraying no alarm. I watched as the edge of the hub grew closer and then we were falling out into free space, with the bulk of the spindle looming beyond. Cane took the ship out and away towards the starfield.

She said little throughout the course of the trip. I ate some of the rations – I did not want to have to worry about food the moment I reached the surface – and the rest remained packed away in the bag. If I was careful and sparing, I might be able to eke out the supply until the pick-up; I didn't want to be bothered with sourcing the local cuisine, though I would hunt if I had to. Then I dozed once more for a while.

At last Cane said, startling me awake, 'There. See, the world with three moons?'

We were flying through a system. A planet lay ahead of us, ochre and blue, wreathed in cloud.

'That's Mondhile?' I reached for the straps that held me in my seat.

'So it is.' She nodded at me, pleasantly enough. 'I'll take

you in as close as I can. Remember what I said about the pick-up.'

'I'll remember.'

Thanking her, I left the cabin and went along the narrow walkway to the pod storage bay. I selected the third pod along – three is a lucky number on Muspell – and opened the hatch. It hissed up, revealing a slender bulge in the side of the craft. For someone larger than I was, it would have been a tight fit. I positioned myself in front of the instrument console and tightened the strapping, then closed the hatch securely behind me and fixed the electrode from the console to the implant entryway just behind my ear. The pod smelled strange, an odd musky smell, and the size was not helping my claustrophobia. I closed my eyes for a moment and thought of the Reach. Cane's voice spoke into my ear, startlingly loud.

'All clear to drop?'

'All clear,' I said, and I heard the snap, tiny as a falling pin, as the restraints pulled away. Then the pod was descending towards Mondhile. I touched the console, willing the parachute-web to open – as always, fearing instrument error. Sometimes fear can make things happen, I am certain of it. But the drop went smoothly. I did not look to see the ship veer away, concentrating on the world ahead of me instead.

The implant was directing the navigational system, keying what I knew of our destination into the pod's console. We fell towards the northern hemisphere and I watched with fascination as a ragged coastline appeared through the clouds, a fringe of white lace around it. Fjords and mountains; it could almost have been Muspell. I felt a sudden twinge of longing and suppressed it. The pod was gliding downwards, twisting and turning to compensate for the information fed into it by my implant. I could only watch; the pod knew where we were going. We flew over a range of mountains – ragged crags falling into the snowline – and the pod swung from side to side, buffeted by powerful winds.

Now, the sky above me was dark, filled with racing snowcloud, and a blue knife of lightning split the western horizon. The thought of coming down in a storm was a grim one, but there was nothing I could do. It also was inauspicious; I felt as though Frey had somehow stolen my luck – a wholly irrational notion. For all I knew, he'd made landfall in worse weather. But the knowledge that the landing details had been given to me by a vitki did not inspire me with confidence.

The pod lurched as though struck by a giant hand. The strapping prevented my face from hitting the viewscreen, but only just. I caught a glimpse of a long stretch of forest, blue-green and black trees illuminated by a sudden stray shaft of sun, touched with a bloody tinge. Then the gap in the clouds closed and the trees bent forward, lashed by the wind. The pod began to slow until I was sure I could hear the whine of the wind in the webbing. It tumbled slowly, cartwheeling above the treetops. I resisted the urge to close my eyes. And then we were floating through a haze of rain towards the ground. The pod had guided itself into a clearing, where it lay still.

The strapping had prevented me from striking the sides of the pod, but I still felt bruised. I lay encased in the pod, catching my breath and waiting for the worst of the rain to stop. It was hammering down on the viewport, heavy thunder drops that gradually slowed to sleet, and then to snow. The pod was cramped and still making me feel claustrophobic; I had to find other shelter. Opening up the hatch, I stepped shakily onto the world of Mondhile.

The cold hit me like a hammer-blow, but it was familiar. The air smelled fresh and strange, filled with resin and ice and other scents that I was unable to identify. I stood for a moment, trying to get my bearings. A peak rose above the trees to the south, an immense glacier wall, half hidden in the clouds. Apart from that, I could see only forest. But I had the coordinates of Frey's pod, and the upload from my own pod would tell me where to find it. I set the map implant to *display*, and walked towards the trees to find shelter.

When I woke, the sky had cleared and the forest was covered with a blanket of stars. The air was cold and bracing and I could feel the approach of the dawn, a kind of rising in my blood.

Then something shrieked. It was a high, thin cry that fell away into nothing and it froze me to the rock. It sounded like fenris, but there was a peculiar kind of sentience to it, as though whatever had made the sound had not merely howled, but cried out a word. The seith rushed through me like a prickling wind. I seized the pack and headed through the trees. The cry came again, and it was as though not only my skin, but my bones, shivered. Something about it touched me to the core. I stood still, sending out my senses to the edges of the seith. Something was coming, hammering at the seith, but I could also hear them now, many heavy bodies crashing through the undergrowth.

The memory of the fenris' attack sent my head reeling. I gasped, and they were nearly here. I flung the pack over my shoulder, grasped the lower branches of a slippery black-barked tree and swung myself upwards. I did not stop, but kept climbing until I was a third of the way up and surrounded by forest. It felt like sanctuary, but I had no way of knowing whether or not this was really the case. What if these things could climb?

I took the projector out of the pack and held it tightly. My nightsight, which was adequate but not excellent, was settling into the seith now, providing me with a clearer view of the forest below. They were coming fast, no more than a few yards away now. As I watched, one of the moons glided out from behind a cloudbank and I saw them.

They were long, low creatures, perhaps ten feet from nose to tail, and covered with silvery fur that gleamed in the moonlight like water. Their heads were narrow and pointed; I could see the open jaws, the solid ridges within that glistened wet. They ran swiftly, flowing around the base of the tree. As they did so, each one looked up, but when I gazed down into their faces, I saw with a shock that they were eyeless. There were no sockets, nothing but seamless fur. They made no sound and they did not pause. I crouched in the branches, paralysed, until they had gone.

When the creatures reached the edge of the clearing, however, they stopped. I saw them form into a pack, then fan out into a circle. I could not see anyone, but the seith told me that someone was there; a presence stepping out from between the rocks. Whoever it was carried with them a sense of the cold and the dark, a hollow emptiness that crashed in over me as though I had been picked up and flung into an abyss.

It felt a little like vitki, like Frey or the man I had met in Darkland, but it was far more powerful and I knew that I had never met this person before. Other than that, the seith could tell me nothing. But the beasts knew; I could hear the faint but unmistakable whine of welcome, and the murmuring reply. This voice made me shiver almost as much as the earlier cry had done, and I realized then that the voices were one and the same. Whoever had shrieked had been calling the beasts to them.

And then both human and pack were gone, so suddenly that I blinked. The sense of them was receding swiftly into the distance. The forest around me was empty except for the stir of waking birds and the rustle of the trees in the dawn wind. I dropped cautiously to the ground and went on.

There were no signs of the creatures in the clearing ahead, but their tracks were evident and there was a strong, pungent odour, heavy with musk. In addition, I found bootprints, presumably human, which scuffed about until they vanished into the rocks. But I also found something else that disturbed me, on the sharp rims of the stones – traces of blood. It was fresh, and had not had time to congeal.

I wondered at first whether the person – assuming it was human blood – had carelessly cut themselves climbing up onto the ridge, but the angle and the shape of the droplets seemed wrong. It was more likely that the person was already wounded, and had bled as they walked. They clearly did not care that their trail was visible to anyone who might care to follow them, or perhaps they were not wise to such things. That seemed improbable, though. If we were on a less primitive world, I might have considered it likely, but on this kind of planet people took note of such things as a necessity for survival.

I took the pack from my shoulder, found a swab and an analysis sachet from it, and touched it to a drop of blood, just in case. The presence in the clearing had borne no resemblance to Frey, but I wanted to make sure. However, the indicator on the analysis sachet, keyed into the sample of Frey's DNA that Idhunn and I had been sent from the hospital on Muspell, drew a blank. A native, then. The incident had disturbed me. I thought of those eyeless heads, glancing upwards.

Frey's pod must be around somewhere; he would not

have had the resources to conceal it very effectively, unless by some means of the vitki that I did not know about. I wondered if one could supply the parachute pods with a stealth function; I saw no reason why not. I set the implant to a 'locate' setting; the seith was not particularly helpful when it came to technology. Frey would have turned off any locator beacons, but there were signature traces that the pod would emit.

I climbed to the top of the ridge, keeping a cautious lookout for any signs of life, but there was nothing apart from flocks of what looked like water-birds, heading in v-formation over the forest. I wondered, and hoped, that the forest creatures I had seen were nocturnal. That raised the question of where they might go to ground during the day – they were surely too big for burrows, but with alien life-forms, one never knew. I did not want to risk stumbling over a lair. But there were no traces of their having passed up here. Perhaps they had headed into the deeper forest and rested amid the undergrowth during the day.

By now, the red rim of the sun was rising just above the mountains. It was cold, but pleasantly so, and a long way from freezing – though I could see snow up on the distant peaks and along the glacier wall. Beneath the ridge, the black-branched trees had a red glaze; when I walked down to investigate I found buds, crimson-tipped but ebony-coloured within. Shoots of a coarse golden grass were beginning to creep up through the earth. This, the temperature, and the movement of birds, suggested spring was on the way. A good time to visit Mondhile, I told myself. It would have been all too like Frey to carry out his mission in the depths of winter.

Standing on the spine of the ridge, I looked out across the forest. Patterns in the treetops suggested clearings, and there were other outcrops of the glossy dark stone, rising like pyramids from among the trees. I could see no score-mark from where a pod might have fallen, but perhaps, similar to my landing, Frey had brought his craft down gently into the forest. I set off along the ridge, scanning the land using all the resources that the Skald had given me.

It was early in the afternoon when I found the first traces of Frey's pod. Initially, I thought that the marks represented nothing more than storm damage, high in the spines of the black trees, but the scatter of burnt branches on the forest floor told me otherwise. I estimated the direction of its trajectory and followed it. The thorny undergrowth that had so plagued me in the less dense parts of the forest was no longer visible here, starved of sunlight and possibly deterred by the acidity of the soil, if these trees were anything like the conifers of Muspell. I thought with dismay of the candle-trees and the creature in the forest outside Hetla. Shed needles littered the ground like rust. I followed the trail of scorched wood until I came to a clearing, and there was the pod, standing upright with its surface colouring set to camouflage – russet and black.

It was reasonably well hidden. It seemed doubtful that people, or any of the native wildlife, would come this far into the deep wood without good reason, and at a casual glance the pod was invisible against the trees, but then I remembered the pale predators I had seen that morning; however, there were no tell-tale tracks in the needle-litter and I could smell nothing except resin and a faint dampness.

The seith lay alert but serene, revealing nothing, and I stood motionless among the trees, letting it move out from my body until it enveloped the trees themselves. To another person, I would be hard to see, but not invisible. To the more limited visual array of the pod, I was reasonably sure that I could not be seen. The implant was set to neutralize motion sensors.

My first action was to attempt to disable the pod. This would have to be done carefully, as it was probable that Frey had placed a trace on the craft to inform him if anything happened to it. I took a sensor from the pack, keyed it into the map implant, and ran it cautiously over the surface of the craft, taking care not to touch its shiny surface. I found one sensor on the base of the pod, which I deactivated, and another attached to the side of the transmission spire. A further search revealed no others. I ran a wire from the tabula into the spire and whispered the deactivation codes – a scramble, translated to me in turn by the implant.

It took some time: the pod had an inevitable sequence of firewalls and lockouts, relaying limited feedback into the tabula, but eventually I got there. There was a sizzling, satisfying hum as the pod uploaded its databank into the tabula and then powered down. It would not be permanently disabled, but I did not want to interfere with it further. If he needed to, Frey could key-in the codes, but he would have to re-set the navigational array and this would take time. If he made a run for it, it would at least slow him down. And more importantly, I now possessed information as to where Frey was heading.

When I uploaded the data into the map implant, his destination turned out to be a spot some distance to the north, perhaps five miles or so. Frey had a number of maps of the landscape that, though sketchy, were helpful enough. I found the ridge along which I had walked that morning and saw that it led to a string of small round lakes, nestling in the foothills that towered up to merge into the glacier wall. The implant put this into holographic display, so that I was looking into a tiny representation of the landscape where I stood. One of the maps was of the coastline, some ten miles away, detailing the area over which Frey had evidently flown; the edges merged into a misty vagueness, but now I had a firmer idea of where forest met sea, where a river lay, and the general lie of the land.

The last map, however, made no sense to me. I studied it from a number of angles, trying to work it out. It showed the same section of country as the previous maps, but criss-crossed with lines and blotches. Mineral deposits? They would not be paths, leading as they did through the deep forest. One of them ran parallel with the ridge, for instance, and I had seen no evidence of any man-made track that morning. Unless they were animal trails – though I did not see why someone with Frey's abilities would bother noting these. Most of the lines were depicted as faint, silvery traces, but some of them were black and red, and these led to a central nexus; a small circle high in the hills.

I did not know what this might mean, but it was clearly of significance to Frey. And anything that was of significance to him was relevant to me, too. I set off in the direction of the circle.

Although the place – if it was a place – lay only a few miles away, it was hard going. The dense conifers soon gave way to more deciduous forest, white-barked trees with thick roots that arched out of the soil. In summer, or the equivalent season, the canopy was probably dense, but now the crimson buds were only just beginning to show through and the forest floor was a mass of burgeoning vegetation: tall plants with pulpy leaves and delicate cups, in which insects struggled in a sticky fluid; curled golden ferns like bracken, which grew closely packed; thick treacherous moss surrounding swampy pools; some of these were covered by a dense mat of a lily-like plant, the buds swollen and ready to burst.

I slipped once, trying to avoid a knot of roots, and went into water up to one knee. I was unhurt, but my boot came up black with a clinging, stinking mud. Cursing, I carried on. This would be a botanist's paradise, like so many uncharted worlds. This class of planet, not so very dissimilar to Muspell, had the usual botanical analogues, but then I came across something that was unique in my experience, and very strange. At first, I thought it was a patch of mist, a low-lying vapour from the swamp. It hung in the air like a shadow, swallowing the light that filtered through the branches. But as I stepped past it, I had to look ahead to see where I was putting my feet, and out of the corner of my eye it resolved itself into a plant; a tall, pale thing with white fronds. I turned to look at it directly, and there was only the mist.

I did not want to touch, so instead, I picked up a fallen branch and prodded it, glancing at it obliquely. I saw the fronds draw back into themselves and puff out a dozen or so clouds of spores. Looking at it directly once more, the mist thickened. I was careful not to breathe any of it in, and kept watch on myself for the next few minutes. Who knew what toxins might be lurking in this uncharted territory? I was reminded of the bracket fungus in Darkland, the narcotic cypress that lined the streets of Hetla. It struck me that perhaps Frey's interest in this world might be botanical after all.

At last I came to the edges of this swampy stretch of forest. The white trees once more gave way to scattered conifers, and the black outcrops of stone that I had seen from the ridge. As I made my way among them, I became aware that I was climbing. The conifers became more and more infrequent until I was once more standing on a bare spine of rock, high above the treeline.

And that was when I first laid sight on the tower.

It stood on one of the outcrops, backed by the forest and eventually, in the distance, by the glacier wall: a massive, squat rise of pale stone. As I shifted position, however, the tower's colour changed, shadowing to black. Fascinated and unnerved, I moved to and fro, watching it alter with the light. I had no idea if this was deliberate – perhaps to confuse attackers – or whether it was simply some quality of the local stone. I had never seen anything like it before.

Looking at it, the tower was no more than a typical fortification, of the kind that was common to a dozen medieval worlds and had once been usual on Earth. The ancient brochs on Muspell had been similar. Defensive strategy dictated structure more than mere aesthetics, not to mention limited architectural capability. But the tower terrified me, and I did not know why. It might have been something to do with the way it changed with the light, yet the seith was screaming. I wanted to leave, now – forget about Frey and revenge and whatever he might be planning for this world; go back to the pod and float around in space for the next few days until Cane came to pick me up. Anything would be preferable to standing and staring at this thing. It was like looking into the eyes of the fenris. Any moment, I felt, and it would reach down and devour me.

I stumbled back down the slope to the nearest outcrop, narrowly avoiding a fall into the sharp scree, and huddled there with my back against some comforting, ordinary stone. I let the seith enfold me, merging me into the fields of the stone and the trees, and even though this was an alien world, they felt familiar; enduring and growing; enveloping me in their natural cycle. Gradually, the sense of panic receded, like an ebbing wave, and eventually was almost gone. Almost, but not quite. I could still feel the presence of the tower, an unnatural thing squatting in the midst of the natural world.

It must be some kind of defence, I thought, when I was able to consider things more clearly. It was something that affected the seith; which could mean that it was either technological, or psychological. There were ways of inducing panic and terror by means of devices. Military engineers had been developing them for thousands of years and some of them, on worlds such as Taman and Hatha-Khar, were extremely sophisticated. To the best of my knowledge, this was hardly a technologically advanced society, yet there had been mention of 'house defences' in the anthropologist's report. Perhaps the Mondhaith were one of those societies that had developed certain technical abilities faster than others; there was no inevitable linear progression of scientific knowledge, after all.

Tech aside, however, the only people I knew of who could disrupt the seith through mental effort – apart from the Skald – were the vitki, and this did not bode well. So the question arose: was this some naturally occurring phenomenon, a social product of local tech, or something that Frey had brought with him and was now trying out? And if the latter, then why do it here and not in Darkland, which certainly had few reservations about more dubious forms of experimentation.

I did not want to face that tower again, but I would have to. Studying the map implant, there was no question that it was the place indicated by the black circle. And I knew, at the visceral level of intuition – that had as much to do with vengeance as it did with the seith – that Frey was here. I had not known him as Aldur, but I knew him now.

It was growing late. Dusk was drawing over the land, casting the forest into indigo shadow. The glacier wall glowed above with the last light of the sun, then fell into silhouette. I did not want to approach the tower in darkness, nor did I want to risk another encounter with the pale predators. I climbed as high as I could among the rocks of the vitreous outcrop and settled down in the pad-bag with my back to stone. The first stars began to flicker out, but Grainne was not amongst them. I should have felt a longing for Muspell, but the seith was beginning to do its work, the field integrating into that of the landscape around me, knitting me into the world. It would not, I thought, be a seamless fit.

I ate some of the rations, waited until Grainne floated up above the glacier wall, then fell asleep under the distant light of my own sun.

I had a dream. I was back on Muspell, in another kind of forest. The conifers here were cloud-grey, and it was early summer. The short grass of the clearing was soft and damp beneath my bare feet and the light was falling. I could hear the howl of fenris far off to my left and knew that I was in Darkland.

I was not alone. A child sat on the grass, a short distance away. She was perhaps four years old. She wore ordinary clothes; a short-sleeved top and trousers. She, too, was barefoot. The grass around her was scattered with torn flowers, but she was no longer playing with them. She was staring at me, unblinking, but then I saw that she was blind. Her eyes were a silvery blankness, as though covered by an iridescent cataract.

'Who are you?' I asked.

'You know who I am,' the child said, and I stumbled back, for the voice was Frey's.

'You're Frey,' I said.

'No, but I am vitki. Look.' She held out a fragile hand and lightning shivered along her arm, a sudden blue electricity that shorted out on the damp grass and made the tattered flowers wither into ash.

'I have seith,' I said.

'You have nothing. It will not help you. It has passed you by.'

'I don't know what you're talking about,' I said.

'It's too late,' the child said. Her face was elongating, the eyes slanting outward, until a girl with the head of something that looked a little like a fenris, and a little like a pale predator was staring back at me. She opened her jaws and gave a high, strange cry. Fenris swarmed out of the trees and each one carried an eye in its teeth. I turned to run, but the child was standing directly in front of me and I fell over her, falling heavily to the ground.

I woke. It was close to midnight. All three moons had risen and were casting a pallid light down onto the forest. A child was indeed crouching some distance away; blank-eyed and naked. Its hair was a matted mass that reached the ground, concealing any evidence of gender, and its nails had grown to become long curving claws. It hissed at me, displaying sharp teeth, and then it turned and bolted away, down among the rocks.

At first I thought I was still dreaming, but when I eased myself out of the pad-bag and went to investigate the place where it had been crouching, I found scuff marks and small footprints in the soil. Even after studying the anthropologist's report, it was a shock to see a child in such a condition, out alone in this wilderness. I went slowly back to my shelter at the summit. It occurred to me that I might have taken the child's hiding place, and I wondered uneasily whether there might be others, and if so, whether they might take it into their heads to attack. On another level, it was reassuring to see that this land apparently supported human life. Mondhaith children might be different, but they were still kids. If a child could survive out here in the wild, then so might I.

I slept again, but lightly, with the seith on full alert. But nothing more disturbed me, and I did not wake again until just before sunrise.

TWENTY-SIX

PLANET: MONDHILE

When Gemaley came to him that night, Ruan said nothing to her of the conversation he had overheard. But he could not get the stranger's mocking words out of his mind, even when Gemaley lay naked in his arms.

'Do you often get other travellers here?' he asked, in a tone that he hoped was casual.

'Sometimes. People pass through, traders from over the Otrade, heading for the coast. Why?'

'I just wondered. I wondered if you've ever seen a migration.'

Glancing down at her, as she lay with her head on his shoulder, he saw her smile.

'We don't migrate, my kind.'

'What do you mean? You're human, aren't you? Everyone migrates, unless they're crippled.'

'We don't,' Gemaley said. She raised herself on one elbow to look at him. Her eyes were hard and icy, though her voice was idle enough. 'I told you. We're different.' She ran a hand down his chest, then lower, until he hardened in her grasp and forgot whatever it was that he had been about to say.

Later, however, he woke to find Gemaley gone, and the memory of the overheard conversation returned to plague him. He lay in the half-darkness, moonlight streaming in through the window, and thought of the stranger's words. What if this was what Gemaley did? Lured people to her, like some spirit out of legend, seducing and destructive? But if so, there would surely be evidence. The man in the forest had spoken of cellars . . . Ruan decided once more to go exploring.

The tower was silent, and again it had that empty-forever feeling. Nonetheless, Ruan was careful, and took particular pains to be quiet when he passed Gemaley's door on the ground floor. But he could hear nothing from within. Logically, the door to the cellar should be located in the stove room, and indeed he remembered seeing a door the day before, half hidden by the stove. The stove room was very dark, out of the moon's light, and although Ruan's night sight was good, he stumbled over the step. He stood very still, hoping no one had heard him. But there was no sound from the hallway.

He expected the door to be locked, but it opened easily enough. That in itself was a relief. If Gemaley had something to hide, surely she would take care to lock the door? A twisting flight of steps led downwards. It was too dark for Ruan to see. He fumbled across the rickety stove-room table until he found a taper and flint. The taper was hard to light and covered in dust, which smouldered up when he lit it. But it provided enough light for him to be able to see down the stairs. Cautiously, he went down into the cellar.

He did not know what he expected to find. At the back of his mind, remembering the stranger's words, he was steeling himself against some grisly discovery. But why would Gemaley bother? It wasn't as though the tower was filled with rich pickings looted from the bodies of her victims and he couldn't think of any reason other than robbery why she should bother to plan to kill. *Unless she was mad*, a voice whispered; let her entire self go into the bloodmind. Ruan ruthlessly suppressed that thought, because of its plausibility.

At the bottom of the steps lay a narrow passage. Ruan inched himself through it, the taper guttering in his hand. He smelled the air, alert for the scent of blood and death. But all that he was aware of was the dampness of old stone, rotting wood; earth that never saw the sun. There was an opening at the end of the passage but no door. Ruan stepped through.

It was the chamber from his dream: round, dank and empty. After a glance around him, Ruan expelled a long breath. The vision of corpses strung up to rot receded and was gone. He felt like a fool for doubting her. But just in case, he dropped to his knees and examined the earthen floor of the chamber. The soil was tightly packed, undisturbed. Ruan sent his senses down into it – sometimes you could feel buried bone – but there was nothing.

Then he was sent reeling, sprawling across the floor.

His head rang as though someone had struck him a great blow. The taper was extinguished in a shower of sparks, hissing out on the damp soil. Ruan got to his hands and knees but was again buffeted back. His mind spun.

Bruised and breathless, he reached out and felt rough, slimy stone against his fingertips. Whatever it was had knocked him against the wall. Then the dream was back again. He watched it happen as though it had been suddenly torn from his body: the soil opening up into a chasm, fathoms deep; a rift of darkness that felt as if the night had stretched out a tongue to gather him up and swallow him whole. His only point of reference was the wall. He dragged himself along it, with that pit swirling at the centre of the room, until his hand touched empty space. He was back at the entrance.

Filled with terror and relief, Ruan tried to roll through, but the space would not let him. He was pulled back into the room and hung for a dizzying moment over the pit. He looked down into an iridescent immensity, as though the whole world had fallen out from under him and left nothing but starlit darkness in its wake. He could feel it moving, snaking backwards and forwards as an unnatural and sinuous form.

The worst thing of all was not the drop itself, but the feeling of something watching him from its depths; something alive and aware, that knew him for what he was and which held nothing but hatred for him. But in the next moment he understood that it was not something in the well, but the pit itself that was watching. It was like the dark energy that he had encountered on his first meeting with Gemaley, and now he knew that this was its source, this sentient thing beneath the tower. And worse even than that was its seductiveness. He wanted it to devour him, to fill him with its power, to consume him utterly. It was, he realized with a dim horror, the same feeling that he got whenever he was with Gemaley.

Then, he felt someone clasp him by the wrist and drag him back. He was through the entrance, cowering on the floor. Light flared above him. He was staring up into the face of a ghost.

TWENTY-SEVEN

PLANET: MONDHILE

Next morning, it took me a long time to work up the courage to even look at the tower. The fear that had filled me on the previous day seemed to have grown overnight until it was almost palpable, and the incident with the child had not been reassuring. I told myself that I was behaving like a fool. The tower was nothing more than a building, half-ruined, probably abandoned. Frey must be using it for a base, nothing more – it was unlikely he would have befriended suspicious locals so quickly, though I knew only too well how manipulative the vitki could be. Doubtless the map depicted his movements, with his base clearly marked within it. He must have scouted it out during his first few days here. That was all the fear was, I told myself. That was all it was.

I packed up my meagre equipment and walked round the rocks at the outcrop's summit. There was the tower, squatting in the morning sunlight, shifting as I looked at it. My mouth was as dry as a bone. The tower was looking at me. I could feel it staring, just as one can sense eyes on

275

the back of one's neck. I forced my eyes closed – though it was like shutting one's eyes in front of a predator – and called on the seith. The seith curled outwards, unfolding like a leaf, incorporating me again into the fields of rock and air and trees. I stood there as calmly as I could, letting the seith do its work. When I opened my eyes again, I felt as though an invisible barrier had been placed between myself and the inimical presence of the tower. It was not quite enough to protect me from the revulsion I felt at its presence, but it was sufficient to allow me to look at it without wanting to run, and to permit me to walk with a reasonable degree of care down the slope towards it.

It was easier once I got among the trees. I could still feel the tower, but now it was almost out of sight behind the reddening treetops and I no longer had to look at it apart from the occasional glimpse through the bare branches. I knew, however, that I had to go to it. I was sure that this was where Frey was to be found.

In the months of my convalescence, I had spent days fantasizing about what I would do to Frey when I caught up with him. In some of these daydreams – or nightmares – I simply killed him. I had no plans for torture, though I thought he deserved it, and I was certain that Idhunn had agreed to its use. She had said as much to McGuirey, during the long course of my convalescence – though I did not think she had meant me to overhear. Torture was not a method used, or approved of, by the Skald, quite apart from its illegality on Muspell. Here, I was far from

Muspell, and no one would ever know, but the thought still revolted me. A quick clean killing would be best.

In some of my fantasies, however, Frey begged for my forgiveness, told me that it had all been some terrible mistake. He had been too late to save me from the fenris, maddened with grief, believing me to be dead. I knew that this was sheer nonsense, but in my weaker moments it comforted me a little to believe this. And in the true nightmares, it simply happened all over again: I was once more on the ice, with the beast's teeth tearing at my flesh, but sometimes it was Frey who stood over us, dispassionately watching, and sometimes the fenris was raping me; and then sometimes Frey was the beast itself.

I had not had one of these dreams for a long time now, despite the events on Nhem. The growing use of the seith had dampened it in me, and for that I was grateful. I had to allow for weakness when I saw him again. I told myself that I was prepared. I just wasn't sure whether I believed it.

I stepped through a gap in the trees and there was the tower again, high above me on its crag. There was no sign of any life around it and when I probed with the seith, cautiously, the tower felt old and dead, yet with that dreadful awareness clinging to it. Half of Muspell was said to be a home to ghosts, but I had never seen a place that was so obviously haunted. I could see a door, set some distance up the wall and reached by a short flight of steps. It was shut. In any case, there was no way that I was going through the front door. I crouched behind a grove of the black-barked trees and studied the tower.

It was still having an effect on me, but the seith was helping, and familiarity was rendering the sight of the building more bearable. I was not sure that I liked that: it was as though the tower was dulling my suspicions, luring me in.

I took a deep breath, turned my back upon it, and began searching the surrounding area for signs of Frey. I found none, but I could sense him: a lingering trace that rippled along the edges of the seith. For an instant, it was as though he was standing in front of me, and I caught my breath. But there was no one there, and nothing to betray where he had been, not even the last trace of a footprint.

But I did find signs of someone else. A long, pale hair clung to a thorn branch, gleaming like a silver thread. There were bootprints in the moist soil; a small, light tread that I was sure had been made by a woman. For a moment, the old flicker of jealousy came back, but I let it go. She had stood here, moving slightly; and here, where the black bark was a little flaked and crumbled, she had leaned, perhaps rested a hand against the tree. I could almost see her, tossing back the long hair with a careless hand.

I reached out and placed my hand an inch or so from the tree. She was slightly taller than I, it seemed. But she had not only left physical marks behind her. Like Frey, I could feel her in the air, the drifting linger of another soul. And the soul was a dark one, complicated, leaving patterns behind her that made the seith field flinch, as though someone had reached out to draw a chilly finger up my spine. I had never met her, and I disliked her already.

I stood, feeling her move around the trees, sensing the traces of the interaction of two people. They had stood and talked – and touched. I felt a connection that made my heart leap painfully. Then it was gone, so swiftly that I was not sure whether I had imagined it. That was the trouble with the seith: the impressions one picked up were often so subtle and faint.

It occurred to me then that I had invented this woman, summoned her up out of lost love and present hate – but then there was the silver thread, and the footprints. No, she was real. I remembered the person I had seen among the pack of pale predators, and wondered then whether they might be one and the same. But there was no sign here of the predators. Perhaps they did not like to come so close to habitation, if the tower was indeed still someone's dwelling place and not just a ruin – though the latter seemed more likely.

I scouted around the perimeter of the tower until late morning. I found another strand of hair and more footprints, this time leading down along a ridge that ran from the crag on which the tower stood. I was tempted to follow the ridge, leave the tower behind, but forced myself to clamber down from it instead and into the surrounding forest. I did not think the footprints were Frey's. The person who had made them was shorter and lighter than he was, but heavier than the woman. Even out of direct sight of the tower, I still could not help feeling that I was being watched. The sense of eyes upon me was very strong, but the seith held. I did not know whether the peculiar impression came from the tower itself, or from something else. Or someone. It was as though the forest was waiting, an electric anticipation which remained constant, neither growing nor decreasing.

I also found traces of the animals. Small slivers of fur clung to the lower branches of the thorn trees and the air around them smelled sour. When I plucked some of the fur from the thorns and examined it, I saw that it was fine and silky, a creamy white, banded with fawn along its length and black-tipped. There were pellets along the track, too; balls of skin and hair, containing a mesh of fine bones. These were substantial and seemed too large to have been regurgitated by a bird – unless it was a damn big bird.

I glanced uneasily upwards to the empty sky. The only avian life I had seen had been the water-birds, and I did not think that these bones were those of fish. They looked more like a rodent, being without the characteristic barbs of fish bones. But this was an alien world and I had to be wary of making unjustified assumptions, in spite of appearances.

Later, indeed, I came across a feather in the track, sticking bolt upright like an arrow. I crouched down to look at it. It was as black and glossy as the tree bark – a slender, pointed thing. It looked like a wing feather, a pinion. I ruffled it and the barbs immediately sprung back into place. If this had been Muspell, I might have taken it with me for luck – but that was a superstition from a world I knew and here I did not want to disturb anything more than I had to. Perhaps it was no more than the way it had fallen, but I could not help feeling that the feather had somehow been deliberately put in place. The seith prickled at the thought, reinforcing my intuition.

Standing once more, I considered what to do. I wanted to find a way into the tower, but the prospect presented me with a dilemma. I was terrified of the tower after dark, and it would be stupid to try and get into it during the day. I resolved to return to the outcrop and wait for twilight. It was not a happy medium, but it gave me more of a chance of meeting Frey. The vitki preferred the dark; as the name of their nation suggested, it suited their talents. Just as I had made this decision, however, I heard a sound.

It was not the sound of wind, or of a bird or animal. It was a very human noise: a door, creaking open, then slamming shut. I scuffed my footprints, then dived behind one of the black-barked trees and crouched, concealed in its new haze of scarlet needles. Once there, I sent out the seith field, imagining it spreading outwards from my body like a pool of water into which a stone has been thrown, layer upon layer of concealment. I could feel someone approaching through the undergrowth and I was suddenly certain that it was Frey.

My heart shrunk and withdrew within me, and my fingers clasped the grip of the projectile weapon. Now would be a good chance, I thought, when I was the person he was least expecting to see. There would be no confrontation, no explanations or justifications of his approaching death, no dialogue. I would simply shoot him, preferably in the back. And then it would be over and done with, and I could go home to Muspell and continue with my life. Even on the brink of war, a Frey-less Muspell would be a fine world, one less vitki for Darkland. I raised the weapon in preparation.

But the person who came into view was not Frey at all. It was a woman; a tall girl, perhaps in her early twenties. Her long braids were draped across her arm, out of the way of the thorns, and I saw a glitter from their tips, some kind of clasp. Her face was a pale oval, beautiful and cold, with blank blue eyes. I could see the curve of her long nails against her sleeve and they were more like claws. She looked as though she should have been portrayed in an ancient tapestry, in a long floating dress. Instead, she wore leather: trousers and a heavy coat that was tightly buttoned, even though it was not particularly cold.

She was smiling slightly, a small smug smile that reminded me immediately of the vitki. Her slight form seemed to be casting a greater shadow than it should. The forest darkened. I could feel her very strongly at the edges of the seith and I had to fight the fear back in order to prevent it from disrupting the field. Even a momentary flicker could betray me. I did not even understand why I should be so afraid; I was the one concealed, the one with the weapon most readily to hand.

But she did not glance in my direction. She walked on, dodging around the thicker clusters of thorns and stepping easily over the fallen branches that littered this part of the forest. She moved with the grace of familiarity. This place was known to her – somewhere she understood without even having to think about it. When she was a safe distance ahead, I ducked under the shower of red needles and followed, first checking to make sure that there was no one else behind her. But the forest was undisturbed in her wake, apart from the shadowy chill that she left behind her.

I followed her through the forest. She was heading for the outcrops, pushing her way through the trees and marching up the slope of scree. Even though she never glanced back, and gave no sign that she was aware of someone following, it was harder to pursue her unobtrusively even with the aid of the seith, and I was forced to take a roundabout route through the trees. I lost sight of her once and my heart sank, but then she appeared again at the top of the outcrop. She stood there for a while, legs braced, apparently quite at ease, though I wouldn't have risked standing so close to the edge of that sheer drop. She stared out across the forest. I wondered what she was looking for. I was certain that she was the figure I had seen before, and I expected to see the pale predators come swarming out of the trees. But nothing happened. After some twenty minutes, without making a sound, she climbed swiftly down the outcrop and went back among the trees. Again I followed her, as far as the edges of the crag on which the tower stood.

This time, however, she did not re-enter through the front door. She walked to the side of the crag, to a narrow crack where some of the rock had split away, then vanished behind it. I waited for her to come out again, but she did not appear. I stood behind a tree, gaze fixed on the crag, but she had gone. I sat down and waited. By late afternoon she still had not emerged and I was growing increasingly certain that this was a way into the tower, but the continuing daylight prevented me from acting immediately. Impatiently, I remained there until the sun cast its low and bloody light across the forest, and dusk began to fall. Then, I slipped through the shadows towards the crag.

Up close, the gap was wider than it appeared, angling deceptively out from the stone. Its edges were fire-blackened, suggesting a lightning strike, but other than an earthquake, I did not know of a natural force powerful enough to fragment solid rock. I could feel Frey, a strong, lingering presence, analogous to the odour of a fenris. And I could feel the girl, too.

It struck me that over the course of the afternoon, I had grown to hate and fear her, and I did not know why. Just a girl, that was all, but a girl from that tower. I could feel it above me as though it were about to fall and crush me under it, a dizzying moment of dismay that drew out into a prolonged nightmare. I tried to push it out of my mind and was only partially successful. I had to go on. I told myself that I had endured far worse than this – rape, betrayal, injury, loss . . . but the presence of the tower felt like violation, more so even than the Hierolath's actual assault. I remembered the anthropologist's report speaking of house defences; what if something was active here? The seith was alert, but was not warning me of anything.

Yet despite all this – indeed, because of it – I found another powerful emotion emerging within me: curiosity. What did the tower contain, to give it such force? It was that curiosity that drew me forward, into the gap.

By now, the sky had deepened to blue-green and I could see the first faint prickling of stars. I inched forward, trying to avoid leaving any traces on the walls, but it was hard going. The gap narrowed alarmingly at one point and I had to squeeze myself through. I could not sense anything beyond, but that did not mean that nothing was there. At last the gap widened again. By now, I could barely see but it had become apparent that the gap – created by whatever means – led to a man-made passage. Rock closed over my head, low enough to reach up and touch, and the walls were smooth, as though they had been worked with some kind of tool. Like the outcrop, the crag was glassy – the legacy, perhaps, of long-ago volcanic action. I moved cautiously on, listening out for anything ahead, grasping my weapon. I did not want to risk a light, but the darkness was increasing. Just as I was about to lose my nerve and head back, however, the tunnel itself changed abruptly to an archway in the rock. Ahead, I saw a glimmer of light. I peered through the archway. A lantern stood on a low table of stone, casting a flickering gleam across the walls of a long room, really more of a cavern. I dodged back as the shadow of a figure appeared against the wall.

This time, though, there was no sense of Frey, nor of

the woman. I looked cautiously through the arch and saw a young man, crouched over a lantern. My first impression was that he looked ill. He bore a striking resemblance to the girl: the same oval face; pale hair; lean figure. But his face was pinched, the cheeks hollow and sunken, and his hands were shaking as he reached for the lantern. He spoke in a stream of liquid syllables. I leaned back against the wall of the passage and keyed the map implant into the tabula.

The device took a while to connect, though I could now hear two voices. One was that of the young man, the other, a breathy female voice. I could not see who this belonged to – the person was standing out of sight – but somehow, I did not think that it was the girl who I had seen earlier. At last the tabula made the link, brought in the brief vocabulary download that had been in the anthropologist's report, and began relaying a fractured conversation into my inner ear. Gradually, as the tabula 'learned', the conversation became more comprehensible:

'. . . don't know where it is . . .' That was the boy.

'. . . isn't . . . she knows . . .' the female voice whispered.

'. . . won't tell . . .'

'. . . of course not . . . trust either of us.'

'I know that!' The woman sounded as if she would have liked to have been indignant, but did not have the energy.

'. . . wants it for herself . . .'

'What about him?'

'Who?' the young man said. 'Ruan, or the other one?'

'The other. I'm afraid of him. She says I have no reason

to be, but I am. She leaves the defences down for him, he can come and go as he pleases.'

'He isn't human,' the young man said, as if he were agreeing.

'He wants us dead.' She spoke with a solemn conviction that was almost amusing, a childlike exaggeration.

'You don't know that.' But the young man did not sound sure to me. There was the sound of movement and then the lantern light swung upwards. 'It isn't here. There's no point in looking for it.'

'We should go back,' the woman said. I got the impression that she was relieved, as though he had brought her down here, persuaded her against her will, perhaps, and now she was secretly pleased at their failure to find it, whatever it might be. Her next words confirmed that impression. 'She'll be angry, if she finds us down here.'

I expected the young man to brush aside her fears, but instead he whispered, 'Yes, I know. And we should go.'

I slipped after them as they retreated through the cavern. There was another passage at the far end of the chamber and I took it. Still there was that sense of Frey . . . Still I could feel the tower above me, but its animosity seemed buffered by the rock; there was the sense of dampened power, like a roaring behind a sealed door.

At least with the lantern up ahead, I was able to see. The pair did not look back, evidently not anticipating pursuit. I caught sight of the woman – a girl in fact, with a slight, frail figure, trailing along behind the boy, and half-concealed in a cloak with a ragged hem that dragged along the floor, as if it had originally been intended for someone taller. She looked like a child, dressing up, but I remembered the child I had already seen and it made me shudder.

They turned a corner and I was alone for a moment in the flickering dark. In all probability I would have to make my way back through here, so I began taking more careful note of smells – the dampness of the floor, patches of mould – and the textures of the wall beneath my fingertips: rough, then smooth, then slimy . . . There was the light again, bobbing ahead. I heard a door opening, then being quietly closed. I waited for the click of a lock or bolt, but there was only the receding sound of footsteps. I waited by the door for a few minutes, then gently opened it.

A long room, lit by the embers of a dying fire. Heaps of fur covered the floor and I remembered the long, fine hair that I had held in the forest, brindled fawn and cream. A number of the predators had ended up as rugs and I wondered whether this was one of the reasons why the girl had summoned them to her; a method of hunting, a lure. I'd heard of such things on Muspell – and they said Frey was a beast-caller, after all. Perhaps the predators served as food, too, for these more primitive societies tended not to be primitive at all when it came to using resources. There were few enough folk that were carnivores, but remembering the girl's talons, and the shadows that had clung to her presence, the notion did not entirely surprise me.

There was little furniture, only a chest, which was locked. It looked as though someone had tried to break it open; the wood was splintered and cracked. I wondered what it contained. I stood beside it and listened to the seith for a brief moment. Oppression of age, and the weight of the tower above and below me, were tearing me in two; and *presence*. There were people here, many of them. The room was suddenly crowded with the clamour of voices; hands clawing at my face; the stink of desperation as though the long hall were nothing more than a tiny cell. I stumbled back, closing myself into the seith as I did so, and the sensation ceased. But the oppressiveness of the building remained. I forced myself to go to the end of the hall and through a door.

The front door of the tower stood at one end of an atrium. I entertained a fleeting idea of bolting out into the darkness. Whatever horrors the night might contain, they would be an improvement on this building, I felt. I might actually have acted on this impulse, if I had not heard footsteps coming down the stairs.

I dodged back into the hall and peered through a crack. It was very dark. I had to rely on the other-sight of the seith to allow me to see properly and I felt, as so many times before, that despite the loss of my eye, it was the seith that gave me the more reliable vision.

Another young man was standing in the atrium, looking about him with apparent indecision. I saw a narrow face with a curved nose, the same sweeping, angled features as the girl in the forest, but something told me that this was a racial resemblance, not a genetic one. He wore similar clothes, but they looked as though they had been cared for, and the sleeves of his shirt were decorated with stylized embroidery. After a moment, I realized that it depicted birds in flight. I could make out wings and long, curling beaks.

His eyes were soft and black, and there was none of the girl's cold presence about him, just a weariness and pain that seemed at odds with his years. He had a gentle face, I thought, and he felt to me as though he did not belong to the tower. But in that case, where had he come from and why was he here?

The young man appeared to make up his mind. He turned and walked towards a door at the far end of the atrium, then vanished through it. Curious, I followed. He dithered about in the kitchen for a moment, then a light flared up. He shoved the stove aside and tugged at a small door that lay behind it. I waited until he had disappeared into the shadows beyond, then followed.

Immediately, the oppressive atmosphere worsened. Gasping, I leaned back against the wall for a moment. The light ahead of me swayed. I focused on its floating presence and steadied myself, then went on. The young man led me back down a flight of stairs into a passageway. How was it, I thought, that he could not feel what lay at its base? For it was here, the seith told me, that the tower stopped – indeed, the world itself came to an end, as though we were approaching the edge of a gulf of empty space. And yet, it was not empty. Something was living in it, something that knew me – and hated.

I could not believe that this gentle-faced young man knew what he was walking into. If he did know, then that was even more worrying. But in the next moment, the seith impacted with his terror as he was pulled through into what lay beyond. I had the choice to run back. Instead, I ran forwards, trying to blank out the hating thing ahead of me, under an arch. The seith would not let me go any further; it was as though two curved glass shields had struck one another and then ricocheted off. I staggered back, looking into the maw of the world, but the young man was sprawled at my feet. One hand was flung through the arch; I grabbed him by the wrist and pulled as hard as I could. He fell heavily against me and I jumped back, but he was safe, away from the maw. It battered the space of the arch like a thundering wave.

'We have to go!' I cried. I heard the tabula echo it, in the language used by the two people earlier. I hoped that he understood.

'You are a ghost!' I heard him exclaim.

'What? I don't mean you any harm. Come with me.' I hauled him upright. He clambered to his feet and I dragged him up the stairs. He was shaking, and even behind the protection of the seith, I was not much better. Together, we made our way back through the passage and up the stairs. Even with the other-sight, I almost fell, and took the young man with me. We stood against the wall for a moment, our breath loud and ragged in the silence.

The door to the kitchen was locked. Dismayed, I hammered on it, and it shot open. The kitchen beyond blazed with light. It dazzled me. I flung up my hand to shield my sight, and when at last it adjusted, I saw that someone was standing in front of the door, holding a burning torch. The smell of pitch was strong, thick and tarry. Through the smouldering smoke, I saw that it was the girl from the forest. Her eyes were fixed on me and she was smiling, her head a little on one side. The look on her face was almost enough to send me back down the stairs.

'So,' she said, and the tabula faintly echoed, 'we have another visitor.'

TWENTY-EIGHT

PLANET: MONDHILE

'You thought you'd go exploring, I see,' Gemaley said. They were back in the bedchamber. She reached up and curled her arms round Ruan's neck. 'That was very brave of you.' He could not tell if her tone was contemptuous or not.

'What is it under this place?' Ruan whispered. He detached her grip and pushed her away, holding her a little distance from him. There was a sudden spark in her eyes, but he still could not read her expression; as ever, she wore the same smiling mask.

'What is what?' There was definitely a touch of mockery in the echo.

'That – thing. Down below the tower. There's something living down there.'

'Oh, Ruan.' She ducked her head and looked at him askance. *Now you're just being silly*. Her cruel coyness irritated him. 'It's only a well. Hundreds of years ago, so my clan told me, the tower was built over a shaft in the rock, and they excavated it so that there would always be fresh water in times of siege. It's a wonder that the tower hasn't fallen down, really, with such foundations. But it's not very wide. We don't use it now. There was a tremor in the land, long before anyone in my clan remembered, and the water level shifted. Now, it comes out as a spring, a little distance down the crag, and we don't need the well.'

'It's more than a well, Gemaley.' He wanted to say: *It's alive, and it hates me* – but up here in the bedchamber, with the morning light streaming in, it seemed so melodramatic.

Gemaley frowned. 'But what else could it be?'

'I don't know.' He stared at her. She sounded so reasonable and he was beginning to feel foolish. 'What about your house defences?'

She looked blank. 'They're just the defences, nothing more. They're drawn from the energy line. We leave them down half the time, anyway.' She gave a sudden little laugh. 'Nothing comes here unless they're *meant* to come, anyway.'

He decided to ignore that. 'And what about that – the ghost?'

'There was no ghost, Ruan.' Now she was frowning in earnest.

'But I saw her. She was tall, with dark hair. She touched me and she felt real. She felt like—' he was going to say, *like the stranger from the forest*, but something stopped him.

'There was no one there. You came up the stairs and fell out into the stove room. You kept saying something, but it

294

didn't make any sense.' She stepped forward and put her hand on his arm. 'Gith and I took you upstairs. Ruan, are you water-sensitive?'

'Yes, to some extent. I can feel springs under the rocks, channels. It's a trait in our clan.'

'I think you must be particularly sensitive. If there's a body of water – which there is beneath this crag – then with some people, it can cause confusion. I'm not a water-tracker, myself. I'm more of a mineral person. But Tian suffers from it, sometimes, depending on her cycle.' Her eyes were wide with earnest concern and he wanted so badly to believe her.

'You think that's what it was, then?'

'I'm sure of it. And the ghost you saw – sometimes one sees people from the past here, from the ancient days of this clan. Their essence gets trapped in the landlines, so that they can't enter the world of the dead. But they're just shadows, nothing more.' Her grip on his arm tightened a little. 'You've been unconscious for several hours now. It obviously had a powerful effect on you. You mustn't go down there again, Ruan. The body's energies are all directed into healing when one has suffered an injury, and it can weaken you, especially if you're already sensitive to something. You ought to rest today.'

'I think I will,' Ruan said. He felt exhausted and bruised, but more than that, her words made it possible for him to once more defer the decision whether to stay or go. When she had gone, he sank back onto the bed and slept. He did not wake again until the late afternoon, with the shadows lengthening across the floor. When he went to the window, it was to discover that the air outside was mild, and he had a sudden longing for space.

To his relief, the door was unlocked. He went straight down to the hallway. The front door was wide open, letting sunlight and freshness through into the musty dimness of the hall. The tower seemed like a different place today and Ruan's spirits rose. Those persistent wishes came back: of staying here with Gemaley; restoring this place; looking after her. If he had to care for Gith and Tian as well, Ruan told himself, he would do so. He felt expansive, filled with the generosity of potential responsibility.

He walked down the path that led from the crag and sat on a nearby rock, looking out over the woods. As he did so, even at this little distance from the tower, it was as though a mist lifted from his mind and reality crept in like refreshing waves from the sea, to douse his dreams. He had a clan and a home of his own, people who must be concerned about him, family who must surely think him lost or even dead. Ruan blinked. It seemed unbelievable that he had not thought about this before. And Gemaley herself, so strange. He was suddenly sure that the ghost had been no mere figment of his imagination, but a real person, as real as the mysterious man from the forest. And as for the well – there was a horror beneath the tower, not just a shaft for water. He had known all along, ever since the line of dark energy had snapped and held him. Yet somehow, he had stopped paying attention . . .

Ruan stood, in sudden decision. It was no more than

late afternoon. He would keep walking, in the direction of the mountains, and follow the river down to the estuary, and home. He knew the way. All he had to do was take it. If he saw Gemaley again, he knew, the impulse would be gone; she would talk him out of it – no, not even talk. The will to leave would drain from him like water, leaving him compliant and empty. No farewells. He was leaving.

Ruan stood, and just as he took his first step into the woods, the scream came from the tower. His first thought was of Gemaley. He ran back up the crag, hardly noticing that his ankle was now entirely free from pain, and through the door.

It felt as though the scream was still echoing around the walls of the tower, but the place was silent. The sudden crash of the heavy wooden door slamming shut behind him made Ruan leap around. Gemaley stood by the door.

'What are you doing, Ruan?'

'I heard something. A scream. Was it you?'

'Of course not,' Gemaley said.

'Then it must have been Tian.'

Gemaley shrugged. 'I've just been up to see her. She was fast asleep. If she screamed, perhaps she was having a nightmare.'

'But didn't you hear it?'

'I heard nothing.' She was gazing at him in innocent incomprehension. He was immediately, crushingly certain that she was telling the truth. 'If someone had cried out,' Gemaley went on, 'then I would have been certain to hear it.'

'Perhaps I imagined it,' Ruan heard himself say.

'It might have been a bird or something. There are ghaiths in the roof of the tower – they make a noise sometimes. They don't often wake during the day, but things can disturb them.'

'It sounded human.'

'It can't have been.'

There was a pause. Surely Gemaley was right. A last thought of returning to the clan floated to the surface of his mind like a bubble, then evaporated. Gemaley stepped forward and took hold of his arm. 'I have something for you.'

'What is it?'

'Come and see.'

She led him into the stove room, where three plump oroth lay upon the table, their eyes glazed in death. They were big birds, larger than the little oroth down by the estuary, and still clad in the last of their winter feathers.

'I went hunting this morning. I found them on the lake. And I sent Gith out to get some proper wood,' Gemaley said. 'I thought we could build the fire up and roast these over it.'

'That's a good idea,' Ruan said, startled by this sudden domesticity.

'I thought we should start living better.' She sounded almost shy. 'Don't you agree, Ruan?'

'Yes, of course. You should be a proper family, Gemaley.'

She looked up at him, her slanted eyes bright beneath the fall of her hair. 'But we are, Ruan. Aren't we?'

Later, however, it was clear that Gemaley had little idea how to cook properly. She kept poking the oroth with the end of a blade, frowning as she crouched by the fire. Tian, murmuring under her breath, fumbled with the end of the spit.

'Let me do it,' Ruan said. He could not bear to see either of them manage this so badly. Another moment and the birds would be in the fire. He could feel the girls watching as he flicked the spit around and prodded an oroth's stout leg. Clear juice, still slightly tinged with blood, trickled out and hissed into the embers.

'They're not quite ready. A little while longer, perhaps.'

'You're good at this,' Tian whispered. She sounded surprised.

'Of course I am. We all have to take turns at cooking, at the clan house.'

'We never cook,' Gemaley said. 'There's not much point, is there?' Her earlier enthusiasm seemed to have disappeared. 'There's nothing you can't eat raw.'

'But it tastes better cooked,' Ruan said persuasively. They both looked unconvinced. The oroth were done now. He slid the birds from the spit and divided them onto a platter that Gemaley had found in the stove room. Ruan had had to snatch it from her and wash the dust and vermin droppings from it. Gemaley had looked at him with quizzical amusement, as though he were prone to eccentricities that she could only tolerate, not understand.

'Where's your brother?' He had divided the birds as evenly as he could into four portions. Gemaley shrugged.

'Gith's busy.'

'What's he doing?'

'I don't know.' Her face was hidden behind her hair. Tian shot her a glance that would, Ruan thought, have been nervous if the girl had not continued to look so vague.

'Just eat,' Gemaley said. 'Gith can have something later, if he wants.' She sounded indifferent, and again Ruan could not help contrasting this to the close-woven concern of his own clan, where everyone looked after everyone else. He could not imagine failing to do so. It was the only way that a clan could survive – but of course, Gemaley's family had not survived. They ate in silence.

After the meal, Gemaley muttered something, rose abruptly and went through the door. Ruan thought that she had probably gone to the stove room, but when she did not come back, he went after her, taking the remaining bones of the birds with him. The stove room was empty. Ruan put the platter down on the table and wandered back to the main hall. As he did so, Tian bolted up the stairs.

'Are you going back to your room?' Ruan asked, with a smile. It was important to be kind to Tian, he felt. She was like some small wild animal who ought, eventually, to respond to patience.

'Yes.'

'Don't you want to stay by the fire? It'll be warmer.'

'I don't want to be around when— I don't want to hear.'

Ruan frowned. 'Hear what?'

'You know.'

'I don't understand—' But she was gone, fleeing up the spiral stairs with her ragged skirts swirling around her. Ruan went back into the main hall but Gemaley was not there. It felt as though everything was falling apart. The memory of the place he had found underneath the tower lay at the bottom of his mind – an unhealed wound. He went in search of Gemaley. She was nowhere to be found and he did not dare open the door in the stove room again. Instead, he went out through the back door and onto the crag. The defences were still down.

The sky was the water-green of twilight, already bright with a scattering of stars. Ruan could hear the sound of birds drifting up from the crag, and then realized that they were not birds at all, but voices. Gemaley and the stranger from the forest, perhaps? He followed the sounds, fearful of what he might find. They led him down, the way to the forest, but they were coming from under the crag itself. Ruan investigated and discovered a narrow gap leading into the rock. Here, the voices were louder, echoing from the walls.

'*Who is she?*' This was Gemaley, sounding furious.

Someone laughed; a male voice, the stranger. 'Someone I knew, a long time ago.'

'And you brought her here, to my home?'

'I didn't bring her, Gemaley. She followed me. Just as I hoped she would.'

'It is the same thing, then,' Gemaley said, sullenly. 'You brought her.'

'I brought her for you,' the stranger said, and his voice was suddenly infused with a warmth that made the hair rise at the back of Ruan's neck.

'For me? For the well?'

'No, not for the well. You have to begin thinking in a wider context, girl. For you yourself.'

'But—'

'Don't argue with me, Gemaley.'

'She's strange,' Gemaley said, after a moment. She sounded even more sullen. 'She's like you. A ghost, and yet not a ghost. She is not human, all the same. She has no clan markings. But she has all the senses she should have – I can tell.'

'Of course she has those senses. She is my sister.'

'Your *sister*?'

'Not my sister in blood. We come from different places, different families. But she is my sister in spirit and in ability.' The stranger's voice had become lingering, and Ruan liked this even less. 'But she ran away from me, to a place where I could not follow her. To a place of witches.'

'Witches?'

The word was unfamiliar to Ruan, and also evidently to Gemaley, if the questioning note in her voice was anything to go by.

'The tabula doesn't seem to have an analogue,' the stranger said. 'Ah. Satahrach.'

'A place of elders?' Gemaley said. 'Why couldn't you bring her back, if she means so much to you?'

'They wouldn't let me. They don't trust power. Not like you.'

'And she can't have trusted you much either, if she ran away.'

'She didn't understand what I was trying to do.' Ruan did not know whether he was imagining it, but there seemed to be an uneasy note in the stranger's voice. 'She should have done as I told her, and then everything would have been all right. But she thought she knew best.' The threat was clear, at least, Ruan thought. 'So she ran away.'

'At first I thought her wound was a new one,' Gemaley said, consideringly. 'Her face was falling off. But now I see that it is old, and she is wearing someone else's face upon her own.'

The stranger laughed again. 'It's not her face. It's just a mask, a disguise. See? It's like a soft shell.'

'I've never seen such a thing before.'

'No, I don't suppose you have. But they're common enough, where we come from.'

'She must have been badly hurt,' Gemaley murmured. 'Her eye is missing. And these scars . . . they look like the marks of claws.'

'Very good, Gemaley. That is exactly what they are.'

'What kind of animal was it?'

'The kind that is an ally. You understand that, don't you?'

'Of course I understand.' Gemaley's voice had once more grown cold.

'Yes, I know you do. And that's why I'm going to take you away, Gemaley.'

'What about her?'

'She's coming too.'

'But I thought—'

'You don't understand. Vali will be your teacher, until such time as you don't need her any more.'

'I don't need teaching!' It was a hiss. 'I know all that I need to know.'

'For here, maybe. For the tower, and the woods, and the mountains and lakes. For your visen pack. For the place where you will grow old and bitter and narrow if you remain in it. But there is a wider world out there, Gemaley, and you should play a part in it. In my world. You don't want to stay here forever, do you? With your weak brother and sick sister? With the waifs and strays that you entice from the path . . .'

'No,' Gemaley said after a moment. 'I do not.'

'Very well, then. I think we will begin your training.'

And that, Ruan discovered, was when the screaming began again.

TWENTY-NINE

PLANET: MONDHILE

At first, I thought I was dreaming. I was in a place I recognized: one of the chambers in the depths of the Rock, where the tide enters. I glimpsed wet walls and I was sure that I could hear the boom and crash of the sea. Soon, I thought, the tide would come in. I even thought I could feel the salt spray on my face. I reached out with the seith, but it was in tatters, fraying out from me like ribbons of gauze to dissipate into the air. I might as well have been naked, stripped down to sinew and bone. The side of my face felt raw and exposed as though the skin had been torn from it, and the next moment I realized that this was exactly what had happened. The synth mask had been ripped away and to me, all this meant only one thing. Frey had found me.

I did not need the seith to tell me that he was here. I could neither see nor hear him. There was a rushing sound filling my ears and my head was locked in one position, secured by some kind of bond so that it was tilted at an angle, looking upwards. But I could feel him; the old sense of his presence. Wherever we had been, I had always been able to tell exactly where he was – except for Nhem. I do not know whether it was some latent function of the seith, or simply a lover's paranoia, but I had known then and I knew now.

He was moving around the chamber, treading with animal lightness. Surreptitiously, I tugged at the bonds that secured my wrists and ankles. There was no give in them at all.

'Frey?' I said. He had not bothered to gag me. He did not reply. 'I know it's you.'

'Of course you do,' he said, and I felt my heart start at the sound of his voice. 'I knew you'd follow me, Vali. You did a good job. Of course, I made it easy for you.' Had he always sounded so condescending? But that, too, was making it easier for me now; honing old emotions into newer hate. 'So,' he went on. 'Did the Skald send you, or did you come on your own?'

'The Skald, what do you think?' If he thought I had support elsewhere, it might delay whatever he was going to do. But I did not really believe this.

'The Skald. I'm sure you've proved a great asset to them.' He sounded almost approving. I said nothing. 'Like Nhem, for instance. An effective operation. Subtle, very risky, but it worked.'

'You should know. You were there. Why, Frey? What did you want from Nhem?'

'You should take it as a compliment. I went to a lot of trouble to see how you'd – developed.' Now, he was reproving: a teacher chiding an ungrateful student. 'I didn't mean to abandon you on Nhem, but I had no choice. The special forces militia started sniffing around shortly after you'd gone; I wanted to draw them away from you. I don't expect you'll believe that.'

'That's a lie. You went to the laboratory. The one in the mountains. Why?'

'Oh, you're quite wrong about that, Vali.'

'And the only trouble you've gone to is to try to have me savaged to death by a wild animal and then murdered by a bunch of atavistic barbarians.'

'Is that what you think?'

'It's what I know, Frey.'

'You've never entertained the possibility that that episode on the icefield was just an accident? That I tried to save you, but it was too late?'

His voice was warmer and rougher than it had been a moment ago. This was the conversation I had dreamed of having with him, in the early days of my recovery, before the hate hardened like ice in the winter dark. But if this was what I had longed to hear him say, then why was I filled with such sick, sinking dismay?

'I don't know, I—'

'Well, I don't suppose you'd believe me about this, either, even if I knelt at your feet and pleaded.' His tone was back to indifference. 'And I don't want to return you to traumatic memories, so we ought not talk of it further. But you should know this: I hoped you'd come here. I hoped you'd follow me. Not for revenge, or to finish what you think I started.'

'You wanted me here? Why?'

'Because I need your help. I wasn't sure what I'd find here, but it's much as I suspected. And you and I both have the chance to be so much more than Muspell could offer us. More even than Darkland's petty concerns can give.'

'I don't understand.'

'You will, Vali. You will.'

And then it started. At first, I did not understand what was happening. I could no longer see. The vision in my good eye was blanked out as swiftly and abruptly as if someone had put out the sun, and I was unable to see through the seith. It was the rape on Nhem, the Hierolath's hands crawling over me; an insect rustling that stirred my hair and skin into a burning itch. But this time I was the Hierolath, filled with obscene excitement and the anticipation of pain. I could see down the filthy channel of the Hierolath's memories and it was like peering into a sewer – with all that had been done to him as well as all that he had done, and wished to do. And under all that was the memory of my brother.

I knew that it couldn't be real. The seith would not have picked up so much over the course of the rape, and in any case, I had rid myself of it on Muspell, at the broch – long ago in the case of my brother. I tried to tell myself that whatever psychological contamination I had been infested with during the rape was gone, down into cold salt sand and the fresh air of the sea. I told myself this, but I could not believe it. It was too immediate, too real; I could smell the Hierolath, the lanolin stink of unwashed hair and skin. I could smell myself.

And under it all was the presence in the tower – something that sucked all the pain and anger through me, and wanted more, and shrieked inside my head, thunderous, when it did not get it. When the memories of the rape had drained away, I knew it would go looking, hunting further back, to the carefully managed recollections of the fenris attack.

'Stop!' I heard myself cry out from a great distance away. 'Stop it! I can't take any more.'

'All right, for now,' Frey said. He sounded frustrated and annoyed, but I did not know why. The draining sensation did not cease. Then, more sharply, 'Gemaley!'

It stopped. I lay gasping within my bonds. I felt hollowed-out and empty, and at the same time, horribly full of emotions that were only partly my own.

'It's not working,' Frey said, and the anger was clear. It took me a minute to realize that it was not me he was talking to.

A woman's voice said, with feral spite, 'What did you expect? I told you, didn't I? It will not come yet. Do you think I am a fool, who does not know what she's talking about?'

'Then we will try again.'

'No!' I had not meant to speak. Frey laughed.

'All right. We'll let you be for the moment. Don't want to wear you out, after all.'

'Why is she like this?' I heard the voice say and now I was certain that it was the girl I had seen in the forest, the girl from the tower.

'Like what?'

'So strong. She can take pain, and take and take.'

'But the bloodmind still does not come, does it?'

'But it is there, in her. I can feel it. How does she take so much?'

'It's an ability called the seith. It's a kind of extra sense. You have it yourself – you can sense water and minerals. But there are disciplines by which it can be honed, to give personal protection, and that's what Vali here has undergone.'

'I would like to learn that,' the voice said, with a calculation that made me colder than her eagerness had done. I could hear the humming of the tabula underneath her words: they must have placed it nearby, unless it was Frey's own device that I was listening to.

'And so you shall,' Frey said, indulgently. I heard her give an impatient hiss of breath; she did not like being treated like a child. But remembering the anthropologist's report, I wondered even what that meant here. 'But give it time. There are other things that must be put in place. The well, for instance. You have to learn to draw on the well. Vali is not an inexhaustible resource. You mustn't use her up just yet.'

Don't eat all your sweets at once.

Had he spoken to *me* like that? I could not remember, but it horrified me to think that I might not even have

310

noticed. Had that accounted for the occasional amused glances that other people had given me, when Frey and I were together? Even under these circumstances, and years later, I felt myself grow clammy with shame.

'When, then?' Her voice had grown remote, and even colder.

'Soon, Gemaley.'

A light footstep and then she was bending over me. I looked up into her pale, etched face, the winter-blue eyes that had no whites, only a faint frosting like ice over a lake. She smiled, showing small sharp teeth.

'Well,' she said. 'So you are my new teacher. Welcome to the tower.'

'Who are you?' Her presence was as oppressive as that of the tower and in the next instant I wondered whether it was really the tower itself that had such an atmosphere of darkness about it, or whether that came from this girl.

'I live here.'

'This is Gemaley,' Frey drawled. 'You'll be seeing quite a lot of her, in the days to come. Now say good-bye, Gemaley.'

She did not speak, but gave a slight nod, as if satisfied. Then they both went away. I heard their footsteps retreating along the stone. And they seemed to take all my will with them. I could feel it draining away, as though they had opened a vein in me and let the blood seep out to spill across the floor. I tried to summon the seith, but it was like trying to grasp strands of mist. I gave a half-hearted tug at my bonds, but they remained firm. I slumped in their grip, a passive, blank thing, until Gemaley returned.

Despite my numbed state, I knew at once when she came back. I could feel her approaching presence like a cold slap against my skin. Then she was once more standing over me. This time, she was not smiling.

'You're awake. That's good.' From its place on a nearby ledge, the tabula once more began to hum, translating her words. 'That thing, the little box. It translates what you say into Khalti – so Frey tells me – and what I say into *your* language, whatever that may be. Can you understand me?'

'Yes.'

'Even better.' She ran a sharp nail down my unscarred cheek. I felt it split the skin and I gasped at the sudden pain. 'There, that's better. Soon, both sides will match.'

'Why are you doing this to me? What do you gain from it?'

'You don't plead with me not to hurt you. I like that. Frey likes to hear pain and pleading, but I prefer strength.'

'I'll ask you again,' I said through gritted teeth. 'Why?'

'Why? For power.' she said, as if I were simple. 'This is how I get it.'

'Why do you need it?'

Above me, I saw Gemaley frown, as though this was the first time she had ever considered such a question. 'Why do I need it?' she echoed. 'Because it is there for the taking. What else would I do with it?'

'But what do you actually do with it, once you have got

it? You live here in this ruin, dress in old clothes . . . Why don't you use the power that you have?'

Gemaley was still frowning. 'Those are good questions. Obviously you are not a stupid person. I enjoy power. That used to be enough. Then Frey came, and he told me about other places, far from here, where I could use what I had gained, to my own advantage.' She paused. 'Do you know, at first I was not sure whether I wanted that. The power – the sensations that it gave me – they were all that I needed.'

'You are using the past tense.' At least she was talking to me. And if we could talk, perhaps some connection might be made between us – all the old adages about hostage situations came straight into my mind.

'It's not enough any more. It doesn't give me what it used to.'

'And what was that, really, Gemaley?'

'Pleasure,' she whispered. She reached down and I felt her hand working its way into my tunic until she touched bare skin. The cool hand slid up my breast. I lay very still, rigid, hardly daring to breathe. She pinched the nipple, gently. 'There,' she murmured. 'Isn't that better?'

'Don't touch me!'

'Don't you think it's hot in here?' She shrugged off her long coat and let it fall to the floor. Then she was unfastening my tunic, baring my breasts, and her long hair swished over them like silky water.

'Gemaley, don't—' But she bent her head and her mouth was trailing across my skin, licking and sucking.

313

'Much better,' I heard her say. And I could not do anything to resist. I had never been attracted to women, but under this light touch I wanted Gemaley as badly as I had ever wanted Frey. But through it all I could still feel her sipping at the place within my mind where the seith lay, taking and taking, until my vision went dark and I could no longer see, only feel. Her hand was between my legs, touching bare flesh, and then her fingers were inside me. I felt her claws slide out, tearing the membranes within me. I could hear myself screaming, though I tried to hold it back. At last the pain stopped. I lay gasping and my sight slowly cleared. Gemaley was once more standing over me. Her eyes were as blank as the holes of a skull. Blood and vaginal juices were smeared across her lips. Slowly, step by step, she walked backwards from me, out of sight, and left me to pain and shame.

THIRTY

Planet: Mondhile

Ruan watched from his hiding place, spellbound, as Gemaley bent over the ghost. Of course women did such things together, that was natural, but there was still a dreadful lingering wrongness in this. He could see that Gemaley was hurting the ghost, for the woman's body stiffened and twisted even as she responded. He wanted to step forward and stop Gemaley, but he was rooted to the spot. It was as though Gemaley was throwing out a kind of force. Ruan's vision swam and darkened through the haze of his own arousal, and the humiliation of watching and being unable to do anything. He tried to break free, but he could feel Gemaley behind him, even as he watched her, holding him in a vice. She was in several places at once; he could not understand it.

The ghost arched and twisted against the strips of leather that secured her to the bench, a mockery of climax. By now, Ruan was painfully hard, but his own desire disgusted him even though he could feel the bloodmind starting to rise. He saw blood on Gemaley's claws and

315

mouth, and she licked at the ghost with as much avidity as she had ever shown with Ruan, but her face remained closed and cold. Then, as stealthily as she had arrived, she withdrew from the room, leaving the ghost panting and hurt.

'She didn't like that,' someone said in Ruan's ear. He hit his shoulder painfully against the wall as he jumped. Tian was standing immediately behind him, holding a lamp covered by a piece of cloth.

'You startled me,' Ruan hissed.

'Did I?' Tian frowned.

'What are you doing down here?'

'Gith brought me. But then he went away, to follow the stranger. I could not see well enough to keep up with them.' Her eyes were wide in the dim light.

Ruan drew her further into the passage so that they could not be overheard. 'Tian – what Gemaley is doing, it isn't right.'

'Gemaley does as she pleases,' Tian said, indifferently. 'If she has her distractions, then that means less for Gith and me.' She fell silent and held out her arm, drawing back the torn sleeve. In the lamplight, Ruan could just make out the criss-crossing of old scars. Claw marks.

'Gemaley did this?'

'She used to. Then she grew bored. But she still torments me, sometimes.' There was a curious kind of pride in Tian's voice, as though this made her special.

'Tian – we have to make her stop. You know that. She's feeding whatever lies under the tower with other people's pain.' As he spoke, Ruan felt his throat constrict, as though he had given voice to something forbidden.

'We can't.' Tian spoke decisively. 'She's too strong.'

And as she spoke, Ruan thought: *Yes, you're right. Best forget about it. There's nothing we can do.* But then he thought of the ghost's screams. They cut through the mist in his mind like a knife. The person who he had been – the one who had put an arrow in the visen that threatened his sister – seemed suddenly to flood back.

'We have to set the ghost free,' he said.

'What if Gemaley comes back?'

Ruan almost said *you go and distract her*, but the thought of sending timid Tian back to her sister, with Gemaley in this mood, was unacceptable. 'I'll find her and keep her occupied. You set the ghost free.'

'I can't.' For the first time, the fragile shell cracked and he saw her mouth tremble. 'And even if I could set her free, I can't lead her out. I can barely see. Gith always helps me when we come down here.'

'Our satahrach is half blind,' Ruan said, 'but he manages quite well—' and it was then that he remembered the glass in his pocket. Arrath had said that it did not work, but all the same . . . 'Tian?' He took the piece of glass from his pocket and held it up to her left eye, then stepped back so that he stood at arm's length. 'Look at me.'

Tian became very quiet, and very still. 'Tian?'

'I'm *looking*,' she said at last, in a whisper. 'I can see you.'

'It works?' Ruan said, startled. In a lightning motion, she snatched it from him and held it behind her back.

'I want it.'

'Then you can keep it. But in return, you do something for me. Untie the ghost, or I'll take it from you. And make sure that the house defences are down, if you can.' He did not want to have to wrestle the thing from the frail girl, but he would if he had to.

After a moment, she gestured assent. 'All right.' Perhaps, he thought, the glass might give her enough confidence to defy her sister.

'Go and do it, then,' he said. 'And I'll find Gemaley.'

For a moment, he thought she would refuse, and he held himself back from trying to snatch the glass from her. But then she gave an imperceptible gesture of assent. 'All right.' She crept past him into the chamber like a little spirit. Ruan took a deep breath and went in search of Gemaley.

At first he was afraid that she might be with the stranger, as he could not find her anywhere in the lower rooms of the tower. Heart hammering, he climbed the stairs and suddenly came face to face with her, coming out of Tian's room. Instead of the smugness that he had somehow expected, she radiated anger and frost.

'What do you want?' she snapped.

'I just wanted to see you,' Ruan said, trying to keep his voice placatory and submissive. To his continuing shame, it was not difficult. Gemaley's eyes were like splinters of winter.

'You're lying,' she hissed.

'No, I'm not, I—' but next minute she grasped him by the shoulders and was forcing him up against the wall.

'Have you been spying on me?'

'No, why would I?' he managed to force out, but she snarled, 'You've done so before, I know you have. You and Gith. Everybody lies to me, everyone.' It was a howl of pain and hate and he did not understand what had triggered it. But the glaze that was growing across Gemaley's eyes was horribly familiar. She was going into the bloodmind.

'Gemaley,' he said, very carefully. 'Listen to me—' and greatly to his surprise, she did. She let go of his shoulders and stepped back. The rage on her face was replaced by a remote, chilly calm.

'So,' she said, and she sounded startled. 'So, someone has not lied, after all.' Then she turned on her heel and before Ruan could make a move after her, she had vanished down the stairs.

THIRTY-ONE

PLANET: MONDHILE

At first, I thought she had come back again, but then I realized through the haze of pain that it was not Gemaley who was standing over me, but the other girl. She began picking at my bonds, staring into my face as though she could not see me very clearly.

'Who are you?' I whispered.

'I am Tian.' She shot a frightened glance over her shoulder as though afraid of being overheard.

'Where's Gemaley?'

'I don't know. Ruan's gone to find her.'

'Ruan?'

'The boy she brought here.'

'Are you Gemaley's sister?'

'Yes.' I felt a sharp prickle against the skin of my wrist. Tian had sliced through the leather strap and my hands were free. I twisted upright and freed my ankles. Tian was gazing at me through a piece of smoky glass, held up to one eye. It gave her an odd, comically lopsided look, and despite the pain I could not repress a smile.

'Where did you get that?'

'Ruan gave it to me. I—' Again, that terrified glance. 'Someone's coming.' And she was gone into the darkness, disappearing through the arch. I heard a soft footfall, coming through the passage. I ran swiftly through my options. Even if I got away from the force and through the arch, I could not walk very quickly, thanks to the wounds that Gemaley had inflicted. I also did not fancy my chances of being able to defend myself against her in my current state. I needed to take her by surprise. The bench was in full view of the entrance. She would see that I had escaped and would be prepared. She was perhaps a minute away. I thought of the guard in the cell in Darkland, but I did not trust myself to use the seith this time. I had another weapon. I reached into my jacket pocket and found the pen. I lay down on the floor, sprawled out, and drew it in a bloody swirl across my throat. Then I lay still.

My eye was closed, but I heard Gemaley exclaim as she came through the door to find me lying in an illusory pool of blood with my throat cut. I waited as she bent over me, waited more – and then struck upwards. I felt bone fracture under the blow and then I was standing over her crumpled form. I had dislocated her jaw. She was unconscious, but not dead. I was shivering with cold and shock, so I stripped her leather coat from her prone form and was reaching down to finish her off when I heard more footsteps. I was too afraid to linger in case it might be Frey – and he would not fall for the same trick. I was certain that he knew about the pen; the other vitki had known. I grasped the tabula from the shelf, rushed towards the arch, and fled through it and along the passage as swiftly as I could.

Someone was following me, moving quickly and decisively, but I could not tell who my pursuer was. I'd hoped that the discovery of Gemaley's unconscious form would delay them, but it seemed that this had not happened. I was certain it was Frey. The wound made by Gemaley was pumping a steady trickle of blood down my leg, but at least she had avoided the artery – in that case, I would have long since been dead.

Finally I reached the end of the passage and stumbled out into near darkness. As I did so, someone grasped my arm and pulled me back. I struck out and almost fell.

'Wait!'

It wasn't Frey. It was the young man.

'Ruan!'

'She's not dead,' he said.

'No, I know.' I would have gone back and killed her, but I was too afraid of running into Frey. I clasped Ruan's shoulder, more to keep myself upright than out of any real fellow feeling. 'I'm leaving. Come with me. I don't think it's safe for you here.'

'It isn't.' In the dull moonlight, he was very pale. 'But I can't go.'

'Why not? Because of Gemaley? You think she cares what happens to you?'

'I don't know. No, but—'

'Help me, Ruan. And help yourself.'

I could feel him wavering. 'It won't be long before she comes back,' I said.

'I don't—' He glanced over his shoulder, as Tian had done. I knew desperation when I saw it.

'Come with me, Ruan,' I said firmly, and gave him a little shake.

'Very well, then,' he said. He took me by the arm and together we made our way into the forest.

THIRTY-TWO

PLANET: MONDHILE

The forest was filled with shadows, but the air was soft and mild. And as they went further from the tower, Ruan's mind seemed once more to clear, the mist lifting from it as though burned away by the sun. The events of the last two days were tinged with nightmare, producing that heavy, almost sick feeling that one has on waking from a bad dream, that can colour a whole day until night. He still thought of Gemaley with longing and desire, but now, in memory, she possessed a sharpness, a cruelty. And a calculating madness, that was somehow worse than the blood-mind itself. He could no longer shut out the memory of what he had seen her do – she and the stranger from the forest. Just as before, it now seemed incredible to him that he had given so little thought to so much.

'Vali?' he said, trying out the name. 'That's what he called you, wasn't it?'

The woman who stumbled by his side turned her head. 'Yes.'

'That man – the stranger – you said you knew him.

Who is he?' The words broke the hush of the forest, seeming startlingly loud.

'He was my mentor.' The box she carried spoke its echo: satahrach.

'Your satahrach?' Ruan asked, bewildered. 'But he isn't old.'

'No, but he has a lot of knowledge and a lot of power. He taught me much of what I knew and he was also my lover. Then he tried to have me killed.'

'Why? Were things going badly between you?'

'I don't know.' She gave a grim laugh. 'They must have been, mustn't they?'

'It seems very—'

'The word you're looking for is "extreme".'

'Did he . . . say anything, when he was with you?'

She shot him a sideways glance through the gathering darkness. 'You saw him with me? And the girl?'

Ruan decided that honesty was best, if shameful. 'I watched. I'm sorry. I should have – stopped her, but something prevented me. It isn't a good excuse.'

'I wish you had stopped her,' Vali said, softly, and without reproof; but that was worse than her condemnation would have been. 'But maybe you should not judge yourself too harshly. I've seen enough of Gemaley to know that she has a powerful hold. She can make people do things they would never think of doing. I don't know where she gets her power from – there's some kind of well under the tower . . .'

'There's a sink of energy beneath it. A dark line runs through it.'

'Stop a moment,' Vali said. 'I need to catch my breath.' She leaned against a tree, hand pressed to her lower abdomen.

'Vali?'

'I'll be all right. It's a stitch, that's all. When you say a "dark line", what do you mean by that?'

'The energy of the world. Sometimes it's positive – it can sustain you – but sometimes it's negative; it sucks the life out of you, steals your own energy. That's what the tower is like. I found out the hard way – the energy trapped me and I could not move. I managed to break free, and would not have gone back there, but then I injured my ankle and Gemaley found me.' He did not like to tell her, even now, that it had been half in his mind to go in search of Gemaley. 'Once I had been in the tower for a few days, I no longer felt the dark energy. And I— did things that I've never done before.' Memory returned in a hot, clammy rush. He could feel Vali watching him and he looked away, embarrassed. She had had no choice, whereas he . . .

'We ought to go on,' Vali said, quietly. 'You don't want to go back there, do you?'

'No.' As soon as he said it, he realized that it really was true. 'I want to go home. To my clan house.'

'Your family? Do they live far away?'

'No, not so far. Half a day's travelling, perhaps. It depends which way you take.'

'Ruan, I would take you there if I could. I have a— cart.'

Ruan frowned at this; it seemed somehow unlikely. 'A cart? But the stranger said that you're from another world.'

Vali gave a small hiss of frustration. 'I'm not sure if that got translated correctly. I have a means of transport, but it's too small for two people.'

'I can make my own way home. But where will you go? To your home?'

'I don't know, yet. I need to find something that will heal me, but I can't leave just yet, not while Frey – the stranger – is still here. I want to know what he and Gemaley are planning.' She paused and he saw her head go up. 'What was that?'

Ruan listened. A long, low humming was coming through the forest, at first distant and barely audible, then growing in volume, like a wind gathering strength. Ruan recognized it at once, with sudden fear.

'Visen!'

'What?'

'An animal pack. Can you climb?'

'I think so, but Ruan – we can't hide in the trees.'

'Why not?'

'Because I think those creatures are with Gemaley. We have to run.'

'You can't outrun the visen!' The murmuring was growing louder, rushing onwards through the forest. Then he heard the bell-cry, the summoning note that the pack leader used in order to direct. 'They've found a scent.'

Vali touched him on the arm and was off, running awkwardly through the undergrowth. Ruan followed. She was bleeding heavily. He could smell her, and if that were the case, then so could the visen. They were leaving a trail as bright as sunlight but there was nothing to be done about it. He remembered, only then, that his weapons were still in the tower – what had Gemaley done with them? He had not thought about them ever since he had been there. But you could not hold off a whole pack; first they would send the weaker members at their victim – the expendable old or injured – then wait until the prey had weakened one by one.

Vali was slipping sideways down a bank, grasping at roots and branches to slow her progress.

'Do you know where you're going?' Ruan called.

'Yes. They weren't able to take that away from me.' She seemed very sure. He followed her along a stream, tumbling in full spate over rocks slippery with moss.

'The water won't make any difference,' he told her. 'They can smell you on the air.'

'It's the quickest route,' she panted back.

'Where to?'

'You'll see.'

She led Ruan, by now wet and breathless, up the bank again. Here, the trees were thinner, and eventually thinned out into a clearing. 'Over here!'

Even in the darkness, he could not think how he had missed it. It seemed to shimmer out of thin air, a narrow, tapering cylinder of some spongy black substance, lying among the plants on the clearing's floor.

'What is that?'

'It's my vehicle,' Vali said, but it bore no resemblance to any cart that Ruan had ever seen.

'You said it could not take me.' Distrust washed over him. Perhaps she was planning to leave him here to face the visen alone. He could not blame her.

'We can't travel in it. But that's not all it does. Stand there.' She pointed to a spot immediately next to the cylinder. Ruan did as she told him. He could smell the visen now, a musk on the wind, and their murmuring filled the forest. It was supposed to be a slow death. They played with their victims before devouring them, ensuring that the prey evacuated their bowels and that the meat would be tender. Vali was fumbling inside the cylinder. And then there was a flashing across his vision, as though a hundred little bolts of lightning were sizzling through the air.

'What—'

'Be quiet,' Vali whispered. The scene in front of Ruan seemed strangely blurred, as though he had developed an age-bloom over his eyes. Through the haze he saw the first of the visen enter the clearing.

'Vali! They cannot see. They hunt by smell.'

'I know. Keep quiet. The field will disturb our scent as well as hiding us from view.'

Ruan watched as the long, pale shapes slunk outwards in the hunting fan and the visen murmured to each other in their soft, uncanny voices. Swiftly, more and more of the pack spilled into the clearing, casting around them. Soon they were surrounding the cylinder, but the invisible lightning held them back. Ruan took a sharp step back and knocked against the side of it. It made no sound, but Vali's furious, warning glance was enough. He looked down onto an arched back, the spinal ridge clearly visible through the dappled fur. The visen was no more than a few feet away, the long jaw slack. The teeth ridge inside glistened with toxic saliva that, Ruan knew, would burn if it touched you.

The eyeless head swung slowly to and fro, seeking its prey. It was so big that Ruan thought it must be the leader and next moment, his suspicions were confirmed. The visen stood on its hind legs, scenting the air, and he glimpsed the pale bulbs of its egg sacs along its belly, each filled with a squirming embryo.

Ruan held his breath for so long that his chest began to ache, but at last the pack leader turned. Its head went up and it gave the bell-cry. The pack all moved as one and flowed smoothly from the clearing into the forest. Next moment, they were gone. The last Ruan saw of them was a tall figure at the very edge of the clearing, scenting around her like the visen themselves. It was Gemaley. The sight of her flooded him with shock and longing. He almost ran to her, but Vali's hand on his wrist was like a vice. She held him back, only for a second, but it was enough. His eyes watered and Gemaley was gone, swallowed by the night-dark woods.

THIRTY-THREE

PLANET: MONDHILE

I had not been in such pain since the attack by the fenris, and it felt worse than just laceration and tearing, out of proportion to the wound itself. From what I had seen of her, Gemaley was not the most hygienic girl, and I did not like to think what germs her claws might have been crawling with. As soon as the visen had swarmed out of the clearing, I dropped to my knees beside the pod and groped inside it for the medical kit. In this were salves and blood-clotting agents, as well as a small box full of epidermal layers. It might be hard to apply these vaginally, due to the viscosity of the membranes, but I had to try.

Telling the clearly embarrassed Ruan to turn his back, I dropped my trousers. My bruised wrists ached. When I touched it, gingerly, the whole of my genital area was a mass of bruising, swelling, and congealing blood. It felt as though the scratches had stopped bleeding, for the moment at least, but it seemed like all the days of a menstrual period had come at once.

I cleaned off the worst of it with a medical wipe, applied

the salves – which at least had the advantage of numbing the ripped flesh – and managed to attach an epidermal layer. I did not know how long it would last, but it was worth a try. It should, at least, allow the skin to knit together again.

But I did not say to Ruan – and barely allowed the admission to myself – that it was not the wounds that so disturbed me, bad though they were. What I now found so unsettling was the fact that in spite of what she had done to me, when I had seen Gemaley standing at the edge of the clearing, in the wake of her visen pack, I had wanted her . . . in the same way that my brother had made me feel the desire for him. I forced that thought away. It was she who had done the most damage, and because of it, I never wanted to set eyes on her again. Another rape. I forced the feelings away.

I pulled up the trousers, soaked with blood as they were, and fastened them. When it was light, I would suggest to Ruan that we return to the stream and get cleaned up. I was concerned less about my appearance and comfort than the possibility of the blood attracting more predators.

'You can look now,' I told him. Uneasily, he turned round.

'If you are planning to sleep here, I suggest we climb a tree. But you should rest.'

I did not disagree. I felt exhausted, as though every muscle in my body had been struck repeatedly with hammers. I let him lead me to the edge of the clearing, away from the lingering smell of the visen. Here, he stopped by a stout deciduous tree surrounded by the black-barked ones.

'This is embla. Better than satinspine – the needles are too sharp to be comfortable.'

He climbed swiftly up the gnarled bark and reached down to pull me up after him. With an effort, I managed to clamber up in his wake until we were perched on a thick branch some twenty feet from the ground. 'This is as safe as any. It's out of reach of the visen.'

. . . *and of Gemaley and Frey?* I wondered, but did not say. But I closed my eye and leaned back against the trunk. It was a relief to be so far away from the tower, away from the girl and my former lover. Their contaminating presence receded a little. I drew strength from the tree, from its endurance throughout what must have been a long winter, from the sap rising within it to meet the spring and the sun. Very faintly, as distant as the palest star, I felt the seith return to me, as though someone had drawn the ghost of a veil across my face. I leaned further back into the brace of the tree, and slept.

When I woke, it was to find Ruan leaning over me. I had to swallow the urge to push him away, but the concern in his face was very clear.

'Vali?'

'I'm all right.' I was by no means sure that it was true. I sat up, cautiously. The wound in my groin still burned and stung; I wondered whether that, too, would scar. Since it seemed unlikely that I would be using that particular part of my anatomy ever again, I thought grimly, it hardly seemed to matter now. What was worse was that I felt feverish; aching and hot. Gemaley's claws had almost certainly been filthy. Ruan put a tentative hand to my forehead.

'You're very warm. Are you sure you're all right?'

I did not want to spend the rest of the day in a tree. I wanted to get on the move.

'I'm fine,' I said, lying. I slid down the trunk and stood there, looking at the ground. It seemed suddenly very close, as though it had become magnified. I could see the outline of each little fallen leaf, each speck of mould, each tiny insect. I stared at the forest floor in wonder, and felt myself fall through it.

I was looking at the stars. Each one seemed very low and very bright, hanging just above my head as though I could reach up and pluck them, like cold fruit. I blinked and the branches above me swung away. I rolled over and found myself facing empty air. Scrabbling to get a purchase, I realized that I had come close to falling out of the tree. The pain was a constant presence, but had eased, enough for me to slide down the trunk to the ground. I don't know where I thought I was going. Ruan was nowhere to be seen and I remember thinking that he'd abandoned me, and that this was probably a good thing. He would be better off without me. But he had obviously taken the trouble to haul me back into the tree and, for that, I was grateful.

I shrugged Gemaley's heavy coat around my shoulders and set off into the woods. In the moonlight, everything was silver and red, a world of blood and bone. I thought of the woman I had seen in the forest in Darkland, sitting staring at me over the skull in her lap. She seemed the only real thing in the world, along with the vitki in Hetla. I remembered him very well and I thought that I should go and look for him, that he would be able to tell me what to do since he was, after all, the one who sent me here.

I felt very clear, not at all delirious; but of course I must have been to think such things. It did not occur to me to activate the map implant; I don't know why. But it would not, in any case, have been of much use to me.

I went on until I came to the edge of a great cliff, looking out over an expanse of ocean. This, too, was illuminated by the moonlight, a wash of mercury from horizon to horizon. I thought I was back in the Reach, stepping from one forest to another. It came to me that all the woods on the worlds were one, and that one only had to find the way through them to pass between, regardless of the span of stars.

I crouched down at the roots of a huge tree – surely almost falling from the cliff, as the roots clung to the granite edge and were themselves as hard as stone. I sat there, clutching Gemaley's stolen coat around me, watching the scenes of my life drift out like shadows across the silver sea. None of it seemed real, or important. None of it touched me any more. I do not know whether I slept, but I resolved distantly to wait until dawn and then make my way down the coast. I do not know what I thought I would find there, only that it might lead to Hetla and the vitki. It struck me again that I should see him, talk to him, there was something that I should remember to tell him . . . but I was roused by a warm breath against my face. I turned and froze. The beast was standing no more than a foot away from me, the eyeless head swinging slowly from side to side. In the light from the moons, her coat was the colour of the sea, as though she had been water-born. I wondered whether she would sing for me, and the thought made me catch my breath. But then I realized, through the haze of confusion and pain, that she was not one of the selk. This was not Muspell. I was lost and far from home, and this alien beast was a predator.

The visen reached forward and touched her muzzle to my ear. I flinched at the rank wash of breath. The visen took a strand of my hair between her jaws, very gently, and pulled. I rose, fearing what the creature might do, thinking of the fenris, and expecting at any moment to feel the rip of teeth in my flesh. It occurred to me then that I had never really stopped feeling it. But my fear was so consuming that I let the pack leader draw me back through the woods, my hand on her mane, moving swiftly and surely through the maze of alien trees to the clearing. I don't remember anything more.

When I next woke, it was to see light streaming in through the window. It was pleasantly warm and the blankets that covered me were soft, slightly rough, in the way that home-woven garments tend to be. They smelled greasy, like lanolin. Above me, the weathered beams were hung with herbs. I had been dreaming, I thought: about Frey and a fenris and a girl who had done her best to rape me; about Darkland and a world named Mondhile; a beast that had come to me in the forest and led me home. But it had been nothing more than a dream and now I knew where I was – in that house in Yetland, on the edges of the ice.

'Vali, are you awake?' The voice was male and familiar, a little uncertain. Idhunn? I wondered – but the voice had been a man's, and immediately I was reminded of Frey. I blinked and twisted round in the bed. Ruan sat next to it, staring at me anxiously.

'I think so.' I spoke clearly, or so I thought, but he frowned.

'I'm sorry . . . I didn't hear you.'

'Where am I?' The room in which I lay was a mess, but it was a mess of which I approved. Jars of what appeared to be pickles sat on a bench, glowing green and golden in the sunlight, and the floor was covered with pieces of parchment, on which someone had energetically scribbled diagrams and just as energetically crossed them out again. The air smelled of a hundred different things, not all of them pleasant. I was among the latter. Regardless of Ruan's presence, I surreptitiously put my hand between my legs and found it covered with something sticky and unfamiliar.

'It's a salve,' Ruan said. He looked away. 'I'm sorry, but you were unconscious and the satahrach did not want to delay treatment. One of the women put it on.' Then, presumably remembering Gemaley, it clearly struck him that this last comment would not be as reassuring as it might otherwise have been and he rose abruptly to his feet and went to the window.

'This must be your clan house. How did I get here?' I asked. He turned in relief, clearly glad to have had the subject changed.

'We brought you. You went down the tree and collapsed. The place where you took me is not so far from the clan house, as the bird flies. I put you back in the branches. I did not know whether I was doing the right thing, but I wanted to put you up high in case the visen came back – then went back and told my family what had happened. My sisters came back with me and fetched you and the speaking box. You were unconscious all the time we were with you.'

'Ruan.' I did not know what to say. 'Thank you. You've almost certainly saved my life. I'm so grateful.'

'You were the one who got me out of the tower.' He was standing with his back to me; from the tension in it I sensed that he did not want to turn and face me. 'I couldn't do it on my own. She made me so weak and I wanted to be weak, too. I let her, because I wanted to stay with her. I should have left earlier.'

'Your family must have been very relieved when you turned up again.'

'Yes, they were. *And* they were furious.'

'They must have been worried.'

'They thought I was dead. I had to tell the satahrach what had happened. He thinks I'm an idiot. I think I'm an idiot.'

'If you had found the strength to leave,' I said, 'then you would probably have gone before I came to the tower, and I would still be there, with Gemaley and Frey doing to me whatever they chose. Even if I had escaped, I would not have had the strength to make it through the forest on my own. I might even be dead. Instead, I am here with you and your family. Everything works out for the best.' I spoke firmly, but I did not feel strong, at all.

But he turned at that, and smiled. 'That makes me feel better. Thank you.'

'We owe one another.'

He looked down at the floorboards as if embarrassed. 'My family don't know what you are. They say you look like a ghost but you feel real.'

'I just come from – somewhere else. I'd like to talk to someone about all this, though. If that's possible.'

'The satahrach wants to talk with you. He's fascinated, actually. But my sister is standing by the door and not letting anyone in until you are feeling better. She said to ask if you are hungry.'

Now that he mentioned it, I found that I was. 'Yes. Very.'

'Then I'll bring something in,' Ruan said and disappeared through the door. I heard the murmur of voices outside. Ruan's sister sounded like a bird. I pictured a small, fragile person, like Gemaley's sister, and wondered what had become of Tian. She had also helped to save my life but at the moment there seemed no way of repaying her.

I threw back the covers and found that someone had dressed me in a linen shift, which fitted – more or less. I wrapped myself in a blanket and went over to the window. I could see mountains, which allowed me to orientate myself somewhat. The implant informed me that we were about ten miles from the landing site and this was reassuring. Outside, the air held the hint of spring.

I watched as a small fawn-coloured animal crossed the yard and sat down to scratch a tufted ear. I had no idea what it was. But I was pleased to note that, if I needed to, it would be an easy climb down from the window to a low roof and then to the ground. This was not a tall house, although I could see steep gables surrounding the place and for some reason this came as a surprise. I had somehow got the idea that Ruan's clan house stood alone, but this looked like a small town.

'Ruan told me that you're awake. I have something for you.' It was the bird-voice belonging to Ruan's sister, but when I turned round I saw that she was a tall, rangy woman, with a gaunt face. Her arms were bare and as tightly muscled as a fisherwoman of the Reach – hardly the fragile person I had imagined. She was carrying a steaming bowl. 'This is fish. I hope you can eat it – some people eat just meat, but the women will not go hunting until this afternoon.' She brushed a mess of papers aside and set the bowl down on the table. 'Arrath, the satahrach, wants to speak with you, but first you ought to eat.' She smiled. 'He can be exhausting.'

'Thank you,' I said, trying to hear the words she was using beneath the humming translation of the tabula. She sat down on the side of the bed and looked at me expectantly with pale green eyes. She looked nothing like her brother. Clearly, she wanted to make sure that I ate whatever was in the bowl, but she did not need to worry on that score. I was hungry enough to eat her out of house and home.

If she had not told me that it was fish, I would have taken the lumps in the bowl to be some kind of pale venison; they had a texture I associated more with game than with seafood. She was watching me anxiously.

'It's very good,' I said – and fortunately could mean it. It was flavoured with something that tasted like a combination of mustard and dill. Green fronds floated between the chunks of flesh.

'If you want more, there's plenty,' she added after watching me chew for a few moments.

'Thank you, but I'm all right.' It was certainly protein-packed and was starting to make me feel human again, after the floating sensation of shock, injury and lack of food.

'I'll bring you some tea,' she said and was away through the door before I had a chance to protest. In any case I was, I realized, ragingly thirsty.

I sat down on the bed to digest the food, but in what seemed like moments I opened my eyes again and found that a soft spring dusk was beginning to fall. My mouth tasted like an old sock. A pot of tea stood by the bed with a small round cup, and when I laid my hand against its earthenware side I discovered that it was still warm. I sipped – some kind of fragrant concoction of herbs – and wondered whether I should go in search of Ruan, but the peace and silence were too precious. I felt myself start to gather the shattered remains of the seith around me, as though I were knitting the fragments of myself back together again.

By the time the door opened again, it was dark. Ruan's tall sister stood in the doorway, accompanied by a man. When Ruan had spoken of the elder, I had assumed that he meant someone very aged, used as I was to the life expectancies of the Reach. But this man looked only as though he were in his early fifties, with the same pointed, angular face that I was starting to recognize as typically Mondhaith – or at least, common to this particular region. He had white-on-white eyes and long grey hair. He was smiling. He also radiated an aura of enthusiasm and I felt my heart sink. Ruan had brought something interesting home, as a hound might, and his master was pleased.

'So you are Ruan's ghost.' He walked across the room and stood studying me, from a distance of a few feet. At first, I had assumed that the blank eyes were as good as anyone else's, but something about the way he was squinting led me to think that he might be short-sighted, as I had suspected. It made me think of Tian.

'I am the stranger, yes.'

'From another world.'

'Do you believe that?'

'Such things have been known before. Rarely, it's true. But why not? We know that there were once folk on the moons. We see vessels in the sky, passing to and fro. But all those who claimed to have come from other worlds – and there have not been many – were ghosts, only half-human. They might have been from the land of the dead, for true spirits are capable of great trickery. You are not a ghost. You feel real.'

I knew it was the seith that he could sense; it was as if it was becoming harder around the edges, more solid. 'You understand what it is to be a person. You have extension.'

I could tell from its scratchy stutter that the tabula was having problems translating this. 'I have been trained in a particular discipline,' I said.

'And trained well. What is your element, your speciality?'

The tabula was still stammering. 'I'm not sure what you mean.'

'Can you sense water? Particular kinds of rock? Are you sensitive to the flight of birds or the passage of animals? Can you feel the presence of others?'

'I am a tracker,' I told him. 'And I have experience of the sea. I grew up on a coast, with boats.'

'A sea-reader!' The tabula, programmed in Gaelacht

and the *lingua franca* of the common worlds, was using Reach terminology, but I wasn't sure whether this was what the satahrach had actually meant.

'Yes, I think so. I understand the tides and currents.'

'And you can follow a man, or an animal, by the signs that they leave? You're a woman. You must surely be able to hunt.'

'I can follow, yes, and sometimes I hunt.'

'Very good. And how did you lose your eye? Was it an accident, or were you in a fight?'

'An animal attacked me. Something like a visen, but larger.'

'Then you are lucky to be alive. Did you kill it?'

'No, but someone else did. Why do you ask?'

The satahrach frowned. 'It would be better if you had killed it, and then its spirit would be truly dispatched instead of waiting for another chance. There is a cloud around you.'

'You can feel that?'

'Oh yes. It's very strong. It feels like a loose thread fluttering in the breeze, as though part of you has become detached and longs for death because it does not know what else to do. But I can also sense that your chance is coming.'

'My chance?'

'To weave yourself back together again.' The satahrach stood looking at me for a moment, head on one side as if listening. But I did not know if he was picking up anything real, or whether this was simply the usual performance made by folk-tellers and shamans – obfuscation to impress the gullible. I did not know what to say and so said nothing.

'Well,' the satahrach said, with no trace of disappointment at my failure to reply. 'Tell me about your world, then.'

So I talked a little of Muspell and the Reach, trying to put it in terms that the tabula would not easily confuse. It was a good thing, I thought, that I did not come from anywhere that was solely dependent on high tech. But anyone could understand boats and fishing and hunting. I did not speak of Frey at first, but then the satahrach said, 'And there is another here, Ruan tells me. Your lover, yes?' Not any more.

'A man called Frey.'

'Do you know why he has come?'

'No. Ruan's told you about the tower?'

'Ruan has told me, yes, and I think we should be grateful to you for getting him away from it, stupid boy that he is.'

'I think *he* got *me* away from it. And you shouldn't be too hard on him,' I said. I, too, had trusted someone I shouldn't have, when I was about Ruan's age. 'It's a powerful place.'

The satahrach gave a snort. 'All the more reason to stay well away from it, then.'

'There's something under the tower.'

'Of course there is. Black energy.'

'But what *is* "black energy"?'

The satahrach stared at me. 'What an odd question. That's like asking "what is water?"'

'But you must have theories for what these phenomena are? Explanations?'

'Why should we have an explanation for something that simply is? Black energy is black energy. It won't be changed by my having ideas about it.'

'So you've no idea why it occurs in some places and not in others?'

'All energy is produced by the world itself. Its lines girdle the world, from pole to pole, and around the equatorial region – or so I am told. I have never been there, but I have spoken to folk who have. Apart from these great meridians, there are many lesser ones, just as there are smaller rivers that form the tributaries of larger ones. Some energies are light, some are dark, and some are neutral. Most of our settlements, as you can probably feel, are built in places where the earth energy is positive. But sometimes those who are weak, or wicked, are drawn to places of negative energy and choose to build their dwellings there, to use that energy for the house defences. Gemaley's clan are one such.'

'Defences?'

'Every settlement draws on earth energy to protect itself.' I must have looked blank, so he continued, 'When a child is born in a place, that energy is imprinted upon it. The child is sent out into the world, and when it is half-grown, it returns. Crossing the line of the defence restores it to conscious awareness and it becomes fully human.'

'How does this work?'

It was the satahrach's turn to look blank. 'It just does. But black energy – that can infect a person.'

'Are you saying that Gemaley is . . . possessed?'

'Possessed?' The satahrach frowned and once again I felt that the tabula had translated incorrectly.

'Like being inhabited by an evil spirit.' Even as I spoke, I realized that I had no idea whether the Mondhaith even used concepts like this, though they spoke of ghosts. A pity that there wasn't more information in the anthropologist's records.

'I've heard of such things, but the girl is more like a vessel that has nothing to fill it, and so it becomes filled with the first thing that anyone pours into it, whether that is water or wine or vinegar.'

'Or poison.'

'Exactly so.'

'And because of that she has become – what? Filled with the desire to do harm?'

'I think it is more that she either does not reflect at all on what she does – and simply does it – or that she fails to understand that what she is doing is wrong.' *Ignorant*, the tabula added after a moment, revising its previous translation. I realized that I knew nothing of Mondhaith morality, either.

'But she is driven by the energy that lies under the tower?'

'Yes.'

'And what if you took Gemaley away from the tower?'

'She would probably not live very long,' the satahrach said.

'Why not?'

'Because the energy of the tower has imprinted itself upon her, as I told you. Infected her.'

'So if *you* left this place for any length of time, you would die?'

'No, because the energy here isn't harmful. I live in equilibrium with it, and so does everyone else who lives here. We can come and go as we please. But those like Gemaley – she is *fed* by the energy, it has become her nourishment, even though it will probably cause her to waste away, like someone who eats a slow-poisoning food.' He paused. 'And Ruan tells me that she told him that she and her siblings were never sent out into the wild like normal infants, but remained at the tower with their clan, all through their childhood. Have you ever heard of such a thing?'

At some point, I was going to have to have a serious discussion with someone about Mondhaith child-raising practices, but now was not the time. I muttered something non-committal.

'Of course, she could have been lying, but it seems such an unbelievable claim,' the satahrach mused.

'Extraordinary.'

'But if it is true, perhaps it has caused her to become addicted to the energy beneath the tower, which attached itself to her as a child and now will not let her go.' The satahrach looked at me. 'In any case, it is an evil place and you are well free of it.'

'I could not agree more. And thank you for looking after me,' I said.

'Oh, think nothing of it. It's interesting to meet someone from so far away.' From the way he spoke, I did not think that he had entirely grasped that I was from another planet, even though he had mentioned habitation on the moons. To him, I suspected, it was as though I merely came from a distant land. He went on, 'We would do the same for any traveller, especially at this time of year.'

'What time is that?'

'The spring tides are on the turn. The town is about to enter masque.'

The tabula had a brief struggle to translate that word, I noticed, and the little screen was flashing a warning.

'I'm not sure if I understand you.'

'Within a few days, when the moons enter phase. I've been calculating it. No one else bothers, of course. They just let it all happen. Bit of a nuisance, actually. I have things I want to get on with and this will just get in the way. But I have no choice, and the signs are that it will be a brief one, this time.' He rose from the side of the bed. 'It's getting late and you are tired. I should stop indulging my curiosity in this fascinating conversation and let you rest. I've told Ruan to leave you alone for now, but tell his sister Eleshtra if you need anything. She's in the room next to this one.'

349

'Thank you,' I said. 'You're very kind.'

The satahrach made an airy gesture with one hand and was gone through the door.

So, there was some kind of festival coming up. I wondered if it was a religious occasion, but the satahrach had mentioned spring and it was possibly something a little similar to Beltane in the Reach. Under normal circumstances, that would have been interesting, perhaps even fun, but I had no time for frivolity, not now. I still had to find Frey.

Yet again I woke. It was past midnight and Frey was standing over me, his golden eye glittering like fire. I started upright, moving back against the wall with such force that I banged my head on the plaster. Frey turned and strode through the door. I wanted to hide under the blankets, but instead I threw them aside and ran after him. By the time I reached the end of the landing, he was already down the long flight of stairs that led through the house. I followed, noting dark, polished panelling, thick rugs, a jar of fragrant herbs placed carefully on a ledge halfway down the stairs. This was nothing like the ill-kept ruin of the tower. This was a home. I thought of the satahrach's words as I padded after Frey: light and dark, negative and positive. Could one be affected so strongly by a place as all that? Or was that just an excuse for torture and sadism?

The doors of the clan house were open and when I went through I saw that I was standing in the courtyard that I had seen from above. It was cold, but the stone under my feet was free of frost and the sky above was clear, sparkling with stars. Two thin crescent moons hung over the tiled ridge of the roof.

Frey was going through a gate at the end of the courtyard, striding fast, not looking back. I cursed the lack of weapons, wishing I'd had time to find Ruan and ask for the loan of a bow. And how had Frey got into the house in the first place? I remembered the vitki, stepping out of the air on the beach in Darkland, and shivered.

I stood little chance of killing Frey, but this time I could not help following him. It was as strong as my compulsion to cut – and as destructive. It was as though he was drawing me on, reeling me in by some unseen thread. I pursued him up through the town, past tall houses with shuttered windows, across a narrow bridge leading over a chasm. I saw the glint of water, silver in the moonlight, hundreds of feet below and smelled the rank salt of the sea.

The town itself was empty of anyone except myself and Frey. No lights showed behind the shuttered windows and the only faces that looked down at me were the faces of demons and gargoyles, carved on eaves and guttering, poised halfway along the tiles or snarling up from doorposts. This town felt ancient: steps worn into a curve by generations of feet; paving stones polished across the centuries; old wooden beams buckled beneath the weight of ageing houses. The style of architecture was very different – high and thin rather than low and solid, ornamented rather than functional – but it reminded me nonetheless of places in the Reach. As we continued up through the town the buildings grew more ornate and, it seemed to me, even older. Lacy balconies overhung the street and some of the houses had walkways between them: thin bridges of slats hung on ropes. Coming up between two black wood mansions, the street stopped abruptly at a flight of steps and when I climbed them I realized we were at the town wall.

Frey had halted and was standing some distance along the wall, staring up the hillside. When he caught sight of me, standing hesitantly below, he made a little gesture of impatience.

'Look at this.'

I did not want to go near him. I could feel his presence pulling at me, and this time I managed to solidify the seith, and successfully resisted the impulse to run to his side.

'Very well, then, don't.' Frey said. 'But look there.' He pointed up the hill. A long bare slope led to the edges of the forest. At first it was hard to distinguish the moonlit shadows, but then I saw them. The visen pack was coming out of the forest, circling the town. I saw their long, gleaming bodies slinking under the wall, some forty feet or so below. Each one raised its head as it approached the point under which I was standing, scenting the air with a whispering eagerness. I could hear them calling to one another in their soft, sinister voices. Then they were gone. The pack poured up the hillside and back among the trees, in response to some signal that I had failed to hear.

'They're waiting,' I heard Frey say, but when I looked along the wall he, too, was gone. I did not want to stay there in the dark with the visen close by. I made my way back through the silent town to Ruan's clan house. The doors were still open. I went up the stairs and into bed like the clockwork soldier that the vitki had named me, and once there, I sank into a kind of ethereal sleep, like death.

In the morning, waking late, I was unsure whether or not it had been a dream. My feet were filthy and covered in blisters, but I could not tell if these were the result of my flight from the tower or from the night's wanderings. It had not felt like a dream, but that is one of the powers of the vitki: to make unreality appear to come alive. I should have been glad that it was morning, with the sun already risen, but the night's fears spilled out into the day and gave me no peace.

Someone, perhaps Eleshtra, had left a bowl of bread – and what tasted vaguely like a thick curdled milk – by the bed, along with a larger bowl of water and a facecloth. It was good to be clean again. Having washed and eaten, I put on the clothes laid out for me – trousers and a shirt – and went in search of Ruan.

The house was a muted hive of activity. I got the impression that there were a great many things going on just out of sight. I passed a woman on the stairs with a basketful of washing. She smiled at me, but in a distracted way. The doors were wide open, letting a flood of sunlight into the hall. A girl was polishing the floor, with a mutinous expression that suggested she had been forced to do it. She did not look up.

I found Ruan down in the courtyard, surveying a pile of logs with equal glumness.

'Good morning,' I said. The tabula mumbled something equivalent.

'Good morning.' Ruan pushed his hair back from his eyes. 'There's going to be a masque. It starts this evening. Did the satahrach tell you?'

'Yes, he did. So what will happen in this masque?'

'Oh, you know. The usual sort of thing,' he answered.

'I'd like to stay for it, but I've got to find Frey.'

'I understand. You'll need to leave before sunset, in that case.'

'Why is that?'

'They'll seal off the town, in case any travellers stray in.'

I frowned. 'It's not allowed for outsiders to take part?'

'It isn't really a good idea. *You* know. If you were staying, we'd make sure that you were safe inside.' He shot me an uneasy look. 'But it's up to you, of course. If you feel well enough.'

This was beginning to sound less and less like some harmless revel.

'Ruan, what exactly happens during a masque?'

'I'm not really sure. You know why,' he said again. 'The bloodmind is like that. Sometimes there are – well, sometimes people get hurt, or worse.'

I suspected that it got very crowded. And thinking of

the layout of the town that I had seen in my dream – or night visit – of the thin bridges and long drops, I was not surprised to learn that there were accidents. 'Well,' I said, dismissing it, 'in any event, I won't be here.'

'You're going back to the tower?'

'If that's where Frey is, then I must. But I know what to expect this time. I plan to be prepared. I'll need weapons, Ruan. And boots. And if your satahrach can teach me anything about dark energy, then that will be a help, too.'

He started to say something, but he was interrupted by a high snarling cry. It sounded as though it was right in my ear. I must have leapt a foot in the air.

'What was *that*?'

Ruan looked at me as though I'd gone mad.

'Just one of the mur.'

'The what?'

'The riding beast.'

It sounded unlike any horse I'd ever met. 'Show me,' I said.

Ruan looked vaguely surprised. 'If you like.' He led me across the courtyard to the far end, to what looked like stables. But they did not smell like the stables I had been used to on Muspell. There was none of the warm smell of straw and dung, and grass-eating livestock. What I could smell now, coming from the low dark building at the courtyard's end, was raw meat.

Moments later, when we walked through the door, I saw that the smell was emanating from a bucket set down on the stone floor. There was no sign of any straw, but the place was very clean. The bucket was filled with bloody chunks, half-covered with fur. At least, I thought, it did not look like anything that might have been human, but was then surprised at myself for thinking that these people, who had been so kind to me, might be feeding human flesh to their riding beasts. It made me wonder what I myself was perhaps starting to become.

When I set sight on the thing that had made the unnatural shriek, I realized that my estimation had been even further from the truth. It not only looked completely unlike a horse, it was like nothing I had ever seen. The beast had a long, narrow head on a snaking neck, the oddly arched back that seemed to characterize the beasts of Mondhile, little red eyes like a fiery dragon, and a vertebrate tail that it was thrashing from side to side – presumably to express its displeasure at setting eyes on me. It had clawed feet rather than hooves and it was covered in a thick, indigo pelt that I immediately coveted. It growled, then emitted another piercing yowl. I stepped back.

'Are they all this ill-tempered?'

'I suppose so,' Ruan said, surprised. What concerned me, however, was the glint of awareness in the thing's eyes; it did not have an animal look. Had the visen not been eyeless, I wondered whether I might have noticed it in their gaze, too. I thought of ancient genetic engineering and as though he had read my mind, Ruan said, 'We are supposed to share ancestors, from the very oldest times, when humans were beasts and beasts were human. There are legends about it.'

'Do you believe them?'

Ruan thought about this, frowning. 'I don't know. I think they're just stories, but some people are closer to the mur than others. They have a language, you know. But not everyone can understand it.'

It was not the time to tell him that the planet's colonists, far in the past, had apparently undertaken more than their fair share of genetic tinkering with both local and imported fauna. Once more I looked at Ruan, and wondered how human he really was. In Gemaley's case, it was not a question I had to think very hard about.

The mur shrieked again and it was beginning to make me nervous. The slats around its pen did not look especially secure.

'Let's go back outside,' I said.

'Of course.' I did not think Ruan was reluctant to leave, either. The mur watched us go, from little angry eyes. I could feel its stare between my shoulder blades all the way out of the door.

As soon as we were once more in the sunlit courtyard, and I had begun to breathe more easily, Ruan turned to face me. 'If you are truly determined to go back to the tower, then you will need weapons.'

'I have no intention of going unarmed. Do you have anything that I could borrow?'

'Weapons won't be a problem,' Ruan said. He took me to a small room on the ground floor of the house. It was filled with fighting gear, like any weapons room in the Reach, but here the weapons were bows and swords instead of guns. It made for an interesting change of pace, although I was not versed in sword-fighting. The prospect of taking on Frey in hand-to-hand combat was not an appealing one, and I planned to shoot him from as safe a distance as possible.

Whenever I thought of Gemaley, a rush of conflicting emotions came over me: shame, fear, hatred, desire . . . If I got the opportunity to kill her, too, then I would do so, but she had to be regarded as a bonus. However much I might want to – and I did – I was not going to make a point of hunting her down. And from what the satahrach had said about the energy-sapping nature of the place in which she lived, it might not even be necessary. I could find it in me to feel a little pity for Gemaley, but not much. I regretted leaving her alive, hoped she would soon be dead, and considered that this world would be a better place for it.

Some of the weapons looked ancient, tarnished silver scabbards chased with fantastic configurations of animals and leaves. Some of it looked a little like the old Celtic forms that were found in the Eirelander parts of the Reach, but with its own particular character. So much time had gone by, after all. I wondered what racial types had first colonized Mondhile, and glanced at Ruan: the pale skin; paler hair; the slightly slanted, blank dark eyes and strong bones. Impossible to tell now, without a DNA scan, and why would anyone care? Perhaps the vitki, with their atavistic notions of a special people might, but I did not. The past mattered, but not in that respect.

'Which ones are best?' I asked Ruan.

'This one is a good bow. It's my sister's, but she said last night that you could use it if you wanted to.'

'You spoke to her about this?'

'Oh yes. She understands why one might want to kill a lover.' Ruan looked troubled, but said no more on the matter. 'She had this bow made in the south – see? It has a different look to the rest.'

Examining the weapon, I saw that he was right. It had a long, sleek curve and the inlay was a pale golden metal that I did not recognize. The decorations on it were different, too. A multitude of human faces – shadowy against the sunlit curve of the bow – stared out at me. I liked the weight of it in my hand, the easy pull of it, and also the fact that it had been used by a woman before me. The knowledge gave it a slightly mythical quality – foolish, I know, but we live by the stories we tell ourselves. Looking more closely, I noticed something about the weapon: the faces were all female. I pointed this out to Ruan.

'It's a woman's bow,' he said. 'Made *by* a woman, *for* a woman. I think you should take it.'

The bow came with a matching quiver. It felt strange to be strapping it over my shoulder, to be hunting down Frey with this old form of weapon. When I'd imagined our final battle, I had envisaged myself holding a pulse rifle, not this antique. But something about it was fitting, all the same.

I turned to see that Ruan was sizing up one of his own bows; a light, slender thing made of wood.

'My weapons are still at the tower,' he said, running a finger along the curve of the bow.

'Are you planning to go hunting?' I asked.

'I'm coming with you.'

'No, you are not.'

A young man of the Reach would have been indignant and bridled at such an order, but Ruan only gave a brief, apologetic smile and said, 'It's only fair, Vali. If you are going after Frey, then surely it's right for me to go after Gemaley.'

'Is that what you want?'

'She— took too much from me. I think you understand. I'm not just talking about the weapons. I need to get it back.'

'I do understand. But Gemaley has a lot of power, even if it isn't really her own. You saw her at the tower, and in the forest with the visen. She has capacities for control of others that I don't think I really understand. And, if you'll forgive me, I've had more experience of this kind of thing than you.'

'I know,' Ruan said, still apologetic. 'I don't want to get in your way, and I won't.'

'Ruan, tell me something. Do you hate her?'

He paused. 'I don't know. I hate what she made me do. Do you hate Frey?'

'I am like you. I hate what he made me become – but then again, I was complicit in it. I let him change me . . .'

I swallowed painfully, '. . . because of what someone had done to me before. I don't think I was *his* victim, until towards the end. I think I was my own. And because of that – yes, I think I do hate him.' *And myself*, a voice reminded me, fragile as a thread; but I did not want to listen to that.

'At first I thought I could save her,' Ruan said. 'But when I spoke to our satahrach, he told me that she is probably past saving. So the best I can do is to make sure that she doesn't get the chance to draw anyone else into the tower. There were the dead there, you know. I don't know who they were, but I could feel them in the hall.'

'They might have been other travellers.'

'Or her family. I don't understand what would make someone build on such an unwholesome place to begin with.'

'Some people have a fascination for darkness,' I said, thinking of the vitki. They would love such a place as the tower, and they would probably understand it better than Gemaley, and be able to use those energies . . . It struck me that this might have been why Frey had come here. But if that was the case, what did it mean for Darkland? What did it mean for the Reach?

'I don't understand that,' Ruan said, but he sounded uncertain. I looked into his perplexed face and before I could stop myself I reached up and touched his cheek, trying to reassure him.

There was a look there that I had not seen in a man's eyes for a very long time. I had to resist the urge to put my hand up and cover my ruined eye. He leaned forward a little and I was suddenly very aware of him, but then he drew back.

'I'm sorry,' he said. 'I didn't mean to—'

'It's all right.' I was not, I realized, all that much older than Ruan, but I felt older, by years and years. My heart was pounding, but not with desire. I felt a cold trickle down my spine. A flickering memory of the Hierolath whisked through my mind . . . and earlier memories . . . to be replaced by Gemaley. I blinked and all were gone.

'If it were not for—' he stopped, awkwardly.

'I know.' This time I did touch the eye. 'I don't expect you to . . . to be able to deal with this, Ruan. There are enough pretty girls around. I know what I look like.'

'What?' He seemed genuinely bewildered.

'What were *you* talking about?' I echoed. My voice sounded more ragged than I would have liked.

'I didn't mean your eye.' He made a dismissive gesture, very much like the satahrach. 'That's nothing. Everyone's got scars or their teeth are missing or their hair is falling out because they had water fever or whatever. I meant: because of Gemaley; because of what she did to you.'

'Oh, I'm tired of thinking about Gemaley,' I heard myself say and, without giving myself time to think, I reached up, linked my arms around the back of his neck and kissed him.

It had been seven years since I had touched a man. The kiss did not last long. The door was flung open and we sprang apart like a pair of guilty lovers.

'Oh, sorry!' I heard Eleshtra say, sounding like a startled bird, and then she slammed the door shut. Ruan and I stared at one another for a second, embarrassed. I kept wanting to laugh, or perhaps cry, but knew that if I started, I would not be able to stop.

I spent a moment silently and violently cursing Frey. If it hadn't been for his presence – out there and scheming who knew what – I could stay here for a while in this fascinating society with this pleasant young man and maybe start thinking about that vow of celibacy, which had once seemed so necessary. Instead, Ruan and I found ourselves obliged to pack up and get started, to dispatch our respectively treacherous lovers. What a bore that was. But beneath it all, I knew it was all just wishful thinking, a bravado fantasy.

We ate before we left, in the main hall – a very different place to the tower's hall; full of firelight and conversation, even in the middle of the afternoon. Eleshtra came up to me when we were eating and apologized again. She seemed to consider that she had committed some grave social solecism instead of discovering her raddled guest in the process of seducing her little brother in the weapons room. I felt as though I ought to be apologizing to her, under the circumstances. It struck me, with some force, that kissing Ruan had been an extremely stupid thing to do. There was also the issue of the sudden need to deal with cultural variables. I had no real understanding of how the Mondhaith regarded relationships between the sexes. I spent a few minutes working myself up to a difficult conversation, put down my spoon and began.

'Ruan, what happened between us in the weapons room – it can't happen again.'

'That's up to you,' he murmured, though I thought he looked flatteringly disappointed.

'It isn't that I don't want to. I just think that we need to concentrate on Frey and Gemaley. And also—' I hesitated. This culture did not seem to have traditionally conventional views toward women, but one never knew. To my own horror I heard myself say, 'Do you think I'm a slut?'

'A what?'

Failure to translate, the tabula said, suddenly and tinnily. *No known analogue*. I suppose that answered that question.

'If we want to get out of town before sunset,' Ruan reminded me, 'we'd better start now.'

We left the hive of the clan house behind and started to walk up towards the city wall. The houses that we passed were familiar, but I did not see the narrow bridge. Instead, we climbed a long flight of stone steps, leading between the tall houses. In daylight – or rather, not dreaming – I could see that the place was indeed old, with most of the woodwork weathered and flaking. I looked back to see that a bright line of sea had appeared over the rooftops. A chain of islands curved around the edge of a wide bay, blue and distant in the afternoon light. The colours were different: a deeper sky; sharper shadows; a sun that was more crimson-tinged than Grainne's gold, but which still reminded me of the Reach – an arrow-sharp bolt of memory. I wanted to linger, but I turned away and followed Ruan.

The town, so quiet in my dream – or my wandering – was now thronged with people. Many of them were masked, looking out from curls of feathers, or leather in the shape of leaves, or spirals of tinsel made to fall like water. Some were almost naked, in spite of the spring chill, while others wore mantles of velvet over what was clearly armour. And there was an 'edge' to the town, a palpable air of excitement and anticipation.

To me – held within the partially restored senses of the seith – it felt dangerous, in spite of the festive clothes. The street was filled with smells: hot burning coals; thick coal-tar from braziers at street corners; sea-salt and flowers of the scarlet creepers that spilled over the balconies; and musk from perfume worn by the women. Yet there was something missing, and eventually, as we made our way up through the town, I worked out what it was. I could not smell food. No meat on the fire, or fish, or baking, and this seemed strange, especially given that festivities in the Reach revolved around food. Despite what Ruan and the briefing had told me, another peculiarity was the absence of children; everyone here was an adult. The youngest person I saw looked about sixteen.

'Ruan,' I said, when I caught him up at the top of the steps, 'no one seems to be cooking anything.'

'What would be the point?'

'Don't people eat during this thing?'

'No,' he said.

'What about alcohol?' *Some party this was likely to be,* I thought.

'No one needs it.'

I was going to ask Ruan what they used instead – drugs? Or dancing? Or did they just get happy? – but he was already walking along a street that seemed vaguely familiar. We were, I thought, drawing close to the town wall and presumably the gates. I wondered again whether I had really made that night journey, or whether it had only been my spirit that had wandered here. For a moment, looking around me, I lost sight of Ruan in the crowd, but then I saw him again, heading down an alley which was a little quieter than the rest. Movement attracted my attention and I looked up. Three women were standing on a balcony above me, their smiles quickly hidden by fans. A feather drifted down to rest at my feet, as blue as a summer sea.

'Remember me when the time comes, bow-woman,' one of the women cried.

'No, *me* – remember me,' and then their voices were lost in laughter. They disappeared inside like puppets on a string. I bent to pick up the blue feather. When I straightened up again, Gemaley was standing in front of me. She was wearing her leathers and the stars sparkled in her hair as she tossed her head back. She was carrying a bow of her own, an arrow notched, and pointing at my throat. She gave a slow, ragged smile and abruptly vanished.

'Ruan!' I was not even sure that I had called out until he came running.

'What is it?'

'I saw Gemaley.'

'What? Where?'

'Here – just in front of me.'

We looked quickly around, but the lower windows of the houses were tightly shuttered and there were no openings into which she could have stepped. I reached out with the seith, but all I could sense was Ruan, and a growing tension in the air that snapped back against the edges of the seith like a rebounding bowstring.

'We have to get to the gate,' Ruan said, but he sounded uncertain.

'If she's here, Frey might be with her, in which case there's no point.'

We stood indecisively in the street for a moment.

'Can you sense either of them?' Ruan asked.

'No. Can you?'

'No.' But he looked nervous and I could not blame him.

'We'll go on to the gate,' I said.

I was now beginning to feel more certain that Frey had really been here last night and had led me out to see the visen. But why – as a warning? As a threat?

Just before we reached the gate, I felt his presence. A taut ripple ran along the edges of the seith, making me catch my breath.

'Vali? What's wrong?'

'He's here.' I was suddenly very sure. I stood still,

listening. I felt cold within the confines of the seith, as though it was turning to ice, but when I put out my hand and touched the wood of a door frame, it was warm in the spring sunlight.

'Are you certain?'

'I'm certain.'

There are negative and positive energies, the satahrach had told me. Most settlements had been built on the positive ones, to sustain the community. Just as I had used the power of the land under the broch, perhaps I could use this earth-energy, too. I leaned my hands against the sun-warmed wood and closed my eye.

'Vali? I'll keep watch.'

I liked the fact that Ruan did not attempt to question me, or interfere, though it was a little worrying he seemed to have acquired so much trust in me. I hoped it would be justified.

Reaching down through the stones beneath my feet, I could feel the energy that the satahrach had spoken of. It ran right through the middle of the town, parallel with the coast. It was like putting a hand over a huge, humming wire; I could feel its vibration all the way up my spine, reverberating around the bones of my skull. I imagined it being drawn up through the soles of my feet, travelling up my backbone, following the vibration and reinforcing the seith. And imagination made it real.

I opened my eyes. I could still feel the connection with the energy meridian underneath the streets and it was as though I had acquired a whole new set of senses. I could see Ruan's personal field around him; a calm colourless shimmer. Behind me, the narrow street was filled with traces and patterns left by passers-by – and two streaks of shadow. This, I knew, was where Gemaley and Frey had been. It was as though I had suddenly gained the senses of an animal, seeing scents in the air. The shadows led round the corner.

'They went this way,' I said to Ruan. He reached out and touched my arm.

'I will ask again – are you sure? Because in a little while, they will close the gates and the town defences.'

'I can see where they passed,' I said.

'Then you lead, and I'll go with you.' He did not ask any more questions. By now, the sunlight was starting to sink and deepen, casting ink-black shadows across the streets. I looked up at slanting eaves, half expecting to see Gemaley astride the roof ridge like a hunting falcon. With Ruan beside me, I followed the street to its end and then up a flight of steps. The traces of Gemaley and Frey were still lingering in the air, like dark mist, but as I came to the top of the steps, the trail split. They had separated and headed off in different directions, and now that they were apart, each trail was fainter. I explained this to Ruan.

'You go after Frey, then,' he said. 'And I'll take Gemaley.'

'You won't be able to see her. And it's best if we stick together.' I was not entirely convinced of the truth of this, however. I did not like hunting in company, having to watch out for someone else's back as well as my own.

Reluctantly, Ruan said, 'Very well, then.' There was a tension in his face which, now I came to think about it, I had last seen when we were in the tower.

'What's the matter?'

'Vali – if we have to stay in town, I'm not sure how long I can hold it off. Maybe you have some way of dealing with it – the satahrachin do – but I don't think I can.'

'Hold what off?'

'The bloodmind.' The tabula hummed and whirred, denoting uncertainty.

'Ruan, I have no idea what you're talking about.'

'The change. When we lose consciousness.' He was staring at me askance. 'You really don't understand me, do you?'

'You mean you're likely to pass out?'

'No, not that. *Change*.'

A finger of coldness was beginning to creep up the length of my spine. 'Ruan, what sort of change? Into what?'

'Into our other selves. Our animal selves.'

I realized I was gaping at him with my mouth open. 'You change *shape*?'

'No,' he snapped, clearly frustrated. 'Of course not. We lose our awareness, follow our instincts. We stop being human.'

My first thought was: *oh, great!* Another hour and I would be surrounded by – what? A town full of lunatics? Those sentences in the anthropologist's report that had made no sense suddenly fell into place; the missing pieces of a puzzle.

I knew now what these people reminded me of, too. The selk, who altered and changed with the tides, from sentient to animal, and back again. I thought of the sheds outside Hetla and of Frey, here on Mondhile. I remembered the women of Nhem, made compliant, stripped of their awareness through the breeding programs which the women of the resistance were so frantically trying to resolve, and the laboratory that Frey had raided. I thought too of the mysterious Mondhaith house defences, making feral children into human beings.

And then I finally thought I knew why Frey had come here.

'Ruan, tell me,' I said, trying to get a grip on it. 'How – functional – are you going to be when this happens? Will you know who I am?'

'I doubt it. I won't even know who I am.'

'How long have we got?'

'Until sunset? Perhaps an hour. But it's already beginning.' He gave an uneasy shrug. And now that he mentioned it, I could see it in the faces of the people who were passing: a strange wildness behind the blank eyes; a touch of feral animation. The seith shuddered, as it had done when I had been surrounded by the visen. It was responding to the presence of beasts, not other human beings.

'And there's no way of stopping this – *bloodmind*, once it's begun?' I asked.

'No.' He shifted his weight onto the other foot, clearly unsettled. 'I wish you had not seen them. I wish we had been able to get out of the town.'

I refrained from pointing out that we might have had a similar problem as soon as he reached the tower – given its effect on him – but it did not seem very productive to say so.

'Vali – when this really begins, I will be worse than useless. I might even pose a threat to you. We kissed, and I think you are— anyway, if I—' he paused.

'If you what? Want me? Are you saying that you might turn on me?'

He shifted uncomfortably. 'It's a possibility.'

'All right,' I said. 'Maybe it's best if we separate, then.' A thought struck me. 'Ruan – will Gemaley be going through the same process, or whatever it is?'

'Yes. She might have uncommon abilities, but she's still human.' *As you are not.* The unspoken words hung over the tabula's translation like a shadow. But at least Frey would be having the same problems with his sidekick as I would be having with mine – assuming of course that he regarded it as a problem. With the vitki, who knew?

'Go, then,' I told him. 'If you want to look for Gemaley in the time remaining to you, then I think she went down there and round the corner.' The mist was still hanging in the air. I could see it in the waning sunlight, like dust, but it was slowly starting to evaporate. I watched Ruan run lightly along the street and disappear, and could not refrain from a sigh of relief when he had finally gone. Now that I was on my own again, responsible only for myself, I could concentrate once more. But I could not help worrying as to what would happen when he encountered Gemaley.

I made my way up onto the town wall. There were not so many people here, and those that I passed drew away from me, sliding into the deepening shadows to stare out, bright-eyed. If these people became animals, even though the transformation might not be a physical one, then what sort of animals would they become? But I already knew the answer to that. Humans were predators at heart, and these people had been engineered to be more predatory still. I kept a close grip on the bow and checked the long knife at my belt. It was not just Frey and Gemaley that I had to worry about.

I glanced over the wall into the forest. Either I had come up at a different point, or I really had dreamed the episode of the night before, because I did not recognize the landscape that I saw. Here, the trees grew as thickly as they had done just beyond the tower, and created a carpet of branches some feet below the top of the wall. I now had the chance to study the wall itself: a structure with round keeps and arrow-slits; like something from old Earth or the more ancient parts of the Reach. Like the tower.

There was no point in lingering. Frey's trace, fading fast with the daylight, led along the wall towards the west. I went after it, looking down onto crowded streets on one side – filled with the glowing colours of the masque – and the silent forest on the other.

The wall took me in a long curve round the town, along the boundary of the trees to a point where I could look out to sea. I took a moment to gaze towards the islands, now changing swiftly to shade as dusk swept across the land. Far beyond the town, the distant peaks caught the sunset, turning to fire, and glowing. To the west, the red sun hung low over the sea, linking the town to the horizon with a path of blood. As I watched, it slipped over the edge of the world, leaving a flash of gold imprinted on my retina, then was gone. A sudden hush fell over the murmuring streets. The only sounds were the breeze rising in the forest and the hissing snap of coals in a brazier below. It was as though the whole town was waiting.

I felt an unseen touch upon the edges of the seith, a tremor running through my bones, but then it was gone. Twilight had fallen; beyond, the town came alive again, and any trace of Frey had vanished from the air. But I could feel something else: a kind of trembling far beneath my feet.

The seith drew inwards to envelop me, a strange protective sensation. It was as though the land underneath was reaching up to encase me in a pocket of air, to keep me safe. It was almost like the brush of another consciousness against mine, as though I was standing facing someone. Perhaps for the first time, I began to appreciate that my ancestors had not merely been superstitious when they spoke of the spirits of a place. But then the other consciousness, too, was gone; rushing past me and down into the town. I thought this must mean that the settlement's defences had been raised. When I looked after it, I saw Gemaley.

This time, she was quite visible. She was standing at a street corner, the bow still notched in her hands, looking about her with a terrible eagerness. I could see the mottled bruising along her jaw, where I had dislocated it. And there was something else in her face as well: an odd, wondering naivety: the country girl, come to town. I must have worn the same expression myself, once. It occurred to me that she might never have had the chance to visit such a town before.

She turned and went swiftly down the street. I dropped from the wall onto the edge of a flight of steps and followed her. I did not think she had seen me – shrewdness did not appear to be Gemaley's forte – and there was no sign of either Ruan or Frey.

She was moving fast, almost running, and as she sped on she slung the bow back over her shoulder with an impatient movement, as though it was bothering her. The streets were emptying now, people swarming down through the town towards some unknown congregation point, but a few remained, crouching in the shadows like panicked animals. I gave them a wide berth. One woman hissed at me and I dodged aside. Gemaley must have heard it; she threw a glance back over her shoulder and I ducked into a doorway. When I looked out again, she had disappeared.

Although twilight had fallen fast and the stars were coming out over the roofs, the town was still brightly lit. Lanterns, painted with the faces of demons and animals, hung from the eaves and the overhang of balconies, and the braziers cast their own light and warmth. I could no longer see the trail that Gemaley was leaving behind her, but I could feel it. When I held out my hand, it grew cold, as though I had laid it in an icy stream. I chased her along another street and it was there that I saw her meet Ruan.

He was standing outside a house, looking bewildered, as if he did not understand what was happening to him. From the subtle changes on the faces of those around me, I suspected that this was probably the case. He did not immediately see Gemaley, but she certainly spotted him. Her face grew tight and drawn; intent, like a cat hunting. She slipped into the entrance of an alley. I was not close enough to hear what she said, or see what she did, but the light and the air around me seemed to slow and thicken. Ruan's face grew slack. He walked swiftly and without hesitation into the alley.

Cursing, I ran forward, but by the time I reached the alley, they had both disappeared. I looked up and down, searching vainly and unable to shake off the impression that Gemaley was still standing there, watching me from some unnatural hiding place. Then I was picked up bodily from behind, spun round, and dumped against a wall.

'Frey! No!' The voice did not sound like mine, but when I looked up I saw that it was neither Frey nor Gemaley, but a total stranger. I experienced a quick rush of sheer injustice and then, with a snarl, the man fell on me. I was not sure whether it was rape or murder he had in mind and I did not wait to find out. I felt sharp teeth graze my throat and his grip on my wrists was strong. I twisted round, kicked up and felt my foot connect with his knee. He fell back with a gasp.

I scrambled to my feet and kicked him in the jaw. He dropped like a stone. I spent a moment checking to see that I hadn't killed him – he might have just tried to murder me, but I couldn't help thinking that it wasn't entirely his fault – and ran back out into the street. I could hear a voice coming from one of the upper floors above me. It had a raw, pleading note which I recognized as Ruan's. I would love to have believed that Ruan could take care of himself, but I didn't think he could.

I tried the front door but, sensibly, someone had bolted it shut against the mayhem outside. I couldn't work out how Gemaley and Ruan had got up there; the balcony was a good fifteen feet above the ground. In the end I shinned up the door frame, jumped for the balcony and hauled myself over the edge.

The doors to the balcony were open. I stepped through billowing curtains into a dim, smoky room. Gemaley's eyes glared out of the shadows like lamp-lit ice. She had backed Ruan onto the bed and was crouching over him on hands and knees. He did not seem to be objecting.

'Gemaley!' I shouted, without any great hope that she would even understand me. 'Leave him alone!'

Her lip curled back in a snarl, with her hair falling all

over her face – a visen would have looked more human. I raised the bow but she skittered backwards, spider-swift, through the curtains at the other end of the room. Ruan lay where he was, wearing an expression of mild bafflement. He would not, I surmised, be good for much at the moment. I drew the knife, fought the curtains aside and ran after Gemaley. I trapped her in the hallway; she was in a corner, spitting and hissing. It was clear that any real awareness she might have possessed had been burned away by the effects of the masque; there was certainly no sign of any behind her pale eyes.

I did not hesitate, and raised the bow. Better to kill her from a distance than risk closing in on her with the knife; I had seen how quick she could be. Deep inside me, there was still that dreadful, unwilling, ache of desire, but I refused to listen to it. I notched the arrow, took aim, then the front door burst open. Frey was immediately between us. I fired. The arrow sang through the air and buried itself in someone's elegant tapestry. Frey and Gemaley were both gone, out into the night.

I ran back up the stairs to discover that, ironically, Ruan had disappeared as well, and the doors to the balcony were blowing about. I did not bother with the stairs but dropped from the balcony onto the street. There was no one to be seen, but I sensed Frey. I ran in the direction that my instinct told me, and once again came out onto the city wall. At this rate, I could have just stayed put and let Frey come to me. I could not see anyone, but at that moment a flare of light from one of the braziers set against the wall illuminated one of the little keeps and I saw movement within.

I crept closer, grasping the bow. They were both inside the keep, but as I edged into the cloak of the shadows, Gemaley emerged. She was staggering and Frey moved to support her, holding her by the shoulders.

'Gemaley! Can you hear me? I want you to call them. Can you do that? Can you understand me, you feral bitch?' His voice was urgent. She slumped over his arm, head lolling backward. Her eyes were a translucent white in the glow of the brazier and there was a wet redness about her mouth.

'Gemaley?' Frey slapped her hard across the face. She hissed, but stood upright and stayed there, swaying. 'Call them!'

Slowly, her mouth opened. I saw her lick her lips. Frey swung her round towards the forest, which by now lay completely in darkness, with only the thin light of the moons striking the occasional damp branch. He shoved her behind the curve of the keep, making it impossible for me to get a clear shot. From Gemaley's throat came the sound that I heard before; the cry that had brought the visen running from the trees, pouring obediently into the clearing to their mistress' feet.

Surely they could not be hoping to draw the visen here, into the town – but then I remembered the fenris standing over me, my blood running down into the snow, and I grew cold and shaky and still. The forest started to rustle as though the wind was rising. It was a sound I knew. The visen were coming, Gemaley's animal army, and there was nothing I could do about it. There was no one I could tell: the inhabitants of the town; Ruan; Ruan's family – everyone had gone beyond the human, beyond speech and comprehension.

I ran along the wall, heading for Gemaley. The cry echoed around the walls of the town, bouncing back from the forest, and the pack answered; a long ululating cry rose from a hundred throats to fill the air. Even if she had managed to draw them here, surely they would be unable to scale the wall. But even as this thought occurred to me, I saw a pale body hurtle up into the treetops. It seemed that visen could climb after all, if they chose. The first beast leaped, hitting the wall not far from Gemaley and scrambling over. The arrow was already notched, so I fired.

Eleshtra's bow was a powerful one; it sang as it loosed the arrow. The arrowhead struck the visen just behind the rib cage, sending it rolling over and over to lie still on the wall. Gemaley shrieked and Frey spun round, but I was already dropping over the wall to land in the street. It was a hard fall, but I was down behind a buttress and out of range of Gemaley's bow.

It was, in any case, too late. The visen were over the wall, a pale flood streaming down into the town. They ignored me as they passed and I wondered why. I glanced round the side of the buttress. Gemaley and Frey were nowhere to be seen. Holding the bow at the ready, I followed the visen.

Turning a corner, I came face to face with a middle-aged

woman, swathed in crimson robes. Under normal circumstances, I thought, she might have been a gracious, serene person; I could see the vestiges of it in her face. But now her expression was distorted, lips drawn back against her teeth, eyes shining. The visen came from behind me. There was a sudden heavy softness against my legs as it brushed against me and sprang. The woman went down, but she went down fighting, clawing at the beast's flank, teeth aiming at its throat. I put an arrow in its neck and dragged her out from beneath a fountain of blood. She struck out, sending me reeling against the wall, and took to her heels, still growling.

Further down into the town, carnage was taking place on both sides. I saw old women and young girls fighting in close combat with the pack, a seething mass of no-longer-humans. Coming down some steps, I almost tripped over another prone body of a visen, paws curled in death like a sleeping cat, but most of the corpses were of the townspeople.

To fight something like this, you needed weapons and cunning, not bare hands. A visen outweighed a human by a long way. I had the bow, but a limited stock of arrows and I wanted to save two of them, at least, for Frey and Gemaley. I used all the arrows I dared, then tore them bloody from the carcasses, but in the main I used the knife. The visen growled at me, and one swatted with a casual paw, but they did not attack and I could not think why. I felt in greater danger from the Mondhaith.

The first was a woman, old, with a skein of white hair.

She could have been my grandmother, apart from the hissing. She turned, then came at me so swiftly that she became no more than a blur, her face a fixed mask of hate, striking out at me with long slivers of claws. I turned too slowly and felt her talons rake down my cheek. The sudden burn brought back the memory of the fenris' attack. I staggered, striking my shoulder blades painfully against a wall. Distantly, a small cold voice within told me that what with Gemaley's earlier assault and then this, I was now likely to have scars on either side of my face. At least they'd match.

She struck out at me again, and this time I blocked the blow and punched her. I caught her on the side of the jaw and she crumpled to the floor. I looked around to see if I could put her safely away from the tearing jaws of the visen. I did not want to leave her in the street. Eventually I forced a door open and hauled her behind it, dragging her towards the door as I closed it, as best I could. I hoped it would keep her safe.

My face was stinging, but the cut did not seem as deep as I'd feared. I turned to go back down the street when a heavy body jumped on me from above. I cried out, convinced in that instant that it was one of the animals. But it was another man. His weight felled me, and this time it was obvious that it was not murder he had in mind, at least, not immediately. I could feel his erection against my thigh and his eyes had a darkness in them that conveyed a total clarity as to his intentions.

My arms were pinned and recent panic filled me, along

with the pain of my wounds. I twisted, rolled, tugged them free and clapped both hands to his ears. If that didn't work, I would try an eye gouge, but I still felt handicapped by the desire not to do any substantial damage to anyone. He reared up, and I rolled to my feet, then rabbit-punched his neck. He collapsed forward and lay still. But I did not have the time to pull him to safety, as the visen pack was pouring in from the end of the street. I did not stop to see what they might do to his fallen form. I ran.

And all the time I was conscious of Frey or Gemaley suddenly appearing while my back was turned. I saw no sign of Ruan and I was terrified for him. None of these people were in any condition to withstand this kind of attack, which was presumably why Frey had arranged it. But why the attack in the first place? What purpose was all this serving, aside from mayhem?

A girl ran past me, face contorted, mouth and hands covered with blood. I looked back to see one of the visen loping towards me; a much larger beast than the rest, with a marked black mane striping down its back. The girl must have seen the pack behind me, and cried out, a shrill, desperate shriek, beyond fear. I swerved down an alleyway and I must confess I was hoping that she would distract them. But if they killed her, then it wouldn't take long.

I can't remember now where I ran. Buildings passed by in a haze of terror, lit red by lamps and fire. I remember the sudden reek of smoke on the wind and thinking that this was too strong to have come from one of the braziers, and that a part of the town must be on fire. Here, in this place of wooden beams and carved balconies and boarded bridges, fire would be a disaster, and it filled me with a fear that was as old as humanity.

I no longer had a direction, and any shielding that the seith might have given me was gone, tattered and torn by panic. I should have ducked into a building, hidden myself behind walls and doors, but the fear was too great and too old and it drove me on. Then I turned down yet another alleyway and saw the town wall rising straight ahead. It was a dead end, and the pack was right behind me.

The top of the wall was lost in darkness. I leaped, scrabbled for a handhold, and found none. I did not have the laser piton that had served me well enough in Darkland, nor the fibreline that I had used on Nhem. Only my own hands and my wits, and they were not enough. Slowly, the great brindled pack leader came forward.

THIRTY-FOUR

PLANET: MONDHILE

Ruan knew only glimpses; shadow and flame and desire. He ran past glittering eyes and clasping hands, not noticing whether they belonged to women or men. The only thing that mattered, the only thing that drew him on, was her, and he had scented her on the wind. He could see her scent, too – a faint gleaming trail in the air ahead of him, growing brighter and fiercer with every step he took. It was almost as though she ran beside him, just as she had moved with such sinuous grace by his side on the day they had met.

He knew, now, that he should never have left her. He was not capable of putting it into words, for language had drained from him like the rain after a storm, but he was part of her, belonging, wanting only to sit at her feet or lie in her arms. Without her, he was nothing more than a shadow, halfway to the world of the dead, a landless spirit.

The beasts seemed to recognize that he was less than flesh, for they left him alone. At one point, he found himself running with them, moving with their water-flow, and he understood then that they ran according to certain patterns; following the water under the earth just as a human might do, drawn by the tides of the moon and pushed by the swell of the sea. He had not realized before that the visen migrated, as humans did, but their migration season was not yet upon them and they were drawn by the same thing that he was – by her.

She was their lodestar, their north, and Ruan ran with the visen in perfect accord for a time, until they seemed to catch another scent, something stranger, out of place, foreign and yet familiar. It was not strong enough to distract Ruan from his goal and he ran on as the pack slipped silently away. Dimly, he was glad when they vanished, for now he could concentrate fully upon her, and would not have to share.

And then, at last, he found her. And she was not as he had expected.

THIRTY-FIVE

PLANET: MONDHILE

The pack leader stalked forward with the same stiff movement that I had seen in predators elsewhere. I raised the bow, but I had only three arrows left. I began, through the haze of fear, to set targets: one for the leader; one each for the two biggest visen on either side. I raised the bow but my hands were shaking. Memories of the fenris were flooding in, flashback-swift, hallucinatory in their intensity.

And then the pack leader spoke to me.

She did not speak in words. She communicated through the seith, which was suddenly back around me and yet opening up, as though a hole had developed in the heart of the world and let me see through into another realm. I could not only feel the pack, but was part of it, and it was inviting me in. The emotions relayed to me were not human; not even close to human. They spoke to me of the land, and connection with it; a seamlessness with the world, a swaying on the world's tides, and those of the moon and the sea, all of which I could feel around me.

I remember wondering why the Mondhaith even bothered with language, why any of us did, why we insisted on this artificial separation between ourselves and the real nature of things, and I knew that self-consciousness was curse as much as blessing. And for the first time I understood the visen: the hierarchies that existed between them; the connectivity of the pack. I realized, too, that I had been basing my reaction to the pack on assumptions that were not correct. The pack leader was not female; none of them were, or male either. Their gender shifted and changed with the moons, and currently, apart from a few with egg sacs, they were all neutral. Remembering Nhem, I recall thinking that this fluidity, too, might be no bad thing.

I reached out my hands to the pack leader and it came forward and licked them. I had expected roughness, but the beast's tongue was soft and slippery; not at all pleasant. It raised its head, which reached the level of my jawline, and licked the blood from my face as gently as a kitten. Its breath stank of human blood and I took a step back.

The visen padded after me patiently, as though I were a cub that did not yet understand. The others waited, a silent mass, thinking the same thoughts. The leader's tongue slid once more down my face and it was as though it was try-ing to heal what the fenris had begun, licking the scars away. I turned my head to escape its attentions and caught a flicker of movement from the corner of my eye. Frey stepped out of the shadows.

'Very good,' he said.

I raised the bow. 'I've been expecting you.'

'Of course you have. I've been here a while. You can put that down. It should be obvious by now that I don't mean you any harm.'

'No? You had me savaged by one wild animal, and now you're scheming to have me savaged by another?'

'Do they look as though savagery is their aim?'

'No. Are you controlling them?'

'No. Are you?'

'What do you mean?'

'This is what it has always been about, Vali. Your breakthrough, into your heritage. You think I've been trying to kill you. That isn't true. I've been trying to change you, but I couldn't say so in front of Gemaley. She gets . . .' he paused and smiled, '. . . a little jealous. I suppose that when you've never had much, you want to keep what you have, clutch it close.'

'I can't imagine *you* responding well to that.'

'No, I don't. But Gemaley's useful, just as you are. I was so delighted when you showed up here, Vali. You cannot imagine . . .'

'*Useful.* It's a very vitki thing to say.'

The pack leader whined, as if seeking my attention, and without stopping to think about it I found myself reaching down and scratching the thick mane, as though the visen was nothing more than a dog. The coat was not coarse, but very thick and fine, floating through my fingers like down.

'But vitki is where you come from, Vali. You have

Darkland blood in you. I don't know where or when, but there are traits bred into you that are pure vitki and you only have to use them. You're not meant for the Skald. You're meant for us. And I mean to take you back.'

'That's not true.' He was quite mad. I could see it in his eyes. He couldn't bear it that I had slipped away from him, and it had nothing to do with love for me. He would have been the same with any woman.

'Isn't it? You've let the Skald constrain you, not train you. All of your talents could have been there for the using if you'd only acknowledged them. You are part predator; you have the ability to use senses that are not available to everyone, and that makes you special. I could smell it in you the moment I walked into the room and we first met. Why do you think I chose you for my apprentice?'

'Then why did you try to kill me?'

'I *wasn't* trying to kill you, Vali. I was trying to wake you up. The journey we made onto the icefield was supposed to be your initiatory journey, your ingsgaldir, but where I went wrong was in underestimating the degree of resistance in you to your abilities. I thought the fenris would break through your prejudices and trigger your non-sentient side, just as the Mondhaith enter the bloodmind – just as you've connected with the pack leader. That's what happened with me. I ran with the fenris on my ingsgaldir, Vali. I ran with the pack. But you showed too much fear and the fenris attacked. It was too young, as well. A more mature beast would have held back. If you'd

390

only listened to me, become my shadow in truth instead of resisting, you would have been able to connect with your own instincts and mastered them.'

'So it's all my fault? My injuries?'

'Partly, yes.' He sounded gently reproving, as though I was a student who had gone astray. 'But now, you see, you've finally come into your own. You've become part of a pack. Wasn't that worth it?'

'If I've made some kind of breakthrough,' I said, slowly, 'it's because of the training that the Skald has put me through, not through anything you've done or because of anything I innately am.' And it still did not answer the question of why Frey had come here in the first place, but I had thought I was starting to understand the answer to that.

'You ought to thank me.' His head tilted back, with that old challenging arrogance. There were many things I could have said. *Who are you to tell me what I am and what I should become, to change me without my consent or knowledge? What right do you have to do that, to withhold information about me that should be automatically mine, to play the magician over my life?*

But I said none of this. Words are just words, empty on the wind. If the visen were indeed my pack, and this the result of my ingsgaldir, then I may as well use these things. Instead of more talking, I reached out through the seith into the mind of the pack, and asked them to work my will. The pack leader sprang forward and the pack followed, almost bowling me over as they poured around me. I saw an instant of dismay on Frey's face, a moment of uncertainty, and that was all the revenge I needed, short of his death. But then he was gone, sailing up over the wall. Trust a vitki to have an escape route. It didn't matter. We followed.

The pack was practised in climbing, presumably a legacy of their mountain heritage. They swarmed up on one another's backs. I climbed a ladder of bony spines, springing upward until I was standing on the wall. I looked from side to side but could not see Frey. It didn't matter. The pack could scent him and so, therefore, could I.

We ran along the now-familiar wall, the pack holding back a little so that I could keep up; two legs are always going to be slower than four. But Frey was the quarry and I did not need them to wait for me; I could sense where they were going and what they were up to, even if I had been on the other side of the town. I urged them on and the pack went. Only the leader remained, gliding silently by my side. I could sense what it was feeling: *I will not leave you.*

Silently, I indicated that the leader should go, but it did not react. And so, as swiftly as we could, we followed the pack along the walls of the town. They took me over the wall, down through the trees, and with them I felt only the faintest shiver of the settlement's defence. We headed into the forest, following Frey.

THIRTY-SIX

PLANET: MONDHILE

Gemaley was crouched against the wall, huddled in a ball, shivering. A great wave of protectiveness filled Ruan and he dropped to his knees beside her. The energies of the masque were fading, ebbing away. He did not yet have the words to ask her what was wrong, but he put his arms round her and she sank into them. It was only then that he felt complete. He knew that he could stop running, stay here with her. He looked up and saw a moon over the shoulder of the town wall, a thin crescent of light that seemed to illuminate Gemaley's own face, so that the girl and the moon were one. He bent his head and nuzzled her cheek as her trembling arms crept around his neck, and that was when she struck him.

He was moving. There was a lurching, uneven sensation beneath him. He was lying on his back, facing the stars. There was another moon in the sky now, little Elowen, and it looked hard and cold and distant. The bloodmind had ebbed, leaving him hollow, but language and awareness had come back to him. So had memory, in contorted fragments. He raised his head and found himself looking along his own body to a long, whisking tail. His arms and legs were bound to the back of a mur; he could see the knobbed vertebrae of the tail as it switched from side to side.

'Gemaley!' He had no doubt as to who had so bound him and taken him from the town. 'Gemaley, where are we going?' But he had no doubts about that, either. There was no reply.

The beast snorted, evidently disliking the sound of an unfamiliar human voice. Gemaley must have stolen it from one of the pens in the town.

'Gemaley!' He was determined to make her acknowledge him. He cried her name over and over again, until at last the beast came to an abrupt stamping halt and Gemaley's face, incandescent with fury, appeared alongside Ruan's own.

'*What is it?* You are making enough fuss to bring back the dead!'

'What do you expect me to do?' Ruan snapped. There was love and longing there, somewhere, but there was also a dawning, growing rage, as though Gemaley's own fury had been the spark that had touched his own alight. 'You strike me, kidnap me, carry me across country to that damned ruin of yours and why? Because you haven't got anything, Gemaley. Everything you manage to possess goes to feed that thing underneath the tower. You have nothing of your own – no real family, no real clan, no real childhood. You are nothing. All that you have and are is one great gaping pit.' The words tumbled out on a torrent of anger, as though the bloodmind had simply served to dam them up behind a wall of unknowing.

Gemaley stared him, open-mouthed. It struck him that perhaps no one had ever questioned her like this before, except perhaps Vali's former lover. And indeed, there were few enough people to question. She cared nothing for anything save her own desires, unaware that others were as real as herself.

Then, Gemaley appeared to compose herself. He saw her force the rage from her face, until it was as white and remote as the moon.

'But I do have something, Ruan,' she said, sounding utterly reasonable. 'I have *you*.' Then she turned away and he heard her click her tongue to the mur and they were moving on.

THIRTY-SEVEN

PLANET: MONDHILE

Running with the visen, I lost track of the time, and I think this may have been because their own sense of its passage was so fluid, drawn only by the seasons and the turning of the day. Thus it was with a distinct shock that I realized the long night was approaching an end and the sun was coming up over the distant wall of the mountains. Then it was at the summit and the forest was flooded with light. I had no idea where we were. The pack moved silently and swiftly, the leader always close by my side, pausing with a strange graciousness as I stumbled over logs and splashed through pools. If it had possessed hands, I thought, it would surely have reached out and offered me one. It would perhaps have been easier if I had been able to ride on its back, but the arched, bony spine made it an impossible mount.

Around us, the forest was coming into its morning life. Dew dripped from the bracket fungus that thronged the red bark, sparkling down onto thick webs and into the long columns of the ferns. The air sparkled around pitcher plants and the visen avoided these, skirting carefully around them. I remembered their hallucinogenic effects and was careful to keep close to the pack. But linked to the pack's senses as I was, the place already possessed an almost hallucinatory quality: every little thing magnified to twice its degree of brightness and relevance. This must be what it was like to be an animal; heightened attention and awareness, all the time, for life depended on it. Everything else – Ruan's safety, the whereabouts of Gemaley, the state of the town now that the visen had left and the bloodmind had, perhaps, worn away – all of these concerns had dwindled until the slightest movement of an insect among the fern fronds had eclipsed them. The pack's single focus was now its own security, and its prey.

Like the pack, I could see Frey's scent on the air and I understood now that my earlier glimpse of it had little to do with the actual seith, and a great deal to do with my growing link to the pack. The visen had recognized it before I had; this had been, of course, why they had not attacked me. If this was the result of the ingsgaldir, I began to understand why the vitki prized it so, but I still did not believe that it made me special. I had a particular genetic heritage, nothing more.

I was certain that Frey was heading for his pod, and I tried to communicate this to the pack leader, but without success. It was not only the lack of words, but the lack of concepts, and I did not expect this of them. Theirs was a closed and insular world, a sealed system, with no room for anything new. They had absorbed me, but I could not be the pearl in their oyster. I must become just another part of the pack, to be assimilated, not to command change.

It seemed to me that whatever genetic engineering might have been committed upon them, the visen had been this way for thousands upon thousands of years, highly successful predators, and I could neither anticipate nor count on an alteration in them. I was trying not to think of what would happen when we had accomplished our goal and it became time for me to leave. I was not sure that they would let me.

As time wore on it became clear that Frey was not heading for the pod after all. The forest was starting to grow familiar and I felt a distinct sense of satisfaction from the pack leader, as if everything was gradually coming into place. The red-and-black trees thinned as the rocky outcrops grew more frequent, spiralling unevenly up into the morning light. Frey was making for the tower.

As soon as I realized this, I stopped dead. The pack leader hung back anxiously, ears flattened with concern. I sent images of the tower, my fear of it, memories of the injuries I had sustained there. And the pack sent back a flow of understanding, reassurance: *you are with us now. You will be safe. This is our place.* To them, it was home and I finally understood. The caves underneath the tower were their lair. And Gemaley had been part of the pack, too, fulfilling the same role that I now did, being part of the pack, bringing them in and feeding them. But if we were going to the tower, what of Gemaley? I did not think there was room for two queens in one pack, and that meant, or so I thought, that one of us would have to kill the other, or at least battle for dominance. And if I killed her, how would the pack react? But the leader was pulling me on now, teeth gently locked round my wrist. Deal with Frey first, I resolved, and then we'll think about Gemaley. Yet I did not think Gemaley was the kind of woman to wait in line.

Another few moments and the tower came into sight. This time, it filled me with conflict – accustomed terror at the very sight of the place, fuelled by memories of pain and humiliation, and a fierce, flooding relief: *now we are home at last*. My own self was at war with my pack self and it was tearing me in two. I slowed down, again, and it was perhaps fortunate for my dilemma that it was at this moment we set eyes on Frey.

He was standing in front of the tower, on the worn steps, looking back over the forest. Even from this distance, I saw that fierce smile, and knew that this had been his intention all along, to draw us here. But I did not yet know why. When he saw that I had seen him, he ran lightly up the steps and into the tower, leaving the heavy door open behind him. It was a deliberate taunt.

The pack saw none of this. Their sole focus was on Frey and his death; they did not have the conceptual apparatus to consider a trap. I tried to pull them back, frantically searching for a way to communicate my fears. I sent images of traps in the earth, leg irons, every means of securing an animal that I could think of, but the visen simply did not understand and it was at that point that I realized that they had no experience of such things.

Perhaps another pack, in a more populated part of the world, might do, but this group was entirely wild. Yet Gemaley must have found some way of luring them to her bidding; but then maybe her role was no more than mine. The pack surrounded me, encouraging, evidently mistaking my misgivings for simple fear. They surged on, carrying me with them towards the tower.

THIRTY-EIGHT

PLANET: MONDHILE

By working his hands against the leather bonds that held him, Ruan was at last able to free a claw. He began to slice through the thongs, taking careful note of the landscape around him. It was now past dawn and much colder than it had been down in the town. They were back into the high country now, with snow still lying along the spines of the ridges and the gleam of icy water from the lake below, away to the left. They were traversing one of the ridges, a thin arch of rocks above the snowline. Then the thong finally parted against Ruan's claws and gave way.

He lay still for a moment, estimating Gemaley's presence at the head of the mur, then, very cautiously, he uncurled himself from the animal's back and sat up. The mur danced, but only a little. Ruan slid down from its back to the ground. Immediately the mur turned on him, whirling around, teeth bared. Gemaley cried out in rage. He could sense, emanating from her, that same compulsion, an insidious force that attempted to command worship – but this time, it failed. They were too far from the line of energy on which she fed, too far from the tower.

She hauled back on the mur's bridle, just in time to prevent the long sharp teeth from raking Ruan's shoulder. She smacked it across the flank and it snarled at her, the narrow eyes crimson and slitted in the long head. He felt her senses hammer out and strike it – and the mur, crying out, bounded down the slope in an erratic veering path, and away.

Gemaley, her own teeth bared, spun to face him, but finally Ruan was ready. Perhaps the residue of the blood-mind was still somewhere within, but tuned for death this time rather than desire. He did not wait for her to attack him, or try to work her will once more. This time, he sprang at her.

They rolled, snarling, down the slope, locked together. Ruan's teeth met in Gemaley's shoulder and he could taste her blood, curiously bitter, like poison. She bit and scratched and kicked. He felt her claws score his back, scrabbling for purchase on the leather armour and failing to find it. It was a surprise to him to learn that he really was the stronger. She had hidden it well, but now that it had come to this, it was not a fair fight at all.

Finally she grasped him by the hair and he felt her claws rake into the back of his scalp. The sensation was agonizing and somehow he welcomed it – not in the sub-missive way of their sexual games, but with a clarity and focus that could only come from pain and rage. By now they were both falling fast down the slope, a slide of packed snow and ice. A flickering memory of falling into the crevasse crossed his mind and then the thought that this was so much better, because now he would be taking Gemaley with him.

Out on the ice, something was shrieking. He did not stop to see what it was. When they reached the gentler slope of the foreshore, their fall was slowed and Ruan was able to roll over and clamber to his feet, dragging Gemaley after him. He struck her hard across the face, sending a spatter of blood over the snow. She spat and lashed out. The shrieking cries out on the lake intensified. Gemaley, to Ruan's surprise, broke away and stumbled down the slope towards the ice.

'Gemaley!' he cried, or thought he did. He was filled with fury at the thought that she might escape him, that at the last, when he was finally gaining the upper hand, it was Gemaley who should cut and run. He wondered, briefly, if this was how she had felt: a disbelieving rage at his temerity in not agreeing to be taken and slain. But Ruan was not interested in stopping to analyse her motives. Instead, he bolted after her, slipping on the ice at the foreshore and finally sliding out onto the lake.

Gemaley was a little way ahead of him now, and he could see what had been shrieking: a flock of serai in the middle of the lake. As far as he could make out against the snowfield, the birds were all in their white winter plumage; there was no black one among them. Gemaley was crying out to them in a high, thin voice and he realized that she was trying to summon them to her, to attack him.

But the serai were panicked by all the commotion and he did not think at that point that they would have listened to one of their own kind, let alone this sudden human in their midst. They took off in a whirl of wings, soaring up into the morning sky. There were so many of them that they eclipsed the sun and the lake grew dark in their shadow.

Gemaley dropped to one knee and stared after them, but then she recovered herself and turned to face Ruan. By now, he was a little less angry – as though the cold was slowly rising to kill the heat within him – enough to say, 'Gemaley, come back with me. It's not safe. Go back to your tower, do what you will. I want to stay with my clan. It's over.'

But Gemaley, her face twisted with spite and loss, struck out at him again. 'You don't understand! I have to feed the tower. I have no choice; I never have. If I don't feed it, it will come for me, devour me. And I want to live, Ruan. I want to live.'

She lashed out again, claws fully extended and glistening in the light like knives. He pushed her away and she fell hard, going down against the ice, and the thin film at the middle of the lake finally cracked.

Suddenly there was nothing except a fractured pavement beneath Ruan's feet and then that, too, was gone. He was down into icy water, so cold that it sucked the breath from his lungs and the warmth from his marrow. He struck out, managing only a few desperate strokes, but it was enough to bring him to the slabs of thicker ice near the shore and haul himself from the lake. He lay, gasping and winded, for a moment, then looked back.

Gemaley had hauled herself out, too, and lay motionless on the ice. He stumbled back, rocking on what was now a floe, but just as he was about to reach out, everything she had done rushed into his mind. If she herself had reached for his hand, he might have found it within himself to save her. But instead she struck, hissing, and he saw the mindless hate behind the pale blue eyes. He thought of Tian and Gith and Vali, and put a boot in her ribs.

She rolled over into the water with barely a ripple. He waited, balancing on a block of ice, but this time, she did not come up.

He called her name, realizing it to be useless, and sure enough, there was no reply. And he would freeze if he stood here, so he made his way as quickly as he could to the shore and clambered up the ridge to the sunlight. Its meagre warmth felt like the heart of a summer's day after the icy spell of the lake and he basked in it, drawing on the earth far beneath his feet, letting the warmth of spring rise up in him as the satahrach had taught him, but he was as weak as an infant. Slowly, far below, he thought he saw the lake beginning to freeze over. Gemaley did not emerge.

Later that morning, when Ruan was drier and had recovered some of his strength, he went back down the slope to look for her. He was very careful where he trod, noting where the ice looked thinnest; he did not think he could survive another ducking in that green-black water, but he had to know she was dead. Somehow, in the bruised, numb place that had once been his heart, it seemed impossible that she could have died, that he had been the one to kill her. He could not help picturing her waiting under the water, eyes open, ready to pounce upward and out in a shower of cold spray. But she did not do so, and when he finally found her, she did not move.

It was still morning, and the currents of the lake had taken her back toward its edge. She floated just under a clear patch of ice, only a little frosted by cold, and she shimmered. Her eyes were open, as he had imagined they would be, and her face was smiling slightly. She looked more peaceful than he had ever seen her. Even her hands were locked neatly across her breast, perhaps in some last effort to ward away the killing cold. Her long hair streamed out around her in spirals.

She had become ice, Ruan thought. Even if he managed to bring her body from the lake, she would shatter in the sunlight. And so after a long moment he turned and left her there, drifting beneath the ice. When he reached the ridge he looked back once, to see a single dark-winged bird flying in slow circles above the frozen water, drifting down like a dying leaf. He did not wait to see where it landed, but turned his back on the lake and set off down the ridge.

THIRTY-NINE

PLANET: MONDHILE

The pack took me up the steps and into the tower as I struggled to fight clear. I think they took my reluctance for the unwillingness of a pup to face something unknown; there was a palpable amusement in the way they nudged and shuffled me forwards, seething around me to prevent me from reaching the edges of the pack, as though it were all a great game. There was no sign of Frey. The tower felt as ruined and deserted as always, were it not for that presence underlying it – a demanding, pulling force that recognized me as soon as I stepped inside its confines, like something sitting up and taking notice.

The pack's ears pricked up, moving like a single animal, but that was all. We were through the hallway now, and Frey's own presence was very strong, hanging on the air. It was not like smelling someone, but a combination of essences: the feelings he produced in me; the seith sense of him; a mass of intangibles that still managed to generate a sharp and vivid whole.

The thing that lay under the tower was pulling us

downwards. The pack was used to it, and as they huddled me down the cellar stairs I felt the anticipation in them: now we will feed you. Now we will bring you prey. For a terrible moment I thought they meant me, but then I realized that they were thinking of Frey. I wondered why they had not taken him before – but Gemaley had been pack-queen then, and now I was.

We were in the cellar, the caves beneath the tower, its hollow foundation. Surely, I thought, through the mist of that presence, the tower itself could not long survive, perched as it was on this rotten core. A rise in the water level, a shift of the earth, and the tower would crumble and fall. The weight of the building seemed to lurch dizzily above me and only the press of the visen around me prevented me from falling myself.

I could see nothing, but the visen drew me on – and then, all of a sudden, they were no longer there. They had slipped away, as quietly and quickly as lizards into a crack. I could not even feel them and it left me feeling desolate. I stood alone in the dark, with the thing under the tower, and its full attention was on me, now.

'So,' Frey's voice said into my ear, making me start. 'They brought you back. I knew they would. They're very obedient, and of course, it fitted in with their own desires. You are pack leader now, after all.'

I whirled away from his voice, or thought I did, but he was again behind me now and fastening my arms painfully behind my back. I kicked behind, stamping down, but his foot hooked around my ankle and took my weight from me so that I was sagging in his grip.

'Frey? What the hell *do* you want?'

'I want you to come into your power, Vali. Just as Gemaley did, all unknowing. But she's a little savage, really. I've learned a lot from her, but there's no teaching her and she's too much in thrall to this place. I had to lie. When I find her, I'll take her back to Muspell and place her in a Darkland brood-pen. She'll be happy there, if they feed her enough drugs. I don't think she's ever known what to do with this, for example.'

'"This"?'

'The thing that lies here.'

'It's an energy sink.' I wrestled against his hands, but could not part them. His grip on me tightened.

'Stop fighting me, Vali.' It was a command, with the vitki powers of voice behind it, but this time I paid it no heed. I was more afraid of the well under the tower than I was of Frey, which made, I suppose, a refreshing change. 'It's more than an energy well. That might have been how it began, fed by lines of force that were inimical to humans. But over thousands of years, some of the folk who lived here must have become partially immune to it – or, it's more accurate to say, connected – until they couldn't live without it. Or it without them. It's conscious. It feeds from the seith of humans. The pack is linked to it. We're not talking about anything very sophisticated here, Vali. It's little more than a conscious mouth, really.'

'But that wasn't why you came here, was it?' *Keep him*

talking, this time. I was not yet in a position to strike. 'You came for the bloodmind. I saw you out on the icefield that day, controlling the selk. You know how to do that, don't you? Something in the voice, to switch off their sentient minds and change them back into animals again. But you couldn't control them for long. I saw them slip from your grasp. And I saw the experimental sheds outside Hetla, too. Did you get hold of the anthropologist's records about this place, and realize that on Mondhile there were humans who were similar to the selk?'

'Something like that.'

'And if you could learn more about it, find the key, what then? I saw what they did on Nhem. You wanted something like that for Muspell, didn't you? Either switch off people's awareness, or turn them into mindless beasts. I think you've been practicing on Gemaley, on the town. You brought the visen there to see what would happen when humans become unthinking predators and are faced with a foe.' Or perhaps it was simply that he was mad, I thought – half beast himself – and wanted to see blood. *Never mind that now. Keep talking.* 'I don't believe I'm special, Frey. I don't believe you are. That's just a vitki myth. Everyone in the north shares a similar genetic heritage. *What have you been looking for, Frey?* The key to switching off the sentience in "ordinary" humans? Put a few key vitki players into power, once the war-wings have subdued the Reach?'

His grip tightened further. 'You could be one of those

players, Vali. You've shown me that, here.' This time, his voice was soft and persuasive.

'I don't think so.' As I spoke, I was reaching out to the pack, calling them back, calling them in. It was hard, through the dissonance of the energy well. But at last the pack answered, and began to draw close.

Frey laughed. 'I know what you're doing, Vali. Won't work. Their gender changes, as I think you realize. They respond to those who are fixed in gender, but what you don't realize is that ultimately the male is always the dominant one. Just like everywhere else.'

'Not everywhere,' I said, thinking of the Skald, the parliament of the Reach, the women of the north. Idhunn seemed suddenly very close, as though she was standing next to me in the chamber, and the memory of her gave me a small shred of hope.

'Oh, but it's true,' Frey said, patiently, as if admonishing a child. '. . . everywhere where it matters.'

I closed my eyes and reached out to the pack leader, but its now-familiar presence was distracted and growing irritated, too. I was not behaving as I should. It thought that I should be obeying Frey and I was holding back, an ungoverned pup. I felt the needle-fanged muzzle nudge me, hard, in the small of my back. The rest of the pack were grouping around me.

'What do they think the well is?' I asked Frey, stalling for time.

'I have no idea. Their god, perhaps?'

'You don't know? Can't you – ask them?'

'They have no speech, only feelings. They're locked into their own small world, like all beasts, Vali.' He sounded amused, in complete control. 'There's no way out of here. Go on. Try it.'

For a moment, in response to his voice and that tone, the old cowed self I had once been, reasserted itself, and I felt again that he really was my mentor, the person who would make me into what I should become.

'*That's* better,' he was stupid enough to say and everything in me rebelled. No one had that power except myself, and no one was entitled to it except me. I stamped back, striking his instep, and jerked free. I was in the middle of the pack. The visen surged forward, taking me with them to the energy well. In the darkness, I was as blind as they. Frey was calling my name and there was a weird timbre to it; he was aiming at control.

If I had been able to locate him, I would have risked a shot with the bow, but his voice seemed to bounce and echo from the walls. He was taking no chances with me, and that made me feel a little better. I reached out with the seith, but everything was being obliterated by the dissonance of the well.

The pack took me with them. As we passed through the entrance to the chamber, I stepped on something that rolled beneath my feet and threw me to my knees among the pack. My palms hit the ground hard as the visen shifted out of the way and my face was momentarily buried in a mass of soft fur, the coat of the nearest animal.

The visen were milling around something that shifted and rattled and, to the seith, stank.

I reached out a groping hand and found my fingers brushing across something rough and hard, a texture that was immediately familiar to anyone who had spent time on the farm holdings of the Reach. I was surrounded by bones, and the smell was the stench of old and bloody death. For a moment, I could see them, their faces frozen against the dark, the inhuman eyes filled with hate. They looked like Gemaley. They were all that was left of her clan. She must have led the visen to them, used their death-throes to feed the well.

The centre of the energy well lay only a little way ahead, the chamber filled with its silent roar. It seemed to snatch at the seith, pulling me forward, draining it from me until I could feel myself becoming reed-hollow, as empty as the space between the stars. Moments before it was too late, I tore the senses back from its grip. I felt the energy well recoil – as though no one had done such a thing before – but then it lashed back with renewed force.

For an instant, I lost all sense of who and what I was. But when a fragment of consciousness returned to me, I knew what it wanted: information. Gemaley had seemed to think that it desired pain, but this was only one kind of information. The well wanted a mind, something to feed it, to inform it, and I knew also that it was not a natural thing. It had been put there, a very long time ago, and then abandoned. I could feel its loss, a great howling into the void. But I did not have time to analyse what it might be;

I had to fight back. I had to distract it. If it wanted information, I thought, then that is what I would give it.

I had never done such a thing before and I did not even know if it could be done, but I had to try. I activated the map implant and instead of concentrating on the data that was being downloaded – details of Muspell, details of Mondhile – I channelled it out into the seith. The well seized on it, leaving a corner of my mind free for the pack. I drew them to me, surrounding myself with them until we were a single mind. Frey wanted me to demonstrate my control over them; very well, then, that is what I would do. Slowly, I began to build up the image of him as the outsider, the enemy. I told the pack that he was not human, but something else; I called up the image of the fenris, standing snarling over my tattered body.

This is the one who attacked you? The pack leader thought, in images.

'This is the one.'

I could feel Frey trying to draw the pack back to him, establish authority, but I did not believe the myth of the dominant male and my disbelief was so strong that I communicated it to the pack.

'Isn't like us. Is different. Is an enemy.'

I felt a flicker in them and knew I was about to lose them. But they could sense where he stood, and therefore so could I.

I threw myself at him. For all his vitki senses, he wasn't expecting it and he reeled back, stumbled and fell. I lashed out, struck him in the crotch and as he curled, I buried my teeth in his throat. The visen needed no encouragement to join me – and their teeth were better than mine.

It must have been over in seconds, a quick, bloody death, but it seemed to last for ever. Frey's screams echoed in my ears. I would like to say, now, that I was not among those who tore flesh into fragments, splintered bone between my teeth, lapped blood. But I do not feel much guilt, even now. I do not know what that makes me. Perhaps at the last, Frey succeeded.

When we had finished, and there was nothing left except bones, the pack turned back to me to see what we should do. The map implant was coming to the end of its download; we had to get out of there. The pack did not understand why, but I had just delivered prey and they were indulgent. I went with the pack, out and up, relying on their sense of smell to take us into the tower.

Stumbling into the hallway of the tower, I recoiled. There was someone standing in the shadows. I caught sight of a bladed profile and for a second I thought that it was Gemaley. Then the figure stepped forward and gripped me by the shoulders. It was Ruan.

'Vali!'

I stared at him as though he was a ghost.

'You're alive,' I said. 'You came back.'

'What happened here? Did you find him? The outworlder?' Ruan was all that was holding me upright, I realized. I sagged back against the wall, nodding. 'Yes. Yes, I found him. He's dead.'

'Good,' Ruan said. He made no mention of the fact that I was covered in blood. Without wasting any more time on the matter, he added, 'And so is Gemaley. I sent her into the lake, under the ice. I couldn't bring her up again.'

'Ruan.' I did not want to utter some platitude, say that it was probably all for the best, that she would never have been whole, or happy. It would have sounded fatuous, and besides, I was glad she was gone. I thought the neighbourhood was much better off without her. And Ruan, too, was moving on.

'I didn't expect to find you here. What happened in the town—' he broke off. 'I'm worried about my clan, but this place was on the way, and now that Gemaley's gone, I wanted to find her brother and sister. They'll need someone to look after them. They'll be lost without her.'

'I'll help you,' I said.

But it seemed that they were not there. We found no trace of them inside the tower, or in the surrounding woods. I tried to induce the visen to search for them, using a skirt that we thought had belonged to Tian, and the pack were acquiescent enough, but after some indifferent sniffing around the trees, they swarmed back around me.

If I had possessed access to explosives, I would have sent the tower to oblivion and Frey's bones with it, but I did not and besides, something in me said that, though an evil place, it was home not only to the two tattered remnants of Gemaley's clan, but also to the visen. Perhaps they could have found another lair easily enough; I do not know. But it seemed better to let the place sink into ruin on its own. Ruan told me that the water beneath the tower was still rising, leaching away at its foundations, and I decided to rest content with letting nature do its work. He also said something about going back, with his sister, to look for the missing pair.

I still felt some responsibility to Ruan, so I waited until the pack had slunk back into its lair for the day and then we once more made our way west, to the coast, and the torn town.

There had been some twenty deaths, fewer than I had expected, but still enough for a small community. No one from Ruan's clan was among them. The Mondhaith were in mourning, but philosophical about it. They seemed to be a people who took disaster in their stride, and I suppose that they had had enough practice at it.

'Such things happen,' the satahrach said, squinting up at the fire-blackened eves of the murai stable. The beasts had been taken early up to the spring pasture. I was thankful not to have to face more local animal life. He raised a lens to his eye and peered through it.

'My friend has sent me another of these things, but I still cannot get it to work.'

'It depends on your eyes,' I told him. 'You need to grind it, or perhaps thicken it.'

'I do not know how to thicken it. Perhaps I will grind it down as you suggest and see what happens.' He looked at me. 'Do you know anything else?'

I laughed. 'Some few small things.' There are no guidelines for giving out information to primitive worlds. We are all of the same stock, the same heritage, entitled to the same knowledge and the same mistakes. Using my own judgement I kept back what I knew of modern weapons, just in case, but they already had gunpowder, and the strange configurations of the house defences, and something told me that it would not be long before they came up with something nasty.

But maybe I was wrong. They had welcomed me, a stranger, and their violence seemed confined to their episodic lapses of self-awareness. I did not know whether it was better that way, or worse. But I spent an afternoon telling the satahrach what I knew of lenses, and metalworking, and astronomy, and human physiology, though I was careful to try to explain that there were already gulfs between his kind and mine, though perhaps not as great as I had thought. He listened, sometimes intently, sometimes politely, and I did not think he believed everything I told him, which was also a positive sign. And he told me more about the way the Mondhaith were, about the defences of their settlements, and I knew for certain then that I had found Frey's key.

'It's why he came here,' I said to Arrath. 'He must have read the old report, learned of a people who are sometimes animal and sometimes human. Of a forgotten technology that triggers consciousness in feral children, and occasionally surges to switch it off again. Get hold of that technology, and take it home to Darkland, then use it against my people as part of the war effort. But he got distracted by Gemaley and the tower. Perhaps, at least, I should thank her for that.'

We sat silent for a moment. Then the satahrach said, politely, 'Well. This is all very interesting, though I'm sorry for the state of your world. Perhaps we shall come and visit you, one day. But I don't think it will be for many years. And people from your world should come here, when you are at peace again. There was one such once, as you know. I think there should be more. We should all learn as much as possible from one another.'

I agreed. I thought that those visitors should find out what they could about the energy network that underlay the planet, the strange technology that those ancient colonists had employed, and then abandoned, to work its own weird will on the people they had left behind them – their transfigured, altered descendants, forged in a crucible of fanaticism and rigidity to become a race who were at the same time quite odd and strangely reasonable – at least in my prejudiced view.

I asked the satahrach again what he knew about the dark energy lines, and in particular the black well, but he could tell me little more. My own opinion was that some artifact lay under the tower, probably not a computer but some piece of ancient tech, that had once served a purpose and had then become warped across the centuries – a semi-sentient demon, made by man. But something in me said that this was not the right explanation at all, that it had in some manner been a part of Gemaley, a piece of her twisted, projected will. I still could not see her as human, in the same way as Ruan or the satahrach or I, but something else; something eldritch and strange. I did not want to think about her any more.

I took my leave of Ruan in the forest. We did not say a great deal to one another. I did not suppose that I would ever see him again, and I was sorry for that. He said with abrupt apology as I was strapping myself into the pod, 'I would like to go with you. But I can't.'

'I'm afraid it isn't possible. But I would like you to, as well.' He was, after all, the only man whom I had had any time for in all these years, though too young. He had given me back some faith, at least, and for that I kissed him good-bye. The parting was easier than I had thought.

But strangely, when the clearing and the forest, and then the great sweep of the sea had given way to the starfield where I was to wait for the pick-up, it was not Ruan of whom I was thinking, or even Frey, but the vitki of Darkland, the man called Thorn.

EPILOGUE

Spring had come fully to the Reach when I returned to Muspell. The forests along the coast from Tiree bore new green among the conifers and when I piloted a wing out to the Rock, I passed islands that were a carpet of wild flowers. It was too tempting to pass up. I radioed in a call to Idhunn saying that I would be later than expected, set the wing ashore on one of the smaller islands – no more than a dune, really – and walked up through the blowing machair to the grassland that crowned its low summit. It reminded me of the place of the broch, but I did not know its name. It would have had one, for there is a name for every place in the Reach, however small.

Here, there was little in the way of a 'spirit of place'. The dune felt empty, inhabited only by thrift and sea-thistle, with a solitary red-billed rock-runner trundling along the foreshore, rooting in the sand for shellfish. The emptiness suited me. I sat for a long time among the flowers, watching the sun drop lower and lower until it was a great crimson ball over the western sea. It seemed strange to remember that I had seen that sun from space: first the huge shadowy bulk of Fellheim; then the smaller jade sphere of Idhunn's namesake world; and finally the white-and-azure Muspell on which I once more stood, Loki circling it like a slung stone.

Somewhere beyond that horizon, already beneath the curtain of night, lay Darkland. Somewhere there, lay Frey's masters and the vitki Thorn who had plans for me. I thought of how those plans might have changed, with my new knowledge and Frey's death.

Thorn had known me, better than anyone ever had, even myself. Fear and anticipation rose in my throat like cold bile. Whatever was between him and myself was surely not yet over and now that I had returned to Muspell, I could not help but think of those plans. Did he know I had come back, that Frey was dead? Somehow, I was certain that he did, though I could not have said how. It was like an itch inside my mind, a twitch of recognition.

Staring at the sunset, I remembered the selk, penned in their holding tanks under the cliffs of Hetla, and the warwings in their dry docks, waiting for the call to go to war. I thought of the forests, impenetrable, hiding secrets, of the woman I had seen sitting with a skull in her lap. I wondered – with a shiver of premonition that I would have liked to have attributed to the sunset wind but could not – who she had been and whether I would ever see her again. Now, with so much that had passed, she felt even more like a figure from a fairy tale, some grim daughter of the forest, not a part of the modern world at all. She reminded me of Gemaley.

And I remembered Nhem: the shadowy women of the resistance who had first approached the Skald to hire me, the ones who had escaped a breeding program that made women into animals, outraging the Skald enough to meddle in an outworld affair – or at least, that's how it seemed on the face of it. But somehow I did not think that any of us had heard the last of Nhem.

The sun was dropping swiftly now, staining the spring sea with lavender and red. I looked up, to where a skein of sea-birds were heading back towards their roost, and thought again of Gemaley – that strange, sad, twisted girl. It suddenly struck me that she and I were not so dissimilar. She had turned her anger outwards – using it always against others – whereas I had turned mine inwards, against myself. I looked down at my forearms and the tracks of old scars. It crossed my mind that I should visit a surgeon and have them removed, but then I dismissed the idea. I would keep the scars and the memories all; but it was time to stop looking within. Darkland was waiting for me, and I turned my back on the west, taking the wing out of the shallow harbour of the dune, and raced it east over the twilit sea to the Rock.

It did not take long to reach home. Soon enough the pillar of the Rock reared up out of the ocean and I brought the wing into the narrow harbour. There was no one waiting for me as I stepped out onto the wave-lashed platform, but I put this down to my earlier transmission, stating that I might be late. The doors to the stairwell were closed and I had to key in the access codes. The doors were often locked when a storm was coming up and so it didn't occur to me, even then, that something might be wrong. It was not until I passed the door to the Council chamber that I saw someone. I had only a glimpse of a white, set face above a guard's stripe-shouldered shirt, though she almost knocked me back down the stairs in her haste.

'What's the matter?' I called after her, but there was no answer. Around me, the seith felt icy cold. I took the stairs to the lamp room two at a time and when I got there I did not knock. There was no need. The doors stood open and four members of the Skald were there, gathered around something on the floor. Their numb horror echoed from the edges of the seith like blows. I pushed through them, to see Idhunn's body lying sprawled in the centre of the floor. There was no need to check if she was really dead. She lay face down, and her spine had been torn from her. And the only thought in my mind was: Darkland.